THE Canadian ESSAY

Selected and introduced by

GERALD LYNCH & DAVID RAMPTON

University of Ottawa

Copp Clark Pitman Ltd.
A Longman Company
Toronto

ISBN 0-7730-4983-5

Executive editor: Brian Henderson
Editor: Camilla Jenkins
Design: Susan Hedley
Cover: Susan Hedley. Map detail based on "Le Canada," 1653, in turn based on a 1616 map drawn by Samuel de Champlain.
Typesetting: Carol Magee and Marnie Morrissey
Printing and binding: Webcom Limited

Canadian Cataloguing in Publication Data

Main entry under title:

The Canadian essay

ISBN 0-7730-4983-5

1. Canadian essays (English).* I. Lynch, Gerald, 1953–
II. Rampton, David, 1950– .

PS 8365.C35 1991 C814.008 C91-093004-X

Copp Clark Pitman Ltd.
2775 Matheson Blvd. East
Mississauga, Ontario
L4W 4P7

OTABIND
Bound to stay open

Publisher's Note

Otabind (Ota-bind). This book has been bound using the patented Otabind process. You can open this book at any page, gently run your finger down the spine, and the pages will lie flat.

Associated companies:
Longman Group Ltd., London
Longman Inc., New York
Longman Cheshire Pty., Melbourne
Longman Paul Pty., Auckland

Printed and bound in Canada

1 2 3 4 5 4983-5 95 94 93 92 91

CONTENTS

PREFACE

The essay continues to have a distinguished place in English-Canadian literature. But until now no single text has featured a generous sampling of the essays of our most important writers, allowing both students of Canadian literature and general readers interested in their own culture the opportunity to appreciate this neglected genre. *The Canadian Essay* hopes to fill this gap. While the book chronologically surveys and illustrates the continuity of the essay in Canada, the essays themselves cover a variety of fields and subjects, including, for example, Sara Jeannette Duncan on the eminently unliterary character of Canadians, Stephen Leacock on the death of the Devil, W.L. Morton on the role of the North in Canadian historiography, Northrop Frye on the relation between the sciences and the humanities, and Margaret Atwood on "writing the male character." As well, a number of the essays—those by Margaret Laurence, Robert Kroetsch, and Mordecai Richler, for example—provide a more personal, even intimate, view of the lives of some of Canada's major writers. Yet this is only to say that *The Canadian Essay* is an anthology of *essays*, for the genre itself has always offered its practitioners the widest possible range with regard to subject and point of view, on the sole condition that the writer's personality, as expressed in his or her style, prove strong enough to assume the literary responsibility of the freedom granted: to entertain, to instruct, to delight. The essayists represented here fulfil that condition.

For encouragement and advice since the inception of this project, we are grateful to Brian Henderson of Copp Clark Pitman Ltd. We also thank our colleagues in the Department of English at the University of Ottawa for many helpful suggestions, and our families for their patient sacrifices of time.

This book is dedicated to the memory of Hugh MacLennan (1907–1990) and Northrop Frye (1912–1991).

Gerald Lynch and David Rampton
University of Ottawa
March 1991

INTRODUCTION

Compared to tragedy or to the epic or the lyric poem, the essay is a literary genre of recent origin, and one person in particular can take credit for its creation. In 1570, having decided that sixteen years of government service was enough, Michel de Montaigne resigned his post as counsellor in the Chambre des Enquètes at the Parliament of Bordeaux. Only thirty-eight, Montaigne was too involved in public affairs and too energetic to be nothing but a nobleman at leisure, and his temporary retreat from the world was responsible for the birth of the essay as a form. For the next sixteen years, Montaigne "essayed"; that is, he "tried" to articulate in prose what he thought and felt—about sadness, idleness (he had trouble adjusting to it), liars, constancy, pedantry, cannibals, sensual pleasures, smells (a moustache helps convey them to the nose), and so on. He wrote three books in all, more than a hundred essays. He annotated adages or sayings, quoted liberally from classical authors, and recounted historical anecdotes, but the essays endure because they tell us about Montaigne, his likes and dislikes, hopes and fears, actions and reactions. These attempts to communicate the provisional truths of ordinary experience to a sympathetic reader gave rise to the essay as we know it today.

Francis Bacon is generally acknowledged to be the father of the English essay. In works such as *Essays or Counsels, Civil and Moral* (1597), he used the essay as an instrument of empirical inquiry, a more impersonal means of conveying a range of speculations on humanity and the natural world. The eighteenth century was the great age of English prose: Samuel Johnson wrote hundreds of essays for the *The Rambler*, using them to "inculcate wisdom and piety" by conveying his own common-sense morality and his convictions about the vanity of human wishes. Joseph Addison, Oliver Goldsmith, and Sir Richard Steele also made significant contributions to the genre. As the market for periodical literature grew, the readership for the professional writer increased. The Neoclassical principles of the eighteenth century gave way at the beginning of the nineteenth to Romanticism, with its emphasis on individual psychology. Charles Lamb, in both his criticism and his splendid personal essays, strove to convey the emotional aura of his subject, whether that subject was literature or his own experience. William Hazlitt and Thomas De Quincey, the other two indisputably great Romantic essayists, also combined criticism and autobiography in original and evocative ways. Hazlitt extended Montaigne's conception of the essay, defining his métier as "applying the talents and resources of the mind to all that mixed mass of human affairs, which . . . falls under the cognizance of the writer." De Quincey wrote some 215 essays, in which he reshaped the poetic prose of the Elizabethans to create a sonorous, elaborate, and idiosyncratic style.

In eighteenth-century America, Benjamin Franklin and Thomas Paine became immediately popular and influential by using the essay to speak to the common citizen about affairs that affected everyday life. English Romanticism and Yankee individualism combined in the writings of Ralph Waldo Emerson and Henry David Thoreau, who continued to develop a vigorous American tradition for the essay. In such works as "Nature," "The American Scholar," "The Divinity School Address," and "Self-Reliance," Emerson caught the imagination of an entire country by speaking out against the stultifying effects of dogmatism in every aspect of American life. Though less recognized during his lifetime, Thoreau is now regarded as an original thinker and a consummate stylist. Essays such as "Civil Disobedience" and the book-length "Walden," with their arraignment of the "quiet desperation" that characterizes so many ordinary lives, and their analysis of the political, social, and economic systems that have estranged people from nature and from themselves, have continued to be influential in our own century. From the middle of the last century to the present day, the essay has been an accommodating and supple medium for numerous writers, but the best essayists of this period have been novelists or dramatists or poets first: George Eliot, Robert Louis Stevenson, Oscar Wilde, William Butler Yeats, E.M. Forster, Virginia Woolf, D.H. Lawrence, Aldous Huxley, and George Orwell. The list of British writers who have made important contributions to the genre is a long and distinguished one. Any list of important American essayists in our own century would include T.S. Eliot, Wallace Stevens, Loren Eiseley, E.B. White, Joan Didion, John Updike, James Thurber, Lewis Thomas, and Stephen Jay Gould.

In Canada, the development of the essay over the past hundred and fifty years describes an arc, beginning in various kinds of journalism, developing into a form more closely resembling the British and American essay of the eighteenth and nineteenth centuries, and arriving, much changed, at a form that combines a variety of approaches. Writing in *Literary History of Canada* on the essay's Canadian roots, Brandon Conron suggests that even at the outset the transplanted genre showed something of a distinctive quality: "As the essay emerged from its many related forms, it was characterized by a heterogeneous but vigorous individualism that combined the traditional ideals of civilization with the peculiar reactions to a distinctive physical environment and the peculiar problems of a new nation." Glimmerings of something like the essay proper appear first in the mid-nineteenth century, in public speeches of the kind that the politician-poet Joseph Howe delivered to Mechanics Institutes in eastern Canada, in highly wrought political oratory like that of Sir John A. Macdonald on the necessity of Confederation, in literary sketches of the kind written by Susanna Moodie on her life in the bush, naturalistic descriptive pieces like those of her sister Catherine Parr Trail, and in the journalism of poets and novelists such as Charles Mair—inflaming Ontario over the Riel Rebellion—and Sara Jeannette Duncan. From such diverse beginnings, the essay became a more purely literary form that was in fact something of a return to the British essay of earlier times. One can note here essays such as those written by Sir Charles G.D. Roberts to explain the new kind of animal story he was writing or to make reactionary assaults on modernism, or those of his cousin Bliss Carman in such collections as *The Kinship of Nature* (1903), or those of Duncan Campbell Scott on such subjects as the relation between poetry and progress. From February 1892 to July 1893, Scott and his friends Archibald Lampman and William Wilfred Campbell contributed a lively series of essays on everything from holiday excursions to topical literary questions to their "At the Mermaid Inn" column in the *Toronto Globe*. (The entire series has recently been reprinted in book form under the column's title, providing an excellent example of the popular literary essay of the day as well as privileged glimpses into the minds of three of Canada's accomplished Confederation poets.) But the most prestigious forum for the essay in the late nineteenth century was the Toronto magazine the *Week* (1883–1896), which was founded by Goldwin Smith, first edited by Roberts, and contributed to regularly by the likes of Duncan, Archibald MacMechan, and Sir William Osler. The *Week* was that rarity in magazine publishing: respectably literary so as to attract the best writers of the time, yet editorially flexible enough to accommodate all kinds of writing, from the most evanescent observations on the passing scene to the most lasting. In short, it provided the ideal place for the various strands of the essay in Canada to coalesce.

With the advent of such writers as Sir Andrew MacPhail, Peter McArthur, Stephen Leacock, and Frederick Philip Grove, the essay in Canada entered its golden age in the first quarter of the twentieth century, a time when the influence of modern-age mass journalism was still beneficial in the main and when the literary culture of the nineteenth century was still in the ascendant. Yet already the movement away from more traditional styles that are reflected most clearly in the work of Leacock—that is, essays of common sense and humour, demonstrating a range of interests—was heralded by the appearance in 1920 of the magazine the *Canadian Forum*. The *Forum* can now be seen to have replaced the *Week* and all that it represented in the best traditions of the eighteenth- and nineteenth-century humanist essayist. The *Forum* also suggests the influence of the better journalism already present in much of Duncan's and Leacock's work, shifting the tone of the essay from the leisurely discourse of an entertaining individual of strong character and tastes to the terse prose of a writer with an argument to make, an argument often laced with irreverence and sarcasm. Such feisty contributors to the *Forum* as Douglas Bush and A.J.M. Smith typify the kind of essayists who came to dominate the tradition in Canada, writing essays that moved away from the British influence and towards the American—a movement, say, from the style of a Charles Lamb to that of an H.L. Mencken. Smith, for example, in his landmark essay for the *Forum*, "Wanted—Canadian Criticism" (1928), demanded that Canadian literature be judged by international standards of literary excellence, the prescriptions of Anglo-American modernism. Grove, in "It Needs To Be Said" (1929), took a tough, critical look at Canadian art. As well as contributing to the growing influence of journalistic practices, the *Forum* more than any other Canadian magazine shows the effects of the new modernism on the Canadian essay: the economy of style, the polemical tone, the colloquial language, the disparagement of unnecessary ornamentation.

Throughout the middle decades of this century, other magazines and literary periodicals played important roles as forums for Canadian essayists: *Queen's Quarterly*, *Canadian Author & Bookman* (founded in 1921 as *Canadian Bookman*), *First Statement, Preview, Northern Review,* the *Tamarack Review,* the *Dalhousie Review, Maclean's, Canadian Literature,* and such widely popular newspaper supplements as *Weekend* and *Star Weekly*. *Saturday Night*, which is now one of the few outlets for essayists wishing to reach a wide audience, regularly published Leacock, B.K. Sandwell (who was its editor for a period), and Robertson Davies (who was its literary editor), to name but a few. Less widely circulated magazines such as the *Montrealer* remained the choice of writers like Hugh MacLennan who had higher literary aspirations. Today, magazines such as the *Idler* continue to provide a forum for writers who work in this insufficiently appreciated genre. Also, most newspapers still feature columns for the essays of writers with a larger readership in view, humorous writers such as Eric Nicol and Gregory Clark, or, more recently, Erika Ritter, Harry Bruce, and Susan Musgrave, or political commentators such as Allan Fotheringham, Peter Newman, and Marjorie Nichols. In part, the essay thrives in Canada as a result of such newspaper columns. As Conron writes, since the 1920s journalism has had a beneficial as well as a deleterious effect on the formal essay: "Later essayists adapted the directness and force of the journalistic tradition into their own styles, and found that the vigour of the modern idiom was by no means alien to the carefully integrated and unobtrusively artful style of the essay."

This then is the background and the context for the essays included in *The Canadian Essay*, essays that show how Canadian writers have extended a rich tradition and thus established themselves as the equals of other practitioners in what is now literature's most thriving genre.

The editors have deliberately chosen the essays that follow for their diversity as well as for the themes that recur. If it is fair to say that poets write ultimately only of God and love, then Canada's essayists can be said to write only of nature and Canada. In the broadest sense this has been true since at least the middle of the nineteenth century, and it is true generally of the essays in this book. Essays on Canada involve attempts to define Canada, Canadian identity, and Canadians. When these writers ponder the persistent enigma of what it means to be a Canadian (sometimes in unlikely contexts, as in Sara Jeannette Duncan's essay on Thanksgiving), their various provisional conclusions suggest, with few exceptions, that the ongoing exploration of this subject may itself be the defining characteristic of Canadians. It will come as no surprise to readers of Canadian fiction and poetry, or for that matter to those who have read Northrop Frye's "Conclusion" to *Literary History of Canada*, that the country's essayists are also haunted by its immense and empty landscapes. Earlier in this century, such writers as Peter McArthur, E.K. Broadus, H.L. Symons, John D. Robins, and Ernest Brewster wrote essays in a popular bucolic-rural mode, sometimes humorously, as with McArthur, but more often in a nostalgic vein that suited the sentiments of a population rapidly shifting from the country to the city. Other essayists, among them Roderick Haig-Brown and earlier the Grove of *Over Prairie Trails* (1922) and *The Turn of the Year* (1923), demonstrated a more naturalistic, or scientific, approach to nature, displaying a wide knowledge and a meticulous eye for detail that makes their work as interesting today as when it was first published. The North looms largely but differently in the imaginations of such writers as W.L. Morton, Margaret Atwood, Robert Fulford, and Al Purdy. The increasing importance of science and technology, and their problematic relation to the humanities, is considered by George Grant, Marshall McLuhan, and Frye from three distinct perspectives. Mavis Gallant and Atwood take very personal stands on the controversial issues surrounding sexual politics, while D.M.R. Bentley and Linda Hutcheon provide literary critical essays that focus on matters cultural and theoretical.

One of the enduring attractions of the essay has been the intimacy it can offer. (Deprived of a real conversational intimacy by the death of his friend, Étienne de La Boétie, Montaigne felt compelled to find recourse in the literary intimacy of the essay form itself.) In "The Writer and His Audience," the first essay presented here, Hugh MacLennan explores the public and private dimensions of the relationship between essayist and reader—that foundation of trust upon which the complex network of literary communication rests. The essay, observes MacLennan, "depends more than any other form of writing on a relationship between author and reader so close that at times the author at his desk has the illusion that he is lounging in his library late in the evening of a well-spent day, a glass of beer at his elbow and a personal friend in the opposite chair." Many of the essays collected here, especially those of Leacock, Grove, Wilson, MacLennan, Laurence, and Richler, illustrate this observation, providing privileged access to the thoughts and feelings of some of Canada's finest writers.

Even in a collection of writers as diverse as this one, other continuities with the form created by Montaigne can be observed. Graham Good has summarized some of these in his excellent study of the essay, *The Observing Self*, in which he suggests that the essay is often critical of or sceptical about previous learning, that it "cultivates diversity where the disciplines seek unity," and that it has strong links with the novel, emerging as it does from the same intellectual climate and using as its subject matter the lives of ordinary individuals. He argues that dividing the essay according to content reveals four types—travel, moral, critical, and autobiographical—corresponding to "the main essayistic activities: traveling, pondering, reading, and remembering." For the student of the genre, this classification offers a useful alternative to the traditional rhetorical categories of expository, persuasive, narrative, and descriptive essays. Students and readers may note, therefore, that half of the essayists presented here are primarily novelists, and that most of the essays can readily be categorized according to Good's divisions. For example, under "travelling" we would list some essays by Grove, Purdy, and Laurence; under "pondering" a great many, but especially those of Duncan, Leacock, MacLennan, Woodcock, and Fulford; under "reading," Duncan, Grove, Morton, Frye, Davies, Gallant, Kroetsch, Richler, Atwood, Bentley, and Hutcheon; and under "remembering," Leacock, Gallant, Laurence, and Richler. As with any simple system involving complex elements, there is much overlapping, and a number of important essays—sometimes the best—escape easy categorization. Such shortcomings should encourage readers and students to make their own connections, while the system provides a starting point for study and discussion.

Finally, anthologists can always be easily embarrassed by the "What about so-and-so?" question. Because good essayists encourage the intimacy between writer and reader that MacLennan remarks upon, some readers will be disappointed at the exclusion of personal favourites. Of course, the selection of writers depended finally on the interests and tastes of the editors themselves. Nevertheless, when readers consider that, in addition to the names already mentioned, Barbara Amiel, Pierre Berton, Morley Callaghan, June Callwood, Ramsay Cook, Donald Creighton, John Kenneth Galbraith, Sandra Gwyn, Bruce Hutchinson, Michael Ignatieff, Josef Škvorecký, Fredelle Maynard, Lester B. Pearson, Malcolm Ross, F.R. Scott, David Suzuki, and Frank Underhill could have been included, it is hoped they will appreciate the difficulties of the editors' task and, more importantly, begin to acquire a better sense of just how distinguished Canada's contribution has been to the genre that Montaigne created.

The Writer and His Audience

HUGH MacLENNAN

When I was engaged in selecting the essays that later appeared in the book *Thirty and Three* I found that a pattern in the material I had written began to disclose itself. All the pieces I had written for American magazines had lost much of their original vitality over the lapse of time. They had all appeared in handsome formats, accompanied by large and colourful pictures. They had been well received in the months of their publication, and even in Canada a few of them had won some praise. But already they have begun to wither away.

The reason for this was not hard to discover, once sufficient time had passed. Those pieces written for American magazines with big names and glossy pages were written for a public which does not really exist, for a public which is no more than an abstraction invented by politicians, journalists, and the editors of mass-circulation periodicals. Those articles I wrote, with much labour and the expense of time and nervous stability, were designed to make a quick impact on a more or less unknown quantity. They were carefully constructed and scrupulously polished, and contained a great deal of exact information. They were also, in terms of financial returns, big money-makers. But they lacked the essential ingredient of literature, they lacked intimacy. They were bound to lack intimacy because the magazines in which they appeared had a mass circulation. As communications, they were words spoken into dead air confused with static, not necessarily because most of the readers were living in a foreign country, but because no one who writes for that many people living all over the place can possibly know who his listeners are.

A strange thing, this. The writer is one of the most solitary of workers, but when he sits at his desk he must feel that he is writing for friends if what he writes is to be good. If he pretends to write only for himself, he lies, or lets his pride deceive him. Only the diarist does that, and the diarist is not interesting to others unless he is a famous personality or his material scandalous. The professional prose writer cannot possibly write for himself alone. He must convince himself that a personal relationship exists between himself and individual members of his audience. He must think of those individuals as valuable personally, each a person whose soul is inviolate, whose intelligence must never be insulted with clichés or by the kind of propaganda-prose which grabs him by the throat. Unless a writer can be convinced that a decent intimacy exists between himself and those who read him, what he writes may have impact for a day, but it will be dead a week later.

Since rediscovering this truth, which was ancient in Homer's day, I have felt a lot better about the future of that activity which the critics call "Canadian" literature and handle with tongs. I don't feel alone anymore, as the critics try to make you feel, stuck with the job of creating some literature all by myself. I know that Canadian readers are sharing the job with me, and that the state of our culture depends as much on them as it depends on those of us who write. I know that if I respect them they will do their part, and that the way to respect them is to write with them in mind and not to consider them as a roadblock between myself and the huge, lucrative market of the outside world.

So, after many years of continuous writing and experimentation, perhaps I have learned the humility which will turn out to be the beginning of wisdom. The trouble with most critics is that they never seem humble enough to accept the role of the audience in the development of a nation's culture. The higher their brows are, the greater is their contempt for the audience and the vaster their ignorance of it. I don't know how many highbrow critics I have heard say that all a Canadian needs to do to win international recognition is to write a good book, a good play, or a good essay. But I suspect, perhaps wrongly, that what they want us to do is write like Joyce or Eliot or Faulkner, to be in fashion, to comb the Canadian scene in search of a wasteland or a Leopold Bloom. I entirely agree with them that the only way to win international recognition is to write a good book. But since a good book is a good communication, I don't see how it can be written by a Canadian unless it is written primarily for an audience of people he knows well.

This is not to suggest that the Canadian writer should limit himself to regionalism, whatever that is. It is to suggest the very opposite. It is to point to the beaten path followed by all the best-loved writers from Homer's day to our own. All of them wrote with those nearest to them in mind, and in so doing they reached the ears of millions of strangers. Shakespeare has been read by the entire world, but he did not write for it. His audience was a small number of London play-goers, and in establishing an intimate communication with them he even portrayed his Romans and Italians as fair representatives of the Elizabethan Englishmen who were the only people he knew. Lewis Carroll wrote *Alice in Wonderland* for a single little girl and Stevenson *Treasure Island* for a single small boy. Here is the paradox of the literary art. The greater it is, the more intimate it is. The more universally it comes to be loved, the more local has been its origin.

With novels and plays, which depend on dramatic situations, deep emotions, and the revelation of character, it is obviously far easier for the writer in a thinly populated country to transcend his national boundaries and reach individuals no matter where they may happen to live. In a small way even I have done this with my novels. But with the essay it is more difficult.

For though the essay can be a tough and enduring piece of literature, its case is a special one. It depends more than any other form of writing on a relationship between author and reader so close that at times the author at his desk has the illusion that he is lounging in his library late in the evening of a well-spent day, a glass of beer at his elbow and a personal friend in the opposite chair. For this reason, it is almost impossible for a good essay to find its way into a mass-circulation magazine and totally impossible for anyone to write enduring essays with a large audience of foreigners in the forefront of his mind. This does not mean that he cannot reach foreigners if his essays are good. It means merely that he is not thinking about them when he writes. I suppose the best essayist Canada ever produced was Stephen Leacock; he is certainly our only one whose essays have been read and loved far beyond the limits of Canada. Leacock, so I am assured by men who knew him well, wrote some of his best pieces as though he was talking to his cronies at the McGill Faculty Club. Even now when I read Leacock, I can almost hear the chuckles of some of them, whom I know, too.

This same assumption of matter-of-fact intimacy was the secret of the three supreme essay-writers of England, who of course were Bacon, Addison, and Charles Lamb. Lamb wrote primarily for a small coterie of personal friends, and though Addison was extremely interested in making money out of his work, he wrote directly for the gentlemen of London he encountered in his daily relaxation in the coffee-houses.

But as Bacon is the greatest of these three, so also is he the most intimate: more so even than Lamb, for the Bacon of the essays is naked. The sage Lord Chancellor seems never to have had a close personal friend in his entire life. But he associated with scholars, courtiers, and politicians, he wrote with them in his mind, and when he sat down to compose an essay, he assumed that everyone who would read it would think and feel like himself. He wrote as though all his readers were as learned as himself, as experienced in affairs and as worldly-wise, as selfish and idealistic, as treacherous and magnanimous, as noble in aspiration and as shoddy in the means he used for his splendid ends, as delighted with beauty and learning, as fascinated by the mystery of the universe. The fact that nobody who ever lived was such a distilled essence of contradictions did not matter. Bacon assumed that everyone was, assumed it and got away with it, with the result that a young student from the Saskatchewan prairie, more than three centuries later, can read this incredible man and feel close to his spirit.

None of us are Bacons, nor is it likely that Canada will ever again produce a writer with the unique texture of Stephen Leacock. But these men have showed us the way to go. The way is not the one of the highbrow critic who feels ashamed because nobody in Canada writes like Joyce or Proust or with the attitude of Jean-Paul Sartre. The right way is the one which brings the writer and the reader together in a closer intimacy, and the writer cannot travel this road alone. The reader must go along with him, accepting or rejecting his vision according to whether or not he likes it, but accepting or rejecting it himself, without waiting to find out what the American judgment of the man is going to be. After many years I believe this to be true. The future of Canadian literature depends as much on the development of a great, independent audience as on the existence of great, independent writers, for the communication which is literature's essence requires them both.

"Prologue: The Writer and His Audience," from *The Other Side of Hugh MacLennan: Selected Essays Old and New*, ed. Elspeth Cameron (Toronto: Macmillan of Canada, 1978), 1–5. Published earlier in the *Montrealer* (June 1954).

SARA JEANNETTE DUNCAN (1861–1922) was born and raised in Brantford, Ontario. In the 1880s, she worked as a journalist for the *Washington Post* and subsequently became the first female reporter employed regularly by the *Toronto Globe.* She travelled throughout the world, living for twenty-five years in India and ending her rich and varied life in England. Of her twenty-two books, two are set in Canada, with the best known of these being the novel *The Imperialist* (1904). That novel traces the political fortunes of an idealistic young Canadian politician campaigning for the Imperialist cause—that is, for closer ties between Canada and Britain and among the colonies of the British Empire—in a turn-of-the-century Ontario town generally recognized as having been inspired by Brantford. In this novel we also find evidence of a new kind of literary heroine emerging, one who knows her own mind and actively seeks to impress her views upon the world; one who is, moreover, the creation of the Duncan who wrote in an essay of 1885–1886,

> In this golden age for girls, full of new interests and new opportunities, we all—you, the musical girl; you, the literary girl; you, the artistic girl; you, the practical girl; and I, whose appropriate adjective is of no consequence—want to do something; something more difficult than embroidered sachets, and more important than hand-painted tambourines. The sachets and the tambourines are very charming in their way, but as the chief industrial end of life we have begun to find them unsatisfying.

Duncan's skills as a recorder of ordinary experience made her one of North America's earliest practitioners of a type of literary realism. Her ability to portray Canadian society, along with her wit, intelligence, and daunting energy, had already made her a "natural" essayist, and one of the *Week*'s most valued regular contributors in the 1880s. "Before I say anything I must have something to say." What journal of political and literary opinion would not value the writer who expressed such a dictum? Consider, for example, Duncan's view of the reason for Canada's lack of a literary culture towards the end of the nineteenth century:

> In our character as colonists we find the root of all our sins of omission in letters.... Our enforced political humility is the distinguishing characteristic of every phase of our national life. We are ignored, and we ignore ourselves. A nation's development is like a plant's, unattractive under ground. So long as Canada remains in political obscurity, content to thrive only at the roots, so long will the leaves and blossoms of art and literature be scanty and stunted products of our national energy.... A national literature cannot be looked for as an outcome of anything less than a complete national existence.

The following pieces appeared originally in "Saunterings," the column that she wrote for the *Week*.

SARA JEANNETTE DUNCAN

An Eminently Unliterary People

We are still an eminently unliterary people.

Another Canadian summer has waxed and waned; mysterious in our forests, idyllic in our gardens, ineffably gracious upon our mountains. Another year of our national existence has rounded into the golden fulness of its harvest time. The yellow leaves of another September are blowing about our streets; since last we watched their harlequin dance to dusty death a cycle has come and gone. And still the exercise of hope and faith—charity we never had—continue to constitute the sum of our literary endeavour. We are conscious of not having been born in time to produce an epic poet or a dramatist; but still in vain do we scan the west for the lyrist, the east for the novelist whose appearing we may not unreasonably expect. Our bard is still loath to leave his Olympian pleasures; our artisan in fiction is busy with the human product of some other sphere.

And we look blankly at each other at every new and vain adjustment of the telescope to the barren literary horizon, and question "Why?" And our American cousins with an indifferent wonder, and a curious glance at our census returns, make the same interrogatory; whereupon one of them tarries in Montreal for three days, ascertains, and prints in *Harper's Magazine* that it is our arctic temperature! And in England, if our sterile national library excites any comment at all, it is only a semi-contemptuous opinion that it is all that might be expected of "colonials."

Mr. Warner's idea that the Canadian climate reduces the Canadian brain to a condition of torpor during six months of the year may be dismissed with something of the irritation which it inspired in every Canadian who read it, that a writer who observes so keenly in his own country could be led to such an absurd and superficial conclusion in ours. One would naturally suppose that climatic influences which produce the bodily results to be found in the average Canadian, at least conduce toward giving him an active mind as well. Physically, Canadians compare with Americans to the great disadvantage of the latter; that they do not intellectually, alas! is not the fault of the climate.

Nor can we place the slightest responsibility for our literary short-comings upon our educational system. On the contrary, our colleges and public schools are our pride and glory. We point boastfully to the opportunities for intellectual elevation Ontario offers to the children of her navvies and farm labourers; and the ease with which Canadian graduates obtain all sorts of American degrees testifies to the thoroughness of our university training. So great indeed are our facilities for education that our farm lands lie untilled while our offices are filled to unprofitable repletion, and grave protest is arising in many quarters against the State's present liberal abetment of this false adjustment of national energy to national needs. Clearly, Nature and the Hon. G.W. Ross can do no more for us. We are a well-developed and well-educated people; but we do not write books.

"No, for we are not rich enough," you say. "The cultivation of letters demands wealth and a leisure class. We have a professional market in view for our hard-bought college training. We cannot afford to offer it up in unremunerative libations to the muses. We choose between the rustic homespun and the academic bombazin, but there the alternative ends. It is hard work thenceforward in either case. For Canadians to 'sport with Amaryllis in the shade, or with the tangles of Neræa's hair' is an idyllic occupation which, for financial reasons, must be sternly ignored."

This is a comfortable way of relegating the responsibility for our literary inactivity to an economic dispensation of an overruling Providence which finds favour with a great many people. The disabilities of poverty are so easy to assume! But the theory is too plausible to be tenable. A wealthy public is necessary perhaps to the existence of authors who shall also be capitalists. A leisure class is a valuable stimulus to literary production. But money and the moneyed can neither command nor forbid the divine afflatus. The literary work produced solely by hope of gain is not much of an honour to any country. While authorship is a profession with pecuniary rewards like any other, those who are truly called to it obey a law far higher than that of demand and supply. Genius has always worked in poverty and obscurity; but we never find it withdrawing from its divinely appointed labour, and taking to law or merchandise on that account. When the great Canadian *litterateur* recognises himself he will not pause to weigh the possibilities of Canada's literary market before he writes the novel or the poem that is to redeem our literary reputation. Let genius be declared amongst us, and the market may be relied upon to adjust itself to the marvellous circumstance, for a great deal of the talk of Canadian poverty is the veriest nonsense. Riches are relative. We have no bonanza kings; but our railroad magnates are comfortably, not to say luxuriously, housed and horsed and apparelled. We work hard, but the soil is grateful; we are not compelled to struggle for existence. The privations of our Loyalist forefathers do not survive in us. We are well fed, well clad, well read. Why should we not buy our own books!

"We would buy them if they were written." That they are not written is partly our own fault and partly that of circumstances. We cannot compel the divine afflatus; but we can place ourselves in an attitude to receive that psychical subtlety should the gods deign to bestow it upon us. But the Olympians, bending Canada-ward, hear no prayer for their great guerdons. We are indifferent; we go about our business and boast of the practical nature of our aspirations; we have neither time nor the inclination for star-gazing, we say. The Province of Ontario is one great camp of the Philistines.

Apart from the necessarily untrustworthy testimony of one's own more or less limited acquaintance, there is but one proof of this—the newspapers; and in a free and enlightened country there is no better exponent of the character of the people than the character of its press. The influence of the daily newspaper upon public opinion is not greater than the influence of public opinion upon the daily newspaper. In a very great measure we dictate what manner of editorial we shall take with our coffee; and either of our great morning dailies is eloquent of our tastes. Politics and vituperation, temperance and vituperation, religion and vituperation; these three dietetic articles, the vituperative sauce invariably accompanying, form the exclusive journalistic pabulum of three-quarters of the people of Ontario. No social topics of other than a merely local interest, no scientific, artistic, or literary discussions, no broad consideration of matters of national interest—nothing but perpetual jeering, misconstruction, and misrepresentation for party ends of matters within an almost inconceivably narrow range.

"Why do you print no book reviews?" I asked the editor of a leading journal recently.

"People don't care about them, and it interferes with advertising," was his truly Philistinish response. And the first reason must have a certain amount of truth in it; for if it were not so, public spirit would never tolerate the withholding of such matter for the contemptible—in this connection—consideration of "advertising." Our French compatriots have not this spirit. But they have their Fréchette and their Garneau.

▼ ▼ ▼

A SPIRIT of depreciation of such faint stirrings of literary life as we have amongst us at present has often been remarked in Canadians, a tendency to nip forth-putting buds by contemptuous comparison with the full blown production of other lands, where conditions are more favourable to literary efflorescence. This is a distinctively colonial trait; and in our character as colonists we find the root of all our sins of omission in letters. "In the political life of a colony," writes one of us in the New York *Critic*, "there is nothing to fire the imagination, nothing to arouse enthusiasm, nothing to appeal to national pride." Our enforced political humility is the distinguishing characteristic of every phase of our national life. We are ignored, and we ignore ourselves. A nation's development is like a plant's, unattractive under ground. So long as Canada remains in political obscurity, content to thrive only at the roots, so long will the leaves and blossoms of art and literature be scanty and stunted products of our national energy. We are swayed by no patriotic sentiment that might unite our diverse provincial interests in the common cause of our country. Our politics are a game of grab. At stated intervals our school children sing with great gusto, "The Maple Leaf Forever!" but before reaching man's estate, they discover that it is only the provincial variety of maple leaf vegetation that they may reasonably be expected to toast. Even civil bloodshed in Canada has no dignity, but takes the form of inter-provincial squabbling. A national literature cannot be looked for as an outcome of anything less than a complete national existence.

Of course we have done something since we received our present imperfect autonomy in 1867. We have our historians, our essayists, and our chirping poets. And in due time, we are told, if we have but faith and patience, Canadian literature will shine as a star in the firmament. Meanwhile, however, we are uncomfortably reminded of that ancient and undisputed truism, "Faith without works is dead."

From the *Week* 3 (30 September 1886): 707–8.

SARA JEANNETTE DUNCAN

Thanksgiving

THANKSGIVING DAY! There is in some words such a breadth of suggestiveness, that one has only to write them with the necessary and appropriate mark of interjection, and, out of the letters which compose them, will arise as by magic, scenes and circumstances with which they are inseparably connected. "Thanksgiving Day" is one of these language necromancers. Trace it, say it, and instantly it lights and holds a candle in the shadowy brain-attic where we store our impressions and memories, and, despite the flickering of the candle and the prevalence of cobwebs, we may discover much that is both pleasurable and profitable to muse upon. It is rather neutral-tinted, the picture it illuminates for us—that is, the original sketch. Reproductions of the scene glow with warmth and colour, but that is the result of modern influences upon the hand that painted them; and, seductive though they be, we look longest at the canvas of the seventeenth century.

Cold, gray New England skies, bare branches silhouetted against them in the early morning light, which lies drearily across the thin November snow, piles of withered leaves in the primitive fence corners, a light curl of blue smoke from a colonial log-cabin, a church steeple, and Priscilla in the foreground, soberly apparelled in Puritan maiden habit, stepping over the weedy snow-clad fields, Bible in hand, to offer thanks for her unkindly lot. Not purer and scarcely whiter is the new-fallen snow than Priscilla's downcast face, nor is her drooping grace excelled by that of the straight-stemmed young pine tree in her path, its branches already weighted with their winter burden. No thought of vanity lurks in Priscilla's serious eyes; ribbons and gew-gaws have been banished so long as to have fairly ousted that very feminine fabric for lack of nourishment; and contact with aboriginal fashions has not yet been close enough or pleasant enough to bring it back again. She is counting up her blessings, that her prayerful enumeration of them presently may be easier, and among them she numbers an iron skillet by the last supply ship, several bottles of herb medicines prepared by the skilled hand of her aunt Charity, and the fact that she has found new sleeves in an unnecessary breadth of her bombazin gown. If she thinks at all of the froward youth who pressed her hand ever so gently as he helped her over the stile last Lord's Day, after the evening meeting, it is with reprobation; and if her thoughts wander to the more lightsome English holidays she has learned of by report, she summons them quickly back with a shudder for prelacy and unholy mirth. She hurries her staid footsteps past a low-set cabin, through the smoky window of which she catches a glimpse of an ancient crone bending over her gruel-pot, and adds to her thanksgiving memoranda the item that, by Deacon Hathaway's treatment of the cow by prayer and tar-water, Granny Green's evil spell has been finally exorcised, and Satan no longer interferes at milking-time. And so we follow her all the way to the bare little log-church in the gray middle distance, where she sits numb and patient with her uncomplaining sisters, and raises her voice in consonance with the somewhat grim and nasal gratitude of her Puritan brothers, as it was voiced by the thanksgiving psalmody of the time.

Some authorities tell us that the thanksgiving observance idea was absorbed by the Pilgrim Church during its exile in Holland, from 1608 to 1620, the fact adduced in support of this being that a day of thanksgiving was formally observed in Leyden, October 3, 1575, a year from the date of that city's deliverance from siege. But it is not probable that the Puritan mind, antipodal to all such vain merry-makings of the unregenerate as Christmas, Good Friday, or May Day, and anxious above all things to make even carnal desires minister to the glory of God, would have any need of precedent in such an observance, though it would, undoubtedly, approve the action of the worthy burghers of Leyden. Long before the Pilgrim Fathers left home for their short Dutch sojourn, the seed had germinated which blossomed into thanksgiving after the long later voyage was overpast, and the first Plymouth harvest was garnered in 1621, and on the new, kind soil that gave it, the early colonists knelt, and rendered gratitude and praise to the Hand that had guided and the Arm that had encompassed them through all.

Two years later we find a day of fasting and prayer appointed by Governor Bradford, on account of a long and severe drought that had prevailed. The rain that poured down upon the colonists' petition, even before it could have ascended very far, turned the current of their devotion, and the worthy man commanded thanksgiving services to be held upon another day and in a special manner. Some favourable action toward the colonies, taken by the Privy Council in 1632, induced Governor Winthrop, of the Massachusetts Bay Colony, to recommend a day of thanksgiving in the sweet June weather of New England, and to invite the Governor of Plymouth Colony to unite with him in its observance. Few, if any, of the early years of the colonies passed without such recommendation, however the cause for gratitude might seem to fluctuate. Records show that for a long time special circumstances, such as the arrival of supply ships and new colonists, were made the occasion of special thanksgiving, and that the day did not gain its special harvest significance until late in the history of the Pilgrims. During the Revolution, the observance of a day was annually recommended by Congress, but national appointment ceased after the general thanksgiving for peace in 1784, until 1789, when President Washington invited the new republicans to return thanks for the adoption of their Constitution. For many years, however, Thanksgiving Day was observed almost exclusively in the New England States. New York did not become officially and annually thankful until 1817, and the pleasure-loving, Christmas-keeping Southern States delayed much longer. As late as 1857 we find Governor Wise, of Virginia, when asked to appoint a day for such services, declining on the score of being unauthorised to interfere in religious matters; and, naturally enough, Southern participation in the thanksgiving for victories proclaimed by President Lincoln in 1862 and 1863 was not enthusiastic. About this time, however, the custom became as national as it may ever be expected to be, proclamations being issued simultaneously ever since by the President, the Governors of the States, and the Mayors of the chief cities, the date having been determined by custom the last Thursday in November.

The example of our neighbours to the south first occurred to us as being worthy of emulation in 1877, when Lord Dufferin, as most people remember, bade us give thanks upon a certain day in November—His Excellency acting under the mistaken impression that the colonists of Canada waited only for the opportunity. Lord Dufferin had not possibly been long enough among us to foresee the result of this high-handed proceeding upon the free and independent colonial Briton, but he was soon enlightened, and enlightenment brought the first and probably the only lesson on the nature of gubernatorial authority that very popular Earl ever received in Canada. He discovered that he had been guilty of an outrage upon Provincial rights in this dictation of a day upon which all Canadians should render thanks, and suffered the full broadsides of the present Opposition organ for his temerity in usurping a right that belonged to the Lieutenant-Governors, if to anybody. The organ boldly insinuated that for its own part it should grumble quite as much upon the date thus set apart for a different purpose as upon any other day in the year, Sundays always excepted, if not more, and that it considered the attempt to force upon the Canadian people a special day and hour for their assembling together for purposes of thankfulness and praise, simply subversive of the very principle of religious liberty itself. If this were a matter of trade and commerce, then by all means we should have the dictum from Ottawa; if of property and civil rights, then the dullest might see that it should be settled by the Provinces themselves. Fortunately for Lord Dufferin and the institution in so far as Canada is concerned, it became so difficult to decide, on account of the vast number of counsellors that darkened wisdom, under which of these heads the appointment of Thanksgiving Day fell, that the matter was settled without the assistance of Mr. Mowat, or the decision of the Privy Council. But there must ever mingle in the truly loyal Liberal's cup of blessing a hint of wormwood in the fact that he is not quaffing it at the bidding of an authority he wholly approves.

▼ ▼ ▼

With us Thanksgiving Day can never hold the place that it does in the United States, where it is not more an observance of national duty, as a memorial of what was best and worthiest in national life, and is closely interwoven with its very fibre. The day has no sentiment with us excepting that of a purely religious nature; the custom was superimposed upon Canadian character after it had fully developed. The graft seems to be promising, but it is not safe to speculate upon our ability to assimilate it for all time. Even in New England, where it has taken root in the rocks, as new influences assail the old Puritan character its hold is weakening, and the ever-increasing tide of foreigners, especially of Germans and English, in the Western States, is gradually bringing about a comparative disregard of Thanksgiving Day and an increasing respect for older holidays. And while one can see very well the propriety and great gain of preserving a spirit of thankful humility at all times, if possible, and the very great appropriateness of special seasons of thanksgiving when the occasion is manifest, the observance of a certain day in every year for such a purpose seems to deprive it of its voluntary character, and to give it a formal and stereotyped nature quite different from the real fervor with which it was originally observed. After a time of national disaster, moreover, it would not be easy to believe in the sincerity of national thanksgiving, whatever the feelings of individuals might be. Misfortune, we are told, is salutary, and should evoke our gratitude even more effectually than benefit; thankfulness in other words should be chronic with us. Most people have implicit faith in the principle this embodies; but its practice demands to the common mind too much of that other principle of doubtful acceptance involved in the old saying, "Heads I win, tails you lose," for general following. A special thanksgiving has a broad, generous voluntary significance. It means that the nation is not content with the ordinary channels of its gratitude, but must send it up to Heaven in a great wave of joy and praise. And this is what it meant when it rose from Massachusetts Bay two hundred and fifty years ago. But thanksgiving, because the day is set, and it should be the normal attitude of nations, is to a great many people almost devoid of meaning.

▼ ▼ ▼

The old Puritan custom counts many biographers, and among them some of the brightest names in American literature, which may be said to be positively pervaded by the odour of pumpkin pies, invariable accessories to any

Thanksgiving scene. The light, and glow, and warmth, and real affection with which New England writers have filled their Thanksgiving sketches are qualities in their work for which we also, who have given thanks but ten years, are disposed to be grateful. Had our Loyalist great grandfathers but shown a proper spirit on the sylvan shores of the Bay of Quinté, we also might have had such a heritage of association, and Canadian literature might have received at least an edible enrichment. Governor Bradford, we are told, in his observance of that earliest American Thanksgiving, "sent four men out a-fowling that they might in a more special manner rejoice together." This specialty of Thanksgiving has oddly enough clung to the observance. Its tenacity shows perhaps a subtler connection between the soul and the palate than modern science has yet explained.

From the *Week* 3 (18 November 1886): 819–20.

In his book *How to Write* (1943), **STEPHEN LEACOCK** (1869–1944) claimed that his skills had developed to the point where he could "write up anything now at a hundred yards." The claim is as much matter-of-fact advertisement of professional competence as boast, for Leacock wrote his essays and humorous pieces at a time when an abundance of widely circulated magazines were insatiably hungry for the work of writers who could expatiate on a whole range of subjects with style and wit. Thus Leacock, proudly non-specialist, moves competently into the field of relativity in one of the essays that follow, "Common Sense and the Universe" (a title that can itself be seen to describe Leacock's intent as a man of letters). But perhaps even more than for his writerly skills, Leacock remains perennially attractive to readers for his unflinching honesty, and for the bedrock of not-so-common sense upon which all his writings rest, as is attested to by "The Devil and the Deep Sea."

Leacock also wrote, on the first page of *How to Write*, that "Writing is thinking," and doubtless every writer in this book would concur with the sentiment. (Certainly it echoes Sara Jeannette Duncan's "Before I say anything I must have something to say.") Few writers since Leacock have displayed his ability to survey such a range of information and turn it into the kind of brilliant writing-that-is-thinking that continues to engage and entertain a remarkable variety of readers throughout the world. All told, he was the author of some sixty books, on subjects as varied as Canadian history, American humour, the gold standard, Jacques Cartier, Charles Dickens, Mark Twain, the British Empire, economics, the Canadian West, England, liberty, social justice, Lincoln and slavery, Montreal, and much more. Add to this that from 1910 until his death in 1944 he produced a book of humour just about every year and we have the prototypical portrait of the professional writer who could write up any subject at a hundred yards. Any list of highlights from Leacock's humour books would have to include *Literary Lapses* (1910), *Nonsense Novels* (1911), *Sunshine Sketches of a Little Town* (1912), *Arcadian Adventures with the Idle Rich* (1914), *Moonbeams from the Larger Lunacy* (1915), *Further Foolishness* (1916), *Frenzied Fiction* (1918), *The Garden of Folly* (1924), *Winnowed Wisdom* (1926), *Short Circuits* (1928), *My Remarkable Uncle* (1942), and *Last Leaves* (1945). At the time of his death, Leacock left four chapters of his unfinished autobiography, posthumously published as *The Boy I Left behind Me* (1946), an editorially chosen title that is, as Robertson Davies has observed, mistaken, because the nonsense-loving boy was always very much present in Leacock.

He was the English-speaking world's best-known humorist for the period 1910–1925, at one point earning a dollar a word for his work. Born in England, he moved with his family to a bush farm near Lake Simcoe when he was five, and was educated at Upper Canada College, the University of Toronto, and the University of Chicago (Ph.D. 1903). From 1903 until his retirement in 1936, he was Professor of Political Economy at McGill University. He divided his year between winters in Montreal and summers in Orillia, Ontario, the small town that inspired the creation of Mariposa in his best-known work of humorous fiction, *Sunshine Sketches of a Little Town*. In the aggregate, Leacock's writings reveal a man who esteemed the traditional values that he associated with family, charity, and community over materialistic ideas of progress. In *Essays and Literary Studies* (1916), he described these values as "all less tangible and provable forms of human merit, and less tangible aspirations of the human mind." Indeed, Leacock partakes in the tradition of the humanist essayist, which began with Joseph Addison and Sir Richard Steele in the early eighteenth century and continued with such writers as Oliver Goldsmith, Samuel Johnson, Matthew Arnold, and T.H. Huxley. The two essays that follow display some of these humanistic and conservative values in the voice that is uniquely Leacock's.

The Devil and the Deep Sea: A Discussion of Modern Morality

STEPHEN LEACOCK

The Devil is passing out of fashion. After a long and honourable career he has fallen into an ungrateful oblivion. His existence has become shadowy, his outline attenuated, and his personality displeasing to a complacent generation. So he stands now leaning on the handle of his three-pronged oyster fork and looking into the ashes of his smothered fire. Theology will have none of him. Genial clergy of ample girth, stuffed with the buttered toast of a rectory tea, are preaching him out of existence. The fires of his material hell are replaced by the steam heat of moral torture. This even the most sensitive of sinners faces with equanimity. So the Devil's old dwelling is dismantled and stands by the roadside with a sign-board bearing the legend, "Museum of Moral Torment, These Premises to Let." In front of it, in place of the dancing imp of earlier ages, is a poor make-believe thing, a jack-o'-lantern on a stick, with a turnip head and candle eyes, labelled "Demon of Moral Repentance, Guaranteed Worse than Actual Fire." The poor thing grins in its very harmlessness.

Now that the Devil is passing away an unappreciative generation fails to realise the high social function that he once performed. There he stood for ages a simple and workable basis of human morality; an admirable first-hand reason for being good, which needed no ulterior explanation. The rude peasant of the Middle Ages, the illiterate artisan of the shop, and the long-haired hind of the fields, had no need to speculate upon the problem of existence and the tangled skein of moral enquiry. The Devil took all that off their hands. He had either to "be good" or else he "got the fork," just as in our time the unsuccessful comedian of amateur night in the vaudeville houses "gets the hook." Humanity, with the Devil to prod it from behind, moved steadily upwards on the path of moral development. Then having attained a certain elevation, it turned upon its tracks, denied that there had been any Devil, rubbed itself for a moment by the way of investigation, said that there had been no prodding, and then fell to wandering about on the hilltops without any fixed idea of goal or direction.

In other words, with the disappearance of the Devil there still remains unsolved the problem of conduct, and behind it the riddle of the universe. How are we getting along without the Devil? How are we managing to be good without the fork? What is happening to our conception of goodness itself?

To begin with, let me disclaim any intention of writing of morality from the point of view of the technical, or professional, moral philosopher. Such a person would settle the whole question by a few references to pragmatism, transcendentalism, and esoteric synthesis—leaving his auditors angry but unable to retaliate. This attitude, I am happy to say, I am quite unable to adopt. I do not know what pragmatism is, and I do not care. I know the word transcendental only in connexion with advertisements for "gents' furnishings." If Kant, or Schopenhauer, or Anheuser Busch have already settled these questions, I cannot help it.

In any case, it is my opinion that now-a-days we are overridden in the specialties, each in his own department of learning, with his tags, and label, and his pigeon-hole category of proper names, precluding all discussion by ordinary people. No man may speak fittingly of the soul without spending at least six weeks in a theological college; morality is the province of the moral philosopher who is prepared to pelt the intruder back over the fence with a shower of German commentaries. Ignorance, in its wooden shoes, shuffles around the portico of the temple of learning, stumbling among the litter of terminology. The broad field of human wisdom has been cut into a multitude of little professorial rabbit warrens. In each of these a specialist burrows deep, scratching out a shower of terminology, head down in an unlovely attitude which places an interlocutor at a grotesque conversational disadvantage.

May I digress a minute to show what I mean by the inconvenience of modern learning? This happened at a summer boarding-house where I spent a portion of the season of rest, in company with a certain number of ordinary, ignorant people like myself. We got on well together. In the evenings on the verandah we talked of nature and of its beauties, of the stars and why they were so far away,—we didn't known their names, thank goodness,—and such-like simple topics of conversation.

Sometimes under the influence of a double-shotted sentimentalism sprung from huckleberry pie and doughnuts, we even spoke of the larger issues of life, and exchanged opinions on immortality. We used no technical terms. We knew none. The talk was harmless and happy. Then there came among us a faded man in a coat that had been black before it turned green, who was a Ph.D. of Oberlin College. The first night he sat on the verandah, somebody said how beautiful the sunset was. Then the man from Oberlin spoke up and said:

"Yes, one could almost fancy it a pre-Raphaelite conception with the same chiaroscuro in the atmosphere." There was a pause. That ended all nature study for almost an hour. Later in the evening, some one who had been reading a novel said in simple language that he was sick of having the hero always come out on top. "Ah," said the man from Oberlin, "but doesn't that precisely correspond with Nitch's idea (he meant, I suppose, Nietzsche, but he pronounced it to rhyme with 'bitch') of the dominance of man over fate?" Mr. Hezekiah Smith who kept the resort looked round admiringly and said, "Ain't he a *terr*?" He certainly was. While the man from Oberlin stayed with us, elevating conversation was at an end, and a self-conscious ignorance hung upon the verandah like a fog.

However, let us get back to the Devil. Let us notice in the first place that because we have kicked out the Devil as an absurd and ridiculous superstition, unworthy of a scientific age, we have by no means eliminated the super-natural and the super-rational from the current thought of our time. I suppose there never was an age more riddled with superstition, more credulous, more drunkenly addicted to thaumaturgy than the present. The Devil in his palmiest days was nothing to it. In despite of our vaunted material common-sense, there is a perfect craving abroad for belief in something beyond the compass of the believable.

It shows itself in every age and class. Simpering Seventeen gets its fortune told on a weighing machine, and shudders with luxurious horror at the prospective villainy of the Dark Man who is to cross her life. Senile Seventy gravely sits on a wooden bench at a wonder-working meeting, waiting for a gentleman in a "Tuxedo" jacket to call up the soul of Napoleon Bonaparte, and ask its opinion of Mr. Taft. Here you have a small tenement, let us say, on South Clark St., Chicago. What is it? It is the home of Nadir the Nameless, the great Hindoo astrologer. Who are in the front room? Clients waiting for a revelation of the future. Where is Nadir? He is behind a heavily draped curtain, worked with Indian serpents. By the waiting clients Nadir is understood to be in consultation with the twin fates, Isis and Osiris. In reality Nadir is frying potatoes. Presently he will come out from behind the curtain and announce that Osiris has spoken (that is, the potatoes are now finished and on the back of the stove) and that he is prepared to reveal hidden treasure at 40 cents a revelation. Marvellous, is it not, this Hindoo astrology business? And any one can be a Nadir the Nameless, who cares to stain his face blue with thimbleberry juice, wrap a red turban round his forehead, and cut the rate of revelation to 35 cents. Such is the credulity of the age which has repudiated the Devil as too difficult of belief.

We have, it is true, moved far away from the Devil; but are we after all so much better off? or do we, in respect of the future, contain within ourselves the promise of better things. I suppose that most of us would have the general idea that there never was an age which displayed so high a standard of morality, or at least of ordinary human decency, as our own. We look back with a shudder to the blood-stained history of our ancestors; the fires of Smithfield with the poor martyr writhing about his post, frenzied and hysterical in the flames; the underground cell where the poor remnant of humanity turned its haggard face to the torch of the entering gaoler; the madhouse itself with its gibbering occupants converted into a show for the idle fools of London. We may well look back on it all and say that, at least, we are better than we were. The history of our little human race would make but sorry reading were not its every page imprinted with the fact that human ingenuity has invented no torment too great for human fortitude to bear.

In general decency—sympathy—we have undoubtedly progressed. Our courts of law have forgotten the use of the thumbkins and boot; we do not press a criminal under "weights greater than he can bear" in order to induce him to plead; nor flog to ribbands the bleeding back of the malefactor dragged at the cart's tail through the thoroughfares of a crowded city. Our public, objectionable though it is, as it fights its way to its ball games, breathes peanuts and peppermint upon the offended atmosphere, and shrieks aloud its chronic and collective hysteria, is at all events better than the leering oafs of the Elizabethan century, who put hard-boiled eggs in their pockets and sat around upon the grass waiting for the "burning" to begin.

But when we have admitted that we are better than we were as far as the *facts* of our moral conduct go, we may well ask as to the principles upon which our conduct is based. In past ages there was the authoritative moral code as a guide—thou shalt and thou shalt not—and behind it the pains, and the penalties, and the three-pronged oyster fork. Under that influence, humanity, or a large part of it, slowly and painfully acquired the moral habit. At present it goes on, as far as its actions are concerned, with the momentum of the old beliefs.

But when we turn from the actions on the surface to the ideas underneath, we find in our time a strange confusion of beliefs out of which is presently to be made the New Morality. Let us look at some of the varied ideas manifested in the cross sections of the moral tendencies of our time.

Here we have first of all the creed and cult of self-development. It arrogates to itself the title of New Thought, but contains in reality nothing but the Old Selfishness. According to this particular outlook the goal of morality is found in fully developing one's self. Be large, says the votary of this creed, be high, be broad. He gives a shilling to a starving man, not that the man may be fed but that he himself may be a shilling-giver. He cultivates sympathy with the destitute for the sake of being sympathetic. The whole of his virtue and his creed of conduct runs to a cheap and easy egomania in which his blind passion for himself causes him to use external people and things as mere reactions upon his own personality. The immoral little toad swells itself to the bursting point in its desire to be a moral ox.

In its more ecstatic form, this creed expresses itself in a sort of general feeling of "uplift," or the desire for internal moral expansion. The votary is haunted by the idea of his own elevation. He wants to get into touch with nature, to swim in the Greater Being, "to tune himself," harmonise himself, and generally to perform on himself as on a sort of moral accordion. He gets himself somehow mixed up with natural objects, with the sadness of autumn, falls with the leaves and drips with the dew. Were it not for the complacent self-sufficiency which he induces, his refined morality might easily verge into simply idiocy. Yet, odd though it may seem, this creed of self-development struts about with its head high as one of the chief moral factors which have replaced the authoritative dogma of the older time.

The vague and hysterical desire to "uplift" one's self merely for exaltation's sake is about as effective an engine of moral progress as the effort to lift one's self in the air by a terrific hitching up of the breeches.

The same creed has its physical side. It parades the Body, with a capital B, as also a thing that must be developed; and this, not for any ulterior thing that may be effected by it but presumably as an end in itself. The Monk or the Good Man of the older day despised the body as a thing that must learn to know its betters. He spiked it down with a hair shirt to teach it the virtue of submission. He was of course very wrong and very objectionable. But one doubts if he was much worse than his modern successor who joys consciously in the operation of his pores and his glands, and the correct rhythmical contraction of his abdominal muscles, as if he constituted simply a sort of superior sewerage system.

I once knew a man called Juggins who exemplified this point of view. He used to ride a bicycle every day to train his muscles and to clear his brain. He looked at all the scenery that he passed to develop his taste for scenery. He gave to the poor to develop his sympathy with poverty. He read the Bible regularly in order to cultivate the faculty of reading the Bible, and visited picture galleries with painful assiduity in order to give himself a feeling for art. He passed through life with a strained and haunted expression waiting for clarity of intellect, greatness of soul, and a passion for art to descend upon him like a flock of doves. He is now dead. He died presumably in order to cultivate the sense of being a corpse.

No doubt, in the general scheme or purpose of things the cult of self-development and the botheration about the Body may, through the actions which it induces, be working for a good end. It plays a part, no doubt, in whatever is to be the general evolution of morality.

And there, in that very word evolution, we are brought face to face with another of the wide-spread creeds of our day, which seek to replace the older. This one is not so much a guide to conduct as a theory, and a particularly cheap and easy one, of a general meaning and movement of morality. The person of this persuasion is willing to explain everything in terms of its having been once something else and being about to pass into something further still. Evolution, as the natural scientists know it, is a plain and straightforward matter, not so much a theory as a view of a succession of facts taken in organic relation. It assumes no purposes whatever. It is not—if I may be allowed a professor's luxury of using a word which will not be understood—in any degree teleological.

The social philosopher who adopts the evolutionary theory of morals is generally one who is quite in the dark as to the true conception of evolution itself. He understands from Darwin, Huxley, and other great writers whom he has not read, that the animals have been fashioned into their present shape by a long process of twisting, contortion, and selection, at once laborious and deserving. The giraffe lengthened its neck by conscientious stretching; the frog webbed its feet by perpetual swimming; and the bird broke out in feathers by unremitting flying. "Nature" by weeding out the short giraffe, the inadequate frog, and the top-heavy bird encouraged by selection the ones most "fit to survive." Hence the origin of species, the differentiation of organs—hence, in fact, everything.

Here, too, when the theory is taken over and mis-translated from pure science to the humanities, is found the explanation of all our social and moral growth. Each of our religious customs is like the giraffe's neck. A manifestation such as the growth of Christianity is regarded as if humanity broke out into a new social organism, in the same way as the ascending amœba breaks out into a stomach. With this view of human relations, nothing in the past is said to be either good or bad. Everything is a movement. Cannibalism is a sort of apprenticeship in meat-eating. The institution of slavery is seen as an evolutionary stage towards free citizenship, and "Uncle Tom's" overseer is no longer a nigger-driver but a social force tending towards the survival of the Booker Washington type of negro.

With his brain saturated with the chloroform of this social dogma, the moral philosopher ceases to be able to condemn anything at all, measures all things with a centimetre scale of his little doctrine, and finds them all of the same length. Whereupon he presently desists from thought altogether, calls everything bad or good an evolution, and falls asleep with his hands folded upon his stomach murmuring, "survival of the fittest."

Anybody who will look at the thing candidly, will see that the evolutionary explanation of morals is meaningless, and presupposes the existence of the very thing it ought to prove. It starts from a misconception of the biological doctrine. Biology has nothing to say as to what ought to survive and what ought not to survive; it merely speaks of what does survive. The burdock easily kills the violet, and the Canadian skunk lingers where the hummingbird has died. In biology the test of fitness to survive is the fact of the survival itself—nothing else. To apply this doctrine to the moral field brings out grotesque results. The successful burglar ought to be presented by society with a nickel-plated "jimmy," and the starving cripple left to die in the ditch. Everything—any phase of movement or religion—which succeeds, is right. Anything which does not is wrong. Everything which is, is right; everything which was, is right; everything which will be, is right. All we have to do is to sit still and watch it come. This is moral evolution.

On such a basis, we might expect to find, as the general outcome of the new moral code now in the making, the simple worship of success. This is exactly what is happening. The morality which the Devil with his oyster fork was commissioned to inculcate was essentially altruistic. Things were to be done for other people. The new ideas, if you combine them in a sort of moral amalgam—to develop one's self, to evolve, to measure things by their success—weigh on the other side of the scale. So it comes about that the scale begins to turn and the new morality shows signs of exalting the old-fashioned Badness in place of the discredited Goodness. Hence we find, saturating our contemporary literature, the new worship of the Strong Man, the easy pardon of the Unscrupulous, the Apotheosis of the Jungle, and the Deification of the Detective. Force, brute force, is what we now turn to as the moral ideal, and Mastery and Success are the sole tests of excellence. The nation cuddles its multi-millionaires, cinematographs itself silly with pictures of its prize fighters, and even casts an eye of slantwise admiration through the bars of its penitentiaries. Beside these things the simple Good Man of the older dispensation, with his worn alpaca coat and his obvious inefficiency, is nowhere.

Truly, if we go far enough with it, the Devil may come to his own again, and more than his own, not merely as Head Stoker but as what is called an End in Himself.

I knew a little man called Bliggs. He worked in a railroad office, a simple, dusty, little man, harmless at home and out of it till he read of Napoleon and heard of the thing called a Superman. Then somebody told him of Nitch, and he read as much Nitch as he could understand. The thing went to his head. Morals were no longer for him. He used to go home from the office and be a Superman by the hour, curse if his dinner was late, and strut the length of his little home with a silly irritation which he mistook for moral enfranchisement. Presently he took to being a Superman in business hours, and the railroad dismissed him. They know nothing of Nitch in such crude places. It has often seemed to me that Bliggs typified much of the present moral movement.

Our poor Devil then is gone. We cannot have him back for the whistling. For generations, as yet unlearned in social philosophy, he played a useful part—a dual part in a way, for it was his function to illustrate at once the pleasures and the penalties of life. Merriment in the scheme of things was his, and for those drawn too far in pleasure and merriment, retribution and the oyster fork.

I can see him before me now, his long, eager face and deep-set, brown eyes, pathetic with the failure of ages—carrying with him his pack of cards, his amber flask, and his little fiddle. Let but the door of the cottage stand open upon a winter night, and the Devil would blow in, offering his flask and fiddle, or rattling his box of dice.

So with his twin incentives of pain and pleasure he coaxed and prodded humanity on its path, till it reached the point where it repudiated him, called itself a Superman, and headed straight for the cliff over which is the deep sea. *Quo vadimus?*

From *Essays and Literary Studies* (Toronto: S.B. Gundy, 1916), 41–61.

Common Sense and the Universe

STEPHEN LEACOCK

Speaking last December at the annual convention of the American Association for the Advancement of Science, and speaking, as it were, in the name of the great 100-inch telescope under his control, Professor Edwin Hubble, of the Mount Wilson Observatory, California, made the glad announcement that the universe is not expanding. This was good news indeed, if not to the general public who had no reason to suspect that it was expanding, at least to those of us who humbly attempt to "follow science." For some twenty-five years past, indeed ever since the promulgation of this terrific idea in a paper published by Professor W. de Sitter in 1917, we had lived as best we could in an expanding universe, one in which everything, at terrific speed, kept getting farther away from everything else. It suggested to us the disappointed lover in the romance who leaped on his horse and rode madly off in all directions. The idea was majestic in its sheer size, but it somehow gave an uncomfortable sensation.

Yet we had to believe it. Thus, for example, we had it on the authority of Dr. Spencer Jones, the British Astronomer Royal, in his new and fascinating book of 1940, *Life on Other Worlds*, that "a distant universe in the constellation of Boötes has been found to be receding with a velocity of 24 300 miles a second. We can infer that this nebula is at a distance of 230 000 000 light-years." I may perhaps remind my fellow followers of science that a light-year means the distance travelled in one year by light, moving at 186 000 miles a second. In other words, this "distant universe" is now 1 049 970 980 000 000 000 000 miles away!

"Some distance!" as Mr. Churchill would say.

But now it appears that that distant universe has *not* been receding at all; in fact, it isn't way out there. Heaven knows where it is. Bring it back. Yet not only did the astronomers assert the expansion, but they proved it from the behaviour of the red band in the spectrum, which blushed a deeper red at the revelation of it, like the conscious water that "saw its God and blushed" at Cana in Galilee long ago. One of the most distinguished and intelligible of our astronomers, Sir Arthur Eddington, had written a book about it, *The Expanding Universe*, to bring it down to our level. Astronomers at large accepted this universal explosion in all directions as calmly as they once accepted the universal fall of gravitation, or the universal death in the cold under Carnot's Second Law of Thermodynamics.

But the relief brought by Professor Hubble is tempered, on reflection, by certain doubts and afterthoughts. It is not that I venture any disbelief or disrespect toward science, for that is as atrocious in our day as disbelief in the Trinity was in the days of Isaac Newton. But we begin to doubt whether science can quite keep on believing in and respecting itself. If we expand today and contract tomorrow; if we undergo all the doubled-up agonies of the curvature of space, only to have the kink called off, as it has been; if we get reconciled to dying a martyr's death at one general, distributed temperature of 459 degrees below zero, the same for all, only to find that the world is perhaps unexpectedly warming up again—then we ask, where are we? To which, of course, Einstein answers, "Nowhere," since there is no place to be. So we must pick up our little book again, follow science, and wait for the next astronomical convention.

Let us take this case of the famous Second Law of Thermodynamics, that inexorable scroll of fate which condemned the universe—or at least all life in it—to die of cold. I look back now with regret to the needless tears I have wasted over that, the generous sympathy for the last little band of survivors, dying at 459 degrees below our zero (–273° centigrade), the absolute zero of cold when the molecules cease to move and heat ends. No stove will light at that, for the wood is as cold as the stove, and the match is as cold as both, and the dead fingers motionless.

I remember meeting this inexorable law for the first time in reading, as a little boy, a piece of "popular science" entitled *Our Great Timepiece Running Down*. It was by Richard Proctor, whose science-bogeys were as terrifying as Mrs. Crow's *Night Thoughts*, only slower in action. The sun, it appeared, was cooling; soon it would be all over. Lord Kelvin presently ratified this. Being Scotch, he didn't mind damnation and he gave the sun and the whole solar system only ninety million years more to live.

This famous law was first clearly enunciated in 1824 by the great French physicist, Nicolas Carnot. It showed that all bodies in the universe kept exchanging their temperature—hot things heated cold, and cold things chilled hot. Thus they pooled their temperature. Like the division of a rich estate among a flock of poor relations, it meant poverty for all. We must all share ultimately the cold of absolute space.

It is true that a gleam of hope came when Ernest Rutherford and others, working on radioactivity, discovered that there might be a contrary process of "stoking up." Atoms exploding into radioactivity would keep the home fires burning in the sun for a long time. This glad news meant that the sun was both much older and much younger than Lord Kelvin had ever thought it was. But even at that it was only a respite. The best they could offer was 1 500 000 000 years. After that we freeze.

And now what do you think! Here comes the new physics of the Quantum Theory and shatters the Second Law of Thermodynamics into gas—a word that is Dutch for chaos. The world may go on forever. All of this because of the final promulgation of the Law of the *Quantum*—or, shall we say, the Law of Just So Much—of which we shall presently speak. These physical people do not handle their Latin with the neat touch of those of us who knew our declensions as they know their dimensions. Of course they mean *Tantum*—but let it go at that. *Quantum* is drugstore Latin, *quantum sufficit*. *Tantum* is the real thing—*Virgilium vidi tantum* ("I saw something of the Virgil").

At this point I may perhaps pause to explain that the purpose of this article is not to make fun of science, nor to express disbelief in it, but only to suggest its limits. What I want to say is that when the scientist steps out from recording phenomena and offers a general statement of the nature of what is called "reality," the ultimate nature of space, of time, of the beginning of things, of life, of a universe, then he stands exactly where you and I do, and the three of us stand where Plato did—and long before him Rodin's primitive thinker.

Consider this. Professor Hubble, like Joshua, has called upon the universe to be still. All is quiet. The universe rests, motionless, in the night sky. The mad rush is over. Every star in every galaxy, every island universe, is at least right where it is. But the old difficulty remains: Does it go forever, this world in the sky, or does it stop? Such an alternative has posed itself as a problem for every one of us, somewhere about the age of twelve. We cannot imagine that the stars go on forever. It's unthinkable. But we equally cannot imagine that they come to a stop and that beyond them is nothing, and then more nothing. Unending nothing is as incomprehensible as unending something. This alternative I cannot fathom, nor can Professor Hubble, nor can any one ever hope to.

Let me turn back in order to make my point of view a little clearer. I propose to traverse again the path along which modern science has dragged those who have tried to follow it for about a century past. It was, at first, a path singularly easy to tread, provided that one could throw aside the inherited burden of superstition, false belief, and prejudice. For the direction seemed verified and assured all along by the corroboration of science by actual physical results. Who could doubt electricity after the telegraph? Or doubt the theory of light after photography? Or the theory of electricity after reading under electric light? At every turn, each new advance of science unveiled new power, new mechanism of life—and of death. To "doubt science" was to be like the farmer at the circus who doubted the giraffe. Science, of course, had somehow to tuck into the same bed as Theology, but it was the theologian who protested. Science just said, "Lie over."

Let us follow then this path.

▼ ▼ ▼

When the mediaeval superstition was replaced by the new learning, mathematics, astronomy, and physics were the first sciences to get organized and definite. By the opening of the nineteenth century they were well set; the solar system was humming away so drowsily that Laplace was able to assure Napoleon that he didn't need God to watch over it. Gravitation worked like clockwork, and clockwork worked like gravitation. Chemistry, which, like electricity, was nothing but a set of experiments in Benjamin Franklin's time, turned into a science after Lavoisier had discovered that fire was not a thing but a process, something happening to things—an idea so far above the common thought that they guillotined him for it in 1794. Dalton followed and showed that all things could be broken up into a set of very, very small atoms, grouped into molecules all acting according to plan. With Faraday and Maxwell, electricity, which turned out to be the same as magnetism, or interchangeable with it, fell into its place in the new order of science.

By about 1880 it seemed as if the world of science was fairly well explained. Metaphysics still talked in its sleep. Theology still preached sermons. It took issue with much of the new science, especially with geology and the new evolutionary science of life that went with the new physical world. But science paid little attention.

For the whole thing was so amazingly simple. There you had your space and time, two things too obvious to explain. Here you had your matter, made up of solid little atoms, infinitely small but really just like birdseed. All this was set going by and with the Law of Gravitation. Once started, the nebulous world condensed into suns, the suns threw off planets, the planets cooled, life resulted and presently became conscious, conscious life got higher up and higher up till you had apes, then Bishop Wilberforce, and then Professor Huxley.

A few little mysteries remained, such as the question of what space and matter and time and life and consciousness really were. But all this was conveniently called by Herbert Spencer the *Unknowable*, and then locked in a cupboard and left there.

Everything was thus reduced to a sort of Dead Certainty. Just one awkward skeleton remained in the cupboard. And that was the peculiar, mysterious aspect of electricity, which was not exactly a thing and yet was more than an idea. There was also, and electricity only helped to make it worse, the old puzzle about "action at a distance." How does gravitation pull all the way from here to the sun? And if there is *nothing* in space, how does light get across from the sun in eight minutes, and even all the way from Sirius in eight years?

Even the invention of "ether" as a sort of universal jelly that could have ripples shaken across it proved a little unconvincing.

Then, just at the turn of the century, the whole structure began to crumble.

The first note of warning that something was wrong came with the discovery of X-rays. Sir William Crookes, accidentally leaving around tubes of rarefied gas, stumbled on "radiant matter," or "matter in the fourth state," as accidentally as Columbus discovered America. The British Government knighted him at once (1897), but it was too late. The thing had started. Then came Guglielmo Marconi with the revelation of more waves, and universal at that. Light, the world had learned to accept, because we can see it, but this was fun in the dark.

There followed the researches of the radioactivity school and, above all, those of Ernest Rutherford which revolutionized the theory of matter. I knew Rutherford well as we were colleagues at McGill for seven years. I am quite sure that he had no original intention of upsetting the foundations of the universe. Yet that is what he did, and he was in due course very properly raised to the peerage for it.

When Rutherford was done with the atom, all the solidity was pretty well knocked out of it.

Till these researches began, people commonly thought of atoms as something like birdseed—little round, solid particles, ever so little, billions to an inch. They were small. But they were there. You could weigh them. You could apply to them all the laws of Isaac Newton about weight and velocity and mass and gravitation—in other words, the whole of first-year physics.

Let us try to show what Rutherford did to the atom. Imagine to yourself an Irishman whirling a shillelagh around his head with the rapidity and dexterity known only in Tipperary or Donegal. If you come anywhere near, you'll get hit with the shillelagh. Now make it go faster; faster still; get it going so fast that you can't tell which is Irishman and which is shillelagh. The whole combination has turned into a green blur. If you shoot a bullet at it, it will probably go through, as there is mostly nothing there. Yet if you go up against it, it won't hit you now, because the shillelagh is going so fast that you will seem to come against a solid surface. Now make the Irishman smaller and the shillelagh longer. In fact, you don't need the Irishman at all; just his force, his Irish determination, so to speak. Just keep that, the *disturbance*. And you don't need the shillelagh either, just the *field of force* that it sweeps. There! Now put in two Irishmen and two shillelaghs and reduce them in the same way to one solid body—at least it seems solid but you can shoot bullets through it anywhere now. What you have now is a hydrogen atom—one proton and one electron flying around as a *disturbance* in space. Put in more Irishmen and more shillelaghs—or, rather, more protons and electrons—and you get other kinds of atoms. Put in a whole lot—eleven protons, eleven electrons; that is a sodium atom. Bunch the atoms together into combinations called molecules, themselves flying around—and there you are! That's solid matter, and nothing in it at all except disturbance. You're standing on it right now: the molecules are beating against your feet. But there is nothing there, and nothing in your feet. This may help you to understand how "waves," ripples of disturbance—for instance, the disturbance you call radio—go right through all matter, indeed right through *you*, as if you weren't there. You see, you aren't.

The peculiar thing about this atomic theory was that whatever the atoms were, birdseed or disturbance, it made no difference in the way they acted. They followed all the laws of mechanics and motion, or they seemed to. There was no need to change any idea of space or time because of them. Matter was their forte, like wax figures with Artemus Ward.

One must not confuse Rutherford's work on atoms with Einstein's theories of space and time. Rutherford worked all his life without reference to Einstein. Even in his later days at the Cavendish Laboratory at Cambridge when he began, ungratefully, to smash up the atom that had made him, he needed nothing from Einstein. I once asked Rutherford—it was at the height of the popular interest in Einstein in 1923—what he thought of Einstein's relativity. "Oh, that stuff!" he said. "We never bother with that in our work!" His admirable biographer, Professor A.S. Eve, tells us that when the German physicist, Wien, told Rutherford that no Anglo-Saxon could understand relativity, Rutherford answered, "No, they have too much sense."

But it was Einstein who made the real trouble. He announced in 1905 that there was no such thing as absolute rest. After that there never was. But it was not till just after the Great War that the reading public caught on to Einstein and that little books on "Relativity" covered the bookstalls.

Einstein knocked out space and time, as Rutherford knocked out matter. The general viewpoint of relativity toward space is very simple. Einstein explains that there is no such place as *here*. "But," you answer, "I'm here; here is where I am right now." But you're moving, you're spinning around as the earth spins; and you and the earth are both spinning around the sun, and the sun is rushing through space toward a distant galaxy, and the galaxy itself is beating it away at 26 000 miles a second. Now, where is that spot that is here! How did you mark it? You remember the story of the two idiots who were out fishing, and one said, "We should have marked that place where we got all the fish," and the other said, "I did; I marked it on the boat." Well, that's it. That's *here*.

You can see it better still if you imagine the universe swept absolutely empty: nothing in it, not even *you*. Now put a *point* in it, just one point. Where is it? Why, obviously it's nowhere. If you say it's right there, where do you mean by there? In which direction is there? In *that* direction? Oh! Hold on, you're sticking yourself in to make a direction. It's in *no* direction; there aren't any directions. Now put in another point. Which is which? You can't tell. They *both* are. One is on the right, you say, and one on the left. You keep out of that space! There's no right and no left. Join the points with a line. Now you think you've got something, and I admit this is the nearest you have come to it. But is the line long or short? How long is it? Length soon vanishes into a purely relative term. One thing is longer than another: that's all.

There's no harm in this, so far. To many people it's as obvious as it is harmless. But that's only the beginning. Leave space alone for a moment and take on time and then things begin to thicken. If there is no such place as here, a similar line of thought will show that there's no such time as now—not absolutely now. Empty the universe again as you did before, with not a speck in it, and now ask, What time is it? God bless me, how peculiar! It isn't any time. It can't be; there's nothing to tell the time by. You say you can feel it go; oh, but you're not there. There will be no *time* until you put something into space with dimensions to it—and then there'll be time, but only as connected somehow—no knowing how—with things in space. But just as there is no such thing as absolute top or bottom in space, so there is a similar difficulty as to time backward and time forward.

The relativity theory undertakes to explain both space and time by putting them together, since they are meaningless without one another, into a compound called "space-time continuum." Time thus becomes, they say, the fourth dimension of space. Until just recently it was claimed further that to fit these relationships together, to harmonize space and time, space must have a curve, or curvature. This was put over to the common mind by comparing what happens in space with what happens to a fly walking on a sphere (a globe). The fly walks and walks and never gets to the end. It's curved. The joke is on the fly. So was the joke long ago on the mediaeval people who thought the world was flat. "What happened to the theory of the earth," writes Eddington, "has happened also to the world of space and time."

The idea was made plainer for us by comparing space-time to an onion skin, or rather to an infinite number of onion skins. If you have enough, you can fill all space. The universe is your onion, as it was Shakespeare's oyster.

The discovery by Einstein of this curvature of space was greeted by the physicists with the burst of applause that greets a winning home run at baseball. That brilliant writer just mentioned, Sir Arthur Eddington, who can handle space and time with the imagery of a poet, and even infiltrate humour into gravitation—is loud in his acclaim. Without this curve, it appears, things won't fit into their place. The fly on the globe, as long as he thinks it flat (like Mercator's map), finds things shifted, as by some unaccountable demon, to all sorts of wrong distances. Once he gets the idea of a sphere, everything comes out straight. So with our space. The mystery of gravitation puzzles us, except those who have the luck to fall in an elevator, and even for them knowledge comes too late. They weren't falling at all: just curving. "Admit a curvature of the world," wrote Eddington in his Gifford Lectures of 1927, "and the mysterious agency disappears. Einstein has exorcised this demon."

But it appears now, fourteen years later, that Einstein doesn't care if space is curved or not. He can take it either way. A prominent physicist of today, head of the department in one of the greatest universities of the world, wrote me on this point: "Einstein had stronger hopes that a general theory which involved the assumption of a property of space, akin to what is ordinarily called curvature, would be more useful than he now believes to be the case." Plain talk for a professor. Most people just say Einstein has given up curved space. It's as if Sir Isaac Newton years after had said, with a yawn, "Oh, about that apple—perhaps it wasn't falling."

Now with the curve knocked out of it, the space-time continuum, with these so-called four dimensions, becomes really a very simple matter; in fact, only a very pretentious name for a very obvious fact. It just means that information about an occurrence is not complete unless we know both where it happened and when it happened. It is no use telling me that Diogenes is dead if I didn't know that he was alive.

Obviously "time-when" or "place-where" are bound together and coexist with one another. If there were no space—just emptiness—there could be no time. It wouldn't count itself. And if there were no time, there could be no space. Start it and it would flicker out again in no time—like an electric bulb on a wobble-plug. Space-time continuum is just a pretentious name for this consequence of consciousness. We can't get behind it. We begin life with it, as the chicken out of the egg begins with its cell memory. All the mathematics based on "space-time continuum" gets no further, as far as concerns the search for reality. It gets no further than the child's arithmetic book that says, "If John walks two miles every day for ten days," etc., etc. The child hooks space and time with a continuum as easily as the chicken picks up gravel.

▼ ▼ ▼

But, unhappily, we can't get away from the new physics quite as simply as that. Even if we beat them out on space and time, there is far worse to come. That's only the start of it, for now, as the fat boy in *Pickwick* said, "I'm going to make your flesh creep." The next thing to go is cause and effect. You may think that one things causes another. It appears that it doesn't. And, of course, when cause and effect go, the bottom is out of the universe, since you can't tell, literally can't, what's going to happen next. This is the consequence of the famous Quantum Theory, first hinted at by Professor Max Planck about forty years ago and since then scrambled for by the physicists like dogs after a bone. It changes so fast that when Sir Arthur Eddington gave the Gifford Lectures referred to, he said to his students that it might not be the same when they met next autumn.

But we cannot understand the full impact of the Quantum Theory in shattering the world we lived in, without turning back again to discuss time in a new relation, namely, the forward-and-backwardness of it, and to connect it up again with the Second Law of Thermodynamics—the law, it will be recalled, that condemns us to die of cold. Only we will now call it by its true name—which we had avoided before—as the Law of Entropy. All physicists sooner or later say, "Let us call it Entropy," just as a man says when you get to know him, "Call me Charlie."

So we make a new start.

I recall, as some other people still may, a thrilling melodrama called *The Silver King*. In this the hero, who thinks he has committed a murder (of course, he hasn't really), falls on his knees and cries, "Oh, God, turn back the universe and give me yesterday." The supposed reaction of the audience was, "Alas, you *can't* turn back the universe!"

But nowadays it would be very different. At the call, the Spirit of Time would appear—not Father Time, who is all wrong, being made old—but a young, radiant spirit in a silver frock made the same back and front. "Look," says the Spirit, "I'm going to turn back the universe. You see this wheel turning around? Presto! It's going the other way. You see this elastic ball falling to the floor? Presto! It's bouncing back. You see out of the window that star moving west? Presto! It's going east. Hence accordingly," continues the Spirit, now speaking like a professor, so that the Silver King looks up in apprehension, "time, as evidenced by any primary motion, is entirely reversible so that we cannot distinguish between future time and past time: indeed, if they move in a circle both are one."

The Silver King leaps up, shouts, "Innocent! Innocent!" and dashes off, thus anticipating Act V and spoiling the whole play. The musing Spirit, musing of course backwards, says, "Poor fellow, I hadn't the heart to tell him that this only applies to primary motion and not to Entropy. And murder, of course, is a plain case of Entropy."

And now let us try to explain. Entropy means the introduction into things that happen of a random element, as opposed to things that happen and "unhappen," like a turning wheel, good either way, or a ball falling and bouncing as high as it falls, or the earth going around the sun. These primary motions are "reversible." As far as they are concerned, time could just as well go backwards as forward. But now introduce the element of random change. You remember how Humpty Dumpty fell off the wall? All the king's horses and all the king's men couldn't put Humpty together again. Of course not. It was a straight case of Entropy. But now consider a pack of cards fresh from the maker. Are they all in suits, all in order again? They might so arrange themselves, but they won't. Entropy. Take this case. You show a motion picture of a wheel spinning. You run it backwards; it spins the other way. That's time, the time of primary motion, both ways alike. Now show a motion picture of a waiter with a tray of teacups. He drops them; they roll in a hundred fragments. Now run it backwards; you see all the little fragments leap up in the air, join neatly into cups, and rest on the tray. Don't think that the waiter smiles with relief. He doesn't: He can't smile backwards: He just relaxes from horror to calm.

Here then is Entropy, the smashing down of our world by random forces that don't reverse. The heat and cold of Carnot's Second Law are just one case of it. This is the only way by which we can distinguish which of two events came first. It's our only clue as to which way time is going. If procrastination is the thief of time, Entropy is the detective.

The Quantum Theory begins with the idea that the quantities of disturbance in the atom, of which we spoke, are done up, at least they act that way, in little fixed quantities (each a Quantum—no more, no less), as if sugar only existed by the pound. The smallness of the Quantum is beyond comprehension. A Quantum is also peculiar. A Quantum in an atom flies around in an orbit. This orbit may be a smaller ring or a bigger ring. But when the Quantum shifts from orbit to orbit, it does not pass or drift or move *from one to the other*. No, sir. First, it's here and then it's there. Believe it or not, it has just shifted. Its change of place is random, and *not because of anything*. Now the things that we think of as matter and movements and events (things happening) are all based, infinitely far down, on this random dance of Quantums. Hence, since you can't ever tell what a Quantum will do, you can't ever say what will happen next. Cause and effect are all gone.

But as usual in this bright, new world of the new physics, the statement is no sooner made than it is taken back again. There are such a lot of Quantums that we can feel sure that one at least will turn up in the right place—by chance, not by cause.

The only difficulty about the Quantum Theory has been that to make the atomic "orbits" operate properly, and to put the Quantum *into two places at once*, it is necessary to have "more dimensions" in space. If they are not in one, they are in another. You ask next door. What this means I have no idea.

Nor does it tell us any ultimate truth about the real nature of things to keep on making equations about them. Suppose I wish to take a holiday trip and am selecting a place to go. I ask, "How far is it? How long does it take to get there? What does it cost?" These things all come into it. If I like I can call them "dimensions." It does no harm. If I like I can add other dimensions—how hot it is, how much gold it has, and what sort of women. I can say, if I wish, that the women are therefore found out to be the seventh dimension of locality. But I doubt if I can find anything sillier to say than the physicists' talk of ten and twelve dimensions added to space.

Let it be realized, I say, that making equations and functions about a thing does not tell us anything about its real nature. Suppose that I sometimes wonder just what sort of man Chipman, my fellow club member is. While I am wondering, another fellow member, a mathematician, comes in. "Wondering about Chipman, were you?" he says. "Well, I can tell you all about him as I have computed his dimensions. I have here the statistics of the number of times he comes (t), the number of steps he takes before he sits down (s), his orbit in moving round (o), aberrations as affected by other bodies (ab), velocity (v), specific gravity (sp), and his saturation (S)." He is therefore a function of these things, or shall we say quite simply:

$$F\int \frac{s.v.o.sp.S}{t.ab}$$

Now this would be mathematically useful. With it I can calculate the likelihood of my friend's being at the Club at any particular time, and whether available for billiards. In other words, I've got him in what is called a "frame" in space-time. But just as all this tells me nothing of ultimate reality, neither do the super-dimensions of the new physics.

People who know nothing about the subject, or just less than I do, will tell you that science and philosophy and theology have nowadays all come together. So they have, in a sense. But the statement, like those above, is just a "statistical" one. They have come together as three people may come together in a picture theatre, or three people happen to take apartments in the same building, or, to apply the simile that really fits, as three people come together at a funeral. The funeral is that of Dead Certainty. The interment is over, and the three turn away together.

"Incomprehensible," murmurs Theology reverently.

"What was that word?" asks Science.

"Incomprehensible; I often use it in my litanies."

"Ah, yes," murmurs Science, with almost equal reverence, "incomprehensible!"

"The comprehensibility of comprehension," begins Philosophy, staring straight in front of him.

"Poor fellow," says Theology, "he's wandering again; better lead him home."

"I haven't the least idea where he lives," says Science.

"Just below me," says Theology. "We're both above you."

From *Last Leaves* (Toronto: McClelland and Stewart, 1945), 35–51.

Throughout his life in Canada and, indeed, for a long time after, **FREDERICK PHILIP GROVE** (1879–1948) remained a self-styled enigma in Canadian literary history. Until D.O. Spettigue published the truth of his life in *F.P.G.: The European Years* (1973), Grove managed to remain that figure who may well be the envy of many a writer: his own creation. Grove's version of his life is given in the fictionalized autobiography, *In Search of Myself* (1946), which won the Governor General's Award, but the truth eventually emerged and Frederick Philip Grove was proven to be Felix Paul Greve, born in Randomno, East Prussia, on 2 February 1879. Raised in Hamburg and educated in universities at Bonn and Munich, he was a successful poet and translator before getting into trouble with the law and emigrating while under threat of further imprisonment to Manitoba in 1913. There he began a new life as Grove and a new career as a school-teacher. Widely studied today in Canadian literature classes for fiction that is considered one of the first examples of realism in this country, his novels include *Settlers of the Marsh* (1925), *Fruits of the Earth* (1933), *The Master of the Mill* (1944), and *Consider Her Ways* (1947). In his novels, Grove portrays pioneering prairie farmers struggling against a harsh environment, their own ignorance, and a fate that is close to the classical understanding: a mixture of personal choice and unalterable circumstance. In terms of Grove's vision, to succeed in one area of life—as a farmer, say—is always at the expense of some other area, such as in personal relations. Yet Grove's heroes and heroines persist in prototypical Canadian fashion, and valorous persistence in the face of meaninglessness is perhaps the key to understanding Grove's view of human dignity.

His most popular book in his lifetime was a non-fictional exploration of the United States and of differences between the States and Canada. The success of *In Search of America* (1927) was achieved in large part as a result of Grove's lecture tours throughout Canada in the late 1920s. Yet despite this brief period of popular and critical success, and temporary financial security, Grove's life as a writer was one of struggle, poverty, and obscurity. He described his sojourn in Ottawa, where he was lured into assuming a position in an ersatz publishing firm, as "an isolation comparable only to that of an Arctic explorer, one afflicted with smallpox at that, lost in the Barrier, who, at the best, meets a scavenger gull."

As an essayist, Grove is most appreciated for his first book, *Over Prairie Trails* (1922), from which "A Call for Speed" is taken. Nevertheless, he proves himself to be excellent in the form—suggesting that he has in this regard been underrated—in such other collections as *The Turn of the Year* (1923) and *A Stranger to My Time* (1986), from which "Apologia pro Vita et Opere Suo" is taken. Grove considered this essay, written around the time of his disillusioning stay in Ottawa (1930), as "a sort of valedictory to his friends and enemies."

FREDERICK PHILIP GROVE

A Call for Speed

I held the horses in at the start. Somehow they realized that a new kind of test was ahead. They caught the infection of speed from my voice, I suppose, or from my impatience. They had not been harnessed by the hostler either. When I came to the stable—it was in the forenoon, too, at an hour when they had never been taken out before—the hostler had been away hauling feed. The boys whom I had pressed into service had pulled the cutter out into the street; it was there we hitched up. Everything, then, had been different from the way they had been used to. So, when at last I clicked my tongue, they bounded off as if they were out for a sprint of a few miles only.

I held them in and pulled them down to a trot; for of all days to-day was it of the utmost importance that neither one of them should play out. At half past twelve a telephone message had reached me, after having passed through three different channels, that my little girl was sick; and over the wire it had a sinister, lugubrious, reticent sound, as if the worst was held back. Details had not come through, so I was told. My wife was sending a call for me to come home as quickly as I possibly could; nothing else. It was Thursday. The Sunday before I had left wife and child in perfect health. But scarlatina and diphtheria were stalking the plains. The message had been such a shock to me that I had acted with automatic precision. I had notified the school board and asked the inspector to substitute for me; and twenty minutes after word had reached me I crossed the bridge on the road to the north.

The going was heavy but not too bad. Two nights ago there had been a rather bad snowstorm and a blow, and during the last night an exceedingly slight and quiet fall had followed it. Just now I had no eye for its beauty, though.

I was bent on speed, and that meant watching the horses closely; they must not be allowed to follow their own bent. There was no way of communicating with my wife; so that, whatever I could do, was left entirely to my divination. I had picked up a few things at the drug store—things which had occurred to me on the spur of the moment as likely to be needed; but now I started a process of analysis and elimination. Pneumonia, diphtheria, scarlatina and measles—all these were among the more obvious possibilities. I was enough of a doctor to trust my ability to diagnose. I knew that my wife would in that respect rather rely on me than on the average country-town practitioner. All the greater was my responsibility.

Since the horses had not been fed for their mid-day meal, I had in any case to put in at the one-third-way town. It had a drug store; so there was my last chance of getting what might possibly be needed. I made a list of remedies and rehearsed it mentally till I felt sure I should not omit anything of which I had thought.

Then I caught myself at driving the horses into a gallop. It was hard to hold in. I must confess that I thought but little of the little girl's side of it; more of my wife's; most of all of my own. That seems selfish. But ever since the little girl was born, there had been only one desire which filled my life. Where I had failed, she was to succeed. Where I had squandered my energies and opportunities, she was to use them to some purpose. What I might have done but had not done, she was to do. She was to redeem me. I was her natural teacher. Teaching her became henceforth my life-work. When I bought a book, I carefully considered whether it would help her one day or not before I spent the money. Deprived of her, I myself came to a definite and peremptory end. With her to continue my life, there was still some purpose in things, some justification for existence.

Most serious-minded men at my age, I believe, become profoundly impressed with the futility of "it all." Unless we throw ourselves into something outside of our own personality, life is apt to impress us as a great mockery. I am afraid that at the bottom of it there lies the recognition of the fact that we ourselves were not worth while, that we did not amount to what we had thought we should amount to; that we did not measure up to the exigencies of eternities to come. Children are among the most effective means devised by Nature to delude us into living on. Modern civilization has, on the whole, deprived us of the ability for the enjoyment of the moment. It raises our expectations too high—realization is bound to fall short, no matter what we do. We live in an artificial atmosphere. So we submerge ourselves in business, profession, or superficial amusement. We live for something—do not merely live. The wage-slave lives for the evening's liberty, the business man for his wealth, the preacher for his church. I used to live for my school. Then a moment like the one I was living through arrives. Nature strips down our pretences with a relentless finger, and we stand, bare of disguises, as helpless failures. We have lost the childlike power of living without conscious aims. Sometimes, when the aims have faded already in the gathering dusk, we still go on by the momentum acquired. Inertia carries us over the dead points—till a cog breaks somewhere, and our whole machinery of life comes to with a jar. If no such awakening supervenes, since we never live in the present, we are always looking forward to what never comes; and so life slips by, unlived.

If my child was taken from me, it meant that my future was made meaningless. I felt that I might just as well lie down and die.

There was injustice in this, I know. I was reasoning, as it were, in a phantom world. Actualities, outlooks, retrospections—my view of them had been jarred and distorted by an unexpected, stunning blow. For that it did not really matter how things actually were up north. I had never yet faced such possibilities; they opened up like an abyss which I had skirted in the dark, unknowingly. True, my wife was something like a child to me. I was old enough to be her father, older even in mind than in actual years. But she, too, by marrying an aging man, had limited her own development, as it were, by mine. Nor was she I, after all. My child was. The outlook without her was night. Such a life was not to be lived.

There was the lash of a scourge in these thoughts, so that I became nervous, impatient, and unjust—even to the horses. Peter stumbled, and I came near punishing him with my whip. But I caught myself just before I yielded to the impulse. I was doing exactly what I should not do. If Peter stumbled, it was more my own fault than his. I should have watched the road more carefully instead of giving in to the trend of my thoughts. A stumble every five minutes, and over a drive of forty-five miles: that might mean a delay of half an hour—it might mean the difference between "in time" and "too late." I did not know what waited at the other end of the road. It was my business to find out, not to indulge in mere surmises and forebodings.

So, with an effort, I forced my attention to revert to the things around. And Nature, with her utter lack of sentiment, is after all the only real soother of anguished nerves. With my mind in the state it was in, the drive would indeed have been nothing less than torture, had I not felt, sometimes even against my will, mostly without at any rate consciously yielding to it, the influence of that merriest of all winter sights which surrounded me.

The fresh fall of snow, which had come over night, was exceedingly slight. It had come down softly, floatingly, with all the winds of the prairies hushed, every flake consisting of one or two large, flat crystals only, which, on account of the nearly saturated air, had gone on growing by condensation till they touched the ground. Such a condition of the atmosphere never holds out in a prolonged snowfall, may it come down ever so soft-footedly; the first half hour exhausts the moisture content of the air. After that the crystals are the ordinary, small, six-armed "stars" which bunch together into flakes. But if the snowfall is very slight, the moisture content of the lower air sometimes is not exhausted before it stops; those large crystals remain at the surface and are not buried out of sight by the later fall. These large, coarse, slablike crystals reflect as well as refract the light of the sun. There is not merely the sparkle and glitter, but also the colour play. Facing north, you see only glittering points of white light; but, facing the sun, you see every colour of the rainbow, and you see it with that coquettish, sudden flash which snow shares only with the most precious of stones.

Through such a landscape covered with the thinnest possible sheet of the white glitter we sped. A few times, in heavier snow, the horses were inclined to fall into a walk; but a touch of the whip sent them into line again. I began to view the whole situation more quietly. Considering that we had forty-five miles to go, we were doing very well indeed. We made Bell's corner in forty minutes, and still I was saving the horses' strength.

On to the wild land we turned, where the snow underfoot was soft and free from those hard clods that cause the horses' feet to stumble. I beguiled the time by watching the distance through the surrounding bush. Everybody, of course, has noticed how the open landscape seems to turn when you speed along. The distance seems to stand still, while the foreground rushes past you. The whole countryside seems to become a revolving, horizontal wheel with its hub at the horizon. It is different when you travel fast through half-open bush, so that the eye on its way to the edge of the visible world looks past trees and shrubs. In that case there are two points which speed along: you yourself, and with you, engaged, as it were, in a race with you, the distance. You can go many miles before your horizon changes. But between it and yourself the foreground is rushed back like a ribbon. There is no impression of wheeling; there is no depth to that ribbon which moves backward and past. You are also more distinctly aware that it is not the objects near you which move, but you yourself. Only a short distance from you trees and objects seem rather to move with you, though more slowly; and faster and faster all things seem to be moving in the same direction with you, the farther away they are, till at last the utmost distance rushes along at an equal speed, behind all the stems of the shrubs and the trees, and keeps up with you.

So is it truly in life. My childhood seems as near to me now as it was when I was twenty—nearer, I sometimes think; but the years of my early manhood have rushed by like that ribbon and are half swallowed by oblivion.

This line of thought threw me back into heavier moods. And yet, since now I banished the hardest of all thoughts hard to bear, I could not help succumbing to the influence of Nature's merry mood. I did so even more than I liked. I remember that, while driving through the beautiful natural park that masks the approach to the one-third-way town from the south, I as much as reproached myself because I allowed Nature to interfere with my grim purpose of speed. Half intentionally I conjured up the vision of an infinitely lonesome old age for myself, and again the sudden palpitation in my veins nearly prompted me to send my horses into a gallop. But instantly I checked myself.

Not yet, I thought. On that long stretch north, beyond the bridge, there I was going to drive them at their utmost speed. I was unstrung, I told myself; this was mere sentimentalism; no emotional impulses were of any value; careful planning only counted. So I even pulled the horses back to a walk. I wanted to feed them shortly after reaching the stable. They must not be hot, or I should have trouble.

Then we turned into the main street of the town. In front of the stable I deliberately assumed the air of a man of leisure. The hostler came out and greeted me. I let him water the horses and waited, watch in hand. They got some hay, and five minutes after I had stopped, I poured their oats into the feeding boxes.

Then to the drug store—it was locked. I hunted the druggist all over town for nearly twenty minutes. Everybody had seen him a short while ago; everybody knew exactly where he had been a minute before; but nobody could discover him just then. I worked myself into a veritable frenzy of hurry. The moisture began to break out all over my body. I rushed back to the livery stable to tell the hostler to hitch up again—and there stood the druggist, looking my horses over! I shall not repeat what I said.

Five minutes later I had what I wanted, and after a few minutes more I walked my horses out of town. It had taken me an hour and fifty minutes to make the town, and thirty-five minutes to leave it behind.

One piece of good news I received before leaving. While I was getting into my robes and the hostler hooked up, he told me that no fewer than twenty-two teams had that very morning come in with cordwood from the northern correction line. They had made a farm halfway to town by nightfall of the day before; the rest they had gone that very day. So there would be an unmistakable trail all the way, and there was no need to worry over the snow.

I walked the horses for a while; then, when we were swinging round the turn to the north, on that long, twenty-mile grade, I speeded them up. The trail was good: that just about summarizes what I remember of the road. All the details were submerged in one now, and that one was speed. The horses, which were in prime condition, gave me their best. Sometimes we went over long stretches that were sandy, under that inch or so of new snow, with sand blown over the older drifts from the fields—stretches where under ordinary circumstances I should have walked my horses—at a gallop. Once or twice we crossed bad drifts with deep holes in them, made by horses that were being wintered outside and that had broken in before the snow had hardened down sufficiently to carry them. There, of course, I had to go slowly. But as soon as the trail was smooth again, the horses would fall back into their stride without being urged. They had, as I said, caught the infection. My yearning for speed was satisfied at last.

Four sights stand out.

The first is of just such bunches of horses that were being brought through the winter with practically no yard feeding at all; and consequently their healthy outdoor looks and their velvety rumps were very conspicuous as they scattered away from the trail on our approach. Several times we dashed right in among them, and I had to shout in order to clear the road. They did not like to leave the firm footing on the trail, where they fed by pawing away the snow on both sides and baring the weeds. Sometimes a whole bunch of them would thunder along in a stampede ahead of us till they came to a cross-trail or to a farmyard; there we left them behind. Sometimes only one of them would thus try to keep in front, while the rest jumped off into the drifts; but, being separated from his mates, he would stop at last and ponder how to get to them till we were right on him again. There was, then, no way to rejoin those left behind except by doing what he hated to do, by getting off the trail and jumping into the dreaded snow, thus giving us the right of way. And when, at last, he did so, he felt sadly hampered and stopped close to the trail, looking at us in a frightened and helpless sort of way while we dashed by.

The next sight, too, impressed me with the degree to which snow handicaps the animal life of our plains. Not more than ten feet from the heads of my horses a rabbit started up. The horses were going at a gallop just then. There it jumped up, unseen by myself until it moved, ears high, eyes turned back, and giving a tremendous thump with its big hind feet before setting out on its wild and desperate career. We were pretty close on its heels and going fast. For maybe a quarter of a mile it stayed in one track, running straight ahead and at the top of its speed so that it pulled noticeably away. Every hundred yards or so, however, it would slow down a little, and its jumps, as it glanced back without turning—by merely taking a high, flying leap and throwing its head aloft—would look strangely retarded, as if it were jumping from a sitting posture or braking with its hind feet while bending its body backward. Then, seeing us follow at undiminished speed, it would straighten out again and dart away like an arrow. At the end of its first straight run it apparently made up its mind that it was time to employ somewhat different tactics in order to escape. So it jumped slantways across the soft, central cushion of the trail into the other track. Again it ran straight ahead for a matter of four or five hundred yards, slowing down three or four times to reconnoitre in its rear. After that it ran in a zigzag line, taking four or five jumps in one track, crossing over into the other with a gigantic leap, at an angle of not more than thirty degrees to its former direction; then, after another four or five bounds, crossing back again, and so on. About every tenth jump was now a high leap for scouting purposes, I should say. It looked breathless, frantic, and desperate. But it kept it up for several miles. I am firmly convinced that rabbits distinguish between the man with a gun and the one without it. This little animal probably knew that I had no gun. But what was it to do? It was caught on the road with us bearing down upon it. It knew that it did not stand a chance of getting even beyond reach of a club if it ventured out in the deep, loose snow. There might be dogs ahead, but it had to keep on and take that risk. I pitied the poor thing, but I did not stop. I wished for a cross-trail to appear, so it would be relieved of its panic; and at last there came one, too, which it promptly took.

And as if to prove still more strikingly how helpless many of our wild creatures are in the deep snow, the third sight came. We started a prairie chicken next. It had probably been resting in the snow to the right side of the trail. It began to run when the horses came close. And in a sudden panic as it was, it did the most foolish thing it possibly could do: it struck a line parallel to the trail. Apparently the soft snow in which it sank prevented it from taking to its wings. It had them lifted, but it did not even use them in running as most of the members of its family will do; it ran in little jumps or spurts, trying its level best to keep ahead. But the horses were faster. They caught up with it, passed it. And slowly I pulled abreast. Its efforts certainly were as frantic as those of the rabbit had looked. I could have picked it up with my hands. Its beak was open with the exertion—the way you see chickens walking about with open beaks on a swooningly hot summer day. I reached for the whip to lower it in front of the bird and stop it from this unequal race. It cowered down, and we left it behind. . . .

We had by that time reached the narrow strip of wild land which separated the English settlements to the south from those of the Russian Germans to the north. We came to the church, and like everything else it rushed back to the rear; the school on the correction line appeared.

Strangely, school was still on in that yellow building at the corner. I noticed a cutter outside, with a man in it, who apparently was waiting for his children. This is the fourth of the pictures that stand out in my memory. The man looked so forlorn. His horse, a big, hulking farm beast, wore a blanket under the harness. I looked at my watch. It was twenty-five minutes past four. Here, in the bush country, where the pioneers carve the farms out of the wilderness, the time kept is often oddly at variance with the time of the towns. I looked back several times, as long as I could see the building, which was for at least another twenty minutes; but school did not close. Still the man sat there, humped over, patiently waiting. It is this circumstance, I believe, which fixed in my memory the exact hour at which I reached the correction line.

Beyond, on the first mile of the last road east, there was no possibility of going fast. This piece was blown in badly. There was, however, always a trail over this mile-long drift. The school, of course, had something to do with that. But when you drive four feet above the ground, with nothing but uncertain drifts on both sides of the trail, you want to be chary of speeding your horses along. One wrong step, and a horse might wallow in snow up to his belly, and you would lose more time than you could make up for in an hour's breathless career. A horse is afraid, too, of trotting there, and it takes a great deal of urging to make him do it.

So we lost a little time here; but when a mile or so farther on we reached the bush, we made up for it. This last run of five or six miles along the correction line consisted of one single, soft, smooth bed of snow. The trail was cut in sharply and never drifted. Every successive snowfall was at once packed down by the tree-fellers, and whoever drove along, could give his horses the lines. I did so, too, and the horses ran.

I relaxed. I had done what I could do. Anxiety there was hardly any now. A drive of more than forty miles, made at the greatest obtainable speed, blunts your emotional energies. I thought of home, to be sure, did so all the time; but it was with expectation now, with nothing else. Within half an hour I should know. . . .

Then the bush opened up. The last mile led along between snow-buried meadows, school and house in plain view ahead. There lay the cottage, as peaceful in the evening sun as any house can look. Smoke curled up from its chimney and rose in a nearly perpendicular column. I became aware of the colder evening air, and with the chill that crept over me I was again overwhelmed by the pitifully lonesome looks of the place.

Mostly I shouted when I drew near to tell of my coming. To-day I silently swung up through the shrubby thicket in which the cottage and the stable behind it lay embedded, and turned in to the yard. As soon as the horses stopped, I dropped the lines, jerked the door of the cutter back, and jumped to the ground.

Then I stood transfixed. That very moment the door of the cottage opened. There stood my wife, and between her knee and the door-post a curly head pushed through, and a child's voice shouted, "Daddy, come to the house! Daddy, come to the house!"

A turn to the better had set in sometime during the morning. The fever had dropped, and quickly, as children's illness will come, it had gone. But the message had sped on its way, irrevocable and, therefore, unrevoked. My wife, when she told me the tale, thought, well had she reason to smile, for had I not thus gained an additional holiday?

From *Over Prairie Trails* (Toronto: McClelland and Stewart, 1957), 116–28. First published by McClelland and Stewart in 1922.

FREDERICK PHILIP GROVE

Apologia pro Vita et Opere Suo

Both my way of living and my way of writing have been bitterly, even venomously attacked. I have never answered any individual, waiting for some opportunity to say a few words in a less personal and more generally valid way. I will deal with the two in their order, as far as it is possible to separate the two.

For, after all, my way of living is conditioned by my aims in writing; or, in other words, I am a writer first and a living being only secondarily. It remains, of course, true that the total of the writer's work is necessarily determined by the sum of his experience, but with me, who am in my sixtieth year and have been writing and publishing for over four decades, though only recently under my name, the time has long since arrived when I deliberately limited experience in the horizontal, so to speak, and sank my shafts perpendicularly into the depths.

What are my aims in writing? What I have to say will sound presumptuous to many; it is not meant so, for nobody realizes more profoundly than myself how much achievement has fallen short of the aim in the past, and, seeing what life has made of me (a stunted growth, starved, by a relentless struggle for the daily bread, of intellectual food and of leisure), how much it is bound to fall short in the future. But my aim is still what it was at eighteen; and I would today rather live and work with that aim in view, knowing that I must fail of attaining it, than lower the aim and reach a lesser goal.

I aim at building the sort of work which, while like the pyramids, taking time to build, will also stand for some little time after being completed. But since time is a commodity of which few except myself seem to have a supply on hand these days (I have saved it for thinking and writing by the expedient of not spending it on either living or amassing wealth), how could I possibly exist except under conditions of almost total retirement? Metaphorically speaking, I live in the wilderness and cannot afford to take part in the activities of my fellows. Necessarily, in my way of living as well as of my writing, I am a member of the opposition; and whether I belong to a party of yesterday or tomorrow remains to be seen. Thus, though I am a lover of music, I abhor the gramophone and the radio; though I love to talk to my neighbours, I will not tolerate the telephone in my house; though I am keenly interested in the events of the world and the thought of my contemporaries, I read neither the daily press nor the average magazine and very few books (though, truth to tell, I read about as many good ones as I can lay my hand on—a thing which is more fully explained in a little unpublished work entitled *In Praise of Poverty*); for exercise I resort to walking without carrying steel-tipped sticks with which to drive a hard little ball before me; for entertainment, to almost anything but games. Otherwise I claim to be "normal." In a single word, I do not "conform"; and that, I take it, is the unforgivable sin in this our America of today.

We artists—for, whether my work will prove to be art or not, I am that psychological phenomenon, an artist who cares much for his work and little for himself—we artists need solitude above all. Unfortunately, we also need books and life; and in that contradictory need lies our peculiar dilemma. We need solitude because only when we are alone can we penetrate to any kind of truth—to that reality which, in so-called real life, is disguised by thousands upon thousands of inessentials. Not for nothing is the muse of female gender: like any real woman she needs to be wooed in a fury of concentration, not in the intervals of relaxation between the pursuit of a dollar and a dinner party. We need solitude, further, because only when we are alone can we abstain from the narcotics of a social life; we dare not use any stimulant but one, and that is sleep; like women during gestation we care too much for our offspring not to refuse all others, no matter how much we may crave for them. For let it be said that ours is a strenuous task. In the complex, involved, manifoldly conditioned "appearances" of this kaleidoscopic world we have to find what is common to all of them, what is simple and typical: the component parts of all those many patterns in the kaleidoscope which, to the casual observer, constitute the essential pictures. We abhor what makes up nine hundred and ninety-nine per mill of the current imaginative reading matter: all that is exceptional, picturesque, and baroque—the steep gesture, the exaggerated emotion, the florid phrase, the "queer" in character as well as in situation; these are the opiates of a nerve-racked "public." We artists grope for the stars; and perhaps our grasp will not reach them any sooner than the light of some of them reaches the earth; perhaps it will never reach them. We cannot help ourselves; we do not choose our themes nor our methods of treatment; they are imposed upon us. Nor are we greatly concerned about our failure or success.

But we have the consuming desire of that grasp. What, then, could we have in common with those whose dream is of the next movie-ticket or a more expensive radio set?

Our lives, I said, are conditioned by our work. What about that work, since it seems so important to us?

First of all, though we are the children of our day, we are not concerned with any sort of literary school or tradition—which, paradoxically, is our way of fitting ourselves into the so-called great tradition. Nor are we concerned with depicting, realistically or otherwise, the life of modern Canada or of any section of it. We believe that a good deal of truth about Canada may be culled from our books, and of a kind not commonly traded in; but to depict such truth does not enter among our aims. We are concerned with something more fundamental which we might just as well have propounded with a setting of ancient Greece or mediaeval Europe had we happened to live in such surroundings; for only then could we have been sufficiently familiar with that setting to use it. We are concerned with showing, in the casual disguise of whatever setting we have happened to be thrown into, some of the universally valid and generally human, and, we opine, therefore tragic or comic (according as you look at them) conditions of man's life on earth. (Is it not striking how soon mere "humour" becomes obsolescent so that a commentary is needed to expound it? And what is more barren than the expounding of humour?)

It has been said that our work, being stark, is fundamentally ugly. That may well be, though we do not believe it; ideas of beauty change according to the capacity of finding it. We are the heirs of two thousand years of Christianity and of half a millennium of science; and, though, in our aims, we go back into the past beyond both science and Christianity, we are profoundly influenced by both in our methods; meticulously we find a peculiar sort of happiness in finding knowledge; we are very conscientious and refuse to be bribed into compliance with the demands of our day: that is our Christian and scientific heritage which we may curse but which we cannot escape. On the other hand, just as Homer, Aeschylus, and Simonides live today, in spite of two thousand years of Christianity, so we aim at creating that which will live beyond Christianity and in spite of whatever sublimation may take its place. We shall most certainly fail in that; for, as I have explained elsewhere, this is not a time for the production of great art; but we are content to be the forerunners of such a time; and, to say it once more, we are not much concerned about our ultimate failure or success. Failure may be tragic; but we do not shrink from tragedy; we are not loose-lipped women.

Secondly, we consider even such achievements as that, let us say, of Dickens or Thackeray as mere preliminaries, as mere foreground achievements; quite likely their achievement will, in the long-run, outshine any achievement to which we may even approach; but the point is that it was won on a territory which we deliberately repudiate. They were the masters of mixed styles and the heirs of romanticism. The public calls us realists; we call ourselves classicists, perhaps in a merely epigonic sense, to borrow a term from German critics; time will have to tell; we are in no hurry. Much might be said about this opposition between romanticism and classicism; I have tried to say some of it elsewhere; but at the bottom of it all is this: romanticism places a right against a wrong; God against the devil; and we have long come to suspect that there is no devil; or that, at least, he is only one of God's degenerate children and god-like still. It may be well to state expressly that we do not limit the term romanticism to that comparatively insignificant (though, in a lyrical sense, extremely splendid and iridescent) fraction of the movement which, in England, found its supreme expression around the turn of the last century. Romanticism was a European movement and found more typical expression in continental Europe than in England: forms that continue to dominate much thought today. Classicism opposes a right to a right; and we, too, believe that there is no need, in order to arrive at a conflict—the life-blood of narrative art—to resort to a falsification of life. Life swarms with conflicts; in a sense it is conflict; and in every conflict both sides are right, for both sides are human.

The Victorians, I said, were masters of mixed styles. A mixed style softens matters down for a debilitated taste: it is the proper food for a pessimistic age (but, I am afraid, the diagnosis of pessimism has still to be made for that period of British history). We are just beginning to take courage again and to place ourselves beyond pessimism and optimism, where the ancients stood and a few of the moderns. Only ages of real courage, able to face life as it is, have enjoyed tragedy and its unmixed style. Tragedy is the proper food for men with masculine tastes; and so, by the way, is comedy, taking the word in its strictest sense which excludes both irony and humour. The mixture of the two is the food of a feministic civilization: the tear in the eye and a smile on the lip; and the reader divines that, in spite of its antics, the present age is trying to rid itself of the apotheosis of the "eternally feminine."

It has been said that our work is inconsistent in itself. That, too, may be, though hardly in the sense in which the charge has been made: we shall see by-and-by; there is no hurry. We choose *milieus*, so-called critics assert, in which problems are simplified because they arise in their lowest terms: our characters, they say, are primitive, unrefined by the conventions of a complex civilization, and inarticulate; yet, the moment it suits us, we let them express themselves with amazing lucidity. Primitive? Perhaps. But what is meant by the term? Birth is primitive; death is; and all of life between the two except in the inessentials of the methods by which its needs are satisfied. The charge of inarticulacy is, of course, simply nonsense. In a new country nobody is primitive if the word is to convey a lack of complexity in emotional experience. In that sense, the so-called sophisticate is more primitive than the transplanted peasant. The latter is merely silent under ordinary circumstances. That, in an emotional crisis, he shows his complexity with amazing lucidity is due to the fact that he has thought more, and more deeply, than the average dweller in cities. Like ourselves, the artists, he has had time to explore his own complexity. We, of course, assume the right to correct his spelling and grammar; we are artists, not phonographs. That, ordinarily, he does not speak without hesitation and seeming uncertainty, especially of himself, is due to his reticence, his disinclination to reveal himself, his pride. It is not true that what is commonly called education, except in its highest forms, makes for articulacy in a deeper sense; it merely makes for readiness of expression in inessentials.

Another point needs to be touched on here. National characteristics, and therefore the distinguishing features of national civilizations, do not primarily arise in urban centres; they merely crystallize there, provided they are strong enough, developed as they are elsewhere and transplanted to the city, to withstand the levelling and "shallowing" (*sit venia verbo*) influence of city life. Urban civilizations (except where they were urban merely in appearance, as in pre-Periclean Athens) tend to become alike in all countries. Even distinctions of language tend to disappear: see the Europe of, let us say, 1800. But the European peasant remained what he had been: German, Dutch, Swiss, Italian, Spanish, French. When the superficially unifying influence growing out of the cultural predominance of France in Europe, before 1789, had been overthrown (strange to say, by Napoleon), the capitals of Europe became national again, forced into their new (or old) moulds by pressure from below, not from above. Above, in Germany, f.i., stood Goethe, aloof from national aspirations (again, strange to say, this is even today made an indictment against him). We do not mean to say that national differentiation is necessarily a desirable thing; too often it is not; but the cry is today, "Let Canada be a nation," and therefore we repeat the differences in national character are most pronounced in those who are in immediate contact with the soil they sprang from; for they rest on geographic, topographic, and climatic conditions. Again, I do not mean to suggest that rural civilizations are more desirable or of a higher type; I merely wish to point out that in them the origin of national differentiation has to be looked for. In Canada, the fundamentally new things, a new attitude towards life and its mysteries, arise in the country, not in the city. In contradistinction to older countries, the city stands here for the conservative tendencies: the country is in a cultural revolt; the city tries to impose upon it some semblance of a cultural continuity. Between the two tendencies individuals are being ground up as between the upper and the nether millstones. This needed to be mentioned because it, too, is one of our topics.

One of our topics? Oh, the weariness of it all! For, what we are trying to do cannot become clear till at least a trace of the walls of that edifice becomes visible which we are trying to erect: so far, we have put down only a few of the foundation stones. And so we come back to this: either our day has been, or our day will come; we only know that, in our aim, we are not of this day of false fronts and shoddy. But we also know that, if our lives and works are to be of any value whatever (and we sometimes doubt it), they will be so precisely on that account.

From *A Stranger to My Time: Essays by and about Frederick Philip Grove*, ed. Paul Hjartarson (Edmonton: NeWest Press, 1986), 192–97. Published earlier in the *Canadian Forum* (August 1931).

ETHEL WILSON (1888–1980) had an unsettled early life. She was born in Port Elizabeth, South Africa, where her mother died when Ethel was eighteen months old. She then emigrated to England with her father, where at the age of nine she was orphaned, and subsequently moved at age ten to Vancouver to live with relatives. She died there in 1980. For thirteen years, Wilson taught in Vancouver's public school system, and as a young woman she took painting lessons from (as she describes her teacher) "a forthright woman named Emily Carr who lived upstairs on Granville St. at that time." As writer and model, Wilson herself has had an encouraging influence on the generation of Canadian women writers who came of age in the fifties and sixties, including Margaret Laurence and Alice Munro. In her fiction—six novels and numerous short stories—the early instability of her life finds uneasy expression in an atmosphere of the unsettled, of lonely heroines searching for connection and community in a world always one step ahead of dissolution and chaos. The natural scenery of British Columbia figures largely in her work, both as an arena for struggle between people and their physical environment and as provider of a wealth of metaphoric illustrations of the workings of indifferent natural law. Her own novels include *Hetty Dorval* (1947), *Swamp Angel* (1954), *Love and Salt Water* (1956), and the story collection *Mrs. Golightly and Other Stories* (1961).

Though not as well known as an essayist as some of the other contributors to *The Canadian Essay*, Wilson is the author of *The Innocent Traveller* (1949), a book that combines fact and fiction in its portrayal of the fortunes of a number of English women in British Columbia. In her more personal essays, many of which appeared in the early issues of *Canadian Literature*, Wilson creates and wryly promotes her self-effacing persona. As David Stouck has shown, however, this persona of the befuddled housewife-writer is not entirely true to the facts of Wilson's life, especially with respect to her vocation as a writer: she wanted to be a writer from an early age and served a lengthy apprenticeship in the craft; she was ambitious for book publication; and she was as serious as any high modernist when it came to matters of style and revision. The essay that follows suggests that Wilson's non-fictional prose deserves more attention, for the relation it bears to her fiction and for the subtle artistry of the ingenuous voice, always saying more than it humbly lets on.

A Cat among the Falcons

ETHEL WILSON

Let FAME, that all hunt after in their lives,
Live registered upon the brazen Tombes.
And then grace us in the disgrace of death:
When spight of cormorant devouring Time,
Th' endevour of this present breath may buy
That honour which shall bate his scythes keen edge;
And make us heyres of all eternitie.

So William Shakespeare, the worthy Friend and Fellow of his chroniclers Henry Condell and John Heminge—worthy Friends and Fellows too—takes up his pen and tears into yet another play [*Love's Labour's Lost*], and in the rush of the very first words of the play we hear all the winds of heaven blowing through. No one taught him how to do this. There was no need, for he knew. This was one of God's spies, who wrote of the ungentlemanly goings-on of the dog Crab, thrusting "himselfe into the company of three of foure gentleman-like dogges under the Dukes table," yet this was the man who set down the five terrible words, "never, never, never, never, never." His own mark is upon the words he wrote, and the endeavour of his present breath did buy that honour which made him heir of all eternity. This, I think, translated into ordinary talk about writing in our country and about its future, is my theme.

It is about fourteen years since I first put 50 000 or so words down on paper and began, later, to think about the inner workings of a person who writes even an ephemeral book. The writing part was not done in secrecy but in privacy and, as far as I am concerned, conditions of privacy are the only conditions under which writing can be done. I am sure that the business of writing is one of the four or five most private things in the world, excluding the planning of international treaties or crime.

The under-educated person, appearing in a learned journal, has a slight attack of the shivers and is at a disadvantage in educated company, but one soon resumes the pleasure of ordinary conversation. Of conversation, that practical man Henry Fielding said that one of the natural and essential parts of a novelist's equipment is conversation—talking in the daytime, talking far into the night, and with all kinds of people. Conversation is a book of knowledge concerning people. It can be electrically surprising—or not; and there are moments when it is one of the most charming and rewarding of human joys. So is silence.

I will tell you why I have placed at the beginning of this article the noble words with which Shakespeare opens one of his comedies.

To begin with, the words are written by the hand of glory, and that is enough. Further, they were written for a generation of men who loved glory and fame, not coefficients of expansion or statistics. Further, I think of Shakespeare himself and of the great endeavour of his present breath that made him heir of all eternity, and of lesser men than he, whose poetry and prose have made them at least heirs of time. And then I think of our own future, here, in which we seem to take a hand.

When much time has been spent in summoning and examining invisible images, in excitement, progress, recoil, and probable destruction, and at last a point is reached at which the inner note of completion is struck and the manuscript is reluctantly or eagerly passed into the publishing hand—a writer of novels, great or small, has been through a curious private experience. The emotions and thoughts among which he has lived (it may be for months or for years, depending on his own character, powers, and object) have provided a second life which is apart from the life he leads with people, sorrow, amusement, love, breakfast, death, motor cars, illness, satiety and change, and yet it pervades them all. I cannot think that at any point during this immersion in work the majority of writers seriously contemplate the idea of Fame or, as we say, fame. Perhaps these generations are less ardent. Keats, with his tragic fore-knowledge upon him, was a great and touching exception.

But if the writer has some merit, much merit, or astounding merit in which a rich and powerful quality is manifest, if indeed he has the Gift, then, like a thunderclap or like the strong slow movement of waters or glaciers, comes fame. He may by that time be dead. The thunderclap may be a misfortune, its effects transitory, and its sound superseded by other sounds, soon forgotten. Young Colin Wilson received such a thunderclap and his fame was perhaps his misfortune but he still has time, an active acquisitive mind, and possibly little judgment.

▼ ▼ ▼

My hope is that with the help of initially sound and natural individual processes we may in Canadian letters attain that honour which shall make us at least heirs of time.

I say "initially sound" because the chances of our literary fame are joined delicately and strongly to the conditions and progress of our early education at the present time and place. These conditions are so self-evident that we tend not to see them. Before the young student leaves school, he should be early familiar with the function and construction of a sentence (the sentence is a bridge, or it rests), and the paragraph. He should be familiar in a simple way with précis work, which trains thought and manipulation of language. He should begin to recognize that the sentence is something in itself which can be expanded and sometimes reduced in a variety of ways. His spoken and written language should be flexible and fairly easy through the medium of conversation, answers to questions ("True or False" will not help), and through frequent simple well-corrected exercises in the form of tales or essays. Then he can say what he has to say in the way he wants to say it. This is a great deal but not too much, and it can be assimilated, and should be and often is not, before a student leaves school, whether or not he proposes to enter a university. If the student proposes to enter a university he then finds the ordinary use of written language no barrier, but an approach. And if he is the story-teller, here are his tools to his hand.

Early education in the arts of reading and writing, and now a later habit of wide and varied reading (wide and varied enough to enlarge the faculties and prevent derivative writing) sharpen the self-criticism of the person I am considering—the potential writer. But the Gift is the crown, and the lack of the Gift is the lack of a crown.

Assuming that a potential writer of fiction has also the power of observation, that he has something that needs to be said or told, and a sort of osmosis, writing is an art very much to be learned by doing. Not even the judicious commentaries of E.M. Forster (*Aspects of the Novel*), Percy Lubbock (*The Craft of Fiction*), Elizabeth Bowen (*Notes on Writing a Novel*), the contributions to discussion in *Writers at Work* (Malcolm Cowley), or the studies of Lionel Trilling can teach a potential writer *how* to write, whatever provocative pleasures such books may give to either a potential or a practising writer. As Lubbock says, "It is pedantry to force rules upon a novel. We know of novels which everybody admits to be badly constructed, but which are so full of life that it does not appear to matter."

And so, the course known as "Creative Writing" renders me uneasy and year by year I am apprehensive lest the results in our country may be marked by a current mode or—contrariwise—a straining after difference, and lest our writing may become derivative and undistinguished. These courses can stimulate and give pleasure, and that is great gain; but the odds are there. It is a branch of study not indigenous here, I believe, but it is sporadic on this continent and will increase, whether I like it or not. I first recognized, unforgettably and years ago, the echoes of a Thomas Wolfe manqué in productions from our neighbour's house, and I have since heard other echoing sounds.

Of twelve Canadian novelists whom I have in mind, I will mention four dissimilar names—Gabrielle Roy, Morley Callaghan, Robertson Davies, Colin McDougall. I do not know the writing processes, early or later, of any of my twelve writers but I am impelled to think that most of them—equipped with their natural and varied gifts and their early acquired processes of language—travelled their own legendary way. I cannot avoid the conviction that a writer who can already handle his tools and write, is thereafter self-taught by writing (how the view opens out), and thus a literature is made. I am well aware of being what E.M. Forster calls a pseudo-scholar, and I have scholarly friends who disagree with me on this whole subject. It is possible that a preference for early and thorough familiarity with language, for privacy of intention, and the individual road in the matter of "creative writing" (I borrow the term, it is not mine), is a personal idiosyncracy only; but as I look over the wide reaches of writing and at the highly personal art and act of writing, I don't think so.

Something puzzles me—what is the boundary between creation and non-creation? One man writes about Peru and Peruvians; he writes what is undistinguished and true. The Editor of this Review writes about Peru and its people and there is manifest truth, and creation from manifest truth, the outward eye and the inward eye. One man writes about a river, but Roderick Haig-Brown writes about a river that never sleeps; there is truth and there is creation, the outward eye and the inward eye. Here is one of the mysteries that make literature.

With no thought of becoming a writer, I left school to enter life as I found it to be, which included earning a living. Following a hard-working and happy schooling in a spartan boarding school my education became unorthodox, eclectic, spotty, and ceaselessly interesting. The joys of a little learning are very great. My own discovery of John Donne almost before he had again entered the recognized Re-Establishment, dazzled me. My roaming discovery of the First Folio was as intoxicating to me as to the first readers of it (Shakespeare should be read in the Folio). The great blank spaces in my map are too great and I may be trapped there, but I cannot grieve very much. These discoveries of one's own are strong and sweet and lively. A university education is uniquely valuable and to be desired, different in kind from these vagrant discoveries smelling of sage-brush. The record in the U.B.C. Alumni Chronicle, alone, indicates the impressive contribution that graduate students make to our world, nationally and internationally. But here, I think, we are conversing about writers and how they come about and where they go. The absence of an enriching university education does not prevent the practice of the art of writing. A shoddy early education may prevent it and probably will unless one is a natural, like Samuel Hearne.

If we examine a great novel which attains and keeps a measure of fame, we are aware of the flavour of the writer's personality in that work, as a peach tastes like a peach, caviare like caviare, an onion like an onion. Although we rarely find in great works an over-awareness of the writer's self, narcissism, a deliberate self-consciousness, the mark of personality endures. If Henry James had been advised and convinced that *The Wings of a Dove* [sic] is "oh so beautifully" and nigglingly constructed and that conversations beat about the bush (which may or may not be true), he might have faltered in his intricate mode of writing and the pervading continuing essence of Henry James would have departed. If Henry Fielding with his knowledge of life's dark places and his shrewd unpretentious gaiety had been advised that it is against the rules to stop by the roadside and laugh at the customers, he would have smiled his long-nosed smile and continued to make his pertinent and impertinent observations, for that is Henry Fielding. The individuality of a great original writer, set into action by who knows what deep springs and events, produces James Joyce who produces *Ulysses* which William Faulkner does not produce, because he is William Faulkner. The strange man Marcel Proust—not Balzac, whose voice is different—writes *À la Recherche du Temps Perdu*. The unique and inspired idiocy (oh frabjus day) of Lewis Carroll, and no one else, gave us the "Anglo-Saxon attitude," without method but with meaning. I do not enjoy Sir Herbert Read's novel *The Green Child*; but does that really matter? The artist's personal vision and expression are there in his strange story. The unknowable Ivy Compton-Burnett, not the wise and knowable E.M. Forster, exposes *A Father and His Fate*. All these people are different, immensely expert, original, unteachable. I think that is literature. I have shot my arrows very high at these names, because we are thinking of fame, and some of the constituents of literary fame.

Some of the people that I've been talking about sit upon Olympus. Somerset Maugham does not pretend to sit upon Olympus, but I wonder if there is any novelist anywhere in the English-speaking world today who can write a straightforward story like *Cakes and Ale*, full of humanity and dexterous exposure. He is a master of the involuntary revelations of conversation. Henry Fielding would approve.

I wish to talk about Ivy Compton-Burnett because she is an extreme example of the explosion of personality in truly original writing. Some people lay her books down. I read her with almost painful pleasure and incredulous admiration. One had better not read two of her novels in a row, that is too many; a few pages, read with cold chills, will suffice, and then some more. Metaphysical, metaphorical, and real doors open and shut. She plays tricks with time and place. There are sinister reverberations of thought in a closed room. Not a sentence may be missed, for it hooks into a sentence past or to come or it strays into the universal air and the meaning hangs there. There is no landscape. The currents of a mind rise for one moment to the visible surface, taking their place in the story as violently as a railway disaster, scattering the injured. The demons are phoniness and domestic cruelty. Threads of moral beauty appear, vanish, re-appear in the sombre fabric of the tale from time to time, establishing (but elusively) the ultimate facts of good and evil. All this is done with ease, certainty, and a sardonic wit. Who could have taught her these curious powers? No one. No one knew all this before, although the words lay here and there for anyone to use. Let us not have another Ivy Compton-Burnett. One is enough. If this accomplished writer of fiction, who knows so much more than we do, should offer to instruct us (but she would not), should we accept? No, she is too much herself, and rightly.

There is a moment, I think, within a novelist of any originality, whatever his country or his scope, when some sort of synthesis takes place over which he has only partial control. There is an incandescence, and from it meaning emerges, words appear, they take shape in their order, a fusion occurs. A minor writer, whose gift is small and canvas limited, stands away at last if he can and regards what he has done, without indulgence. This is a counsel of perfection which I myself am not able to take with skill, but I must try to take it. I am sure that the very best writing in our country will result from such an incandescence which takes place in a prepared mind where forces meet. (A writer's mind seems to be situated partly in the solar plexus and partly in the head.) We do not look to an earnest mediocrity amongst us but to this personal incandescence in a lighted mind in whatever manner it shows itself. I think it was shown here lately, by Sheila Watson in the small book *The Double Hook*. Such work as that is individual, an emergence from within, not to be copied. We can recognize this phenomenon, great or in miniature, wherever we see it.

▼ ▼ ▼

During the years before the war, 1937–38, I began to write. I did not contemplate a future in this occupation—life as it was seemed already full—yet now, for the first time, I found it imperative to write. In my childhood we had stood, in Vancouver, on a sort of subsoil of a culture which, as the forests came down, had been vaguely prepared by our forebears in the haste of building and earning. They had arrived at the water's edge with their violins and pianos, some books, some pictures, ideas, undoubted aspirations, opinions—or nothing whatever. Many had memories, no money and a dubious future. Suddenly a small public library was housed. Here was this subsoil of theirs and this was where we stood when I was a child.

When, all these years later, it seemed imperative to me that I should write, I knew of no outlet for "my kind of thing" nor for an individual in Vancouver who was so looney as to think of writing, then. I sent some pieces to the *New Statesman* in London and they were published. Then the war closed down on us all. The distinguished, sarcastic, and admired Head of the Department of English at the University of British Columbia said to me during the war, "You are a damfool not to write." I was pleased by the compliment but disregarded the advice as I had other things to do, and one must go one's own way. Life took another direction.

After the war I immediately wrote an innocent novella which was published in Canada and in England and I then became aware of literary criticism in our country. I had long been addicted to the reading of literary criticism with great respect and liking.

When my husband and I were married in 1921, an impecunious cousin sent us the most valuable present of our lives. It cost him ten shillings, sale price—or was it five? This was a six months' subscription to the *New Statesman* with which were later incorporated the *Nation* and the *Weekend Review*. This weekly publication was execrated in all its works by the Right, venerated by the Left, and early banned by Hitler. That was my first introduction to literary and artistic criticism and political polemics. I soon read in all directions, regardless of politics and schools. What would have happened in my own mental life in a geographical area that was then still a periphery, not a centre, if this very fortuitous influence had not arrived and at that time, I don't quite know. Something else, more or less, because of a child's rigorous education and curiosity, for I had become one of Condell and Heminge's "Great Variety of Readers."

Hard years came when literary magazines died—Middleton Murry's *Adelphi*, Cyril Connolly's *Horizon, Orion* in London. Here I wish to pay affectionate and admiring tribute to my friend Alan Crawley and *Contemporary Verse*, to brave John Sutherland and *Northern Review*, and to *Here and Now* whose life was too short; these have taken their permanent place in the record of Canadian letters.

In those years immediately following the war, most (but not all) literary criticism in our country was insipid and uninformed. Now, in that scene, there is divination in Canada. The falcons cruise high above and search the literary plain where the game becomes more plentiful. Looking about us, we see and hear in many places and ways that the art of criticism is in a healthy state. Without that, those of us who attempt to write would be poorer. But with the increasing popularity of this art, there is also a fringe of prentice comment which goes by the name of criticism. It is one of my favourite indoor games—this game of opinion—but I know that it does not qualify as the art of criticism.

Critics of novels, some unkind people say, are disappointed novelists. That is not true. The critic has probably no desire to write a novel, though some have done so, failed, taken the bitter medicine, and they then know more about the peculiar difficulties and vagaries of the task the novelist sets himself. The finely acid or wise or benevolent and instructed pen of a superlatively good critic is the pen of a writer. Whether that critic is writing about a recent novel, a history of Crete, or a reprint of the life of an ant, he has a quality that makes him a tingling pleasure to the reader who may not even care about ants. The written and the deliberately spoken views of V.S. Pritchett stay in the memory.

A wry reflection that decades of reading expert criticism cannot make a writer out of a knowledgeable reader, does not detract from the value of good criticism. Neither does it damn the reader. The reader reads for stimulation, pleasure, and even for information, and by that form of osmosis which true readers share with writers, he acquires perhaps discrimination, perhaps a catholic and adventurous taste, and the gates of perception are held open to him. But however much those years of reading and criticism may enrich his life, they will not of themselves teach him to be a writer any more than years of knowledgeably watching first class tennis will teach him to be a tennis champion. The Gift is imponderable and unpredictable, and there is no satisfactory substitute.

If eminent critics disagree, that makes expert criticism peculiarly interesting and sometimes amusing. Opposite opinions of the unusual Australian novel *Voss* by Patrick White and James Gould Cozzen's wordy novel *By Love Possessed* point to human fallibility on the part of people who are supposed to know everything. That is reassuring for those of us who indulge in non-conformity of opinion or who are early inclined towards scepticism. Wit can be a delight in a serious critic, but not solemnity, the voice of the prophet or the Great Panjandrum. Dullness is a misdemeanour.

I find that in talking about novelists, their lasting or passing fame, and their critics (who are an undetermined factor in fame), I am thinking first and always as one of "The Great Variety of Readers"; in a small but definite degree as a writer; but not at all as a qualified critic. I am not a cat among the pigeons. I am a country cat among my friends the falcons who are handsome, formidable and trained birds, equipped to detect and pounce upon error. It will be better, now, to take my convictions safely indoors and sit looking out of the window at what I can see, and at the sky which is so beautiful.

From *Ethel Wilson: Stories, Essays and Letters*, ed. David Stouck (Vancouver: University of British Columbia Press, 1987), 94–103. This essay was originally written for *Canadian Literature* (Autumn 1959), under the title "A Cat among the Falcons: Reflections on the Writer's Craft," and was reprinted in *Masks of Fiction*, ed. A.J.M. Smith (Toronto: McClelland and Stewart, 1961).

HUGH MacLENNAN (1907–1990) has written novels of nationalist concerns that have made him a central figure in the debate about Canada's identity. As an essayist, too, his primary subject has been Canada and its people. Claude Bissell said it best when he wrote that "MacLennan's various collections of essays constitute, in supple and eloquent prose, a spiritual history of Canada since the end of the Second World War. No Canadian writer has contributed so much to national self-awareness and understanding." Those collections of essays include *Thirty and Three* (1954), *Scotchman's Return and Other Essays* (1960), and *Seven Rivers of Canada* (1961), the latter being a series of essays linked by a common theme, and from which the deservedly much-anthologized "The Rivers that Made a Nation" is taken. That essay and "Confessions of a Wood-chopping Man," along with the one that begins *The Canadian Essay*, "The Writer and His Audience," demonstrate more clearly than could any paraphrase why MacLennan is considered by many critics to be a better essayist than novelist. But such distinctions are finally beside the point in any consideration of a writer who excels in both forms. It might even be said that the only mistaken claim in "The Writer and His Audience" is MacLennan's generous attribution to Leacock of the distinction, "the best essayist Canada has ever produced," for surely MacLennan himself has a claim to that title. Despite his popular image as Canada's first "Canadian" writer, MacLennan finds universal significance in the most local of events and characters. In his essays, he does so with a wit and humanity that rivals Leacock at his best, while displaying an erudition and style completely his own.

Born at Glace Bay, Cape Breton, MacLennan was educated at Dalhousie University, at Oxford as a Rhodes scholar, and at Princeton University, where he was awarded a Ph.D. in Classics in 1935. He taught in McGill's Department of English from 1951 to 1981. His first novel, *Barometer Rising* (1941), and collection of essays, *Cross-Country* (1949), established the view of MacLennan as an interpreter of Canada, a reputation that he was to strengthen with subsequent books of essays and novels such as *Two Solitudes* (1945) and *The Precipice* (1948). His other novels include *Each Man's Son* (1951), *The Watch that Ends the Night* (1959), *Return of the Sphinx* (1967), and *Voices in Time* (1980). Recipient of a Guggenheim Fellowship in 1943, the Lorne Pierce Medal in 1952, and elected F.R.S.C. in 1953, Hugh MacLennan has won the Governor General's Award three times for fiction and twice for non-fiction.

Confessions of a Wood-chopping Man

HUGH MacLENNAN

Pleasure, profit, and beauty from a single afternoon's exercise—what more could a puritan ask, especially when the profit will not be reaped till next year, and the beauty harvested for years to come. As for the pleasure, merely to be alive on an Indian-summer afternoon in my part of the country is as close to heaven as my imagination extends.

After the first frost has turned ferns to brown dust and the birds have flocked south, the woods around my house in the country are filled with the living presence of silence. My feet crunch outrageously in the dry undergrowth as I make my way to the heart of the grove. My jeans are stiff with ancient sweat and my jersey is out at the elbows, the red paint has long ago been rubbed off the bow of my Swedish saw and my axe blade, several ounces lighter than when I bought it nine years ago, is honed sharp enough to sever a hair on my forearm. Looking up to the sky through the leaf-patterns I shame my environment by the academic thought that this scene is the equal of Sainte-Chapelle, but the comparison lasts only a few seconds. A hardwood copse in the Eastern Townships of Quebec in Indian summer can be compared to nothing else on this earth, being itself an absolute. By some recurring good fortune I am here; I am here with the axe, the saw, the wedge, and the determination to alter the landscape a little. It is a moment that involves every aspect of the slow change in my whole view of life over the past decade and a half.

I was born and raised in a part of Canada where nobody is able to change the landscape. Along the Atlantic coast of Nova Scotia you grow up with the conviction that everything in nature here is as it is forever, and that man, living with the shifting immutability of the ocean and the unshifting immutability of granite rocks, can never dominate his fate, never play artist with nature, but must take life and the world as he finds them. The glacier that set the mould of the Nova Scotia coast (and the coast set the mould of the Nova Scotian character) so denuded the rocks of topsoil that for evermore only a spruce will thrive there. From childhood I accepted the belief that summer, spring, and fall are much the same. One is grateful for a spruce if it is the only tree one really knows, but since any spruce is much the same as any other, and since no spruce ever changes its colours, the trees of my childhood helped the granite and the ocean to confirm me in the belief that nature can neither be altered nor improved.

It took me a good many years to respond to the soft luxuriance of the Eastern Townships, where the eye, the ear, and the sense of smell are played upon gently and with subtle variations. It took me no time at all, however, to learn that here the landscape can and must be altered from time to time because it is continually altering itself to your disadvantage. A house in the country for summer living must be tied to the earth by close plantings of shrubs and trees, to give protection from the winds and to take away its aspect of being a brash intruder. But a maple sapling grows eight feet a year in this rich, rainy land, and a small fir that looks like an incipient Christmas tree when you transplant it soon becomes a dense screen breeding swarms of blackflies. Where there was one butternut there is soon a grove, and within a decade the pasture in which your house was built has been taken over by a stand of maples, oaks, poplars, wild cherries, honey locusts, old apple trees, hornbeams, birches, beeches, and even some stray pines. Their roots are now under your cottage, their branches are joined over your roof, and they have made your home as dark as an animal's den.

The year I bought my house, I cut away every cedar, pine, and spruce that crowded it. This was an act with a double meaning for me. I intended to let the sun filter down through the branches of the great hardwoods farther back, and I also needed a symbol of emancipation from the stern acceptance of my youth, I suppose.

"You'll feel naked without some kind of protection, won't you?" said a neighbour. "Now there's only a garden and the lawn between you and the road."

He meant that *he* would; I felt as though cobwebs had been swept from a dirty window. What good to keep other people from looking in, if at the same time I was prevented from looking out? Anyway, I live high on a hill away from the village, on a dirt road that leads to nowhere, and the passers-by are few and friendly. Since my land slopes at a twenty-five-degree angle and the road is below the house, I can overlook any activity on the road and let my eye take in a view that extends for ten miles over a deep lake indented with bays that lap the feet of thrusting hills. I can look across wind-blown farms and red-pine headlands and the shining roofs of new cattle barns.

I began to cut in order to get sun and air into the house and I continued to cut in order to get sun and air into the surrounding woods. The second year

I was mildly surprised to discover that the wood I cut had saved me many dollars. Then I bought a lot across the road and down the hill to protect our view. But the view gradually disappeared behind a wall of rapidly growing trees. They were a fine mixture of greens in summer and an unbelievable blend of colours in the fall, but living with them in front of me was like living behind a seventy-foot hedge.

So, over the years, those rapidly growing trees have given a pattern to my life in much the same way that his rotating wheatfields pattern the life of the farmer. Come the fall and I must get to work on them.

I have a neighbour who thinks it a crime to cut any oak, but what do you do if you have two oaks within six feet of one another? I run my hand over the smooth, olive-green trunk and feel the hard muscles inside the bark. An oak, especially a young one, feels human when your hand strokes it. But more than any tree in the forest, the oak needs room to grow. Its roots spread wide and lie close to the surface of the earth. I look up at this pair and see that they had grown like basketball players, tall, thin, and not much good for anything else but growing tall and thin. Their lowest branches are at least twenty-five feet above the ground, since it was always dark in here before I got busy cutting out the saplings, and the trees had to thrust high in order to reach the life-giving sun. I feel the trunks of both and decide that the spindlier one must go, to give the other a chance to fulfill the destiny of an oak.

So I go down on both knees, set the saw at the trunk of the victim, and get to work. In such a close-grained tree the opening made by the slim saw-blade is almost invisible once the saw has buried itself in the trunk. White dust spurts out, to become brown as the blade reaches the darker heart of the tree. Then comes the crack—hard, solid, vibrating up the entire length of the trunk and echoing through the silent copse. There is a shiver, a twitch in the pinky-brown plumage, a moment of hesitation. As I stand up and watch, one hand on the trunk, the tree nods in the direction I had intended it to fall, then goes down in a swooshing, stately plunge. There is a flash of scarlet as a maple is brushed on the way down. Inevitably the oak comes to rest at an angle, its cascading upper branches caught by the interlocking branches of neighbouring trees.

In the new silence I consider my next move. A fallen tree, even one as modest as this, creates a sizable wreckage. I think of Mr. Gladstone, who used to slay giant oaks, Royal Navy oaks, to relieve his emotions. When Disraeli was extraordinarily witty or the Queen ordinarily rude, another oak on the estate of the Grand Old Man was doomed to fall. And then there was the labour of cleaning up the mess, a job that I know from experience must have taken days. So far as I can discover from my reading, the Prime Minister gave little thought to this aspect of forestry. He was able to sate his aggressions and stalk off, sweaty under the armpits but with his Victorian waistcoat still in place, while humbler men took over the long task of trimming the oak, sawing its trunk into logs, splitting them and trundling them into the woodshed. Humbler men without the need to sublimate a libido must have stacked and burned Mr. Gladstone's slash.

Perhaps the psychiatrist who lives below me on his own tree-enclosed acreage, hearing the crash of my falling oak, thinks I am ridding myself of aggression, too. He may even think I am slaying a father-image. But no matter what he thinks, my oak has merely been severed at the base, it has not been transformed into cordwood.

It was cold last night. It was colder still at six this morning when I peered out at the thermometer and saw that the mercury stood at twenty-seven degrees. When I got out of bed at eight and built a fire there was still rime on the lawn. The day was fine and clear, but it was so cold my fireplace consumed ten logs before one o'clock. This year a short cord sells at seven dollars, a long cord at anything from fifteen to twenty, depending on what kind of wood it contains. No matter what my woodpile represents to a psychologist, it gives me an intense pleasure to use it for warmth, even though (as the countrywoman remarked yesterday when she came in to clean the house) it takes a lot of sweat to build a woodpile.

I think, sometimes, that Mr. Gladstone missed the best part of tree-cutting. Each fallen tree presents its own problems, and the man who walks off and leaves them is as bad a tree-butcher as the one who murders a copse with a power saw. This oak of mine is entangled with two other trees and of course the simplest thing to do is cut them both down so that all three are prone. But the tree supporting the oak on the left is a rowan, a fugitive from an old garden, probably, and under no circumstances, under absolutely none, will I cut a rowan tree in my own woods. The other is a rock maple, a tree which still fills me with wonder and joy because it was scarce in Nova Scotia, and in England almost non-existent. I always have a twinge of conscience when I cut down a maple. But here the maples grow like weeds and this particular one is so close to the rowan it will rob it of nutriment as both try to grow. So the maple goes, and the crack of its fall echoes over the hill.

Still the oak is suspended; when the maple went, its weight was taken by more stuff beyond. There is nothing for it but to cut the oak down to size in the only way left. I start sawing the trunk in eight-foot lengths, each cut about four and a half feet above the ground, which is as high as I can drive a saw. With the entire tree exerting hundreds of pounds of pressure on the saw blade, I must use the wedge. And this means that for the rest of the afternoon these two trees, the oak and the maple, are going to keep me busy.

Toward sunset the logs are piled and split and fragrant, the slash dragged off into a great angular pile to dry and await my pleasure on a future moist day. I come out of the copse and look to see what effect my work has made on the landscape. A little, and the beginning of a lot, because a splendid butternut has now been uncovered and must be given its chance. With that poplar out of the way the sun will slant deeply into the copse and I will have the beginnings of a woodland nave. A forest without sun is like a church without God; I reflect that the thought is corny, but I don't care. Disposing of the poplar will put no burden on my conscience. Along with a ragged spruce, it exists to be destroyed, for if the axe doesn't get to it the insects will, and after the insects will come the flickers and the pileated woodpeckers. Tomorrow afternoon's work is now planned, and it, in turn, will lead to the work of the day after and the day after that. Carving out the raw material of a forest to create a civilized wood is like making a picture or writing a book. One vista suggests another and there is no absolute end to it in a country like ours. But when the season's cutting is over after Thanksgiving, and I go muscle-bound back to the city, I feel as Melville did when he finished *Moby Dick*, as pure as the lamb.

From *The Other Side of Hugh MacLennan: Selected Essays Old and New*, ed. Elspeth Cameron (Toronto: Macmillan of Canada, 1978), 116–21. Published earlier in the *Montrealer* (November 1956), and *Scotchman's Return* (Macmillan, 1960).

The Rivers that Made a Nation

HUGH MacLENNAN

If any modern Canadian is curious to know how his country was valued two centuries ago, all he need do is recall some of the sentiments it inspired among famous men at that time. Voltaire's dismissal of the St. Lawrence Valley as "a few acres of snow" is almost too well known to repeat; it is less well known that Montcalm, who now is a Canadian hero, loathed the country he fought to defend. The British never valued Canada for herself. Just before the peace conference which ended the Seven Years War there was strong pressure in England in favour of trading Canada back to France in return for Guadeloupe. This little Carib isle grew sugar which makes rum, and because many people like rum, rum will always have an economic future.

But in early days few people liked the Land of Cain or the Land of Snows, nor did many believe that it could possibly have an economic future worth mentioning. Had it not been for the strategic necessity of securing the St. Lawrence as a high-road into the Ohio Territory, and also of protecting the northern flank of the rich Thirteen Colonies, Guadeloupe might easily have been England's choice.

Nor would the British of that time have been absurd if they had made such a choice. Canada may have had, as Dr. Johnson remarked of Lapland and the Scottish Highlands, "prodigious wild and noble prospects," but the Age of Reason saw nothing beautiful in wild and noble prospects, and certainly nothing useful. Least of all could the British recognize any economic future in a terrain shaggy with evergreens and horrid (to them the word meant "bristling") with the rocky outcroppings of the Pre-Cambrian Shield. In addition to all these disadvantages there was the Canadian climate.

Once more we cannot consider the British to have been stupid. The gold and practical metals of the Shield were still locked there, hidden, awaiting a twentieth-century technology to make them available to men. Two centuries ago nobody understood the value of petroleum, least of all did they know that a lake of it existed under the Alberta plain. From the servants of the Hudson's Bay Company the English might have picked up some vague information about prairie soils, but they would have presumed them unfavourable to any large creatures except the buffalo which browsed and multiplied in the knee-high grass of a pasture a thousand miles wide. After fearful hardships the Selkirk settlers managed to keep themselves alive in Manitoba, but for decades they were the most isolated farmers in North America. Railways had to be built, farm implements mechanized, grain elevators invented before wheat growing could become the huge industry it is today. As for the timber of the Canadian east, it never transcended a local use before Napoleon sealed off the Baltic ports from British shipping and made it profitable for Canadian business men to export timber for the masts and decks of the Royal Navy. Most of Canada, just like Siberia, had to wait for the age of technology before it could be developed.

Two centuries ago—and this the English understood when they toyed with the idea of exchanging Canada for Guadeloupe—the sole profitable Canadian enterprises were fur trading and the coastal fisheries. Of these, only the former was of real and continuing interest to the capitals of Europe.

Far different was the situation south of what is now the Canadian–American border. With climates ranging from temperate to sub-tropical, the American English soon developed an economy of considerable variety. Towns and cities flourished on the fertile lands between the sea and the Appalachians. The ports were all ice-free and in easy contact with Europe and the West Indies. By the middle of the eighteenth century a mature urban culture had grown in cities like Boston, New York, Philadelphia, Baltimore and Charleston, and its capacity to offer outlets to a variety of human resources and talents was soon proved by the kind of men it produced. The careers, interests and abilities of men like Benjamin Franklin, Thomas Jefferson and John Jay were of a kind that could not have been developed in the Canada of that time, any more than the careers and abilities of men like Peter Pond and Alexander Mackenzie could have been developed within the Thirteen Colonies. Sophistication is the product of universities and the variety of urban life, epic adventures of a society much more primitive.

In the early days the Canadian experience was epic, and the price of such an experience is roughness and lack of education. As late as 1800, James McGill wrote to the Governor of Lower Canada that not one boy in five in the Montreal area could write his own name. Reading and writing was of no use to a canoe man, (nearly all the *engagés* in the fur trade signed with an X) and for a hundred and fifty years young French Canadians had been growing up along the St. Lawrence expecting to earn their living on the rivers leading into the west.

For this reason alone, urban growth in Canada was extremely slow, and the seniority of a few Canadian cities is no indication whatever of a cultural maturity. Though Quebec was founded some dozen years before the landing of the Pilgrims in Massachusetts, and in the mid-eighteenth century had an imposing presence on its rock above the river, it was really more fortress than city. Louisbourg in Cape Breton Island was rightly named the Gibraltar of America: nearly all of its citizens were soldiers. Halifax, founded in 1749, was originally intended as a naval and military base and only developed into a true city after the American Revolution. As for Montreal, up to the end of the Napoleonic Wars, when its population was verging on 20 000, it could almost be described as a supply depot and base camp for the fur trade carried on in the interior.

But early Canada possessed one asset the Americans lacked: the St. Lawrence River. Its rapids halted sailing ships just above Montreal, but the river struck directly through the gap between the Laurentian and Appalachian chains, and the French Canadians used it. While the Americans remained penned between the mountains and the sea, it was the high honour of the French Canadians that their boldest spirits sallied out from the St. Lawrence to explore and map nearly all of the continental interior which Americans and English-speaking Canadians now occupy. Many Americans today believe that their own West was unknown before the mountain men went up the Missouri, but French-Canadian voyageurs had been there long before the mountain men. When Francis Parkman went out on the Oregon Trail in 1846, the epic period of French-Scottish-Canadian exploration was over. But the reliable guides Parkman found in the Missouri country were all French Canadians. They were the last in a long chain of frontier adventurers whose abilities had been developed by the fur trade.

By its very nature this was a river trade. The rivers brought the traders and the Indians into contact with each other, and from the beginning the French had a wonderful naturalness in getting on with the Indians. The tributaries and backwaters of the great river systems were breeding grounds for the animals, and most of the valuable fur-bearing animals are amphibious. In early times the beaver was the animal whose fur was most highly valued in Europe, and for a curious reason: it served as raw material for the hat trade in a period when the wearing of costly hats was deemed essential to a man's status as a fine gentleman. By another of history's ironies—and Canadian history has been a huge congeries of ironies—this wild and dangerous trade owed its support to a temporary fashion in the capitals of Europe.

The dominance of the fur trade conspired with conditions of soil and climate to retard the development of a true Canadian culture. Not only was fur trading a nomadic occupation; it discouraged settlement everywhere because settlement drove off the animals. It could never afford to employ a large body of workers in the field, and the great majority of these were ignorant men who regarded themselves as a class apart, very much like mercenary soldiers in the old days. Since some of the leaders—Alexander Mackenzie, for instance, David Thompson, Alexander Henry and William McGillivray—had intelligence and sensitivity, they hated the harshness and semi-savagery of life in the field, though the goal that urged them onward never failed to give them a mental and moral dominance over the men they led.

Even the habits of the beaver tribe conspired to turn the early Canadians into rovers who departed further and further from civilization. The beaver is not a remarkably prolific animal: if let alone, the beaver population never increases by more than 20 percent annually. When the Europeans first arrived in America there were, according to later computations, about ten million beaver on the continent, their numbers varying between ten to fifty per square mile in the regions where they bred. This was not a large number considering the destructiveness of the trade. The beaver's habits made it impossible for him to escape his enemies because he was not a migrant. He lived in lodges. As David Thompson noted, the beaver "could be attacked at any convenient time and in all seasons, and thus their numbers were reduced."

They were reduced so rapidly that in the Maritime Provinces the fur trade was virtually dead after a few years of European depredation. As early as 1635, only twenty-seven years after the founding of Quebec, beaver had almost vanished in the region about Three Rivers, despite the fact that the St. Maurice is a great tributary which still, for most of its course, flows through uninhabited land. Champlain himself recognized that if he hoped to retain the interest of his home government in the colony of New France, the fur trade would have to be carried into the interior. *His* primary interest may have been to find the Northwest Passage to the Sea of Japan, but he was practical enough to see that if this venture was to be financed, it would have to be paid for in beaver.

It was Champlain who was the first European to recognize that if Canadians were to move in a forested country they would have to forget about horses and even about European methods of navigation. Cartier had been stopped at Lachine, and so was he: "The water here is so swift that it could not be more so . . . so that it is impossible to imagine one's being able to go by boats through these falls. But anyone desiring to pass them, should provide himself with the canoe of the savages, which a man can easily carry."

So began, with Champlain's first tentative journey in a crazy birch-bark canoe above Montreal, the first chapter in the long saga of voyaging. The canoe, as has sometimes been suggested, would make as accurate a symbol on our coat of arms as the beaver, and the birch tree a truer emblem than the maple. Canada is one of the few countries which did not depend for its early development on the horse. In the Canadian bush a horse could neither eat nor move; if you merely tethered him there the mosquitoes and blackflies would kill him or drive him mad. But the birch-bark canoe could go wherever there was a foot of water to float it, and was so light that even the largest could be carried by a few men. The canoe made possible the careers of generation after generation of explorers who were to follow the rivers of America from Montreal to the Gulf of Mexico, to the Beaufort Sea, and finally to the Pacific Ocean.

It was Champlain, as Bartlet Brebner suggests, who invented the strange trade of voyageur, with its even stranger derivative, the *coureur de bois*. The difference between them was technically a legal one. The *coureur de bois* was an individualist who operated without a licence, and when he first appeared in the west, the servants of the Hudson's Bay Company called him a pedlar. But voyaging, as it was conceived by some of the greater spirits who engaged in it, was more than fur trading. Though men like Radisson, LaSalle, La Vérendrye, Samuel Hearne, Alexander Mackenzie, David Thompson and Simon Fraser were certainly in the fur-trading business, essentially they were explorers.

Once Champlain had begun the fur trade along the interior waterways, the voyages multiplied with a rapidity which still astonishes the historian. So mobile was the canoe, so enticing the next bend around the river, so dominant the human instinct to know what lay around it, that within the course of a very few years the voyageurs of French Canada were in the heartland of the continent. The names of some of them ring like bugle calls in the North American story—some of them the greatest in continental history before the age of Washington.

Etienne Brûlé, one of Champlain's "young men," almost certainly reached the Chaudière Falls on the Ottawa as early as 1610. Two years afterwards he became the first European to reach the Sweetwater Sea, as Lake Huron was then called.

Radisson, with his brother-in-law Groseilliers, was probably west of Lake Michigan by the mid-1650s. During this period (the dates are uncertain) the pair entered Lake Superior and *discovered a portage over which other unknown voyageurs, possibly French, had passed before them!* Soon after this they were in Minnesota at the top of the drainage basin of the greatest river on the continent. When the government of New France, which seldom had the quality of its greatest subjects, confiscated the furs of Radisson and Groseilliers on the excuse that they lacked a licence to trade, they went over to the English, and one result of their doing so was the founding of the Hudson's Bay Company.

The two priests, Marquette and Jolliet, descended the Mississippi as far as the Arkansas in 1673, and thereby established beyond doubt the existence of a practicable water avenue from the St. Lawrence to the Gulf of Mexico.

They were followed a decade later by Cavelier de la Salle. In 1680, LaSalle was on the upper Mississippi with Père Hennepin, and in 1682 he reached the delta of the river and claimed the region later known as the Louisiana Territory for the French king.

About two decades later Sieur de Bienville, who may have been born in Montreal, became the first official governor of Louisiana. A road had been found and developed, though it was very thinly held, from Quebec City to the Gulf of Mexico. The French, using the rivers as only they knew how, had drawn a vast loop about the English colonists who still were confined to the Atlantic seaboard.

The last of the supremely great French discoverers, and surely one of the most interesting, was Pierre Gaultier de Varennes, Sieur de la Vérendrye. Born in Three Rivers in 1685 (the same year, incidentally, in which Handel and Johann Sebastian Bach were born) LaVérendrye first served in colonial wars, then went to Europe to fight in the War of the Spanish Succession. After his final return to Canada, a man over forty, he took to the rivers. Armed with a monopoly for the far western fur trade, La Vérendrye was at Grand Portage in 1731 with a party of fifty including three of his sons. He worked out a successful route through the maze of small streams, lakes and muskeg of the western Shield, and in 1734 the first white man's fort stood on the black earth of Manitoba. The vast central plain lay open to him. The Assiniboine and the South Saskatchewan wound across it and led men of the La Vérendrye party to a sight of mountains, possibly the Rockies, a little more than one hundred and thirty years after Brûlé reached the Chaudière Falls.

Nothing in later years was as epic as the sustained efforts of these early Frenchmen. It could not be. In later years the white men were better armed, and though the Indians in the Canadian west could be dangerous, they seldom if ever displayed the appalling cruelty and military vigour of the eastern savages who tortured Brébeuf to death. After the Hurons killed Etienne Brûlé, they ate him.

These facts are familiar: I repeat them only to underline the desperate nature of the early Canadian experience. There was no discharge from this war, at least not for the dedicated man. The isolation of the voyageurs, the knowledge that they were self-condemned to a life of hardship and danger before which, ultimately, their physical and moral powers were bound to fail—these thoughts haunted the bravest and boldest among them. They lacked the consolation of soldiers who risk their lives, for what they did was done without an audience, without the support of a disciplined regiment or army. They could not even communicate their experiences to civilized men, because civilized men lacked the knowledge and background to understand what they meant when they told them that the winter had descended before they could reach a base camp, or that such and such a number of portages had been made or rapids run in such and such a number of days.

Thoughts like these were in Radisson's mind when he wrote a passage with the force of poetry:

> What fairer bastion than a good tongue, especially when one sees his owne chimney smoak, or when we can kisse our owne wife or kisse

our neighbour's wife with ease and delight? It is a different thing when victuals are wanting, worke whole nights & dayes, lye down on the bare ground, & not always that hap, the breech in the water, the feare in the buttocks, to have the belly empty, the wearinesse in the bones, the drowsinesse in the body by the bad weather you are to suffer, having nothing to keep you from such calamity.

When New France fell and was ceded to England in 1763, the control of the Canadian fur trade passed from the French forever. English-speaking men, most of them Scottish Highlanders, now appear in the trade working with the experienced French-Canadian voyageurs who served under them in the North West Company as *engagés*. It was a partnership vital for the future of Canada, and the beginning of the Scottish influence in Canadian affairs.

For it was about this time that the Highland Scotch had finally reached the end of their long, brave but self-damaging struggle for independence against the Anglo-Saxons of the south. The English had conquered them in 1745 and doomed the clansman's way of life. At the best of times it had been a poor life in a poor country: it has been remarked more than once that only the Highlanders and the French Canadians had the necessary background of poverty to qualify them for work on the Canadian rivers. Already the Hudson's Bay Company, scouring the British Isles for men hardy, desperate and disciplined enough to entice into the trade, had been recruiting Orkneymen from the rocks of Ultima Thule, shipping them by the northern route into Hudson Bay and putting them to work there.

Simon McTavish, the master of the North West Company, lived in Montreal like a lord and had something of the temperament and style of a Highland chief of the better sort, though his Scottish ancestry was probably less exalted than he liked to pretend. All of these Highlanders—as distinct from the patient Orkneymen—had the intense personal pride of a race never noted for its emotional balance. This may have been one reason why they had so little sympathy for the slogans of the democratic revolution then brewing in the Thirteen Colonies. That revolution came out of the middle classes, and the Highlands had never had a middle class.

The fire, the imagination and the boldness of these Highland leaders transformed the whole character of the fur trade and turned it into an enterprise in which business considerations, at least as seen by a cool-headed man, very often took a second place to dreams. When the American Revolution broke out, James McGill (a Glasgow man originally) instantly recognized that if the Americans won the war the south-west of the continent would soon be closed to the Canadian fur trade. When he realized that the Americans were on the point of victory, he sold his shares in the company. But Simon McTavish met the challenge by pushing it right over the edge of the map. He bet his fortune on the Athabaska region. The tenacity of McTavish and his colleagues in the face of appalling obstacles can almost be called sublime. Under the best of circumstances, fur trading was a gamble in which the margin of profit over cost was never very great. Though a few large fortunes were made in it, they were acquired by penny-pinching and a driving of the *engagés* to a degree which would horrify a modern labour union. But McTavish and his associates did not hesitate. Not even the complete success of the American Revolution lessened their compulsion to expand. Ironically, it was the blind obstinacy of these Highlanders which limited the plans of some of the shrewdest American statesmen who ever lived.

When Benjamin Franklin, John Adams and John Jay met the English diplomats in Versailles in 1783 to draft the treaty which ended the Revolutionary War, one of their chief objects was to destroy permanently the British ability to threaten the new Republic. The British were still entrenched in Nova Scotia and the St. Lawrence; the Americans had not yet moved out in any large degree beyond the Appalachians. The question of the boundary between the United States and what remained of British North America was therefore the most vital question at this conference.

The boundary to which the British finally agreed was a triumph for the United States and a permanent disaster for Canada. The British were so ignorant of North American geography they did not understand what they were giving away, and they had invited no Canadians to the conference who might have told them. Ever since 1783, the Canadian population has been penned between the Shield and the border in narrow strips. The St. Lawrence and the four northern Great Lakes were split down the middle between the two countries. Montreal was cut off totally from the Ohio Territory and the Mississippi Valley, and as a final touch, Grand Portage was slipped in just underneath the new border so that it reposed in the United States. However, the British did insist on gaining equal rights along the Pigeon and Rainy rivers, and this was to be of vital importance to Canada. It left open a canoe route to the prairies and the far west.

The Montreal fur-traders had few illusions about what this border would mean to them. In time, and the time would not be long, they would be forbidden to do any business at all in the wilderness south of the border which Canadians had explored and opened up to trade. Even Grand Portage would be closed to them. So the North West Company moved their inland base to a new site at Fort William. The cost of doing so came to £10 000.

From this time until the North West Company was absorbed by the Bay in 1821, the Montreal traders met one of the most remarkable challenges in the history of commerce. As they depended on the far north-west for their furs, they were now committed to an operation in which the supply lines were stretched to a limit which would make any normal, hard-headed man of commerce turn pale. The pelts had to be paid for in trade goods conveyed three-quarters of the way across the continent in birch-bark canoes. The pay loads had to be paddled and portaged back to Montreal over a distance of some three thousand miles. The market, nearly all of it in Europe, was still another three thousand miles to the east across the Atlantic Ocean.

Speed and efficiency of the highest kind, supported by an *esprit de corps* among the canoemen as intense as that of a championship hockey team, were the sole possible replies to a challenge so stern. The travel schedules set for the voyageurs seem incredible to the modern imagination.

Leaving Lachine in "brigades" of three to four canoes, with an experienced guide in the leading craft, the voyageurs from Montreal first set out for the Grand River, as the Ottawa was then called. At Sainte-Anne-de-Bellevue they always stopped to pray in the chapel to the saint who protects travellers on water, and this rite gave rise to Thomas Moore's famous poem:

Faintly as tolls the evening chime
Our voices keep tune and our oars keep time,
Soon as the woods on the shore look dim
We'll sing at St. Ann's our parting hymn,
Row, brothers, row! The stream runs fast,
The rapids are near and the daylight's past . . .

This poem, written in soft music by a cultivated visitor to Canada, using the word "oars" instead of "paddles," depreciates its subject. The Homer of the *Iliad* might have risen to the experience of the voyageurs, but not the sweet poet of Ireland.

After paddling and portaging the Ottawa as far as Mattawa, the canoes turned south toward Lake Nipissing, crossed it, and descended the French River into Georgian Bay. Then they paddled west along the North Channel above Manitoulin Island, working in the dead or choppy waters of the lake and often losing several days if the winds were contrary. They called the wind *la vieille* (the old woman), and if she was behind them they could raise a sail. But is she was heavy against them—and the prevailing winds in the region are contrary to west-bound canoes—they often had to put up on the shore because the high, steep waves of the inland lakes would break the backs of their canoes. When they went to Michilimackinac they were expected to reach their destination within a period of from thirty-five to forty days, and the same time was expected when they were bound for Grand Portage and Fort William. This voyage was accomplished with canoes fully loaded with trade goods, and there were thirty-six portages between Lachine and the Lakehead, some of them longer than a "league." In the voyageur's language, a "league" was roughly two miles. If express canoes without cargo were used, as they sometimes were on special occasions, the time was much faster. A letter survives dated in Montreal on May 6, 1817, which was received at Rainy Lake beyond Fort William on June 3.

What these voyages invoked in hardship, labour and moral stamina can no more be revealed by the historian's method of stating the facts than the truth of a battle can be conveyed by the communiqué issued by the high command after the fighting is over and the dead have been counted. From Julius Caesar to the P.R.s of the Pentagon, the truth of life and death has always been hidden behind facts and statistics. That is the trouble with history. It is probably an unavoidable trouble, but it certainly explains why so few people learn much from it.

"Our men moved their camp, marched twenty miles, and at night they placed their camp in a suitable place"—how many of us welcomed lines like these when we studied the *Gallic War* in school! They occurred so often we did not have to pause to work out the grammar. But they told us nothing of the realities.

On every step of that twenty-mile march, probably through hostile country, the legionaries had to carry their weapons and food, their armour and personal necessities, a total weight close to a hundred pounds per man. When the "suitable place" was reached, it was usually on a hill with a forest nearby. While one detachment marked out the lines of the camp, another dug a trench about it and still another went into the woods to cut trees. After the trunks had been trimmed, sawn up and sharpened at one end, they were dragged to the suitable place and staked into the ground just behind the lip of the trench. Only after all this work was done could the soldier wrap himself in his cloak and fall asleep on the ground.

A similar recovery of reality is essential if any modern man is to understand the truth about life on the Canadian rivers in the voyaging days.

On May 25, 1793, a young Scot called John Macdonell set out from Lachine on his first voyage with a brigade of the North West Company. He has left a diary of that voyage written in the usual terse language of the communiqué, and he has also recorded, with the distances distinctly stated, the nature of each of the thirty-six portages between Montreal and Grand Portage—here the carrying place was nine miles long—as well as the character of the streams and lakes. With the help of the imagination, the record is a fascinating one, the more so because this was a routine voyage.

On this stage of the journey into the west, the larger canoes carried loads varying from three to four tons and were manned by crews of eight or ten men. The middle men, using short paddles, sat two abreast while the bowman and steersman were placed higher and were equipped with paddles much longer. The Montreal canoe was thirty-five to forty feet long made entirely of the bark of yellow birch placed over ribs of thin white cedar with thwarts numbering between four and nine and boards four inches wide secured just below the gunwales as seats for the paddlemen. The bark was secured by melted pine gum, and after a heavy rapid or a day's paddling the seams had to be re-gummed to prevent leaking. The canoe used by Alexander Mackenzie, and specially designed for his exploration of the Rockies, was so light that it could be carried by two men. But the weight of a large canoe out of Montreal was much greater than this, and required at least four men on the portage. The whole operation of portaging brings up an interesting calculation in the mathematics of labour, sweat and tired muscles.

Superlatives have bothered me all through the writing of this book, but I cannot avoid them without diminishing what seems to me the truth. Every new thing I have learned about the Canadian voyageur seems to me more incredible than the last. His deeds originated the Paul Bunyan myths of the American north-west, and Paul Bunyan was an inheritor of Hercules and Mercury in folklore. But the true and proved facts concerning the life of the voyageur are such that I can only say that if I, physically, am a man, he, physically, was a superman.

On portages the load that had to be moved, divided up among the crew, usually totalled more than four hundred pounds per man not counting the canoe. Every man of the crew was expected to carry at least two "pieces" of goods, each weighing ninety pounds, but so great was the emulation among them that some individuals often carried three pieces or even four. They did not walk with these loads: *they carried them at a dog trot* bent half-double with the pieces on their backs and secured there by a leather band, called a tumpline, which was passed around their foreheads. More than one traveller conveyed by voyageurs in the canoes has testified that without any load at all he could barely move as fast as these men did with two hundred pounds on their backs. Finally, because they worked at the height of the insect season, the voyageurs were encased over the carrying places in humming, stinging envelopes of mosquitoes and blackflies.

In addition to the portaging there was the tracking of canoes against heavy currents and the running of rapids. The rapids were always risky, and crosses marked the graves of drowned voyageurs on the banks, clusters of them all the way from the Long Sault on the Ottawa to the mouth of the Winnipeg River. Tracking could be a nightmare. The men had to get out and haul by ropes attached to bow and stern (two ropes were essential to prevent the canoe from yawing in against the shore) and this meant slithering over wet rocks slimy with vegetable growth, stumbling over the usual litter of fallen trees and sometimes wading breast high in the stream. As I know from personal experience, the silt along the banks of the Assiniboine, Saskatchewan and Mackenzie is deep and soft, and after rain it has the consistence of porridge and sometimes the texture of axle grease. Along the Fraser when the men had to do a great deal of tracking under appalling difficulties, they wore out a pair of moccasins a day and had to make themselves new ones. While tracking canoes, the men were more plagued by insects even than when they portaged, because there were usually more of them along the water's edge. So paddling in a free river or in an open lake came as a marvellous release, and when the men swung into the stroke they broke into song. That was when time was made up. The mileage from Montreal to Georgian Bay was little more than the mileage from the mouth of French River through the Sault to the head of Lake Superior, and here the figures of John Macdonell tell their own story. It took his brigade thirty-one days to reach Lake Huron from Sainte-Anne. But though they lost a day through a storm on the lake, they reached Grand Portage from French River in just under ten days! Look at the map, remember that most of the time they were travelling against the wind, and try to believe that this was merely a routine voyage!

At Grand Portage or Fort William the Montreal men ended their runs. The Company's agent met the wintering partners from the north-west, and the trade goods were forwarded over the height of land by a special body of men to the Company's fort on Rainy Lake, the eastern terminus of *les vrais hommes du nord* who had come down across the plains from the Athabaska country. At Grand Portage or Fort William the Montreal crews had a brief time for carousing and eating, then they re-loaded their canoes with the furs and set out on the return trail to Montreal with the pay loads. If they did not get back before winter, they were frozen in and had to survive as best they could. A failure to return in time also meant a disastrous financial loss to the Company.

At Rainy Lake the true Northmen took over, and these were the élite of the service. They paddled through Lake of the Woods and by a series of smaller lakes and interconnecting streams (the Winnipeg River was exhaustingly cursed by rapids) into Lake Winnipeg itself. In earlier times canoe parties used to paddle from there up the Red River into Minnesota toward the sources of the Mississippi, but after the American Revolution the goal was the north-western edge of the North American map, Lake Athabaska and the Peace River country. The Saskatchewan and Athabaskan brigades paddled north up Lake Winnipeg to the mouth of the Saskatchewan River and then—after some very severe portages—they worked up against the current of the North Branch to Cumberland Lake and thence to Frog Portage, which made a bridge to the Churchill River. This powerful stream, against which they also had to paddle, led them to the Methye Portage (or Portage LaLoche), a very tough one with a sharp height of land at the end of it. The Methye took them to the Clearwater, a tributary of the Athabaska, and then they coasted down that great river of the north-west into Lake Athabaska and reached their chief north-western base at Fort Chipewyan. In the later years of the North West Company the brigades went even beyond this. They paddled up to Fort Vermilion on the Peace, and later still the fur-traders established themselves in forts on the Fraser and the Columbia.

This final leap across two-fifths of Ontario, across Manitoba, Saskatchewan and some or all of Alberta, all of it trending north, was a race against time even more intense than the run from Montreal to the head of Lake Superior. So close was the margin between the meeting with the Montreal canoes and the coming of frost that a delay of a few days might ruin a whole voyage. According to Alexander Mackenzie, the Athabaskan brigades generally left Rainy Lake on the first of August, and had to reach Chipewyan inside two months.

What of the canoes and of the men themselves?

By the time the North West Company was established, the art of canoe-handling had so matured on the rivers that the French Canadians were much more mobile than the men of the Hudson's Bay Company. British as they were, the Bay men clung for a long time to wooden *bateaux*. The Nor'westers used two types of canoe which they called the *canot du maître* and the *canot du nord*, the former for the run out of Montreal, the latter, which was lighter and carried less than a ton and a half of cargo, for the run west of Fort William where the streams were shallower and tracking more frequent. The *canot du nord* often carried a crew of no more than five men.

But the *canot du maître* was a considerable craft. It had a wide beam, a remarkably high strake and high, curved bows. It was gaily painted and travelled with a pennant blowing out from its stern and often with the picture of an Indian's head on its bows. A variety of pictures of these larger canoes survive and one of them has a feature which—at least to me—was more interesting than the canoe itself.

This was no less a personage than Sir George Simpson, the "Big Bourgeois" of the Hudson's Bay Company, the chief destroyer of the Nor'westers, and in his old age one of the richest men in Montreal. After the Bay absorbed the North West Company they not only employed the skilled Canadian voyageurs; even before that time they had adopted the classic Canadian canoes. In this picture Simpson sits in the middle wearing a top hat of massive proportions, as did many of the bourgeois (this was the old French name for the proprietor or company partner) while *en voyage*. The top hat was a mark of their quality and station. In Simpson's canoe the paddlemen are seated as usual two abreast and the bowman and steersman are in their usual places. But directly behind Simpson, who wears a grim expression on one of the most haughty faces in Canadian history, are a pair of undersized, wild-looking characters blowing bagpipes.

The presence of these pipers in Simpson's canoe gives the Big Bourgeois an extra dimension. People who worked for him knew that he was the toughest employer there ever was in a notoriously tough trade. He pinched pennies, he was ruthless, he squeezed out of his servants the last ounce of work, he paid them as little as he possibly could. One knows that Simpson understood the value of every square foot of every canoe or York boat in the service of his company. And yet, there sits that pair of private pipers! The Scotch are a peculiar people, and never more so than when they try to out-English the English in cold calculation after they have gone into business and made a success of it. But the old wildness never quite leaves the pure Scot. Behind the granite features of George Simpson, underneath his brutal surface callousness, the primitive heat burned, and hence that pair of pipers. Without them, the *canot du maître* could have carried at least two hundred more pounds of trade goods. Yet Simpson sacrificed money for the pipers, and I like to think of him sitting there in his stove-pipe hat, the mosquitoes buzzing in his hair, the canoe swaying down a rapid through the forest wilderness, and that pair of wee pipers behind him blowing his ears off.

But there were no pipers, no luxuries, for the average *engagé*—the paid voyageur of the fur-trading companies. Day after day from dawn to dusk, sometimes for eighteen hours daily, they drove those loaded canoes back and forth across the continent. As they paddled they sang the old French songs and some others of their own making. In favouring currents they could swing the stroke easily, but in adverse currents or dead water their paddles bit hard. The average rate of stroking was forty to the minute, but often they stroked at the rate of one per second, in perfect time and with only a few stops in the course of the day. The stops were called "a pipe," and their length depended on the state of the men. Travellers carried in canoes have testified that after twelve hours' paddling, with only three rests of ten to fifteen minutes each, those incredible French Canadians refused to stop because they were still "fresh." Their sense of competition with one another was Homeric. Duncan McGillivray once witnessed a race in Lake Winnipeg between Athabaska men and a rival brigade. The men paddled all out *for forty-eight consecutive hours without once leaving their canoes!* A steersman collapsed into sleep, fell overboard and would have been drowned had not his own canoe gone back to pick him up; he was sinking under the weight of his clothes and in a state of shock from the frigid water. In this race as the men stroked, the guides cut off hunks of pemmican and thrust them into the mouths of the paddlers.

What manner of men were these—giants? Actually, they were built more like gnomes. In 1826 an American, Thomas L. McKenney, visited the trading routes of Canada and described the voyageurs as follows:

> They are short, thick set, and active, and never tire. A Canadian, if born to be a labourer, deems himself to be very unfortunate if he should chance to grow over five feet five, or six inches—and if he shall reach five feet ten or eleven, it forever excludes him from the privilege of becoming voyageur. There is no room for the legs of such people, in these canoes. But if he shall stop growing at about five feet four inches, and be gifted with a good voice, and lungs that never tire, he is considered as having been born under a most favourable star.

Freedom, T.E. Lawrence once wrote, is man's second need: here is the sole explanation of those men's willingness to engage in a trade like this, which in time was sure to break them. Though there were many instances of river men keeping on working into late middle-age, the voyageurs as a rule died young. They were lucky if they were not double-ruptured and suffering from spastic backs before they were forty. But at least they were free from the forelock-tugging kind of poverty their class had to endure in Europe. They had the pride of champions which is the surest of all proofs of an inner sense of personal value. Freedom has always been the most expensive possession in the world, and the price for it has been paid in different coin from age to age. In the early days of Canada, the coin was hardship and endurance.

There were rains and cold nights, and the only women of the interior were virtual savages. The food the men ate on the rivers makes the diet of a modern Canadian work camp seem like the fare of a Roman emperor of the decadence [sic]. On the eastern run to the Lakehead the voyageurs were called *mangeurs de lard*, or pork-eaters, and the French word gives us a good idea of the quality of the pork. In the west pemmican was the stable diet, and no more nourishing one was ever invented, but even with wild rice added, boiled pemmican at the end of sixteen hours of labour is not much to look forward to. If the schedule was not too exacting, the men fished and hunted and searched for birds' eggs, but if food ran out they would eat anything. Often they literally ate crow. The poor French voyageur, especially in the early days, usually had nothing better to eat than a kind of hominy made of split dried peas or corn impregnated with fat.

But of all the ordeals faced by the river men, that of the winterer was the worst. He was the one who had to stay out in the wilderness perhaps two thousand miles from his base. The Indians brought him furs, and though he often had an Indian wife, he sometimes was entirely alone. If game was abundant he ate well, and there was usually plenty of fish preserved from the fall through the winter. But if game failed or fish rotted, starvation or dysentery was his fate. If he fell sick there was no help for him, and his loneliness was total in a six months' winter when the prairie was nothing but a white death.

Narrow this life was, uncivilized and uneducated, but on the whole it was less brutalizing than the life in the lumber camps in the Victorian era. At the principal bases of the Hudson's Bay Company all the men were required to attend prayers regularly. There is a poignant memorandum dating from the early eighteenth-century records of the Bay which enjoins the Company's servants "to live lovingly with one another not to swear or quarrel but to live peaceably without drunkenness or profaneness." The Nor'westers had a rougher tradition but more personal independence within the service; less consciousness, perhaps, that they were suffering a thankless exploitation by rich men who never troubled themselves to know at what price of human stamina and hardship the profits were earned. Nearly all the Montreal partners in the Company had served at least some time on the rivers. The French-Canadian voyageur, though not fond of washing *en route*, was a considerable dandy whenever he neared a post. Even though the only women in the post were savages, he washed and put on his best clothes. He had a Gallic courtesy to counteract his almost incredible toughness, and Francis Parkman writes feelingly of the human quality of his *Canadien* guides along the Missouri. As for the Highlanders in the service of the fur trade, one of them wrote the "Lone Shieling" poem, possibly the most haunting verses ever composed in Canada.

The fur trade failed in the end; it was doomed the moment the settlers began moving into the west to farm. Long before that time there were men engaged in it who had seen the writing on the wall. Sometimes when I walk up the avenue of the McGill campus and reach the Founder's tomb, I think back on the life he led and the shrewd Lowland caution which prompted James McGill to take his money out of the fur trade in time. He had never been a true voyageur, merely a poor boy from Scotland who had entered the only Canadian trade which offered him a living. He had earned his place in the Beaver Club by a winter spent alone near the headwaters of the Mississippi, but he got off the rivers before the life on them broke him. McGill lacked the transcendent imagination of Simon McTavish and the last-ditch loyalty of William McGillivray, but he had much common sense. Unlike most of his old colleagues in the fur trade, he did not die broke. His life had taught him that civilization could never grow in Canada under the conditions he had known in his youth. Though he was well off by colonial standards, he would never have been accounted an especially rich man in England. He left just enough to make it possible to found a college. Today McGill University lies like a quiet pattern of order in the roaring tumult of modern Montreal, and is by far the most important visible monument to the North West Company's great adventure.

For the economic contribution of the fur trade after the American Revolution has surely been exaggerated. It is a common argument that furs saved the country from being absorbed by the United States because they provided an east–west trade, all Canadian, in a continent where the normal lines of economic communication run north and south with the greater power and population of the United States sucking the wealth of Canada southward. I cannot believe this. The fur trade may have bridged an economic gap for a number of years, but the true reason why it saved Canada from absorption was not economic. It was political.

Not only did the voyageurs explore most of North America; after 1783 they staked out Canadian—or, at that time, British—claims to the whole northwestern hinterland from the head of the Lakes to the Pacific. When the tide of homesteaders fanned out from the railheads in the American mid-west in the nineteenth century, the Canadian west would surely have been occupied by them, and subsequently claimed as American territory by the American government, had not the ancient rights of prior exploration, which the Americans respected, bound the land to Canada. The lonely posts were on the plains, in the Fraser and Columbia valleys, on the Pacific coast, and the Union Jack flew over all of them. Yet only a handful of men achieved this result. At the height of its power the North West Company may have employed as many as five thousand men, but less than two thousand were in service in the field between Montreal and Chipewyan. It was not their numbers that counted, but what they did. And in the long run what was done by the dreamers mattered the most.

David Thompson was probably the greatest geographer ever developed in North America; without his work, backed by Simon Fraser's voyage down the river which bears his name, it is hard to believe that British Columbia would now be a Canadian province. And of course there was Alexander Mackenzie, the prince of all the Canadian explorers.

A dozen years before Lewis and Clark, Mackenzie reached the Pacific through North America. He threaded to the end the Northwest Passage. Its reality bore no resemblance to the European dream of a great gorge which would float sailing ships from the Old World through the continental land mass of the New. It was simply the chain of rivers, lakes and portages which enabled canoes from Montreal to move all the way from the St. Lawrence across Canada to the northern and western oceans.

"Alexander Mackenzie, from Canada, by land, the twenty-second of July, one thousand seven hundred and ninety-three"—this celebrated understatement, scrawled in a mixture of vermilion and grease on a rock in Dean Channel after Mackenzie's passage down the Bella Coola, wrote *finis* to a quest begun exactly three hundred and one years earlier when Christopher Columbus set out across the Atlantic from Palos. The reality found by Mackenzie served only to dissipate the dream. But it introduced a new reality, just as Columbus' lost quest drew an entire hemisphere into the story of civilization. How strange that a Canadian birch-bark canoe without a name, last in a long succession of canoes from Champlain's first one, should have earned a place in the company of ships like the *Santa Maria* and the *Golden Hind!*

From *Seven Rivers of Canada: The Mackenzie, The St. Lawrence, The Ottawa, The Red, The Saskatchewan, The Fraser, The St. John* (Toronto: Macmillan of Canada, 1961), 9–29. First appeared as "By Canoe to Empire," *American Heritage* (October, 1961).

W. L. MORTON (1908–1980) was born in Gladstone, Manitoba. He was educated at the University of Manitoba, and at Oxford as a Rhodes Scholar (B.A. 1934, B.Litt. 1935, M.A. 1937). Morton had a distinguished career as a professor of history and an administrator at various colleges in Manitoba, including his alma mater, before moving to Trent University in 1966. His *The Progressive Party in Canada* won the Governor General's Award for academic non-fiction in 1950. Other books include *Manitoba: A History* (1957), *The Canadian Identity* (1961), *The Kingdom of Canada* (1963), *The Critical Years* (1964), and *The Shield of Achilles* (1967). In his best work he writes with a muted passion, communicating personal involvement in the history he depicts, as when he represents the forces arrayed on the Prairies at the turn of the century against the European immigrants who were trying to hold on to their culture, to any culture, in the face of overwhelming natural opposition. This impression of personal involvement is vividly conveyed in the conclusion of "Seeing an Unliterary Landscape":

> The need to reconcile the actual and the mind's landscape, I think from my own experience, underlies the need, felt at least by the sensitive, of a new country to create its own literature and write its own history. It is a rite of reassurance, certainly. But it is done by that "passionate thinking" ... which fuses the thing seen and person seeing, that reconciles the seer and the seen, that is part of the magic of art, and part also of the historian's craft.
>
> I think, by way of example, that one fall evening I was rewarded in my search for a landscape in which inner and outer vision were

> reconciled. It was on a late afternoon flight from Winnipeg to Edmonton one October day. The air was clear except for a vast swirl of smoky cloud across the western horizon in which the sun was dying to glowing ash. The great globe of the prairies rolled majestically below, incised with square stubble and square fallow, engraved by the vast river valleys, gemmed with lapis lazuli of random lakes. The whole was a Renaissance globe wrought for a Medici, turned by the thumb of old Sebastian Cabot, worked in rough bronze burnished to murky gold, fading off in ridge and coulee into smoky purple or darkening over vast plains in dusky amber—the work either of a Cellini or a Dürer. It was the West of the drifting buffalo herds, of the islanded farmsteads, of Butler, Grove, and even of Margaret Laurence. It was my West completely envisioned.

As an historian, Morton is best known for his sensitive and meticulously detailed studies of the Canadian prairie West. He was the general editor of the seventeen-volume history of Canada in the Centenary series which emphasized the "regional communities" that make up the country. At the same time, Morton always emphasized how the "local" was the product of a diverse cultural heritage that linked Canadians to the rest of the world. Central to his view of our history were the country's "northern character," "historical independence," "monarchical government," and a "national destiny" committed "to special relations with other states." Morton was a federalist and a conservative, believing all his life, for example, that the monarchy was a force for continuity of tradition, the symbol of what makes Canada different from the United States. As he says in one of his most famous essays, "A Northern Nation" (too long to reprint here), "Not life, liberty, and the pursuit of happiness but peace, order, and good government are what the national government of Canada guarantees. Under these, it is assumed, life, liberty, and happiness may be achieved, but to each according to his taste." He was also a firm believer in a pluralistic Canada, which he described as "a partnership of peoples and cultures, of regions and provinces."

Seeing an Unliterary Landscape

W. L. MORTON

The walking-plough, tipped with its point set to slip into the sod, its mouldboard gleaming a lambent silver polished by miles of turning soil, jerks as the horses lean into their collars, and the furrow rolls.

Such is one of the clearest images of my boyhood memory. It is an image drawn from one of the many skills of old-time farming, the breaking every July of a few acres more of new land from meadow and poplar bush. I look back on it with fondness for something gone forever except in fading memory, and am proud that I was once good at the plough. Indeed, sometimes now I find myself falling into the ploughman's halting plod, taking the weight of the share's twist on the right foot every second stride. I could drive a straight furrow and cover every wisp of grass and trash beneath the gleaming furrows, the soil moist with summer rain and turned for the first time since the waters of Lake Agassiz laid it down deep below the now phantom waves.

The image is one which may, moreover, be opened into many petals, each of entrancing colour. Only consider the meanings of that turning mould. For one thing, what an archaism ploughing it was. It was becoming unusual even in those days half a century ago to break land with the walking-plough; the tractor was taking over. In a sense, however, I was fortunate because I was among the last of millennial generations of men who followed the plough, as I knew even then. So I belonged to a human labour force, peasant, serf, slave, whose work fed household, village, and city, and carried the fabric of civilization on their sweating shoulders. A strange boast, if you like, but it is a strong, rich memory.

For another thing, the plough, with its patient, fourteen-inch furrows turned side by side, one by one, till meadow and bush were black and level, was one of the greatest of history's transforming tools. No other, perhaps, has left such a mark on the face of the earth. Grassland and forest, oak grove and prairie steppe, each has eroded before its trenchant share and rending coulter, and the wilderness become field and lawn. It must be ranked with glacial ice and running water as one of the major engravers of the globe. And I used, therefore, to while away the plodding hours by musing on how I too at the plough handles was changing the face of a planet and remaking a landscape.

The image might be further unfolded, but I have come to my theme, the seeing of the landscape I was in fact transforming. It was already largely altered, of course, as I was the third generation to plough the family land. Much of the original landscape of the locality remained, however—the heavy stands of aspen poplar common to the Assiniboine delta, of glacial Lake Agassiz, interspersed with shallow sloughs and alkali meadows, a pleasant parkland country, neither prairie nor woodland, but a varying mixture of both. To early travellers and even to later newcomers, it often suggested the standing parks and sweeping lawns of England, but it was a suggestion only. It was, in fact, a countryside of austere ecological selection, fitted to survive winter, drought, and wildfire.

It could not survive axe and plough, however. Clearing and breaking the parkland indeed was easy compared with the medieval task of overcoming the hardwood forests of western Europe or of eastern Canada. Very quickly, therefore, in fact in less than three generations for the most part, the elegant undress of the wild landscape of poplar bluff and meadow had given way to the prim and level square fields made by the plough.

The new landscape was that standard in North America, the homestead with shelter bluff, square white house, and long red barn usually, perhaps with silo and windmill, although these were not common in a locality that grew little corn and had plenty of water near the surface. Around the homestead the fields and pastures spread out to the fenced limits of the farm, usually the road allowances. They were square or oblong, but always rectangular in response to the insistent demand of the plough that it turn full, square furrows when at work.

It was pre-eminently a landscape of abundance, whether when the fields were green with the new crop, or ranked with stooks at harvest, or black with fallow and fall ploughing. In my earlier years, when the grain was not only stooked, but stacked, and when the hay stacks stood both long and high, and wisps of hay hung from the loft doors, it was a cornucopia landscape, overflowing with abundance. (Sometimes it was not so, of course, when the June rains did not come and the wind drove the soil in banks along the fencerows, scouring the bare fields ferociously day after pitiless day.)

In short, it was a countryside transformed. A new landscape had come into being. That it was standard to a pattern from the Appalachians to the Rockies; that it was square in all its features, mile after wheeling mile; that it had no distinction except to an eye both fond and familiar, were matters of no importance. The remade countryside was well suited to the needs and habits of those who had remade it for their own purposes. Farm and homestead with more or less success furnished food and shelter. The livestock pastured, the crops grew, the children went to school, neighbours passed the time of day. There were the summer picnics and the winter bonspiels and ice carnivals, the Saturday nights for shopping in the local town, the Sundays for church, and such rest as farm life allowed. And the ploughs ran smoothly in the mellowing fields, summer after summer.

The landscape, that is, had been remade by the farm culture of North America. It was at once a material reshaping of the land, and also a firm and confident expression of a way of life, rarely defined, but well understood. It was a landscape in which men could work, could live serenely, even take some ease. They had possessed it, not only with their hands but with their whole being. They had made it, not only into farms, but into townships, school districts, electoral districts, town lots, church yards, cemeteries. It served all their purposes and was a cultural as well as a material landscape.

Landscapes, however—or seascapes, or cityscapes—are not only material. There are also the landscapes of the mind, literary landscapes, for want of a better term. These are formed, not by the play of eye on meadow and forest, valley and mountain, but by books, pictures, television, music. They are cultural landscapes, formed by what the mind, not the seeing eye alone, takes in. As I grew familiar with the actual world in which I chanced to be born, I began, once I learned to read, to enter another and, as it happened, quite a different landscape indeed. I had been prepared for this by conversation, for my mother had been, again as it chanced, raised among hills, and would talk of the joys of long sleigh rides down the valley sides of the Birdtail the enormous distance of one hundred miles to the west.

I was thus quite prepared to accept, perhaps also aided by a liberal education in *Mother Goose*, after which nothing can possibly seem improbable or wholly unacceptable, the new world which reading opened. My early reading, as I try to recall it, seems to me wildly random. My home had no collected library, but books were freely welcomed, and a very odd company of travel-worn and quite unassorted volumes had found refuge in odd corners of the house. An imperfect memory makes that dishevelled company even more nondescript than it perhaps actually was. My first memory is that of Henty's *Deerfoot on the Prairie*, the first book I was to read in the course of a single day—it must have been a rainy day with the usual chores cut off, or perhaps done by others as an enraptured boy followed that noble savage in adventure leading to adventure. For, blessed memory, reading was tolerated in my home, perhaps sometimes rationed, but never treated as mere indulgence, or a flight from reality.

So I was let loose into a literary landscape, rather, a world of strange and varied landscape—the Victorian world of adventure, of Ballantyne and Marryatt, the exotic world of African travel and native conversion, of Baker and Livingstone, Speke and Grant, the utterly odd and incomprehensible world of the *Boys' Own Annual* and the English public school—wholly inexplicable that—the grotesque world of Dickens, and the curiously vivid world of poetry, in which I gained as private booty such oddities as a liking for Anacreon and much puzzlement over Moore's *Lalla Rookh*. It was obviously a rubbish heap of literature in which I rummaged, one deposited by almost geological chance. Nevertheless, it served its purpose. I was forever released. The actual landscape, the world before my physical eyes, that of my boyhood, and of any material landscape I have seen since, some so famous as to be more literary than actual, has always been to me only one landscape among alternates, something I might see, or not, as I chose.

Henceforth, and this is the result of reading, no doubt also of television—hence the appalling error of precious people in condemning television as the visual opium of the masses—I was a master and manipulator of landscape. I could see what I wished. There are aids to seeing: books, pictures, music, travels, dreams; but books were to me the best aid, as I cannot but think they will always be. (The best sometimes does happen and can last forever, and the printed book is one of those things, *pace* McLuhan.) So I hunted books as I hunted partridge and rabbits, with the same care and same pleasure in the kill. After having read and reread all the books to hand, to get a new book was to feel the same fierce pleasure as to bring down a duck on the wing.

So I sought books where they could be found, in the houses of friends, where they were usually dusty, in the school library, unused, or in the odd corners of the attic, so congested that it could be mined repeatedly with ever diminishing, but often exciting returns. The results dismay me now—cheap novels best forgotten, immigrant literature, such as Canon Gill's *Letters of a Manitoba Choreboy*, books prized for their covers, fragments of books, always the dust and mould. The general tone of this literary fall-out was either adventure—I adored Zane Grey and worshipped Hopalong Cassidy—or romance, the last sentimental oozings of the great romantic movement. My most memorable foray, however, occurred when I had become enamoured of Burns, and learned that two Scotch brothers and neighbours had a volume of his collected poems. One was permanently odd with a fixation on religion; the other had just been released from the mental hospital. I dared all, and spent a fearful afternoon in their log house while the simple one took me with rapture through the volume, lovingly brought from Argyllshire and lovingly treasured, while the other strode the floor muttering to himself of his private and incomprehensible woes. At last, overwhelmed by the firm stench of their bachelor housekeeping and by the plain kindness of both, I went off with the sacred volume in my unworthy hands.

The experience itself was a memorable lesson in the strange condition of man, the volume a treasure I would pore over for days, one ploughboy to another, learning how in another land it was not thought strange that a man, obviously a man among men—and women also—could be praised for devoting his life to poetry, much of it poetry about, or at least set against, the local Ayrshire landscape. The collected volume of all Burns wrote, trivia, fragments, and all, with the country songs he took up and improved, was perhaps, or so it seems in giving shape to random recollections, something of a turning point in the growth of my power to see the world as it was and as I in fact saw it. A challenge had emerged. If Burns could sing of Sweet Afton, why not I, or another, of the local stream, the Whitemud? But it was a daunting thought; the Whitemud, even when it ran clear in early summer, ran through raw clay banks, and in any case nobody had ever heard of it.

Thus my actual landscape, the one the neighbours had made and worked in with apparent content, and my literary landscape, from the banks and braes of Bonnie Doon to the long beaches of Coral Island, were in conflict. I had no single vision for both, but had to re-focus like one passing from dark to light. Nor was the conflict to cease for many years.

It was in fact aggravated by the accident of my belated Victorian inheritance. Not only at home, but at school no less, the influence of the Victorian World and the great Romantics was constant and massive. Just as I shall be a Victorian to the end of my days, so was I irretrievably romanticized. The essence of the influence, in the fragmentary and debased form in which it reached me, was that of a deliberate and stylized separation of the authentic actual from the alleged real. A primrose by the river's brim could not be a primrose merely; it was a conceit laid up in the mind of a poet. Thus the literary landscape, the way one saw the world, was always and necessarily distinct from the world as it was.

As my reading widened, and as I came under instruction, I began, of course, to taste of other styles and sample other outlooks. But I quite failed to be rescued by the Augustans, and was too early for the Metaphysicals. I rejected them except insofar as I found some early morning haze of pre-Romanticism in them. I was conditioned not to see things as they were, but only as a Romantic perceived them. Even the pre-Raphaelites did not help; their mannered simplicity pleased, but because it too was a convention. The *Blessed Damozel* is, after all, utterly Tennysonian.

Further on, I encountered Hardy, and his concern for actual landscape and simple folk seemed to suggest a way of escape, and I indeed set out to be an expert in Hardy. It was not a bad goal, but I was to be diverted.

The diversion was an attempt to find in Canadian literature an authentic landscape, a way of seeing that reconciled the seer and the seen. Again the quest was haphazard and intermittent. It so happened that Martha Ostenso's *Wild Geese* was published in these years, and Frederick Philip Grove's novels and essays were to be found here and there. Grove indeed had taught in the little town which was my home, and *Settlers of the Marsh* was placed in the country to the northeast, as were the essays in *Over Prairie Trails*. Oddly enough, for these writings were "naturalistic" in the European and the contemporary American convention, these new outlooks were no more helpful than the Romantic spectacles I had contrived in reconciling what my eyes saw and what my mind perceived. They yielded only another convention, another cultural landscape no more authentic than the Tennysonian.

Even historical reading, the reading of what professed to be true, to be authentic without style, or convention, or art, had the same effect as Keats or Grove. History too, Macaulay on seventeenth-century England, or C.G.D. Roberts on Canada, had the same effect. It too created a landscape no more reconcilable with what I daily saw than was poetry or fiction.

As I look back now, I suspect the way out may have lain in some reading of American literature. Everybody, of course, read *Tom Sawyer* and *Huck Finn*, and somehow, even if one knew nothing of black men or Mississippi steamboats, their landscape was one, one sensed, that had been seen as one wished to see one's own, as it actually was, but more so. But in neither school nor university at that time was American literature taught as such, as an expression of the American experience. American poems and stories one often met, but took them in as they were offered, simply as English literature with perhaps different subjects, such as Whittier's *Barefoot Boy*. Enough wit might have saved one, but I was merely a gluttonous reader. And when I turned consciously to American poetry and novels, I was put off by the realism of *Babbitt*, or of *An American Tragedy*, as starker than I enjoyed in my literature, and in American poetry by an overstatement and cultivated waywardness I found distasteful. I frankly preferred the English Georgians, in fact was rarely to find their successors and displacers, Auden and Spender, as anything but lumberingly dull.

It becomes apparent that, in fact, my tastes were terribly limited and conventional, for all that I read anything I could pry loose. How much the trouble was caused by narrowness of mind and simple ignorance I am unable to say; obviously to some considerable extent. For example, I did not then care, and have not much since cared for urban literature, if, that is, the literature depends on urban background. Witty dialogue divorced from any actual background, or the use of city scenes as mere background, as in *Ulysses* or *The Wasteland*, are of course quite a different matter. But the use of the city as one form of human landscape, as in *Les Misérables*, has always left me unaroused. There may be a reason; a cityscape, after all, is man-made and to that extent humanized. But how to humanize what was not human to begin with? It is this question, perhaps a shallow one, that makes me clash with the city-bred historians of today who condemn my respect for environment in history. They have what I call the pavement mentality. By that I mean in all but accidents—which may be important and consoling—any city is within like any other city. They know neither the revolution of the seasons nor the relevance of time and place, but live contained and self-impelled lives.

The difficulty that puzzled my forming mind, a difficulty no doubt peculiar to particular circumstances, but still possessing a generality that attaches to anything that happens to a human, the difficulty was to reconcile a landscape actually seen and realistically experienced with an internal landscape formed by reading. How could these be brought into a single, authentic vision in which neither would deny, but rather clarify, the other? How was one to see with a single eye that would do justice to a total experience of daily vision and literary perception?

This was not a defined and conscious impediment to me, as it might well have been to a more sensitive person. Nor was it an existentialist imbroglio. A blurred perception did not alienate me from the world. Nor did I feel my environment was hostile, although I knew well enough few of my ordinary associates would take my difficulty seriously, or even understand it. I sought, I think, only two things. One was to see my world only in some more penetrating way than casual sight afforded; the other was that others should also see more in it than met the unaided eye. I wanted, I think, that as the wilderness landscape had been remade by axe and plough into a cultivated landscape, that raw, new landscape should be made into a humane landscape of heightened tone and enriched association. I desired it to be seen not only as it could be seen, but as it might be seen.

In short, I wanted to write about it. This, in fact, proved somewhat difficult, as I soon revealed even to myself that I lacked the verbal skill and sensitivity of imagination to do so as poet, or novelist, or essayist. I turned to the laborious and essentially pedestrian skills of the historian. I have never felt, however, that a historian can succeed without insight and intuition as well as evidence and judgment, or that his history will not be better for the best expression he can shape for it, and the best use he can make of all the resources of literature. His work, to be good, must of course be true to fact, but it ought also to possess its own integrity, the truth of total vision.

I set myself, therefore, to see by reconstruction my actual landscape of the prairie west as it had been seen, in order to arrive at a cumulative sight and insight. This is simply what any student of history does. He tries by reading, seeing, travelling, talking, to re-experience what past men have done, and thought and felt, so that he can see as they saw, think as they thought, feel as they felt. It is of course laborious, but, more important, it is in its own way imaginative and creative. Like plastic art, or imaginative literature, it makes out of things as they were something more that authenticates by enhancing.

If, then, by study of how the landscape had been seen, I might arrive at a simple vision of my own, I might contribute to its being seen as I felt it ought to be, not only in its stark terms, but in the terms of men who knew and lived in it.

The search, only somewhat less fragmented than my early reading, led me through the journals of fur trader and traveller, the books of the explorers, the journalists, the promoters of land sales and settlement, the newspapers, the diaries, the novels, the political speeches, and the doggerel verse and popular ballads—all the way from Alexander Ross and Pierre Falcon to Nellie McClung and James Oliver Curwood. It made up a very motley lot of reading.

But my search was simple: What had any of them to tell me of how they saw the country?

In looking back over the job, I am not sure that I found anything that directly served my purpose. But the search, after all, was cumulative. The question was not, when all was said, whether any particular stick of kindling was especially good; it was whether the whole pile when piled together would blaze. Some passages stayed in mind: David Thompson's rendering of the Indian tale of how the industrious beaver had terraced the slopes of Manitoba until only one hilltop remained dry for the huddled Indian folk; Ross's eyewitness record of the buffalo run in the rolling dust of July; Hind's vivid rendering of the shimmery flight of grasshoppers out of the southwest, or of the Plains Cree warriors riding in file down the slopes of the Assiniboine to Fort Ellice, feathered and chanting; John Tanner's account of hunting moose in the winter forest; Rupert Brooke's comments on Winnipeg and the Winnipeg River; Grove on farm life at Lowe Farm; Nellie McClung on immigrant days at the Black Creek stopping house; the strange outbursts of Riel and his vision of a West ample enough for all people; Butler on the stark silence of the winter woods—the random memories float by.

It was, however, all inadequate in and by itself. It did, however, give all historical reading can ever give, a purging of the vision with which one began. Seeing always with others' eyes, I at least came to the point where I did not see with my own. In some sense, I had read myself blind. Blind, however, only to my narrow and imperfect view of a landscape, now suddenly transmuted and augmented. I could now see Argus-eyed.

So, at least, I thought. How correct I may have been is a matter to be judged from my writings on western history. In them I felt at least I was seeing the western landscape, people with men and women in conflict with, or at home in, the western environment. In them, I found some touch of that intensive joy in making be something that had not been. To me that was a view of the West seen both as it actually is and as it really is. The wilderness, reshaped to men's purposes by men's hands, was to some degree now illuminated by men's minds.

Impersonally and objectively, the process was, of course, the ancient human game of possessing by naming and describing. Nothing, no country, can be really owned except under familiar name or satisfying phrase. To be apprehended by the mind and personal, it requires not only the worn comfort of a used tool or a broken-in shoe; it requires also assimilation to the mind, ear, eye, and tongue by accepted, or acceptable, description in word, or line, or colour. (Is it perhaps the plight of the existentialist and the alienated that they are such because they cannot, indeed we cannot, possess the world of the scientific revelation by describing it in terms mere humans can accept?)

The need to reconcile the actual and the mind's landscape, I think from my own experience, underlies the need, felt at least by the sensitive, of a new country to create its own literature and write its own history. It is a rite of reassurance, certainly. But it is done by that "passionate thinking," to take up a phrase recently used by an American historian in an different context, which fuses the thing seen and the person seeing, that reconciles the seer and the seen, that is part of the magic of art, and part also of the historian's craft.

I think, by way of example, that one fall evening I was rewarded in my search for a landscape in which inner and outer vision were reconciled. It was on a late afternoon flight from Winnipeg to Edmonton one October day. The air was clear except for a vast swirl of smoky cloud across the western horizon in which the sun was dying to glowing ash. The great globe of the prairies rolled majestically below, incised with square stubble and square fallow, engraved by the vast river valleys, gemmed with lapis lazuli of random lakes. The whole was a Renaissance globe wrought for a Medici, turned by the thumb of old Sebastian Cabot, worked in rough bronze burnished to murky gold, fading off in ridge and coulee into smoky purple or darkening over vast plains in dusky amber—the work either of a Cellini or a Dürer. It was the West of the drifting buffalo herds, of the islanded farmsteads, of Butler, Grove, and even of Margaret Laurence. It was my West completely envisioned.

I am aware of the artistic and philosophic connotations of what I have written, although I am not competent to explore or to deal with them. I can only plead that I speak from remembered experience, and that every human being, like the light trail of a meteor, draws behind artistic, philosophic, and theological suggestions, even affirmations, that might, if worked out, refill many libraries. I am bold to say, therefore, that I have shared a common experience with all who have tried, in whatever form of art, to catch some aspect of the once new landscape of Manitoba and the West. Out of that apprehension comes the new environment in which the artist is free to explore the inner landscapes of men, and to find some reconciliation of the known and the psychedelic in that far more challenging milieu.

From *Contexts of Canada's Past: Selected Essays of W.L. Morton*, ed. A.B. McKillop, Carleton Library Series no. 123 (Toronto: Macmillan of Canada in association with the Institute of Canadian Studies, Carleton University, 1980), 15–25. This article originally appeared in *Mosaic,* Manitoba Centennial Issue 3, 3 (Spring 1970): 1–10.

The "North" in Canadian Historiography

W. L. MORTON

This paper attempts two things. One is to suggest how the area and condition loosely called the "North" by Canadians has affected the development of all Canada. The other is to advance the proposition that any satisfactory interpretation of Canadian history must include the influence of the "North" on Canadian history. The latter proposition implies, as it is meant to do, that no scheme of Canadian historiography yet advanced is wholly satisfactory because none as yet takes account of the influence of the "North." Canadian awareness of Canada is the poorer for that lack, as is the significance of Canada in the world.

The "North," of course, in common usage and in literature is not a scientific term; it remains at best vague and even ambiguous. Precise definitions do exist, but they are precise because limited in purpose. Every man and every scientist has his own "North." The "North" of this paper must therefore be defined for the purpose of the paper. The North is exceedingly cold, as measured by the needs of living plants and animals, for most of the year. The frost-free period, if any, is too brief to allow the growth of cereal foods. In terms of that greater part of human history which has rested on the cultivation of cereals, the North therefore does not admit of agricultural settlement.

The North is thus a climatic environment. In the North, environment is a fact of life and a factor in historiography, whatever may be thought of the influence of environment in the historiography of other regions. The North will admit of an extreme form of nomadic living; witness the Eskimo. It admits also of what may be termed an extreme form of urban life: witness, say, Schefferville in northern Quebec, or still more the urban forms adapted to the North which architects have planned. Life is possible in the North, but ever and always on the conditions imposed by it. To say this is, perhaps, to differ with Stefannson's contention that man can live on the country. Stefannson, like the Eskimo, proved his contention, but he wisely refrained from saying how *many* men.

The answer, of course, exists in any head count of northern population. A hunter, however skilled, can support few people. The present population of the North is supported, at a price, by means of transport developed in more favourable regions. It follows that the development of the North, whether of its old hunting economy or its new mining economy, has depended and will depend on high skills or high costs. Both are the toll the North exacts. The development of the North, therefore, has its own characteristics, different in quality, scale, and sociology from the historic development, agricultural and industrial, of southern regions. Population in the North will be concentrated; it will be made up mostly of transient residents; it will rest on dwindling resources. To some degree a northern community resembles a human outpost on the moon or Mars more than one in the south.

If that is so, one must ask what institutions and what cultural life such communities will have. Of one thing it is possible to be sure; they will be as like those of the south as may be. Man may change his latitudes easily enough, but he does not readily change his ways. It seems unlikely, however, that either institutions or culture can be, as they have not been in the past in many significant ways, like those that history has evolved in more favourable regions. Schefferville, or Thompson, is outwardly at least like any town in the south. Inuvik, much farther to the north, is not. A domed city, or a sunken city on a southern hill slope, would undoubtedly require a more regulated, more repressed life than, say, that of Peterborough or Winnipeg. Would it be so much different that new forms of city government and new ways of living would come into being? Would the northern environment press even under the domes, even into the subtly coloured, wall-to-wall carpeted livingrooms of Oilmansville, Banks Island? It is my expectation that it would.

To sum up, then, by the "North" is meant all that territory beyond the line of minimal growth of the known cereal grains. To the northern developer, of course, such a line is meaningless, but it does seem to have meaning in historical perspective, however quickly that perspective may be lengthening, because the society we know, southern society, is an urban society resting on an agricultural base. In the North there can be no such base for living. A northern society, other than that resting on the hunting economy of the Eskimo, clearly must be a society projected into an alien environment, a society in orbit.

The character of the North, then, is firm, decisive, and different from that of the south. Has that character, however, notably affected the historical development of Canada as evidenced today? It is my impression that, on the one hand, it has affected that development, in ways I shall attempt to sketch, and that, on the other hand, it has not been generally incorporated into Canadian history as it is understood. Hence the thesis of these remarks, that this country, insofar as it is distinctive, is a response to the character and influence of the North. To the extent that it has failed, Canadian historiography so far is incomplete and insufficient.

That there should be a hiatus between the history of exploration, with which so much of the historical literature and documents of Canadian historiography have to do, and Canadian history as actually written is not surprising. Much of that history is in one sense not Canadian at all; the voyages of Hudson, Cook, and Franklin are more truly part of British maritime history. The great inland explorations of Champlain, La Vérendrye, Hearne, Mackenzie, and Thompson, properly understood, are not really Canadian either. They are part of French imperial history, or of economic history pure and simple. It is even more difficult to bring the scant history of the North into Canadian historiography. The antiquity of the Northmen's ventures, the lack of hard evidence, the very differences of language, necessarily make the ancient voyages seem at best mere marginalia to an essentially different story. When a former colleague of mine, and a later member of the Royal Society of Canada, Trygvi Oleson, attempted to argue that what had indubitably happened in Greenland, a mingling of people and culture in the North, might also have happened in the Canadian Arctic, he was met with disbelief and rejection. Yet, if the argument attempted here has any validity, Oleson was right in that his argument accorded with the fundamental pattern of Canadian history. What happened beyond reasonable doubt in Canadian history as accepted happened also in the North, because the North is an integral part of Canadian history. Both the contacts of the Northmen and the explorations of the seamen and the explorers were part of Canadian history because they were part of the process of learning and adaptation to the conditions of the North. That some were failures which left no mark is irrelevant; failure is part of success in learning and adaptation.

The fur trade may seem different, and indeed it is not to be dismissed as just economic history. Money made in the fur trade went into the founding of the Bank of Montreal and the building of the Canadian Pacific Railway. Behind the foundation of many of our cities lies a "moccasin ring" of greater or less proportions. Indeed most Canadian cities began as convenient places to grubstake a fur trader, a fisherman, or a miner, or to fit out a settler. Yet the fur trade had an essential character that may be called "northern," even if it revealed elements of that character also in the Carolinas and the Florida Everglades. That was the adaptation of European commercial enterprise to the exploitation of the only readily available resources of the wilderness. Hence it was also a learning of wilderness ways, of dependence on Indian inventions and skills and the use of lands not yet, if ever, habitable. The elements of northern development are discernible in the fur trade of the south.

The history of the fur trade, to some degree, stands apart from Canadian historical development. At most it gathered capital, explored the land, and opened the ways to settlement. But it did these things only in part, in southern

Ontario not at all. For that reason, although it forms the backbone of the interpretation of Canadian history attributed to Harold Innis, it is unconvincing today as the groundwork for the interpretation of accepted Canadian history. The fur trade depended on the wilderness; where the settler, as used to be said, tamed the wilderness, that is, destroyed it, the fur trade retreated with the wilderness, leaving only some half-breed offspring in place of the beaver, a multitude of place names, and Lower Fort Garry.

An implication of the above remarks, and it is intended, is that the accepted history of Canada begins with settlement. (A second implication today, and it is recognized here, is that agricultural settlement leads to urban foundations. This is, in fact, partly fallacious. A good case can be made that the urban foundations preceded settlement; that, in short, Canadian history was metropolitan from its beginnings.) The belief that there could be no history without a farmer to begin it is touchingly revealed in the respect given Louis Hébert and Abraham Martin in the older histories of New France. But the bucolic inclination persists even today. It is this preoccupation with settlement that explains why the North has little, if any, part in accepted Canadian history, and has not been incorporated as yet in Canadian historiography. The North rejects the farmer. If without the farmer there can be no history, it follows that there can be no northern history, and consequently no place for the North in Canadian historiography.

It is not correct, however, to infer that, because the North as here defined is the region where agriculture is impossible, it has not affected Canadian agricultural settlement, and therefore has no place in Canadian historiography. The northern character of the greater part of Canadian territory may not have made agriculture impossible in the remainder of the country. It did, however, limit the character and extent of that agriculture, often severely. The Yankee farmer who told Captain Butler he would not go to Canada because "you cawn't grow cawrn crop up there" may well have explained why there is a Canada. Farming Canada is and always has been at best spring, not winter, wheat, much less corn, country. Only a few very favoured regions—the Annapolis Valley, southwestern old Ontario, the Okanagan and lower Fraser valleys—can safely add orchard to field crops. The North has restricted the diversity, if not the abundance, of the Canadian farm in almost every corner of the country, and acted as a limitation, if not a prohibition.

The North, as defined, moreover, has created another definite feature of the Canadian landscape. As the agricultural frontier moved westward, it left an open flank to the north. This became a permanent frontier, an enduring demarcation line between wilderness and farmland, between North and south. Ragged, flexible, moving far north in the far northwest, it is nevertheless an impenetrable as well as permanent frontier. It may be vaulted; it cannot be removed. The importance of this will be elaborated below.

If, then, the North affected even agricultural settlement in Canada, and is, therefore, part of Canadian history and ought to be part of Canadian historiography, can the same be said to any significant degree of Canadian urban settlement? This matter depends upon whether one thinks of urban settlement as growing out of agricultural settlement or as having independent origins of its own. As I have already suggested, it is notable that in Canadian history the beginnings of our chief cities—Halifax, Quebec, Montreal, for example—antedated agricultural settlement. The last was particularly a place of assembly for trade in its origin and nothing more. In some sense that suggests that there could have been a Canada and Canadian history without any agricultural settlement, as is indeed the case in Newfoundland. The city in itself, the metropolis dependent, not on the riches of its neighbourhood, but on the reach of its commerce over areas of trading, whether extensive or intensive, does not need its own local food supply.

Were such cities, or, to put it another way, Canadian cities, both metropolitan and local, in any way affected by the Canadian North? One possible answer is affirmative insofar as metropolitan Canadian cities—Montreal, Toronto, Winnipeg, Edmonton, Vancouver—have been dependent on extensive trade, as all have been, and insofar as the "North" is to be equated with extensive trade, those cities have been affected by it. But has the North as defined affected all cities, both metropolitan and local, in any significant way? It would seem not, except in the ways all areas of Canadian life, urban as well as rural, are affected by long winters and low temperatures.

Some deeper analysis, however, suggests that the North has also affected the Canadian city as it did the Canadian farm. The essential features of the city are integration of function (an intensive division of labour) and concentration of site, to ensure ready communication. To these are added the concomitants of size and duration. Now, the city so defined is compatible with the North as defined, and we have in fact such cities as Yellowknife, Flin Flon, Schefferville, Wabush, and Labrador City to establish the point. On the first and last points, however, the North does affect cities in the North. They do not have an integration of function as extensive as that of cities in the south, because they all rest on a single economic base, mining. Since there is as yet no apparent reason for carrying on general manufacturing in the North, that limitation is likely to persist. What then of the last point, duration? The future of such cities is, of course, limited, and I am not altogether sure of the engineer's solution of the resultant problem, to move or abandon them. A mining town or village, yes, but a city in its nature demands a deeper commitment of its people, and will strive to survive.

The city, then, is limited by the North in integration and duration. Have all Canadian cities, if in lesser degree, been so limited? The matter would require great study before any confident answer could be given. Yet it is surely "yes." Only consider how few Canadian cities, Victoria in part excepted, have any real *outdoor* urban life. In the favoured cities of the world the life of the street, the park, the plaza, create their social character, and indeed make them endurable for the poor. In the winter Canadian cities are chiefly shelters, and in summer all who can flee them for as long as possible. (In summer the Canadian city is southern indeed, its pavements baking under the long northern sun.) Toronto may be the cultural centre of English Canada, but I live by a highway which every summer Friday evening is choked by people escaping from its heat. Winnipeg may have its Royal Ballet, but one goes to it through the arctic cold of Portage and Main.

More seriously, I suspect the grave and cautious men of business take note of the limitations the North places on most Canadian cities; the engineers certainly do when they plan the factory buildings and the warehouses. And in sum I think we may assume that the North has limited the characteristics of the city, both metropolitan and local, in Canada.

To say so is not to escape the uneasy feeling that one has belaboured the obvious. The North is cold, and cold limits plant growth and certain of man's activities; so much does not have to be established. My purpose, however, does have a certain subtlety. Canadians behave, and Canadian historians write, as though the North did not exist. My intent is not only to affirm that the North exists, but to assert that it is and has been a very active part of Canadian history and should be taken into account in Canadian historiography.

What emerges, I believe, is that the North not only creates a permanent frontier but in Canada it further imposes beyond that line the breakdown of all conventional and historic institutions. New ones may be invented, old ones modified, but the North begins along the line of institutional breakdown: Its influence operates below that line not by breakdown, but by limitation.

Certain other factors, individual and sociological, must also be taken into account in a way different from that in which settlement, rural and urban, has been taken into account in this paper. It may be sufficient to say of Canadian agrarian and city life that the North has affected them by limiting their extent. It is not sufficient to say no more of the effect of the North on individual Canadians. Here the effect, if it is to be significant, must be an effect not only on extent but also on quality. One could argue, for example, that the North has in some ways extended the good life in Canada by giving winter as well as summer sports, or by furnishing that contrast of civilization and wilderness, the result of the permanent frontier in Canada, which underlies the lakeside cottage life, one of the fondest aspects of the lives of many Canadians. If the North, however, had no further effect on Canadians, the argument advanced here would be gravely weakened, if indeed it could stand at all.

On this important point, nevertheless, I must speak with circumspection. Some of my colleagues in this symposium have spoken, or will speak, on this theme of the Canadian experience. Moreover, in approaching it at all, I must emphasize that I do not raise, indeed I repudiate, any thought of the North producing, peace to Robert W. Service, a hardy breed of man. Any influence the North may have had on Canadian life is, for this paper, an objective matter. The influence may have been moral, or immoral, or amoral; which it is, for the purpose of these remarks, is indifferent.

With those reservations made, may I have your indulgence to take up the theme exclusively as a historian? That is, I shall attempt to see what influence the North may have had on the lives of Canadians over time and in terms of change. As historian, I see four areas in which the historical influence of the North may be discerned. One is the contact of cultures. American Indian and European; the second, that of customs and conventions; the third, already touched on, industrial development; the fourth, institutional development.

On all but the fourth, comment of any weight is difficult. With respect to the first, for example, it is well known that the European greatly affected the Indian, and the Indian the European to some degree, perhaps in some ways not yet recognized. But what had the North to do with the matter? In attempting an answer, I discard *castor gras* and the thicker furs of the northern forest, even the four-point blanket. What the North did in a degree ever greater with increasing latitude was force the European to live among the Indians. The most evident result of this intermingling was intermarriage, and the most lasting result the half-breed or Métis of Canadian history and Canadian life. The Métis, after all, are not to be lightly dismissed, although Canadians are prone to do so. They were the only Canadians to bring off a successful rebellion, and the province of Manitoba was the result. Less noted is the fact that the importance of the half-breed is that he makes this country significantly unlike the United States in an important sociological aspect, and makes it in this respect akin rather to nearly all the countries of Latin America.

I think that point might be developed, but I pass on to the next, that of customs and conventions. Is the pattern of Canadian life in any way affected by the North? It is even more difficult to say. I suspect that the Canadian belief that alcohol "keeps out the cold" was imported; at any rate I shall forbear to say that the North has helped make us the serious drinkers that we are. There is, however, one custom and one convention common to all Canadians, French and English, new and old, that points to the influence of the North. I do not mean the practice of going south of the border as fast and often as possible. The custom is that Canadians do something about the weather. That sounds a bit Leacockian, but I mean it literally. Some Americans, New Englanders and Dakotans, join us in this. But for Canadians doing something about the weather is both an annual ritual and a serious business, like the daily siesta of southerners. The purchase of winter or summer clothing, the changing of tires, the fitting on of the storm sash and the taking off—how shall I enumerate the varieties of the custom, persisting even in the great cities, if in reverse in the provision of humidifiers, electric fans, or ultraviolet lamps, and in the cultivation of the African violet and the dwarf cactus? And the convention? The convention of Canadian life is to ignore the North as we ignore the winter climate in our history, our literature, and so far as we physically may our daily lives. We ignore the North, its coldness, its emptiness, its menace, and its promise—why? Because it is too terrible; it is a terror only some of us, those who live "down North," have exorcized and tamed.

So emerges my theme. All Canadian historians, such is my proposition, must go down North and ask themselves, ask themselves, of course, in addition to all the other questions they have raised, what the North has meant in Canadian history.

What has it meant? Has it meant more than a cold climate? How indeed can something which is after all only a freezing emptiness, an arctic void, a blizzard-swept desert, a silent space, dark as the other side of the moon half of each year, mean anything at all?

The first thing to be grasped is that even a vacuum has meaning. Even if the North were as empty as our rhetoric makes it, it would still exert an influence. Ours after all is the age in which the negative has become as active as the positive. What being responsible for a wilderness unoccupied and practically unpoliced involves, the voyages of the *Manhattan* have made clear. For both economics and politics abhor a vacuum and, if Canada does not occupy and develop its North, someone else will.

This is true in fact today, but it has always been potentially true. If the French sought the way to China by the St. Lawrence, the English, and the Danes, sought it by the North West Passage, by the *Manhattan*'s arctic route, and sought it as long ago as 1585, if not 1506. Hence the fighting along the shores and on the waters of Hudson Bay. If, however, explorers like Hudson hoped the North might be empty water free all the way to Asia, it was, in fact, not empty of certain desired commodities—fur, seal and whale oil, eider, ivory—the product of the rich marine life which fed along the margins of its ice. These things it was that brought the first Europeans, seeking timber too, Siberian driftwood if necessary, for roof trees and boat-building; these it was that made America a halfway house to Asia to men who lived in a newly global world as we live in a newly planetary one. One historiographical result was that Canada has its own historical beginnings, not in the late Columban voyages, but in the early Icelandic ones.

If, however, the North is in these small ways a significant factor in Canadian history, is it also more? Does it not only limit the bounds of the Canadian historical enterprise, but also qualify it so as to give Canadian historiography a yet further distinctive quality of its own? I think it does, and here I go beyond anything I have ventured to say before.

By historiography I mean here the way the history of a particular subject has been interpreted. In the history of Canada four such interpretations may be discussed, both in the past and as being more or less active today. The first is that of the mission of New France to extend and preserve the Catholic faith and French culture in North America. The second interprets Canadian history as the victorious spread of British institutions, in the Canadian variant of responsible government, on Canadian soil. The third is the Laurentian thesis that Canada is the child of its rivers, reincarnated in its railways. The fourth and latest is that of the concept of the metropolis, general and local, as the key to the explanation of Canadian history. The exponents of none of these was, or is, thinking of historiography as he wrote, or writes; none would claim that his interpretation, at least so narrowly defined, was complete, or aimed at completeness. To me all four seem to possess validity; all seem at the same time to be limited.

All, moreover, actually if not intentionally, do not encompass the North. Harold Innis, of course, was fully aware of the North, but saw it only as an extension of Canada. He did not see the permanent frontier which the existence of the North created once the great fur trade ended. Donald Creighton is aware of the North, but his triumphant goal, like Canada's and Macdonald's, was the Pacific, and the last notes of his majestic symphony are the clink of Donald A. Smith's hammer on the last spike in the mountain silence of Craigellachie. The North is yet to be incorporated into the historiography of Canada.

In fact this will not be done until much professional historical work has been done on the North, work such as Professor Morris Zaslow has now in manuscript. In theory, however, it is clear how it will be done. First, the North is common to all Canada, except three Maritime provinces. (I hate to make the exception, but the lack of the North is one of the disadvantages of those provinces.) Next, it almost alone gives the federal government a clear and positive role to play; in the North its empire remains and its future may reside. Finally, the North is and has been a constant, if largely unrecognized, factor in Canadian history, a factor even as a void, a factor as a breeder of weather, as a source of treasure, perhaps as a reservoir of clean air in a globe polluted, the last pillar of the biosphere. As such it will enter the consciousness of Canadians—how much it has done in the last year!—and the work of Canadian historians. As it does, we shall come to see that the historiography of Canada includes not only the advance by the St. Lawrence but also the unfolding of the permanent frontier, clear as the line between the desert and the sower on the plain of Damascus, beyond which all conventional institutions break down, beyond which life and wealth are possible, but only on the North's conditions.

In that I see the symbolic meaning of Canadian history. Not only in the North, but in nearly all Canada, life and wealth are possible only on the North's conditions. The North makes necessary an absolute dependence on one's fellows, on co-operative skills, on communal capital. So, in ever-lessening degrees southward, does southern Canada. In the North the average does not govern; the extremes do. So, in degrees ever dwindling southward, do they in the south.

I conclude, therefore, with a paradox: The ultimate and the comprehensive meaning of Canadian history is to be found where there has been no Canadian history, in the North.

From *Contexts of Canada's Past: Selected Essays of W.L. Morton*, ed. A.B. McKillop, Carleton Library Series no. 123 (Toronto: Macmillan of Canada in association with the Institute of Canadian Studies, Carleton University, 1980), 229–39. Delivered to a symposium on "The Influence of Climate on Canadian Culture" and originally published in *Transactions of the Royal Society of Canada* series 4, vol. 8 (1970): 31–40.

MARSHALL McLUHAN
(1911–1980) was called many things during his lifetime: a pioneer in communications, an oracle of the electric age, a pop philosopher, a put-on, an intellectual comet. The list is a long one and it is still too early to say how he will be remembered. Few would dispute that he gave the world a new understanding of its media, and became the embodiment of a whole series of myths that he helped to identify. He was born in Edmonton, the son of a real estate salesman who dabbled in metaphysics and of a gifted and ambitious mother who later gave elocutionary performances in all the major cities of Canada. The prairie landscape of his boyhood made a powerful impression on him, as it did on such essayists as Frederick Philip Grove, Margaret Laurence, and Robert Kroetsch. McLuhan once told an interviewer: "I think of western skies as one of the most beautiful things about the West, and the western horizons. The Westerner doesn't have a point of view. He has a panorama . . . [H]e has at all times a total field of vision, and since he can take this total field at any time, he doesn't have to worry about goals." Such remarks help confirm the impression that it was not by chance the literary movements of realism and post-modernism either had their origins or their strongest basis in the Canadian West.

McLuhan studied English literature and philosophy at the University of Manitoba, and his interest in the essay dates from these years and his discovery of Addison, Johnson, Macaulay, and particularly G.K. Chesterton. Chesterton's love of paradox, his Catholic faith, and his belief in the world's essential mysteriousness and goodness had a profound effect on McLuhan. After Manitoba, he enrolled as an affiliated student at Cambridge, where he was exposed to the work of Richards, Empson, and Leavis, three of the most important figures in twentieth-century literary criticism. He taught at St. Louis University before receiving his Ph.D. from Cambridge (1943), then at Assumption College in Windsor, and finally went to St. Michael's College in 1946. He lived and taught in Toronto for the rest of his life. Here he gave the lectures and wrote the books that were to make his name a household word: *The Mechanical Bride* (1951), *The Gutenberg Galaxy* (1962), *Understanding Media* (1964), *The Medium is the Massage* (1967), *War and Peace in the Global Village* (1968), *From Cliché to Archetype* (with Wilfred Watson, 1970).

His insights into popular culture and television, his status as a guru to the sixties generation, his intriguing, elliptical, suggestive, baffling, dazzling attempts to see connections, meanings, patterns where none had been seen before made him the most discussed critic in North America. Yet the public image, generated by the publicity machine that he anatomized so brilliantly, often consisted of a few slogans ("the medium is the message") and made McLuhan into a mere caricature of what he believed. Those who dismissed him as the communications expert who couldn't communicate, or the writer of book after book that proved books were obsolete were as guilty of misrepresenting him as were his more fervent admirers. Contrary to the popular perception, McLuhan was not particularly interested in popular culture, and did not much like what he did know of it. The man whose name inevitably comes up in any discussion of television as a medium intensely disliked most television programs he saw, and counselled his son to limit drastically the television time of his own children. McLuhan did attempt to forge a synthesis between high modernist culture—he championed the work of many twentieth-century writers when it was unfashionable to do so—and popular culture, but his success was decidedly mixed. Much of the notorious difficulty of his style—the lack of coherence, for example—comes from his attempt to turn traditional prose into a new medium for the new insights he had to convey. As Robert Fulford has written, "His religion . . . was technological determinism. He saw history as a series of unfolding inventions, each of which reshaped humanity according to its own new rules." The superficiality and sensationalism that make a news story acceptable because it is "good *television*" are explained, as Fulford also points out, by this central notion of McLuhan's thought. The visual impression becomes more important than the information conveyed. No one now thinks this idea particularly controversial; like much of the best of McLuhan it has become absorbed into the mainstream of our intellectual life.

The Role of New Media in Social Change

MARSHALL McLUHAN

From the Neolithic age until the advent of electromagnetic technology men have been busy extending their bodies technologically. The fragmentation of work and social action that results from specialized extensions of the body has been given close study by Lynn White, in his *Medieval Technology and Social Change.** He opens with a consideration of the stirrup as it modified social organization in the early Middle Ages. As an extension of the foot, the stirrup enabled men to wear armor on horseback. Man became a sort of tank. But armor was expensive. It required the work and skill of a craftsman for a year to turn out a full suit of armor. The small farmer could not pay for such armor. The result was a change in the entire landholding pattern. The Feudal System was spurred into existence by the stirrup, the mere extension of the foot.

The extensions of hand and arm and back that made up the industrial complex of the eighteenth and nineteenth centuries were meshed with Gutenberg technology to create the great team efforts of assembly-line patterns of work and production. But the industrial complex was based on specialist fragmentation of tasks and extensions of the body which carried to an extreme the division of labor that had begun in the Neolithic period in about 3 000 B.C.

A totally different kind of extension occurred with the application of electro-magnetism to social organization. Electricity enabled us to extend the central nervous system itself. It is a biological kind of event that creates maximal involvement of each of us in the total social process. Electric speed tends to abolish time and space in human awareness. There is no delay in

* Lynn White, *Medieval Technology and Social Change* (Oxford University Press, 1962).

the effect of one event upon another. The electric extension of the nervous system creates the unified field of organically interrelated structures that we call the present Age of Information. With the reduction of time and space in the pattern of events there is not only a great increase in the amount of data for daily experience, but action and reaction tend to become fused. Whereas in the previous technologies of fragmented extensions of the body there had been typically a considerable gap in time between social action and the ensuing consequences and reactions, this gap of time has almost disappeared. We are confronted with a situation that invites simultaneous or configurational and ecological awareness instead of the older awareness of sequential and linear cause and effect. In the mechanical age of the wheel and the lever, acceleration had expanded and enlarged the sphere of action. At electric or instant speeds the same sphere contracts almost to the dimensions of a single consciousness. Listening to a concert with an eminent psychologist, I happened to mention the highly tactile character of orchestral strings as compared with the other instruments. He seemed quite surprised and asked: "Do you mean that an auditory experience can have a tactile component?" Discussing the matter with him later, it became apparent that many psychologists assume that not only is auditory experience merely auditory, but so with the other senses. Visual experience is merely visual, etc. Thus, in such a view, there would be little difference in the experience and effects of TV and movies. And indeed many students of the media assume that it is the content of media, whether of the sung word, spoken word, the written word, that really matters. It is this sort of assumption that has tended to divert attention away from the forms and parameters of the media themselves. The sensory modalities of the media as such have not been studied. The very idea of "content" which obsesses us, on the other hand, is unknown to non-literate societies. Our Western divisions between form and content occur with literacy and because of literacy. Literacy is itself a work of intense visual stress in a culture. When men begin to translate the speech complex into a visual code they have already opted for a division of labor that affects the whole society. They have become settled and have begun to specialize. Writing is impossible for man the food-gatherer but it is inevitable for Neolithic man, the agriculturalist.

In his monumental study of *The Beginnings of Architecture*, Siegfried Giedion has many occasions to comment on the fact that before script there is no architecture. Until man intensifies the visual parameters of his life by writing, he cannot *enclose* space. Before writing, man resorts to hollowed-out spaces. The parameters of hollowed-out space are mainly tactile, kinetic, and auditory. The visual components of the cave are minimal. Such proprioceptive space is almost like that of clothing, an immediate extension of our bodies. In our own electric age, space for the physicist has become a non-visual thing of complex stresses. It is no longer uniform and continuous but diverse and heterogeneous. On the other hand, when Newton's physics first entered the European ken, Pascal moaned: "The eternal silence of these infinite spaces terrifies me." Before Newton our Western space orientation had had a much smaller visual parameter but the auditory components of space-structure had been very high. With the advent of the printed word, the visual modalities of Western life increased beyond anything experienced in any previous society. The parameters of the visual as such are continuity, uniformity and connectedness. These are not the notes or modes of any of our other senses. Today, when our electric technologies have extended far more than our visual faculties, the parameters of sense experience in the Western world have been radically altered. Our new media—the telephone, the telegraph and radio and television—are extensions of the nervous system.

I suggest that the sensory typology of an entire population is directly altered by each and every new extension of the body or of the senses. Each extension is an amplification that in varying but measurable degrees, alters the hierarchy of sensory preference in ordering daily experience and environment for whole populations.

Thus, it is an ancient observation, that was repeated by Henri Bergson, that speech is a technology of extension that amplified man's power to store and exchange perceptual knowledge; but it interrupted the sharing of a unified collective consciousness experienced by pre-verbal man. Before speech, it is argued, men possessed a large measure of extra-sensory perceptions which was fragmented by speech technology.

Until electro-magnetism over a century ago, all the extensions of man appear as fragmentary. Tools and weapons, clothing and housing, as much as the wheel, or letters, are direct, specialist extensions of our bodies that amplify and channel energies in a specialist and fragmented way. Today much study is being devoted to the micro-climates created for our bodies by clothing. Some measurements indicate that unclad societies eat 40 percent more than those that are clad. As a technology of physical extensions, clothing channels time and energies for special tasks. It also changes the patterns of sensory perception and awareness; and nudity has very different meanings in different cultures. So it is with all the other extensions of ourselves.

The problem of dichotomy between form and content, that troubles and confuses our Western perception of media today, is now beginning to yield to new awareness of structures, of total fields in interplay, and to ecological approaches in general. We still need to develop awareness of the pervasive visual parameters and assumptions that phonetic literacy had imposed upon Western culture for 2000 years. Today, even the physicist is often hampered by his unconscious visual bias. This bias is utterly inhibiting to the physicist since his data are almost entirely non-visual. It is thus not at all accidental that physics is mainly cultivated by men from cultural areas in which visual values are at a minimum. The unfortunate effects of highly literate culture on the state of the physical sciences is a theme of Milic Capek's "*The Philosophical Impact of Contemporary Physics*." In the West our intense visual bias and our habit of considering form and content as quite separate derives from the structure of the phonetic alphabet. There is only one such alphabet, among the many kinds of scripts. And the unique property of our alphabet that is unknown to the Chinese or to the Egyptian is its power to separate sound, sight and meaning. The letters of our alphabet are semantically neutral. They can translate the words of any language. But they translate them by semantically meaningless sounds into semantically meaningless visual symbols. This divorce between the visual code and the semantic structure has gradually permeated and shaped all the perceptions of Western literate man.

We have long stressed content and ignored form in communication. But this visual and literate structuring of our perceptions has provided us with very little accompanying immunity to the effects of non-visual form. We were amused in 1900 when the Chinese protested that vertical telegraph poles would upset the psychic equilibrium of their people. We still imagine that the effects of radio depend upon radio programs. Yet such literate assumptions were no protection against Fascism. When radio began in Europe it awakened the ancient tribal energies in their auditory depths, as radio does today in backward countries. The auditory form of radio has, of course, a quite different effect in literate societies from its effect in oral and auditory cultures. Intensely visual and industrial cultures like England and America had few remaining tribal roots and vestiges to be re-energized by the tribal drum of radio. Where such roots still existed as in Ireland, Wales and Scotland, there were marked tribal stirrings and revivals. In the more urban and industrialized England and America radio was mainly felt as a resurgence of the folk arts of jazz and song and dancing. In areas like Germany, where tribal experience had been retained by many linguistic and artistic means, radio meant a revival of mystic forms of togetherness and depth involvement that has not been forgotten.

In the same way, the effect of TV has been very different in Europe and in the U.S.A. The TV image or "mosaic" as it is named by the TV engineers, has a quite different sensory character and effect from the movie and photographic image. The mosaic of the TV image provides, structurally, an experience of what J.J. Gibson calls "active or exploratory touch" as opposed to passive or cutaneous touch.*

The TV mosaic created by the "scanning finger" is visually of low definition, making for maximal involvement of the viewer. The painters after Cezanne, in the 1860s, deliberately set about to endow the retinal impression with tactual values.** In order to involve their audience maximally they resorted to various low-definition visual effects, many of which anticipated the typical form of the TV image. They achieved an effect described by J.J. Gibson in his experiments when he reports, "The paradox is even more striking, for tactual perception corresponds well to the form of the object when the stimulus

* J.J. Gibson, "Observations on Active Touch," *Psychological Review* 69, 6 (November, 1962): 477–91.

** E.H. Gombrich, "*Art and Illusion*," 18.

is almost formless, and less well when the stimulus is a stable representation of the form of the object. A clear unchanging perception arises when the flow of sense impressions changes most."*

At the same time as Monet and Seurat and Rouault were dimming the visual parameters of art in order to achieve maximal audience participation, the symbolists were demonstrating the superiority of suggestion over statement in poetry. The same principle obtains on the telephone as compared with radio. The auditory image of the telephone is of low definition. It elicits maximal attention and cannot be used as background. All the senses rally to strengthen the weak sound of the phone. We even feel the need to be kinetically involved via doodling or pacing. And whereas we complete the strong auditory image of radio by visualizing, we only slightly visualize on the phone.

Dr. Llewellyn-Thomas has used the Mackworth head-camera to study the eye-movements of children watching TV. There is great significance in his discovery that the eyes of the child never waiver from the faces of the actors even in scenes of violence. Maximal involvement is experienced not in the actions of the scene but in the *reactions* of the actors in the scenes. The result is the same as the one recorded by J.J. Gibson concerning tactual perception as most adequate when the stimulus was almost formless. That is, exploratory touch comes into play as the visual parameter is dimmed. It is a normal feature of the comics. Cartoons and comics are visually very dim affairs. The amount of visual data provided is small. But involvement or exploratory touch is at a maximum. Leo Bogart's study of "comic strips and their Adult Readers"** observes how comic strip humor seems to produce a grim, unsmiling kind of amusement for the most part. "Genuine hearty laughs seem to be few and far between." Once more, the involvement is high in these forms just in proportion as the intensity of the stimulus is vague and weak. The same comic scenes projected in high visual definition on a movie screen would evoke much more overt response.

Most people were struck by the TV coverage of the Kennedy assassination. We were all conscious of great depth of involvement, but there was no excitement, no sensationalism. When involvement is maximal, we are nearly numb.

One of the notable effects of the TV image on those in the primary grades seems to be the development of near-point reading. The average distance from the page of children in the first three grades has recently been measured in Toronto by Dr. W.A. Hurst. The average distance is $6^1/_2$ inches. The children seem to be striving to do a psychomimetic version of their relation to the TV image. They seem to be trying to read by proprioception and exploratory touch. The printed page, however, is of high definition visually and cannot so be apprehended.

* Gibson, "Observations on Active Touch," 487–88.

** In *Mass Culture* (The Free Press of Glencoe, 1957), 189–99.

It isn't only the act of reading that conflicts with habits of TV perception. I wish to suggest that the depth involvement characteristic of TV viewing discourages the traditional habit and need of "seeing ahead." The TV child today cannot see ahead, in a motivational sense, just because he is so deeply involved. He needs a totally new pedagogy and a new curriculum that will accommodate his shifting sensory ratios and his natural drive towards depth participation since TV. This returns us to the theme that our Western preference for considering the content of media instead of their configurational features is itself a bias of perception derived from the form of phonetic literacy. I do not need to be reminded of how much we owe to literacy. It has given us our way of life. It separated the individual from the tribal horde. I suggest that if we value this legacy of literacy, we shall need to take steps to maintain its existence by a fuller understanding of the role of new media in social change. Autonomy and freedom are best secured by a grasp of the new parameters of our condition. I would meet you upon this exponentially, as the mathematicians put it.

From *Antigonish Review* 74–75 (Summer–Autumn 1988): 43–49.

NORTHROP FRYE (1912–1991) was born in Sherbrooke, Quebec. He was educated at home by his mother, a gifted teacher, until Grade 4 and left school in Grade 10. He later speculated that one of the reasons he became so interested in primary and secondary education was that he had had so little of it himself. Then came the University of Toronto, where he received a B.A. in 1933 and a degree from Emmanuel College. (He was an ordained minister of the United Church but used his office only for "marrying and burying his students.") He received an M.A. from Merton College, Oxford in 1941. Frye spent his life teaching at the University of Toronto, where he was appointed University Professor (allowing him to teach anywhere in the university), and became Chancellor of Victoria College in 1978.

A recent study of almost a thousand journals showed that Frye was among the most frequently cited authors in the arts and the humanities. His erudition, his humour, his style, his *obiter dicta* also helped make him one of the most readable critics we have. He began his career with a seminal study of William Blake, *Fearful Symmetry* (1947), and *Anatomy of Criticism* (1957), one of the century's most important works of critical theory. These were followed by *The Educated Imagination, Fables of Identity, The Well-Tempered Critic*, and *T.S. Eliot*, all in 1963, in which the insights are as sharp, the range as wide, and the writing as lively as in his earlier works. Reviewers made comments such as "worth a hundred ordinary critical studies" when attempting to do justice to these books. The books that followed, on Shakespeare and Milton, twentieth-century culture, romance and Romanticism, essay collections such as *The Stubborn Structure* (1970) and *Spiritus Mundi* (1976), the volumes devoted to Canadian literature, *The Bush Garden* (1971), *Divisions on a Ground* (1982), and his studies of the Bible, *The Great Code* (1982) and *Words With Power* (1990), made Frye more highly acclaimed and more widely discussed than any other literary critic. His views on education and his analysis of modern culture have been very influential, as has his interest in the cultural context of literature and the images and myths that organize it. Diffident and self-deprecating, witty and polemical, an enormously prolific writer whose lectures were enjoyed by generations of students, a great system builder who detested critical elitism, a man who once told an interviewer that he had few leisure activities because he found his work so relaxing—Northrop Frye captured our imagination as no other critic has done.

Canada: New World without Revolution

NORTHROP FRYE

Canada, with four million square miles and only four centuries of documented history, has naturally been a country more preoccupied with space than with time, with environment rather than tradition. The older generation, to which I have finally become assigned, was brought up to think of Canada as a land of unlimited natural resources, an unloving but rich earth-mother bulging with endless supplies of nickel and asbestos, or, in her softer parts, with the kind of soil that would allow of huge grain and lumber surpluses. The result of such assumptions is that many of our major social problems are those of ecology, the extinction of animal species, the plundering of forests and mines, the pollution of water, as the hundreds of millions of years that nature took to build up our supplies of coal and oil are cancelled out in a generation or two. The archaeologists who explore royal tombs in Egypt and Mesopotamia find they are almost always anticipated by grave robbers, people who got there first because they had better reasons for doing so than the acquisition of knowledge. We are the grave robbers of our own resources, and posterity will not be grateful to us. There is, however, a growing understanding that our situation is not simply one of people against planes, or whatever the current issue may be, but of soil and trees and water against concrete and tarmac.

These spatial and environmental problems have a temporal dimension as well. Our history began in the seventeenth century, the age of Baroque expansion in Europe, where the countries advancing most rapidly into the future were those on the Atlantic seaboard. Rapid advance is usually followed either by rapid decline or by a rapid change in some other direction: even by then Spain and Portugal had passed their meridian of growth, and France soon turned back to its European preoccupations. If the French had held Canada they might well have sold it, as they did Louisiana. What is important is not nationality but cultural assumptions. The Baroque age was an age of intense belief in the supremacy of human consciousness over nature. It had discovered something of the technological potential of mathematics, once mathematics had become attached to a powerful social organization. It was not an age of individualism, as is often said, but an age of relatively enlightened despotism, and in some ways very like the dawn of civilization in the Near East, when the pyramids of Egypt and the ziggurats of Babylon emerged as dramatic witness to what men could do when united under a sufficiently strong social will. Both then and in the Baroque period mathematics, and the appearance of geometrical patterns in the human environment, was a symbol of aggressiveness, of imperialistic domination. We can see the results all over our country, in the grid patterns of our cities, the concession lines that divide up the farmland into squares, the railways and highways that emphasize direction through landscape rather than accommodation to it. Improvement in such communications always means a wider and straighter path through nature, and a corresponding decline of interest in it. With the coming of the aeroplane, even the sense of passing through a natural environment disappears. Our attitude to nature is reflected in our social environment, the kind we build ourselves. Washington was a city designed for automobiles rather than pedestrians long before there were any automobiles; Los Angeles, a city never designed at all, seems to have broken through the control even of the automobile. It was, after all, named after angels, who traditionally do not travel through space but simply manifest themselves elsewhere.

The religion that the British and French brought to the New World was not a natural monotheism, like the Algonquin worship of a Great Spirit, nor an imperial monotheism like that of the Stoics, but a revolutionary monotheism, with a God who took an active and partisan role in history; and like all revolutionary movements, including Marxism in our time, it equipped itself with a canon of sacred books and a dialectical habit of mind, a mental attitude in which the neighboring heresy is much more bitterly hated than the total rejection of the faith. The dialectical habit of mind produced the conception of the false god, a conception hardly intelligible to an educated pagan. All false gods, in the Christian view, were idols, and all idolatry came ultimately from the belief that there was something numinous in nature. The Christian teaching was that there were no gods in nature; that nature was a fellow-creature of man, and that all the gods that had been discovered in it were devils. We have derived many benefits from this attitude, but it had a more sinister side; it tended to assume that nature, not being inhabited or protected by gods or potentially dangerous spirits, was simply something available for human exploitation. Everywhere we look today, we see the conquest of nature by an intelligence that does not love it, that feels no part of it, that splits its own consciousness off from it and looks at it as an object. The sense of the absolute and unquestionable rightness of man's conquest over nature extended to other cultures regarded as being in a "state of nature." The primary principle of white settlement in this country, in practice if not always in theory, was that the indigenous cultures should be destroyed, not preserved or continued or even set apart.

The spokesman for the Baroque phase of this attitude is Descartes, whose fundamental axiom, "I think, therefore I am," rested on a desire to derive human existence from human consciousness, and to see that consciousness as being in a different world from the nature which for Descartes was pure extension in space. This attitude, in itself a logical development from the traditional Christian view of nature, got so far away from idolatry that it became a kind of idolatry in reverse, the idol this time being human consciousness itself, separated from nature. We live today in a social environment which is a triumph of Cartesian consciousness; an abstract and autonomous world of interlocking co-ordinates, in which most of our imagination is focussed not on nature but on the geometrical shapes that we have imposed on nature. My own few childhood memories of big cities are full of a kind of genial clutter: crowds of people on streets, shops with their doors open, theatres with glittering lights; and certainly the exhilaration of this had much to do with the attractiveness of cities for those in smaller centres a generation or two ago. Much of it of course remains, but it is becoming clearer that each advance of technology is accompanied by an advance in introversion, and less sense of public use. Many of the streets now in these same cities, with their deserted sidewalks and cars whizzing up and down the road past scowling fortress-like buildings, show us the kind of anti-community symbolized for me by University Avenue in Toronto and by the areas in Los Angeles where pedestrians are regarded as vagrants. The amount of mental distress caused by living in an environment which expresses indifference or contempt for the perspectives of the human body is very little studied: one might call it proportion pollution.

My own university is in the middle of a big industrial city: this means great masses of box-lunch students, who commute in and out from distant suburbs and take their courses with little experience of a real university community, of the kind that Cardinal Newman regarded as the "idea" of the university. The surrounding streets keep steadily turning into anonymous masses of buildings that look eyeless in spite of being practically all windows. Many of them seem to have had no architect, but appear to have sprung out of their excavations like vast toadstools. City planners speak of the law of conserving the plan, meaning that Bloor Street in Toronto or Sherbrooke Street in Montreal are still where those streets originally were even though there has been a total metamorphosis of the buildings on them. But even this law, which seems at first sight like a concession to a sense of tradition, is really a means of confining change to the inorganic. And as we shuttle from a pigeon-hole in a high-rise apartment to another pigeon-hole in an office, a sense of futility and humiliation takes possession of us that we can now perhaps see in its historical dimension.

As civilization has "progressed" from axe to bulldozer, the growing withdrawal from nature paralyzes something natural in ourselves. A friend of my wife's, an interior decorator, remarked that she had a group of neurotic clients whom it seemed impossible either to please or get rid of, and she suddenly realized that they had something in common: they all lived in high-rise apartments at a level above the trees. A withdrawal from nature extends into a growing withdrawal from human society itself. I mentioned the increasing introversion that technology brings with it: the aeroplane is more introverted than the train; the super-highway, where there is a danger of falling asleep, more introverted than the most unfrequented country road. The international airport, completely insulated even from the country it is in, is perhaps the most eloquent symbol of this, and is parodied in Stanley Kubrick's movie *2001*, where the hero lands on the moon, dependent on human processing even for the air he breathes, and finds nothing to do there except to phone his wife back on earth, who is out.

A revolutionary habit of mind, being founded on the sense of a crucial break in time at some point, the Exodus from Egypt, the Incarnation of Christ, the flight of Mohammed, the October Revolution in Russia, has a hostility to continuous tradition built into it. In Moslem countries everything that happened before Mohammed's time is part of the age of ignorance. Guides in developing countries, especially Marxist ones, want to show tourists the achievements of their own regime, and often get angry or contemptuous when the tourists want to see the cultural products of the old exploiting days. Similarly with our own culture. The Puritans in Massachusetts were in communion with the Puritans in Norwich who petitioned the Cromwellian government to pull down a useless and cumbersome cathedral which was a mere relic of superstition. Even the Jesuit missionaries, for all their zeal and devotion, still assumed that the Indians, so long as they were heathen, were a part of subconscious nature, and that only Christianity could incorporate them into a fully human society. A cultural sense thus got started which was still operative until quite recently. My late friend Charles Currelly, the founder of the Archaeological Museum in Toronto, was horrified by the indifference with which the authorities of his day regarded the British Columbia totem poles, and by the eagerness with which they were ready to sell them off to anyone whom they thought would be fool enough to want them. What we are now beginning to see is that an original belief in the rightness of destroying or ignoring a so-called "savage" culture develops toward a contempt for our own. In Margaret Atwood's very ironic novel *Surfacing*, the heroine, trying to get back to an original identity represented by the Quebec forest, finds that she has to destroy everything cultural that she possesses, or, as she says: "everything from history must be eliminated."

The revolutionary aspect of white settlement extended from religion into economics, as entrepreneur capitalism developed. Every technological change brought with it a large-scale shift in population centres. The skyline of Toronto sixty years ago was dominated by the spires of the great churches: now the churches are points of depression within the skyline. My moral is not the shift of interest from spiritual to financial administration: my moral is rather that the churches themselves are now largely without parishes, the population, at least the church-going part of it, having moved elsewhere. Similarly Canada is a land of ruins to an extent that the less spacious countries of Europe would not dare to be: ghost towns at exhausted mines or the divisional points of old railways remind us how quickly our economy can scrap not merely a building but an entire city. As Earle Birney remarks, the country is haunted by its lack of ghosts, for a ghost town has no ghosts: it is only one of the rubbish heaps that spring up in an economy of waste. We may remember Sam Slick on the beauties of Niagara Falls:

> "It would be a grand speck to get up a jint stock company for factory purposes, for such another place for mills ain't to be found atween the poles. Oh dear!" said I, "only to think of the cardin' mills, fullin' mills, cotton mills, grain mills, saw mills, plaster mills, and gracious knows what sort o' mills might be put up there . . . and yet them goneys the British let all run away to waste."

For Sam Slick the ideal thriving mill town of this sort was Lowell in Massachusetts, where my father started in business, and it was a sad day for both us when I took him there as an old man, after all the mills had been moved to the south, and he saw only the empty shell of the town he once knew. One question that such events raise is obviously: what can or should be preserved of what is no longer functional, and has little interest in itself apart from being a part of our past?

Whatever the answer, our social environment is a revolutionary one in which the main forces are indiscriminately destructive. This has to some extent always been true. Once there was a great city called Nineveh, so great that, according to the Book of Jonah, it took three days to journey across it. Then, quite suddenly, Nineveh disappeared under the sand, where it remained for nearly three thousand years. This kind of destruction, from enemy action without, is a greater danger now, as hydrogen bombs would leave nothing for the sand to preserve; but along with it is the even more insidious sense of destruction from within, destruction that proceeds from the very nature of technology itself, not impossibly inspired by some deathwish in ourselves. The only possible economic alternative to capitalism, we feel, is socialism, but if capitalism is a destroyer, socialism is even more of one, because more committed to technology. In ancient Egypt one of the first things a new Pharaoh often did was to deface his predecessor's monuments: this is still our rhythm of life, but it is largely an unconscious one, except when rationalized as progress.

The violence of our almost unmanageable cities is bringing about another great population shift, as people move out of them and back to smaller centres. We are beginning to see a very large cycle of history turning here, and with this is slowly growing another social vision. Ecology, the sense of the need for conserving natural resources, is not a matter of letting the environment go back to the wilderness, but of finding some kind of working balance between man and nature founded on a respect for nature and its inner economies. As part of natural ecology, we are also developing some sense of the need for a kind of human ecology, of conserving not only our natural but our cultural and imaginative resources. Again, this is not simply a matter of leaving alone everything that is old: it is a way of life that grows out of a sense of balance between our present and our past. In relation to the natural environment, there are two kinds of people: those who think that nature is simply there to be used by man, and those who realize that man is himself a part of nature, and will destroy himself if he destroys it. In relation to time and human history, there are also two kinds of people: those who think that the past is dead, and those who realize that the past is still alive in us. A dead past left to bury its dead ends in a dead present, a society of sleepwalkers, and a society without a memory is as senile as an individual in the same plight.

The very word "preservation" reflects some of the panic that goes with the sense of imminent destruction. Some time ago Eric Arthur produced a book on Toronto called *No Mean City*, full of photographs of its older architecture. If we count the number of buildings that have been destroyed, many of them before the book appeared, we can see that there is something else in the city which is, if not mean, at least reckless and out of control, something that needs strong organizing to resist it. According to John Stuart Mill, there is a liberal and a conservative question to be asked about everything: what good is it? and why is it there? If these questions are asked about public, cultural or historical monuments, the prevailing answer in our day to the question, what good is it? is, no good unless useful to the present owner of the property it stands on; and the answer to the question, why is it there? is, because it is not yet worth anyone's while to remove it. Clearly we need more intelligible answers to both questions. What is called future shock is simply a by-product of the destructiveness of technology: it represents a genuine social problem, and it produces such mental diseases as the conviction among educators (noted by Bernie Hodgetts in his trenchant survey of the teaching of Canadian history, *What Culture? What Heritage?*) that it doesn't matter what we teach, because society is so transient that all one's skills and assumptions will soon be out of date anyway. This is a lethal state of mind to get into. Trying to sharpen one's sense of the future is useless, as the future has no existence; trying to see the present as an interim in which anything may go at any time merely adds to the mood of destruction. Not everything that can happen will happen: we have to understand what kind of people we are before we can begin to guess what we shall do. What kind of people we are is perhaps determined, and certainly conditioned, by what we realize of our past, and sharpening our sense of the past is the only way of meeting the future. Preserving our heritage is a central part of that realization and that sharpened sense.

In the Book of Jeremiah there is an episode that I often return to, in which Jeremiah's secretary is reading, to the King of Judah, the prophecy which consists so largely of denunciations of the royal policy. A fire, we are told, was burning in the room, and every so often the infuriated king would cut off part of the scroll being read with a knife and throw it on the fire. This must have been a papyrus scroll, and what fascinates me is that the king's palace disappeared totally in a few years, and not the slightest trace of it remains, whereas the Book of Jeremiah, entrusted to the most fragile and combustible substance produced in the ancient world, is still with us, and still in reasonably good shape. The inference, or at least the human inference, appears to be that what is easiest to preserve is what has the power of reproduction. Literature has always survived much better than the visual arts for this reason, and now, with recorded music, photography, and tape, an immense amount of cultural material has become preservable. From the Avalon peninsula to the Queen Charlotte Islands, scholars have been collecting ballads, folksongs, folktales, and whatever a tape recorder can preserve of vanishing attitudes and ways of life. Sometimes the collector arrives too late for the crucial things to be preserved, but what is done is better than nothing, and our archives and libraries are growing in cultural importance accordingly. One of the most rewarding of the WPA projects of forty years ago was the Index of American Design, an inventory of the conventions of the popular visual arts, a project which extended into Canada, and this kind of record is still one of our most useful allies in the fight against oblivion.

As part of this development, the contempt for primitive or popular art that so distressed Currelly a half-century ago has largely disappeared: in fact we set so high a value now on such art that we have almost transformed the Eskimos into a nation of sculptors, at least with one hand, even though we may be destroying the sources of their creativeness with the other. Some of our attitude to this, perhaps can be discounted as a patronizing sense of what used to be called the "picturesque," something which appeals to us because we think it comes just under our own standard of sophistication. But this is a minor and expendable attitude: what really attracts us in what we so misleadingly call "primitive" art is rather the recognition of a powerful convention at work within it. Such a convention is in the visual arts something of a parallel to what the ability to reproduce is in literature: it indicates, if it does not guarantee, a continuing vitality in the tradition that will make possible a steady production of high quality. Similar conventions operate, or should operate, in the area generally called handicraft, but the one-sided competition with mass-produced goods has largely reduced this to a boutique culture, or what I think of as the ashtray syndrome. In the past, everything from buildings to clothes and household objects went through a certain cycle of taste: first they were in fashion, then they fell out of fashion and became ridiculous; then they settled into the softer lighting of "quaint," and cultivated people became interested in them again, and finally they began to take on some of the archaic dignity of the primitive. Nowadays, the expanding of the antique market and the growing sense of the possible commercial value of whatever is no longer being produced has considerably shortened this process. The sojourn in this period of unfashionable limbo has to be very brief when an "antique" can be an object twenty years old. Similarly, immigrants from Europe or Asia often reject their own cultural heritage in an effort to adapt to the new country, so that it takes another generation before they turn toward their own origins again, but that cycle is also shortening.

This levelling out of cultural interest is in itself healthy: the wild fluctuations of taste and fashion in the past have done nothing but harm, and any philosophy of preservation has to avoid the value-judgments which are really nothing but rationalizings of a destructive impulse. I think of the Italian Director of Antiquities in Thornton Wilder's *The Cabala*, whose reputation was based on his eagerness to destroy a Baroque church in order to expose a thirteenth-century door. Our attitude to the past needs more of the impartiality of the archaeologist who excavates all layers and cultural periods of his site with equal care. One would be very deficient in imagination and curiosity not to have some interest in relics of the Hopewell culture or in the Norse remains, if that is what they are, at L'Anse aux Meadows in Newfoundland. But the industrial archaeology that uncovers the pottery, glass and brick factories of nineteenth-century Ontario has its importance too, as we need more tangible reminders of our immediate past than the mere fact that many place-names end in "mills."

Despite the best efforts of reproduction, it remains true that any physical artefact is subject to decay, especially if it is an outdoor object in any climate that at all resembles ours. Restoration is an often disastrous solution: tourists in English cathedrals hear a good deal about the vandalism of Cromwell's soldiers, but the devastation wrought by Victorian restorers has been often far worse, however much better the motive. The kind of preservation that we have in Williamsburg and similar large-scale open museums is in a sense almost anti-historical: it shows us, not life in time as a continuous process, but life arrested at a certain point, in a sort of semi-permanent drama. There is nothing wrong with this, but it gives us a cross-section of history, a world confronting us rather than preceding us. Something similar is true of the building which is a historical allusion or quotation, like collegiate Gothic, replicas of European churches, or Georgian residential areas. The tendency to make the past contemporary with the present is part of what Shakespeare means when he says, addressing Time,

Our dates are brief, and therefore we admire
What thou dost foist upon us that is old,
And rather make them born to our desire,
Than think that we before have heard them told.

In a sense every physical artefact is a protest against time, an expression of a desire for permanence in a world of change. This is especially true of the huge monuments put up by kings, priests and dictators, either to their own glory or to the glory of their gods or nations. We notice a persistent association between such monuments and death, and from the pyramids to our own war memorials there has run the constant realization that death is the nearest that life can get to permanence. One of the better chapters in *Parkinson's Law* remarks on the tendency of institutions to put up their largest and most impressive buildings at the moment when they are passing out of existence, so that the building instantly becomes a kind of cenotaph. In a national capital like Ottawa, one could perhaps think of more examples than it would be tactful to mention. In general, the kind of artefact that posterity usually finds the most expendable culturally is also the hardest to remove physically.

In every age great artists attach themselves to the social establishment, and make their living from it, or, at least, live without questioning or quarrelling with it. Many of the artists we most deeply revere today, Bach, Shakespeare, Michelangelo, were busy professional men with commissions to fill and deadlines to meet. And yet, as time goes on, this view of culture, in which the artists are dependent on the patronage of their societies, begins to reverse its perspective. In nearly forty years of teaching literature in a university, I have found that William Morris is a writer and artist whose interest for me has never palled, and whose influence on my own social attitude has remained central. In Morris there is an apparent inconsistency between his fascination with medieval culture and his very left-of-centre political views. The inconsistency disappears when we realize that for Morris the creators of a culture, and those who give it its style, are not warriors or kings or priests, or the political or religious ideas they stand for, but architects and sculptors and poets. The ideal world that he presents in *News from Nowhere* is a world where everyone has become something of an artist, though it is the quality of design in the so-called minor or functional arts that he is primarily interested in, and regards as the essential clue to a culture's vitality. Morris' future world is not very interested in history or in preserving its past: it is too happy designing and making things in the present, though there is an indication at the end of the story that its historical perspective is going to expand. But even without this indication Morris makes an important point for those who do wish to preserve their past. Our sense of the need for preservation has in it a certain distrust in the integrity of our own cultural tradition: once things are gone, we have little confidence in our ability to replace them with new things equally good. The trouble is, once again, not the lack of creative people, but the lack of response to creativeness in our society. The rudder, so to speak, that guides our philosophy of preservation ultimately has to be the continuing vitality of our cultural tradition. Without that, the task of preserving our heritage will have in it a quality of desperation unhealthy both for it and for us.

Our museums preserve objects of the past, and by preserving them, if William Morris is right, they also express a potentially revolutionary view of history. I spoke earlier of the developing countries who are so proud of the achievements of their own regime and so impatient with the culture of their reactionary past. Even in China, deeply interested as it is in archaeology, a friend of mine, inspecting some of the great cultural monuments of Peking a few years ago, was accompanied by a guide who remarked that if she had her way she would cover them all up with posters explaining how badly exploited the workers were in those days. The point is, I think, that the social milieu of any culture will always be full of human folly and cruelty, but that whatever is beautifully designed always remains in the state of innocence, always a symbol of the kind of thing that human struggles for freedom and happiness are about.

In a sense it is a considerable advantage to Canada not to have so much history to live with as the European countries, to say nothing of the Middle Eastern ones. In so small and thickly settled a country as England, archaeology has to be largely a salvaging operation, a matter of keeping one jump ahead of the steam shovel. There is no way out of this, short of an atomic war that would cut the world's population in half, and in the meantime the preservation of visible monuments has its own kind of panic. However strongly we may condemn Henry VIII's dissolution of the monasteries, it might have been a crushing burden for the National Trust if all those abbeys had survived. Similarly, it is exceptional when the actual site of an important or interesting event, like the murder of Becket in Canterbury Cathedral, still remains: most of what historical markers remind us of has vanished forever into Newtonian space. Here again what is of primary importance is the quality of our historical imagination, the ability, if I may try to express something very difficult to express, to see things, not merely as objects confronting us, but as growing in time, as having come out of our own past and moving towards our own future.

The title of my talk speaks of Canada as a new world without revolution. As you have gathered, there is a certain irony in this: we have fully participated in all the social and cultural consequences of the American revolution, and its advantages and disadvantages are equally ours. Even Quebec, so long preoccupied with maintaining the traditions of its past, has gone through a remarkably complete cultural revolution, though alleged to be a quiet one. Yet it is still perhaps the absence of a revolutionary tradition in Canada, the tendency to move continuously rather than discontinuously through time, that has given Canadian culture one very important and distinctive characteristic. This is its respect for the documentary. Canadian painting began with documentary painters like Krieghoff and Paul Kane, who may have kept an eye on the European market but were nevertheless keen observers of what was around them. Group of Seven painting, along with that of Thomson and Emily Carr, was documentary painting to an unusual degree, almost an imaginative mapping and survey of the remoter parts of the country; and we have also the extensive "war records" of painting from both wars. What Jackson and Thomson did for landscape Riopelle and Pellan and their contemporaries are doing for the Cartesian culture that we live in now. Canadian film has always been remarkable for its sensitive documentary feeling, applied to everything from Eskimo and Indian life to the urban cultures of Toronto and Montreal. Canadian literature, in the nineteenth century as well as this one, and in both poetry and fiction, has had a distinctive attachment to a sober narrative technique, a clear sense of fact, and a curious tendency to itemize, to make a functional use of lists and catalogues and inventories. The implication is, perhaps, that the Canadian consciousness is one peculiarly adapted to preserving its own heritage, not like a miser guarding his hoard or a watchdog snarling at a burglar, not like a man living among his memories and reshaping them in a form more attractive to his ego, but like one who understands that all coherent action, as well as all moral integrity, depends on the continuity of the present with the past.

From *Divisions on a Ground: Essays on Canadian Culture*, ed. James Polk (Toronto: House of Anansi Press, 1982), 167–80. An address given at the Royal Society Symposium, 7 October 1975, and published in *Preserving the Canadian Heritage* for the Royal Society of Canada (1975), 15–25.

Speculation and Concern

NORTHROP FRYE

As I understand it, I am being asked to discuss the question: What do the humanities provide for human culture that the sciences do not provide? My own field is literature, and literature seems to belong to two groups: the creative arts, including music and painting, and the verbal disciplines, including history and philosophy. Both may be regarded as humanities, but we have to distinguish them even when we associate them. The question itself is, I suppose, legitimate enough: it is, I take it, simply a matter of trying to indicate the different functions of different things. It is difficult, and perhaps impossible, to contrast the arts and sciences without a good deal of oversimplifying and making some false or half-true antitheses. There may be some value in oversimplifying the contrast, if one has to do that to make it at all: a more serious difficulty is that nobody is likely to approach such a problem with his mind fully made up, his convictions firmly held, and his tentative and exploratory notions outgrown. In what follows I am thinking aloud, expecting the kind of indulgence that is accorded to such improvisation.

It will not have escaped your notice that I have so far said nothing except "harrumph." But there is something to be said for the convention of beginning with an apology, or topos of modesty. This kind of question is often called, as I have just called it, a "problem," and one expects a problem to be solved. A genuine problem is a specific formulation of experience that can be adequately stated in other terms: to use a common analogy, it is like a knot in a rope that can be untied or retied without affecting the identity of the rope. A question like this is only metaphorically a problem: it is actually a subject of study, and the word solution is not appropriate. All I can do with a subject of study is to individualize it, to make a suggestion or two about how it looks from the standpoint of a literary critic who is living in the mid-twentieth century.

As a subject of study, the question can hardly be called new: a whole line of philosophers from Hegel onward have beaten their brains out over the difference between the knowledge of science and the knowledge of what the Germans call *Geist*, and over the methods and techniques appropriate to the study of history or sociology as distinct from biology or chemistry. It is an appropriate question for a centennial celebration, because it was one of the liveliest issues being debated a hundred years ago. The level of debate has not improved notably in tone since then. No contemporary treatment of the subject known to me matches the lucidity of Walter Bagehot's *Physics and Politics*, published in 1867, or the amiable and urbane discussion of Arnold and Huxley about the proportioning of humanities and sciences in the curriculum of a liberal education. A few years ago we had the Leavis–Snow dispute, where neither contribution was in the least amiable or urbane, and where it is hard to say which of the two documents was the more stupefyingly wrongheaded. Other essays purporting to defend the humanities have all too often a querulous and self-righteous air, like that of a striptease performer who informs a newspaper reporter that while all the other girls just take off their clothes, she is an authentic artist. And so, after more than a century of giving answers to the question of what is distinctive about the humanities, it is still quite possible that the real answer is "nothing at all." Freud concludes his *Future of an Illusion* by saying: "Science is not an illusion, but it would be an illusion to suppose that we could get anywhere else what it cannot give us." He was talking about religion, but he may be unconditionally right, beyond the limits of his context, and everything non-scientific, except possibly the creative arts, may be only pre-scientific or pseudo-scientific. And the arts may be an exception only because their function may be a purely ornamental or decorative one. This conference, after all, deals with "The Humanities and the Quest for Truth," and the arts not only never seem to find truth, but do not even appear to be looking for it very seriously.

The best way to approach our question, I think, is to begin by reversing it, as Freud's phrasing suggests. What does science provide for human culture that the arts and the humanities do not provide? The traditional answer, and doubtless the right one, is "nature." What I am saying here is that science gives us nature, not the understanding or conception of nature. This may only be bad grammar, but I mean something more than understanding. The human mind can operate in different ways, but one very obvious way for it to operate is as a subject. That is, it can start by saying: Here am I, and I am here. Everything else is there. As soon as the mind does this, nature springs into being, like Athene from Jove's forehead, and reality appears to the mind as objective, as a field. It seems to me that it is peculiarly the function of science to objectify reality, to present the world in its aspect of being there. The world of science is the world of space: as has often been noted, science deals with time as a dimension of space. The subject itself becomes an object in this process, for there is nothing inside the scientist, from the structure of his spine to his infantile complexes, which is not also available for scientific study. Everything is there: nothing is really here except the consciousness with which he studies nature. And this consciousness, or scientific intelligence, is ideally disembodied. The theory of physics, for example, has been complicated, in its more rarefied aspects, by the fact that the scientist possesses a body, and cannot comprehend nature without physical contact. To see the world as an objective field of operation is also to quantify reality, to make it something measured rather than simply seen or heard. Isaiah praises a God "Who hath measured the waters in the hollow of his hand, and meted out heaven with the span, and comprehended the dust of the earth in a measure, and weighed the mountains in scales, and the hills in a balance." In science man takes over this traditional function of God, replacing the divine balance by the mathematician's equations.

Because science deals with reality as objective, there is no such thing as subjective science. What this means in practice is that science stabilizes the subject. It assumes a mind in the situation that we think of as sane or normal, ready to accept evidence and follow arguments. Thus science assumes a mind to some extent emancipated from existence, in the state of freedom or detachment that we call clarity. The sense of truth as an ideal, and of the pursuit of truth for its own sake as a virtue, go with the process of objectifying reality on which science is founded. The word truth itself carries with it the sense of a recognition of what is there. So does the sense of facts as given, as irreducible data to be studied in their inherent arrangements instead of being arranged. There may actually be no facts of this kind, but it is important to pretend that there are, that facts lie around immovably where they have been thrown, like rocks carried down by a glacier. As Wallace Stevens says,

> The arrangement contains the desire of
> The artist. But one confides in what has no
> Concealed creator.*

What science stands for in human life, then, is the revolt of consciousness against existence, the sense of his own uniqueness in nature that man gets by drawing his mind back from existence and contemplating it as a separated thing. The animal is immersed in existence without consciousness; the human being has consciousness, and consciousness means being capable, up to a point, of seeing existence as external to oneself. Of course, to withdraw from existence means to stop existing, and some philosophers, notably Sartre, even go as far as to associate consciousness with nothingness or non-being. However, it seems clear that conscious human beings can externalize their world and still go on living. Human existence, then, is a complex, of which consciousness is one of many functions, and the concentrated consciousness that produces science is a stylizing or conventionalizing of human behaviour.

* "So-and-so Reclining on a Couch," *Collected Poems.*

I do not wish to suggest that science is founded on a narrowly empirical view of the world: that its end is only to describe and understand what it sees. The physical sciences at least are not simply descriptive, but are based on prediction as well: they see their phenomena in time—or their version of time—as well as space, and their end is rather a vision of nature under law. It is not the experiment but the repeatable experiment that is the key to the understanding of nature in the physical sciences, and the repeatable experiment is what make prediction possible and gives to science a prophetic quality. Telepathic communication, poltergeists, mediums, have been approached experimentally and certain typical phenomena recur, but the experiments are not repeatable (except where they are fraudulent),* no laws can be established, and so science applied to such things never gets off the ground. Where the phenomena are unconscious or where the units involved are small and numerous, like atoms, molecules or cells, so that there is no practical difference between the highly probable and the certain, the language of science is primarily mathematical. From the natural sciences we move toward the social sciences, where the phenomena are relatively large, few, and complicated, like human beings. Here prediction on a statistical basis is as important as ever, but, except for some specialized aspects, the repeatable experiment is no longer at the centre of the study. In proportion as this is true, the subject tends to be organized verbally rather than mathematically. We then move into what are generally regarded as the humanities. History and philosophy are almost purely verbal, non-experimental, and non-predictive. But accuracy of statement, objectivity of description and dispassionate weighing of evidence, including the accepting of negative evidence, are still required. Hence a scientific element is still present in them that distinguishes history from legend, philosophy from rumination, and, as I think, literary criticism from a good many of the activities that go under that name. From there we move into the creative arts proper, where the requirements even of accurate descriptive statement and the basing of conclusions on fair evidence are no longer made, or at least not in the same way, and where therefore we may feel that we have finally escaped from science. But except for the arts, which pose separate problems, all scholars, whatever their fields, are bound by the same code of honour. All of them have to be as scientific as the nature of their subjects will allow them to be, or abandon all claim to be taken seriously.

The philosophers who moved from Kant and Hegel towards the establishing of modern historical and sociological methods were largely preoccupied with the question of boundary lines. At what point does *Natur* turn into *Geist*? Precisely where do the methods that work in the physical sciences cease to become effective or appropriate? But it is surely possible that there are no boundary lines at all, and that this whole way of looking at knowledge as divided into two complementary bodies is wrong. The crudest form of this view

* This refers to what is usually called spiritualism, not to controlled experiments in extrasensory perception and the like, where there is no question of fraud.

is the one that I call the heart-of-darkness theory. It is a type of argument that used to be fashionable in natural theology (perhaps still is), and has been transferred to the humanities from there. There have been theories among religious apologists that religion, like the ghost of Hamlet's father, or the dancing fairies of Milton's Nativity Ode, belongs to a dark preserve of mystery on which the sun of science has not yet risen. Religion, according to this approach, deals with whatever seems at the moment to be beyond the capacities of science: creation at first, then the origin of life or the human soul, then moral values, and so on—it has to keep moving fairly fast, like the lunatic in Blake's "Mad Song," to make sure of staying in the dark while science pursues it. Even yet there is a strong popular belief that if we once get hold of something that "science cannot explain," whether it is extrasensory perception or the principle of indeterminacy or finding underground water with a hazel twig, we have a guarantee of free will and immortality and the existence of God.

The basis of such notions, when applied to the arts, is the assumption that if science deals rationally, factually, impersonally with an external world, the arts can only deal with an inner world of emotion, personality, and value. This really reduces itself to the assumption that if science is objective, the arts must be subjective. But subjective art is as impossible a conception as subjective science. The arts are techniques of communication: they are fostered by schools and groups and depend on convention quite as much as science does. In fact, there seems to be nothing that is really subjective except a rebellion against the stability of the attitude toward the world on which science is based. It is very tiring to keep on being open to involuntary sense impressions, to be detached and clear-headed, to weigh evidence and fit judgements to it, and very easy to relapse into an emotional colouring of experience, such as we get from day-dreaming or bad temper or private memories and associations. But however important and normally human in itself, the individual's emotional colouring of his own experience is not what the arts or the humanities are primarily concerned with. So whenever I read critical theories that begin by saying, in effect, "Poetry is whatever mere science isn't," I flake out very quickly, because I know that some version of the subjective fallacy is about to follow.

The genuine basis of this complementary view of the arts and sciences is the distinction, already glanced at and most elaborately set out in Bergson, between time as externalized by science, where it is really a dimension of space, and time in its other form of the continuous awareness of one's own existence. This latter does elude science, so here is something that science cannot explain. But nothing else can explain it either, so that is not much help. All explanation contains some traces of scientific method, unless the explanation is really a clouding up of the question, like the doctor's explanation in Molière that opium puts people to sleep because it has a dormative faculty. But while the direct awareness of being cannot be explained, it can, up to a point, be expressed, and this expression is the basis of the arts. The role of art, then, is primarily to express the complex of human existence, humanity's awareness of being itself rather than its perception of what is not itself and is outside it. This self-awareness is neither subjective nor objective, for man in himself is both an individual and, no less essentially, a member of the society which is partly inside him; and it is neither rational nor irrational. It does not quantify existence like science; it qualifies it: it tries to express not what is there but what is here, what is involved in consciousness and being themselves. The arts, then, belong to the phase of experience that we have learned to call existential, to an awareness that cannot be external to itself nor have anything external to it.

The production of art is, of course, a stylizing of behaviour like the production of science. As far as the actual man doing the work is concerned, I doubt whether there is any essential psychological difference between the artist and the scientist, any "creative" factors present in one that are not present in the other. Both have to use the entire mind; both have much the same difficulties in getting that very complicated machine to work. But when we consider the finished product only, it is clear that the arts do not stabilize the subject in the same way that science does. Emotions, repressed or mythopoeic elements in the subconscious, the manipulating of data, the summoning up of controlled hallucinations (as expressed in the traditional phrase about poetry, *ut pictura poesis*), all have a function in the creation of art. The stabilized subject of science is usually identified with the reason; the unstabilized subject is normally called the imagination. The individual artist is a representative of human imagination, just as the individual scientist is a representative of human reason. But at no point, *qua* artist, is he outside the human world we call culture or civilization, just as the physical scientist, *qua* physical scientist studying "nature," is never inside it.

I speak, of course, of the arts in the plural because there is a group of them: music, literature, painting, sculpture, architecture, perhaps others. The dance, for instance, is in practice a separate art, though in theory it is difficult to see it as anything but a form of musical expression. It seems inherently unlikely, at the time of writing, that we have yet to develop a new art, despite all the strenuous experiment that there has been, some of it in that direction. Marshall McLuhan says of the new media of communication that "the medium is the message," and that the content of each medium is the form of another one. This surely means, if I understand it correctly, that each medium is a distinctive art. Thus the "message" of sculpture is the medium of sculpture, distinct from the message which is the medium of painting. But, as McLuhan also emphasizes, the new media are extensions of the human body, of what we already do with our eyes and ears and throats and hands. Hence they have given us new forms or variations of the arts we now have, and the novelty of these forms constitutes a major imaginative revolution in our time. But though distinctive arts they are not actually new arts: they are new techniques for receiving the impression of words and pictures.

Of these arts, literature is the art of words, and words are also the medium for the humanities and much of the sciences. This suggests that the arts, besides being arts, may also be informing languages for other disciplines. A painting or a poem is a construct: you look first of all at the associative factors in it, the things that make it hold together. But besides having paintings we have pictures of things: that is, there are things outside painting that we understand pictorially. For centuries philosophers expressed themselves in words, taking words for granted, forgetting that there is an art of words, not realizing that the verbal basis of philosophy constitutes a philosophical problem in itself. It seems to have been only in our own time that philosophers and logicians have really tried to become aware of the limitations of form (as distinct from the mere pitfalls or fallacies) inherent in the use of words. Even now their interest seems to be mainly linguistic rather than properly literary, and some philosophers are so ignorant of the source of their own subject that they regularly use "literary" in a pejorative sense. It is obvious that words lend themselves very readily to being an informing language for a descriptive discipline. Literature was not, up until the Romantic movement at least, regarded as the most impressive thing man does with words, the more objectified structures of theology and philosophy being regarded as higher in status and coming close to what is called the quest for truth. As compared with music, or even painting, there is always some reference to the outer world implicit in every use of words. Even if in the future we leave painting to the chimpanzees and music to chance, I do not see how literature can ever lose its kernel of externalizable meaning. And yet the capacity of words for informing other disciplines is not unlimited. Compared with mathematics at least, words are incurably associative: multiple meanings lurk in them and the structures of grammar twist them into non-representational forms. It seems more likely that words have a certain radius of descriptive power, and that it is important to determine the approximate limits of that radius.

The other arts seem to differ widely in their powers of being able to inform other studies. Painting and sculpture, like literature, can be employed to represent the external world, and, again like literature, their descriptive or representational aspect has had more prestige in the past than their associative or constructive aspect. We can understand what their informing capacity is if we think not only of painting but of the pictorial arts, including illustrations, sketches, blueprints, diagrams, and models, and not only of sculpture but of the sculptural arts, including three-dimensional models. Some modern painters and sculptors, such as Miró or Giacometti, indicate the inherent relation of their arts with diagram and model very clearly. In some areas, such as geometry, the pictorial and the mathematical overlap, and of course the role of diagram in the sciences, as in the structural formulas of chemistry, is of immense importance. The question of whether light consists of waves or particles is surely, to some extent, a picturing problem. In my *Anatomy of Criticism* I have raised the question of the role of diagram in verbal thought as well. But to what extent and in what ways the pictorial and sculptural arts inform the humanities and sciences I do not know, nor have I read anybody who did know.

Music, on the other hand, has often been said to be the existential art par excellence, the hieratic, self-enclosed expression of "pure being" with no relation to an externalized order of any kind. Perhaps this is because it is, as Mrs. Langer* suggests, the art of "virtual time," the closest expression of the continuous awareness of being which is the core of non-scientific experience. Or perhaps it is only because, up to the rise of electronic music, the music we know has been founded on a set of conventions as arbitrary as chess. On my piano as I write this is a sonata of Clementi called "Didone Abbandonata": we are supposed to think of the story of Dido while we listen. The finale is a rondo beginning with what for Clementi is a sharp discord, a minor ninth, and the movement is hopefully marked "con disperazione." But it soon collapses into the ordinary rondo structure, and by the time we reach the second subject it is clear that poor Dido has been abandoned once more. A greater composer would have been more tactful or created a more compelling musical mood, but that is why the mediocre example illustrates more clearly my point, which is that music is not an informing art: it sets up a powerful centripetal force that resists being drawn into the structure of anything outside itself. We do use metaphors from music a good deal ("harmony," "overtones," and the like), and the old fables about the music of the spheres suggest that music may have an unsuspected informing power about it. Perhaps the myth of heaven as a place where harp playing is a compulsory cultural accomplishment will come true, and the theology and metaphysics of the future will be understood musically rather than verbally. When I read or try to read Heidegger I get the same feeling that I get when trying to read *Finnegans Wake*, of language dissolving into a mass of associative puns, and language of this kind is surely heading in the direction indicated by the squeals and groans of electronic music.

If words can be used both to construct an art and to inform some of the descriptive disciplines, there seems no reason why we should not think of mathematics, which informs so much of the physical sciences, as an art too. It is a self-contained construct like the arts, and I do not see how it is possible to frame a definition, of even a description, of the arts that would include the five I have listed and exclude mathematics. But mathematics is the art of numerical or quantitative relationships, and so it has a unique capacity for giving order and coherence to the sciences, of providing their descriptions and experiments with the repeatable element of law. In contrast to the other arts, it stabilizes the subject on a "rational" level, as science does, and is so constantly informing the physical sciences that it is often regarded as simply a part of them. Hence some of the more speculatively minded scientists and philosophers are occasionally surprised to discover that nature has a mathematical

* Susanne Langer, *Feeling and Form* (1953).

form. Of course it has: they put it there. And because it informs science so readily, mathematics practised as an art in its own right is a rare and esoteric achievement, though its tradition can be traced from the semi-occult use of it associated with the name of Pythagoras down to the later work of Einstein.

The rise of modern science involved a new way of looking at the external world which is most lucidly set out in Locke, though it had been there at least since Galileo. According to this the world has secondary qualities which are experienced by sensation, and primary qualities independent of such experience, which can only be weighed and measured. This distinction has a rough but significant analogy to the role of words in rendering the external world as compared with the role of mathematics. Mathematics is the language that can render the world of primary qualities: words never lose their connection with human action and human sensation on which the two primary categories of words, verbs and nouns, are based. To the extent that an electron, for instance, is given a name and made a noun, it becomes a potential object of perception, unlikely as it is that it will ever be an actual one. The radius of verbal information, then, apparently runs between the human body and its environment as perceived and experienced by that body. The non-literary function of words is thus, in the broad Kantian sense, critical: words can be used to explain the human situation, instead of merely expressing it as literature does, but they always remain connected with that situation.

The conception of science, as a systematic understanding of nature under law for which the appropriate language is mathematics, is, of course, a relatively recent one. For thousands of years before the great scientific explosion of the last few centuries, thinkers had been making constructs of the outer world, mainly verbal and pictorial. In these constructs the associative characteristics of the arts from which they were derived are very obvious. Poets find it much easier to live in the Ptolemaic universe than in ours, because it is more associative; modern poets turn from science to occultism because the latter still features associative patterns. Very early the two great containing conceptions of the scientific attitude made their appearance: "substance," or the objectified world visible and invisible, and "soul," the ideally disembodied intelligence which contemplates it. These parents then peopled the world with various offspring, ideas, essences, universals, atoms, and the like. The great difficulty with using words, when attempting to deal with primary qualities, is the readiness with which words adapt themselves to what we may call, altering Whitehead's phrase, pseudo-concreteness. Adam named the animals because he could see them, but, as Theseus says in Shakespeare, it is just as easy to name airy nothings, to bestow nouns on and make verbal objects out of things that are not there, or cannot be proved to be there. Again, the prestige of the subject–object relationship meant that attempts to express what is genuinely existential, the human situation itself, could take the form of the *metaphorically* objective. The conception of a spiritual world is a metaphorical verbal object of this kind. With the rise of modern science, words have become more limited in their range. Metaphysics seemed for a time to be taking the form of a verbalized general science, expressing for its age some sense of what scientific activity as a whole is doing. It is more at home, however, with the assumptions on which scientific work is based, because those assumptions are part of the human context of science, and so they can be dealt with critically, which means verbally.

The principle of metaphorical object is of central importance when we try to see what the place of content is in the arts. The activity of consciousness, of externalizing reality, is always part of the whole existential complex. The aspect of painting that reproduces or "imitates" an outer world exists in painting, as, so to speak, a metaphor of externality. Even music has, in the witty and paradoxical form of "programme" music, a metaphorical external world of this kind, and literature has it in everything that we call realism. We are constantly using quantitative expressions (e.g. "I love you very much") as metaphors for things that are not quantities. Aristotle, who approached the arts from a scientific point of view (one of his most illuminating comments on art is in the *Physics*), spoke of the arts as imitative of nature. But as soon as we examine this conception of imitation, the notion of a continuous relation to the external world begins to dissolve, and we can see that "nature" exists in the art only as the content of art, as something that art surrounds and contains. So while science deals with the consolidating of what is there, the arts deal with the expanding of what is here; the circumference of science is the universe, the circumference of the arts is human culture. In our time the sense of cleavage between the expression of what is here and the study of what is there is very sharp. We tend to feel that whatever is objective or external belongs only to the spatial world of science: every other "there" is a metaphor derived from that spatial world, and such metaphors no longer carry much conviction. Theology, for example, or at least the Protestant versions of it that I am more familiar with, is now trying to come to terms with the fact that nothing it is talking about is actually "there." God is certainly not "there": he has been deprived of all scientific function and he has no status in the spatial world of science, including the temporal world that can be divided and measured. So whatever the present or future of theology may be, it cannot be the queen of sciences as we now think of science: science deals only with It, and can take no part in an I–Thou dialogue.

For a long time, of course, it was assumed that the study of nature was also the study of a revelation of God, the order and coherence of nature being assumed to be the result of divine design. This view was contemporary with the view that the models of human civilization themselves, the city and the garden, were also of divine origin. But just as man came finally to believe that he had created and was responsible for his own civilization, so he came also to believe that the real basis of science was the correspondence of nature and human reason. Whatever is there in nature, the mind can find something in verbal or mathematical reasoning that will explain, assimilate or inform it.

"The external world is fitted to the mind," as Wordsworth says. So although nature is an externalized reality, it is not, for science, an alien one. In fact, science, as a form of knowledge, could even be thought of as a gigantic human narcissism, the reason falling in love with its own reflection in nature. Whenever there have been anti-scientific trends in human culture, they have usually seized on some aspect of this principle, though their target has been less science itself than the kind of essential philosophy that preceded it. Existentialism, for example, insists that if we think of the external world as a human world, certain elements become primary that are carefully kept out of science: the imminence of death, the feeling of alienation, the pervading sense of accident and emptiness, and the direct confrontation with something arbitrary and absurd. Once we take away from externality the rational structure that we have put into it, it becomes what Milton calls a universal blank. All science is founded on the equation A equals B, where A is the human reason and B the rationally comprehensible element in nature. The existentialists may be described as the people who have discovered that if A equals B, then A minus B equals nothing.

We notice that existentialists have some difficulty in making their philosophy self-sufficient. Most of the best of them have incorporated it into a religious attitude, and of the atheistic ones, Heidegger went along with the Nazis and Sartre has recently collapsed on the bosom of the Church Marxist. It looks as though the attitude, along with whatever anti-scientific bias it may have, belongs in a larger context which is normally either religious or revolutionary, or both. That larger context is a view, found in very different forms in Blake, Kierkegaard, Nietzsche and D.H. Lawrence, which might be paraphrased somewhat as follows:

Reality is primarily what we create, not what we contemplate. It is more important to know how to construct a human world than to know how to study a non-human one. Science and philosophy are significant as two of the creative things that man does, not as keys to the reality of the world out there. There is a world out there, but science sees it as a world under law, and no vision under law can ever give us the whole truth about anything. Science moves with greatest confidence, and makes its most startling discoveries, in a mechanical and unconscious world. If we remove science from its context and make it not a mental construct but an oracle of reality, the logical conclusion is that man ought to adjust himself to that reality on its terms. Thus moral law imitates natural law, and human life takes on the predictable characteristics of nature as science reveals it. What begins as reason ends in the conditioned reflexes of an insect state, where human beings have become cerebral automata. The real world, that is, the human world, has constantly to be created, and the one model on which we must not create it is that of the world out there. The world out there has no human values, hence we should think of it primarily not as real but as absurd. The existential paradoxes help us to do this, and they thereby reduce the world to the *tohu-wa-bohu*, the waste and void chaos of a world which man has once again to create.

In science applied to the human world, that is, in applied science and technology, we see the mathematical shape of science itself, from the pyramids of Egypt and the highways and aqueducts of Rome to the chessboard cities and cloverleaf intersections of our day. For Blake, and in some degree for Lawrence, these mathematical shapes in human life are symbols of aggression: human life is at its most mathematical and automatic in military operations, and in Blake the pyramid, and more particularly the "Druid" trilithon, the ancestor of the Roman arch, are symbols of imperialistic hysteria and malevolence. Every advance in technology is likely to cause an immense legal complication in life, as the automobile has done, and the sheeplike panic-stricken stampeding of modern life, of which the totalitarian state is a by-product, is part of a technological way of life. Popular fiction has been exploiting the figure of the mad scientist for over a century, and there really does seem to be such a thing as mad science: psychology used to enslave people, nuclear physics used to exterminate the human race, microbiology suggesting even more lethal methods of trying to improve it. However, even in their most anti-scientific pronouncements such writers as Blake and Lawrence seldom if ever say that science is the direct cause of the sinister will to slavery in modern times. They say rather that man has lost his nerve about taking charge of his own world, through a false theory of knowledge in which he is "idolatrous to his own shadow," as Blake says, and that this loss of nerve expresses itself as a perversion and parody of science. The world out there is real, but if we *deify* its reality, if we make it an object of imitation, it takes on the outlines of Satan the accuser, belittling us with its vast size in time and space, contemptuous of our efforts to be free of its colossal machinery.

The contrast I am paraphrasing is more conventionally phrased in other writers, and is often put into the form of an antithesis between values and facts. But the word value still has something prefabricated about it, a suggestion of something immutable laid up in a Platonic heaven. It is man's right to create his world that must be safeguarded, and every creation is likely to require a transvaluation of the past. Besides, values are really for the most part still forms of law, and do not get us out of our dilemma. The same is true of the moral categories of Kierkegaard, the "ethical freedom" of the man who has passed beyond speculation. It would be better to use the existential terms engagement or concern to express the contrast between a reality which is there to begin with and the greater reality which, like religious faith or artistic creation, does not exist at all to begin with, but is brought into being through a certain kind of human act.

Science is increasingly a communal and corporate activity. The humanities are more individualized, and the arts are intensely so: schools and isms in the arts are a sign of youth and immaturity, of an authority not yet established in the single artist. When we think of the scientist as voyaging through strange seas of thought alone, as Wordsworth did Newton, we are probably thinking of him primarily as a mathematician. We are, in contrast to

Communist countries, extremely permissive about a writer's loneliness: we allow our writers to retire into what sometimes seem very neurotic fairylands, because they may also be areas of the unstabilized imaginative vision. The result is that communication in and from the arts is a slow and cumbersome business, and that is why we need the dimension of criticism, the vision of artists as a society engaged in a communal enterprise.

As soon as we take this critical perspective on literature, we see that literature is organized by huge containing conceptions which establish the literary societies and the family resemblances among large groups of writers. We call these containing forms myths, and it is in these myths that the nature of man's concern for his world is most clearly expressed. Our own age expresses itself chiefly in the ironic myth, and irony marks the ascendance of a technological society and the tendency of man to imitate the natural law outside him. It is in the ironic mode that the writer deals with the human situation as though it were external to him and as though he were detached from it, and in this mode that he sees human behaviour as mechanized, frustrated, and absurd. If one were to say to almost any serious contemporary writer: "But I don't like the characters and situations you present to me," he would almost certainly answer: "That's because I'm trying to tell the truth as I see it." In our day the writer defends himself in language parallel to the language of science and other objective disciplines. These myths also inform the structures built out of words that exist outside literature, that is, in general, the humanities. Existentialism, with its conceptions of anguish, nausea, and the like, is an ironic philosophy, a fact which accounts for the lack of self-sufficiency I spoke of before. Irony, in literature, is a sophisticated myth, best understood as a frustration or parody of the more primitive comic and romantic myths in which a quest is successfully accomplished. These romantic and comic myths are those that inform Christianity and the revolutionary myth of Marxism. Earlier in this paper I quoted from Freud's *Future of an Illusion*. Religion was a subject Freud had a Freudian block about, mainly because he wanted to be a lawgiving Moses in his own right, contemplating the back parts of his own God. As a literary critic, I am interested in the fact that Freud and Marx are the two most influential thinkers in the world today, that both of them developed an encyclopedic programme that they called scientific, and that nine-tenths of the science of both turns out to be applied mythology.

These mythical expressions of concern, in which man expresses his own attitude to the culture he has built, are subject to a disease of thinking which is best called anxiety, in the Freudian and not the existential sense. We often find that those who are committed to a religious or revolutionary faith have a peculiar difficulty in being intellectually honest in their arguments: their commitment wants to twist and manipulate facts, to maintain tendentious lines of reasoning, to rationalize or simply assert things for which there is no evidence. The record of Christianity is full of persecution in the name of absurdities, and Marxism is also an anxiety structure, with a sensitive nose for heresies and deviations. The reason for this kind of anxiety is, again, a failure of nerve, a refusal to accept the fact that man continually creates his world anew, a desire to have it fit something outside himself. What is outside, in this sense, cannot be in space: it can only be in time, a pattern established in the past, or to be established in the future, to which all facts and discoveries somehow must be adjusted.

In the sciences it is possible to carry on one's studies with an undeveloped sense of concern. There are scientists who irritably brush off the suggestion that what they are doing may have momentous consequences for good or evil, and that they should be concerned for those consequences. A sense of concern would make such a scientist more presentable as a human being: it would also unite him to the community he lives in, and work against the dehumanizing tendency inherent in all specialization. There is no way of overcoming the barriers of specialization, no way of making a Romance philologist and a solid-state physicist intellectually intelligible to each other. But they are united by being both citizens of their society, and their realization of this makes both Romance philology and solid-state physics liberal arts, studies that liberate mankind. In science this social concern affects the scientist as man, but not so much *qua* scientist. But in the humanities the great poetic myths are also shaping forms: in history, in philosophy, in criticism, a scientific detachment and a humane engagement are fighting each other like Jacob and his angel. That is why the humanities are difficult to characterize, not only in methodology, but even as a distinctive group of studies in themselves.

To sum up, then: it does not seem to me that the really important difference between the humanities and the sciences is in the difference in their subject-matter. It is rather that science exhibits a method and a mental attitude, most clearly in the physical sciences, of a stabilized subject and an impartial and detached treatment of evidence which is essential to all serious work in all fields. The humanities, on the other hand, express in their containing forms, or myths, the nature of the human involvement with the human world, which is essential to any serious man's attitude to life. As long as man lives in the world, he will need the perspective and attitude of the scientist; but to the extent that he has created the world he lives in, feels responsible for it and has a concern for its destiny, which is also his own destiny, he will need the perspective and attitude of the humanist.

From *The Stubborn Structure: Essays on Criticism and Society* (London: Methuen, 1970), 38–55. Published earlier in *The Humanities and the Understanding of Reality*, ed. Thomas B. Stroup (Lexington, KY: University of Kentucky Press, 1966).

GEORGE WOODCOCK (1912–   ) was born in Winnipeg and brought up in England. He was educated at Sir William Borlase's School and at Morley College in London, but it was the English literary climate in the thirties and forties that was to have a profound and lasting effect on him. He edited *Now* and *Freedom*, two anarchist publications in the forties, and was an active member of the Freedom Defence Committee. Woodcock published six books while in England, including studies of William Godwin (1946) and Aphra Behn (1948), and *The Writer and Politics* (1948). He returned to Canada in 1949 and began to make a living as a radio dramatist and commentator. An extraordinary variety of books followed: studies of Oscar Wilde (1950), Pierre-Joseph Proudhon (1956), George Orwell (1966; this book won the Governor General's Award for English non-fiction), Gandhi (1971), Aldous Huxley (1972), Gabriel Dumont (1975), Thomas Merton (1975); travel books on western Canada (1952), Mexico (1956), Peru (1959), India (1964), the South Seas (1976); and books on Canadian history and literature such as *Canada and the Canadians* (1970), *The Hudson's Bay Company* (1970), *Odysseus Ever Returning* (1970), *Peoples of the Coast* (1977), *The Canadians* (1979), *The World of Canadian Writing* (1980), and *Confederation Betrayed* (1981). He has also written hundreds of talks and scripts for radio and television, and published books of poetry and numerous academic articles. As editor of *Canadian Literature* from its founding in 1959 until 1977, he presided over the most significant outburst of literary activity in our history and established the critical standards that have brought that journal great distinction.

The most important theme in Woodcock's work derives from his interest in libertarian thought and his sympathy for those who share his anti-bureaucratic, fundamentally independent outlook. Characteristically, his adherence to anarchism, the political creed with which his name is associated, is qualified by his desire to make its tenets useful for shaping contemporary society. "Our aim should be to preserve as much freedom as possible for men as they are," he has written, "rather than dream of a hypothetical total freedom for men as they at present are not." Woodcock opposes those of our institutions that threaten personal liberty, but he insists that only "institutions rising organically from the needs of men" will guarantee society's freedoms. The following essays give some sense of Woodcock's interests and style, and of the qualities that have made him one of the most deeply respected writers and thinkers in Canada.

The Tyranny of the Clock

GEORGE WOODCOCK

In no characteristic is existing society in the West so sharply distinguished from the earlier societies, whether of Europe or the East, than in its conception of time. To the ancient Chinese or Greek, to the Arab herdsman or Mexican peon of today, time is represented by the cyclic processes of nature, the alteration of day and night, the passage from season to season. The nomads and farmers measured and still measure their day from sunrise to sunset, and their year in terms of seedtime and harvest, of the falling leaf and the ice thawing on the lakes and rivers. The farmer worked according to the elements, the craftsman for as long as he felt it necessary to perfect his product. Time was seen as a process of natural change, and men were not concerned in its exact measurement. For this reason civilizations highly developed in other respects had the most primitive means of measuring time: the hour glass with its trickling sand or dripping water, the sun dial, useless on a dull day, and the candle or lamp whose unburnt remnant of oil or wax indicated the hours. All these devices were approximate and inexact, and were often rendered unreliable by the weather or the personal laziness of the tender. Nowhere in the ancient or mediæval world were more than a tiny minority of men concerned with time in the terms of mathematical exactitude.

Modern, western man, however, lives in a world which runs according to the mechanical and mathematical symbols of clock time. The clock dictates his movements and inhibits his actions. The clock turns time from a process of nature into a commodity that can be measured and bought and sold like soap or sultanas. And because, without some means of exact time keeping, industrial capitalism could never have developed and could not continue to exploit the workers, the clock represents an element of mechanical tyranny in the lives of modern men more potent than any individual exploiter or than any other machine. It is therefore valuable to trace the historical process by which the clock influenced the social development of modern European civilization.

It is a frequent circumstance of history that a culture or civilization develops the device that will later be used for its destruction. The ancient Chinese, for example, invented gunpowder, which was developed by the military experts of the West and eventually led to the Chinese civilization itself being destroyed by the high explosives of modern warfare. Similarly, the supreme achievement of the craftsmen of the mediæval cities of Europe was the invention of the clock, which, with its revolutionary alteration of the concept of time, materially assisted the growth of the middle ages.

There is a tradition that the clock appeared in the eleventh century, as a device for ringing bells at regular intervals in the monasteries which, with the regimented life they imposed on their inmates, were the closest social approximation in the middle ages to the factory of today. The first authenticated clock, however, appeared in the thirteenth century, and it was not until the fourteenth century that clocks became common as ornaments of the public buildings in German cities.

These early clocks, operated by weights, were not particularly accurate, and it was not until the sixteenth century that any great reliability was attained. In England, for instance, the clock at Hampton Court, made in 1540, is said to have been the first accurate clock in the country. And even the accuracy of the sixteenth-century clocks is relative, for they were equipped only with hour hands. The idea of measuring time in minutes and seconds had been thought out by the early mathematicians as far back as the fourteenth century, but it was not until the invention of the pendulum in 1657 that sufficient accuracy was attained to permit the addition of a minute hand, and the second hand did not appear until the eighteenth century. These two centuries, it should be observed, were those in which capitalism grew to such an extent that it was able to take advantage of the techniques of the industrial revolution to establish its economic domination over society.

The clock, as Lewis Mumford has pointed out, is the key machine of the machine age, both for its influence on technics and for its influence on the habits of men. Technically, the clock was the first really automatic machine that attained any importance in the life of man. Previous to its invention, the common machines were of such a nature that their operation depended on some external and unreliable force, such as human or animal muscles, water or wind. It is true that the Greeks had invented a number of primitive automatic machines, but these were used, like Hero's steam engine, either for obtaining "supernatural" effects in the temples or for amusing the tyrants of Levantine cities. But the clock was the first automatic machine that attained public importance and a social function. Clock-making became the industry from which men learnt the elements of machine-making and gained the technical skill that was to produce the complicated machinery of the Industrial Revolution.

Socially the clock had a more radical influence than any other machine, in that it was the means by which the regularization and regimentation of life necessary for an exploiting system of industry could best be assured. The clock provided a means by which time—a category so elusive that no philosophy has yet determined its nature—could be measured concretely in the more tangible terms of space provided by the circumference of a clock dial. Time as duration became disregarded, and men began to talk and think always of "lengths" of time, just as if they were talking of lengths of calico. And time, being now measurable in mathematical symbols, was regarded as a commodity that could be bought and sold in the same way as any other commodity.

The new capitalists, in particular, became rabidly time-conscious. Time, here symbolizing the labour of the workers, was regarded by them almost as if it were the chief raw material of industry. "Time is money" was one of the key slogans of capitalist ideology, and the timekeeper was the most significant of the new types of official introduced by the capitalist dispensation.

In the early factories the employers went so far as to manipulate their clocks or sound their factory whistles at the wrong times in order to defraud the workers of a little of this valuable new commodity. Later such practices became less frequent, but the influence of the clock imposed a regularity on the lives of the majority of men that had previously been known only in the monasteries. Men actually became like clocks, acting with a repetitive regularity which had no resemblance to the rhythmic life of a natural being. They became, as the Victorian phrase put it, "as regular as clockwork." Only in the country districts where the natural lives of animals and plants and the elements still dominated existence, did any large proportion of the population fail to succumb to the deadly tick of monotony.

At first this new attitude to time, this new regularity of life, was imposed by the clock-owning masters on the unwilling poor. The factory slave reacted in his spare time by living with a chaotic irregularity which characterized the gin-sodden slums of early nineteenth-century industrialism. Men fled to the timeless worlds of drink or Methodist inspiration. But gradually the idea of regularity spread downwards and among the workers. Nineteenth-century religion and morality played their part by proclaiming the sin of "wasting time." The introduction of mass-produced watches and clocks in the 1850s spread time-consciousness among those who had previously merely reacted to the stimulus of the knocker-up or the factory whistle. In the church and the school, in the office and the workshop, punctuality was held up as the greatest of the virtues.

Out of this slavish dependence on mechanical time which spread insidiously into every class in the nineteenth century, there grew up the demoralizing regimentation which today still characterizes factory life. The man who fails to conform faces social disapproval and economic ruin—unless he drops out into a nonconformist way of life in which time ceases to be of prime importance. Hurried meals, the regular morning and evening scramble for trains or buses, the strain of having to work to time schedules, all contribute, by digestive and nervous disturbance, to ruin health and shorten life.

Nor does the financial imposition of regularity tend, in the long run, to greater efficiency. Indeed, the quality of the product is usually much poorer, because the employer, regarding time as a commodity which he has to pay for, forces the operative to maintain such a speed that his work must necessarily be skimped. Quantity rather than quality becoming the criterion, the enjoyment is taken out of the work itself, and the worker in his turn becomes a "clock-watcher," concerned only with when he will be able to escape to the scanty and monotonous leisure of industrial society, in which he "kills time" by cramming in as much time-scheduled and mechanical enjoyment of cinema, radio and newspaper as his wage packet and his tiredness will allow. Only if he is willing to accept the hazards of living by his faith or his wits can the man without money avoid living as a slave to the clock.

The problem of the clock is, in general, similar to that of the machine. Mechanized time is valuable as a means of co-ordinating activities in a highly developed society, just as the machine is valuable as a means of reducing unnecessary labour to a minimum. Both are valuable for the contribution they make to the smooth running of society, and should be used in so far as they assist men to co-operate efficiently and to eliminate monotonous toil and social confusion. But neither should be allowed to dominate men's lives as they do today.

Now the movement of the clock sets the tempo of men's lives—they become the servants of the concept of time which they themselves have made, and are held in fear, like Frankenstein by his own monster. In a sane and free society such an arbitrary domination of man's functions by either clock or machine would obviously be out of question. The domination of man by man-made machines is even more ridiculous than the domination of man by man. Mechanical time would be relegated to its true function of a means of reference and co-ordination, and men would return again to a balanced view of life no longer dominated by time-regulation and the worship of the clock. Complete liberty implies freedom from the tyranny of abstractions as well as from the rule of men.

From *The Rejection of Politics, and Other Essays on Canada, Canadians, Anarchism and the World* (Toronto, New Press, 1972), 46–50. Published earlier in *Politics* (1944).

Gabriel Dumont, the Forgotten Hero

GEORGE WOODCOCK

There is one hour in the history of Louis Riel that has haunted me more than any other moment in Canadian history. It is not one of the more obviously dramatic hours: not the time of his execution, or of his condemnation, or of the illusory triumphs that punctuated his existence. It is the moment when the fugitives met in a gully of northern Saskatchewan, and among the leafless willows Riel and Gabriel Dumont talked for the last time. There is only a fragmentary account, in Dumont's brief narrative, of what they said, and that is unrevealingly laconic; neither Riel nor any of the witnesses left any account at all. Yet it has always seemed to me that there must have been an extraordinary dramatic tension in that scene when the prophet met the man of action who had allowed faith in his leader to overcome his practical judgment and who now knew, in defeat, that it was he who had been right.

Not only has the relationship between Riel and Dumont had a peculiar resonance for me, as if it contained some special secret relating to the way our history has developed, but I have been fascinated by our own attitude to the two men, which I think reveals a great deal about the view of themselves and their world Canadians hold. Riel is one of the perennially attractive figures in Canadian history, inside and outside Quebec. He has been the subject of histories, poems, plays, and at least one opera. Gabriel Dumont has gone almost uncelebrated as a follower of Riel, a kind of Sancho Panza to the Canadian Don Quixote. It is worth mentioning that the one book on Riel—and perhaps the best book yet on him—in which something near justice is done to Dumont was written by an outsider; it is the American Joseph Kinsey Howard's *Strange Empire*.

I am one of those who wrote a play on Riel. I wrote it as one of a series which the CBC had commissioned from me in 1967, the year of the centennial, and I included the story of Riel to counter in some way the kind of bland complacency which marked and marred the patriotic face we were expected to wear in that year, just as I included a play on Isaac Brock to show that I saw a point in the realistic kind of patriotism that recognized perils and enemies. So far as Riel was concerned, if others were celebrating Sir John, I preferred to celebrate his victim, to draw attention to the crimes against individuals and minorities that were part of the fabric out of which the union of Canada, like almost every other major political achievement, was constructed. I gave Dumont—not Riel—the last words in the play; my own feeling spoke through them.

They will hang him. They dare not let him live.
But they will not escape his shadow
darkening across their future.

It was a play called *The Defender of the Past*, and the title expressed the view I have always held of Riel. He belonged to a culture against which all the forces of the nineteenth century were aligned; even if he had survived, the way of life to which he belonged was doomed, and this was one of the reasons why he decided to die. Yet in a negative way it did live on, for Riel's death and the destruction of the Métis culture, as distinct from the culture itself, represented something in our own new world which in the end we could not wholly accept. In this way, while Riel's own will was rooted in the past, his involuntary destiny belonged to the future which in Canada today has become our present, the present in which the disinherited whom Riel still symbolically represents—the Métis, the Indians, the French Canadians, the poor, the minorities—rise up against the world that defeated Riel and his past.

But why, in such a situation of resurgence, is it Riel who becomes the symbol? While I was working on my play I was disturbed by this curious fact, and in a book I wrote at the time (it appeared as *Canada and the Canadians* in 1970 and has just been reprinted) I speculated, before Margaret Atwood got round to the subject, on the ambivalence of the Canadian attitude towards heroes and on the kind of epic literature it had produced. I pointed out that what epics we had—the stories of the fur traders' journeys, the building of the Canadian Pacific, the sailing of the *Saint Roch* through the Northwest Passage in a single season, were really "epics of endurance, epics of imagination, not in any true sense epics of heroism," and I would accept the further argument which Margaret Atwood developed in *Survival*, that such heroism as does appear in our epics is *collective* heroism.

I went on in *Canada and the Canadians* to discuss the broader question of our attitude towards heroes, and reached the conclusion that

> the few recent attempts that have been made to fabricate heroes out of the men who made Canada have usually had the opposite effect;

> Alexander Mackenzie and Simon Fraser and their kind stand revealed as a set of capable anti-heroes who would endure anything to pave the way for trade but risk nothing at all for the sake of glory. Counting out Wolfe and Brock as born and bred outside the local tradition, there are probably only two men in Canadian history who might fit the pattern of the hero in the high romantic vein. One is Norman Bethune; but it is in China that Bethune is venerated as a hero, not in Canada. The other is the Métis military leader in the Northwest Rebellion of 1885, Gabriel Dumont; but it is about Riel the martyr, not Dumont the hero, that plays have recently been proliferating on the stage, television and radio.

I might perhaps have extended the list of authentic heroes slightly, but the picture would have been the same. Dollard des Ormeaux was an authentic hero in the old epic style, his last fight at the Long Sault comparable to that of Roland in the Pass of Roncevaux, but it is Brébeuf the passive martyr who has caught our attention. Chénier who died fighting against the British at St. Eustache was undoubtedly another of the kind, but only recently have Quebec militants begun to pull him out of the shadow cast over him by the fame of Papineau, who ran away and then returned to live out his days in the aura of a victim of English tyranny.

The pattern in each case is the same. Canadians distrust heroes, perhaps because heroism is always a kind of imposition; the hero is dominating us by his strength, by his brute courage, and we have become suspicious of such qualities, particularly as we see ourselves generally imposed upon or (as Atwood puts it) colonialized, but more than that, we suspect the sheer gigantic irrationalism of the heroic, for we consider ourselves a reasonable people.

Still, why should we identify so easily with the martyrs, who after all impose on us in another way, by their weakness rather than their strength, by a kind of resigned and destined obstinacy rather than by a wilful courage? Both heroes and martyrs succeed—even if they die in the achievement—through their power of *shaming* other men, of making them lose face with themselves, and that is an irrational appeal that can lead to totally negative ends, that can be and is exploited. "The blood of the martyrs is the seed of the Church" is a statement not only about faith, but also about power. And Riel's body was hardly cold off the gallows before his martyrdom was used for the ends of power by Honoré Mercier and others.

Yet the interesting thing about Riel is not only that he plays such a dominant role in the imagination of modern Canadians seeking a symbol to express their frustration and their sense of being imposed on, but that a man like Gabriel Dumont should have been so influenced by Riel's character that even when he saw the struggle had been lost by his leader's preoccupation with martydom, he fought until everything was finished except his own life and only then departed in the hope of fighting on another day that never dawned.

For Dumont had everything that went to make the kind of folk or frontier hero that has been a contemporary equivalent of the great windy braggarts of Homer and Shakespeare. In the United States he would have acquired legendary status. As long as the buffalo lasted, he was the greatest of the Métis hunters, unrivalled as a sharpshooter and as a breaker and master of horses; he never troubled to learn English, but he knew all the languages of the prairie Indians, their traditional medical skills, their lore of the hunt and the trail; he even knew the ancient skill—dating from the days before the horses reached the prairies—of calling the buffalo; few Indians by the 1870s knew as much of the lore of the wilderness as Gabriel Dumont. He was virtually illiterate; he had no need of books.

Dumont, in fact, was the natural man *par excellence*, adapted perfectly to the life of the wilderness, and in this alone he was profoundly different from Riel, who was as alienated as any modern Canadian from that existence. Here, indeed, is already one of the reasons why Canadians in the 1970s—and not merely French Canadians—find Riel so appealing. He moves out of his narrow historical context, and even out of the French-Canadian legend that Mercier and Bourassa built around him, and appears as a hirsutely appropriate personification of the very anxieties we ourselves are projecting in our renewed concern for the wilderness and in our addiction to ecological and environmental mystiques. Riel, as the title of my play suggested, may have been a defender of the past, but like most such defenders he did not belong to what he defended, the real life of the prairie hunters; his education had separated him from it. He was rather like the westernized Africans who nowadays try to make sense of the tribal cultures they rule, and in the attempt to do so invent past civilizations that never existed because they are incapable of believing that any good exists outside civilization. In the same way, his head filled with the chatter of nineteenth-century Europe, Riel invented a Métis *nation*, which—if one looks at Dumont and the people he led before Riel came up from Montana in 1885—seems to have been a contradiction between word and reality. Riel was trying to impose the theories of a man educated in a classical college, and marred in the contest with a modern state, on the life of a people whose education was in the arts of a pre-agrarian and certainly pre-national way of life.

The fact is that there was a wide division between the Red River in 1869 and the Métis region of the South Saskatchewan in 1885. On the Red River, Riel was involved not merely with recently nomad hunters but with a miniature modern society. Fort Garry and the other settlements along the river may have appeared rustic in comparison with Montreal or the lakeside towns of Upper Canada, but the region had its structure of authority in the Council of Assiniboia, its magistrates and newspapers, its steamers puffing upstream from the railhead south of the border, its Scottish farmers descended from Selkirk's settlers, its Canadian immigrants, its American intriguers, its Fenian conspirators. The whole infrastructure, in other words, of the West as it was to become after Confederation swallowed it. Only the Mounties and the CPR were yet to come.

Riel spoke indeed for the grievances of the Métis, and used them as the armed force by which new political orders often establish themselves. But what he tried to create was not a traditional Métis order based on the traditions of the hunt; it was a government on the same lines as the responsible colonial governments in the Canadian provinces. There is no reason to suppose that when the province of Manitoba was created Riel was disappointed with the constitutional result of his actions. The fact that the rights of the Métis would still be unprotected did not immediately occur to him. He was a very modern man in his illusion that the vanishing splendours of a free and natural life could be recaptured in a cage of political action.

Dumont, on the other hand, was so much the free and natural man that even in 1869 the Red River seemed over-civilized to him. He preferred the farther prairies where the buffalo hunt had still a half-generation to go. The people whose leader he became in 1868 were not refugees from the Canadian takeover on the Red River, though many of those came later. They were the hunters who had moved farther into the west as the buffalo herds were hunted out in the eastern prairies. Unlike the men who provided Riel's support, they had not yet adopted a farming life when they elected Dumont leader of the hunt. But they had established semi-permanent camps around Duck Lake, and two years later, when the priests moved in and a year-round settlement congealed around the mission of St. Laurent and the ferry established by Xavier Batoche, Dumont became its undisputed chieftain. A man with as much practical sense and common foresight as events show Dumont to possess cannot have been unaware of the bleak future that faced the hunting life—the great herds were visibly dwindling—and it was probably he who first led his followers to establish farms along the riverside.

Dumont took no part in the events at Red River, though it is said that he offered to lead his hunters to Riel's aid. Riel did not send for him, just as he did not accept the offer of the Indian chiefs at Lake of the Woods to ambush Wolseley's column; he trusted the Canadians, which Dumont never did. Dumont did not come into direct contact with the Canadian authorities until 1875 when, as chief of the hunt, he arrested a Hudson's Bay hunter who had broken the code by attacking the herd before the pre-arranged signal, and confiscated his carts and fined him. The Mounties were called in; they decided that the rules of the hunt on which Dumont had acted were necessary for the preservation of order on the prairies. Despite his later conflicts with the Mounties, Dumont retained even their respect:

> One might travel the plains from one end to the other and talk to the Métis hunters, and never hear an unkind word said of Dumont [wrote the famous Sam Steele]. He would kill bison by the score and give them to those who were either unable to kill or had no buffalo. Not until every poor member of the hunting-parties had his cart filled with

> meat would he begin to fill his own. When in trouble the cry of all was for Gabriel. His father and uncle . . . were great hunters, though very old men, and were very much respected, but all turned to Gabriel when there was any grave crisis, the oldest paying attention to his word.

Obviously, Dumont was in command of his world while it remained the world of the hunter. It was the sudden changing of that world towards the end of the 1870s that destroyed his security and his authority alike. With no real conservation, the buffalo were nearing extinction. And when the Métis turned to the land they faced the speculators who were infiltrating the prairies and against whom they had no title to flourish; they were even worse off than the Indians, who at least had their reservations to live on.

It is understandable why Dumont called in Riel. An illiterate son of nature, however efficient in his own world, could not compete in the world of legalities and petitions. Riel, who had at least been partly successful in Manitoba, presumably could. What Dumont and his comrades did not take into account was the veering in Riel's mind during the many years since he had ridden away from Fort Garry as Wolseley's troops appeared on the other shore. The Métis expected a political leader; they received a prophet, an *exalté*, a prairie Gandhi without Gandhi's consistency, for Riel developed desperate policies that could only succeed by means of violence and yet shrank from violence when it came.

Dumont's solution to the problem was appropriately heroic. If it had to be rebellion, then let it be total rebellion, with a guerrilla warfare in which a few hundred Métis and Indians would paralyse the eight thousand Canadians and thoroughly confuse that archetypal Blimp, General Middleton. If historical examples like that of Ireland between 1919 and 1921 are anything to go by, such a strategy stood at least a sporting chance of success. Riel's attempt to win by a show of violence without the reality was doomed from the start.

And this—which makes the amazing part of the story—Dumont understood. From the beginning he urged action, and the plans he made—and which Riel always frustrated—show him to have been a very resourceful guerrilla leader. And yet, to the end, he obeyed Riel. He had the last of the hero's qualities: once he had given his fealty, he was totally loyal, and not with the mindless loyalty of the Light Brigade. He *did* reason why, and yet was ready to do or die as commanded until the moment Riel abdicated command.

Dumont fled when there was no point in risking his life any more; he plotted Riel's rescue and failed; he returned to die in the place where he had fought. The only impressive thing left in the bleakness of Batoche is the rough chunk of rock that lies over Dumont's grave, a fitting monument to the nomad chieftain Dumont was for the best years of his life.

But why do we prefer Riel, as we obviously do? Why don't we make plays, poems, and postage stamps about Dumont? Partly, I think, because we have ceased to live in a black-and-white world, and simple and direct people embarrass us with the unspoken demand that we imitate their virtues. Riel has more ambiguities, more shades of intent; he belongs in this world in which we are more conscious of twilight than of dawn. He is the personification of a besieged minority, and most Canadians see themselves as members of besieged minorities. He is a victim, and most modern men (not only Canadians, *pace* Atwood) like to see themselves as victims. And Riel is the kind of victim who enables us to enjoy that role vicariously; he is the *sacrificial* victim who really dies and gives us time to slip over the border and return to die in our beds. For most of us, in that hour of defeat at Batoche, would have made Dumont's choice.

Yet if Dumont had stood beside Riel at the gallows in Regina, we should now remember him in the same thought as Riel, as we remember Sacco and Vanzetti. Dumont would have been the same man, with the same life; only the ending would have been different. And that is the crux of the issue. We see public figures not as men but as functions. It is not Riel himself we admire, for in many ways he was a man impossible to admire. It is Riel the symbol and what he symbolizes is our inner condition, our consciousness of deprivation and alienation from meaningful existence, our sense of rebellion without hope. Which, paradoxically, may be a good thing, for the end of hope is often the beginning of resolution, and when resolution rises we may yet make a symbol of Dumont.

I am still haunted by that last meeting in the gully at Batoche. Did Riel merely talk of his mission? Did Dumont merely say I told you so? As they were men, that is probably all that did happen—that and a tense farewell. But we always expect more of symbols than of men, and rightly so. And I suspect that, after all that has been written about Riel, there remains a book—perhaps the best book—to be filled with the resonances of his encounter with Dumont.

From *A George Woodcock Reader*, ed. Douglas Fetherling (Ottawa: Deneau and Greenberg, 1980), 120–27. Published earlier in *Saturday Night* 88, 7 (July 1973).

Journalist, dramatist, commentator on Canadian culture, professor, novelist—through his many different roles **ROBERTSON DAVIES** (1913–) has become one of Canada's best known and most highly esteemed writers. He is in large measure responsible for the international recognition that has finally come to Canadian literature, but to help gain that recognition he had to serve a long apprenticeship. Davies was born in Thamesville, Ontario, the son of intellectually gifted parents with strong personalities. He learned his craft by writing articles for his father's newspaper, the *Renfrew Mercury*, at age ten: "We all wrote things. It was part of the day's work. . . . [W]e never thought of it as a special kind of accomplishment. . . . You had to do it accurately and concisely because [my father] was extremely persnickety about that." Davies was educated at Upper Canada College, Queen's University as a special student, and then at Balliol College, Oxford, where he received a B. Litt. in 1938.

After a year of acting with the Old Vic company in London, Davies returned to Canada, where he worked as the book editor for *Saturday Night* (1940–1942) and then as editor-publisher of the *Peterborough Examiner* (1942–1960). There Davies wrote editorials and reviews under his own name, as well as the "Samuel Marchbanks" weekly column which served as an outlet for the more fun-loving and iconoclastic aspects of his temperament. During this time, he produced a steady stream of books about the theatre, plays, and novels, including *Eros at Breakfast and Other Plays* (1949), *At My Heart's Core* (1950), *Tempest-Tost* (1951), *A Masque of Aesop* (1952), *Renown at Stratford* (with Tyrone Guthrie, 1953), *Leaven of Malice* (1954), *A Jig for the Gypsy* (1955), and *A Mixture of Frailties* (1957). In 1960, he became a professor of

English at the University of Toronto, and in 1962 was appointed the first master of Massey College. His reputation was secured with the publication of the Deptford Trilogy, *Fifth Business* (1970), *The Manticore* (1972), and *World of Wonders* (1975), which won him both critical acclaim and a large readership. In these novels, Davies uses the characters from his small-town Ontario world to explore magic, Jungian psychology, and the nature of evil, providing along the way his typical wealth of arcana in matters as diverse as saints' lives and travelling theatre companies. Writing has been a major part of Davies' life for seven decades now, and with the recent publication of such novels as *What's Bred in the Bone* (1985) and *The Lyre of Orpheus* (1988), he shows every sign of continuing to be extraordinarily productive.

As a reviewer and essayist, Davies has been a wide-ranging, incisive, and influential critic. The 1960 collection, *A View from the Attic*, provides students of Canadian literature with an engagingly idiosyncratic perspective on their subject, as does his early influential chapbook on Stephen Leacock (1970). The publication of other collections of Davies' non-fictional prose—*One Half of Robertson Davies* (1977), *The Enthusiasms of Roberston Davies* (1979), and *The Well-Tempered Critic* (1981)—have helped make readers better aware of how much sensible and sensitive criticism he has written. The wry humour and keen awareness of the comic potential of cliché that characterizes his persona Samuel Marchbanks also informs the following essay, in which Davies examines the difficulties involved in articulating what it means to be a Canadian—a subject that has long fascinated him.

ROBERTSON DAVIES

Keeping Faith

The soul of Canada—does the idea seem strange to you? Does it embarrass you to have it mentioned? But can you seriously think that Canada, unlike every other country in the world, lacks an essence that is the outcome of the history it has undergone, the races who have lived in it, the unique land and climate that are its geographical being? I am convinced that Canada has a soul, and should get on better terms with it, because at the moment it is a sadly neglected aspect of our inheritance. And that is why I am sitting at this moment in St. James's Cathedral in Toronto, trying to bring my thoughts together in the hope of involving you in this neglected reality. But how, and where, should we begin?

The tried and true method, I suppose, is to attempt some definition of terms. What does "religious" mean, and what does "spiritual" mean, and to what extent are the two definitions linked? The word "religious" gives trouble at once, for it is definable in two ways. The authority of the Christian Church is on the side of a derivation from *religare*, meaning to reconnect, or link back; in fact, to restrain or bind. But classical etymology prefers to find the root of the word in *relegere*, meaning a careful observation and heedfulness toward the numinous—whatever inspires awe or reverence. The two derivations may be linked, but it seems to me that there is an advantage in keeping them separate for such a discussion as this. In Canada the power and authority of churches to bind their members to a particular form of belief and conduct are easily assessed. Any discussion of what moves Canadians to awe and reverence leads us farther afield.

"Spiritual" opens even broader realms of confusion, for it implies that which is neither physical nor temporal, and one does not go far in discussing it without needing to use the word "soul"—which is, for many people, the most objectionable of four-letter words. Do Canadians, even those who acknowledge the binding of particular faith, pay much attention to their souls, or do they confide their souls (and the psychology that is bound up with the soul) to their churches for guidance and safekeeping? Has Canada a national soul, like the Soul of Holy Russia which was once so hotly discussed? Let me confess at once that I think Canada has a soul, but it is a battered child among souls; it needs nourishment, exercise, and fresh air, and, above all, love, if it is to reach maturity.

If religion, in the sense of binding creed and way of life, is to be found in Canada we must look to the Orthodox Jews, to the Doukhobors, to the Sikhs, and to the fundamentalist sects for examples. The experience of life, of economic well-being, of a wide-ranging (if vague) concept of education available to most Canadians does not dispose them toward restrictive disciplines rooted in a belief in God. Our houses of Parliament open their sessions with daily prayers, asking for divine guidance, but what they discuss is necessarily broadly materialistic, sometimes quasi-scientific, and when prayers are over God is rarely invoked. Among our people generally cries for freedom are often heard, whenever some particular group wants its own way, and it is often freedom in areas where religion—or some variety of it—denies freedom. But the realms where Canadians may demand freedom are restricted to moral matters; our governments do not bother their heads much about morals, but they are firm in their insistence on controlling anything to do with money. Our country is only one among many that submit to hitherto undreamed-of burdens of taxation in order that gigantic sums may be spent on enterprises of which the ordinary citizen has only the vaguest understanding.

The state will permit us freedom in realms where the church used to deny it, but the state is as rigorous and condemnatory as any authoritarian church in the parts of our lives which it values, meaning our ingenuity and our labour and the fruits thereof. There is a substantial argument to be made that the state is the real religion of our day, and perhaps the new God, and it is only the unimpressive, non-numinous quality of its priests—our politicians and civil servants—that conceals the danger from us. Indeed, in some situations, such as war or preparations for war, the state does become numinous, demanding and getting awe and reverence in a high degree. The move toward the state as God is still comparatively slow in its growth in Canada, but it may be seen in an advanced condition in supernations, one of them being our nearest neighbour. The parson has lost his control over us but the squire moves on from strength to strength.

There are a great many religious denominations in the Christian population of Canada, and to a casual observer they seem to be active and well supported. They may not be as flourishing in terms of the total population as they were fifty years ago (when it was insisted by the census-takers that everyone must be registered as an adherent of one faith or another) but they are strong in the realm that most of them have taken for their own, which is social betterment and the redress of obvious social wrongs.

The Roman Catholics, the Anglicans, the Lutherans, and the Orthodox churches still, as sacramental churches, form a link with historical Christianity, but many of the other Protestant groups insist on their "relevance" to the world of today, and often contribute to social advancement. They have firmly, and sometimes clamorously, put good works before faith as the path to salvation.

Even among Roman Catholics the cry for "relevance" is heard, and the reforms within that Church have caused astonishment and occasional regret among those who assumed that the Church was really unchanging. The changes have not been in doctrine, but in form, and much of the splendour and beauty which Protestants covertly envied has disappeared. The heaviest loss is undoubtedly the poetic splendour of the Latin Mass, which was truly numinous. The Mass in English has missed the vernacular beauty of the Anglican Prayer Book, and it seems that Rome has turned her back on the poetry in which lay much of her power.

Some Protestants have also gone mad for "relevance" and their ministry is likely to be performed by a bead-wearing, guitar-strumming shaman, whose poverty of spirit and intellect is no longer cloaked in a formal order of worship and a dignified, if sometimes archaic, language. "The merriment of parsons is mighty offensive," as Dr. Johnson phrased it, and their improvised, U-Haul wedding and funeral services cannot be taken seriously.

The most numerous Protestant congregation in Canada is that of the United Church, founded in 1925, and Canada's only substantial religious creation. According to the 1981 census it has sixteen percent of the Protestant churchgoers of Canada, out of the Protestant total of forty-one percent of the whole. Its congregations vary in their approach to worship, ranging from an almost sacramental observance of forms to an evangelistic enthusiasm that reminds us that the Methodist Church was the chief element from which the United Church was assembled.

No discussion of the religious life of Canada can avoid reference to the Methodist Church. On the positive side it gave strength to the forces that sought a mitigation of the colonial status of Canada and the often oppressive ambitions of the Church of England; its work to relieve poverty and improve the conditions of the working class was exemplary. As a negative force it was often anti-intellectual, and displayed a sanctimoniousness that was disgusting to people who were by no means foes of morality. My own mother left the Methodist Church when she was "preached against" from the pulpit of her church because she liked dancing; dancing, cards, drink, and the theatre were all lumped together as works of the devil. Of the arts only music, with special emphasis on what was called "sacred music" (meaning any composition, however wanting in distinction, that lugged in God), was permissible, but even music had to be carefully watched.

The Methodist Church, however it might have laboured in social causes, never forgot John Wesley's emphasis on personal holiness and the need for private prayer and examination of conscience, and in this way it left the path open for numinosity to enter the life of its members. But when it entered the United Church, this aspect of Methodism seems to have been obscured. There was no escape for those Methodists who did not wholly approve of the new creation; their church was in serious money trouble and union with the wealthy Presbyterians had all the attractions of a rich marriage. It would be unfair to stress this element in the union unduly but it was a factor, as was the desire to form a Protestant church which might hope to rival the Catholic Church in its influence—an aim it has not so far achieved.

Those Presbyterians—about a third of the whole—who refused to join with the United Church did so on theological grounds. The United Church offered no firm theology, and has never done so, permitting its detractors to accuse it of a flabby benevolence, of being a theological boneless wonder. The Presbyterians knew exactly where they stood; it was narrow ground, but it was firm. The Shorter Catechism, which they had embraced in 1647, allowed of no doubts or arguments on fundamental things. Its first question was: *What is the chief end of man?*, and the answer was: "Man's chief end is to glorify God, and to enjoy him forever." Take heed that in 1647 the verb "enjoy" meant that man was to give pleasure to God at least as much as God was expected to make man's lot pleasurable. The fourth question was: "*What is God?* ("What," not "who," is important here.) The answer was: "God is a Spirit, infinite, eternal and unchangeable, in his being, wisdom, power, holiness, justice, goodness and truth." There are 107 questions which each Presbyterian child—I was one—had to get by heart and hear expounded and enlarged by an instructor. Such instructors were not always precisely what the formulators of this creed in 1647 may have foreseen. I remember my own Sunday-school teacher, a genial physician, telling us: "It's hard work to get it all by heart but you'll find it invaluable when you get into an argument—in the smoking car in a train, for instance, where there is always a lot of talk about religion, especially at night; if you have your Catechism cold, nobody can get the better of you." True indeed. Even though I deserted Edinburgh for Canterbury when I became free to choose, I have found the Shorter Catechism a rock at my back and a sword in my hand.

It is understandable that the sterner Presbyterians would not abandon this rock and this sword for what seemed to them to be an ill-defined faith. Their ideal was the Christian of Bunyan's *Pilgrim's Progress*, not Mr. Nice Guy. They did not enter the union and are a strong, if small, denomination commonly called Continuing Presbyterians.

It is of interest, and certainly not irrelevant to our purpose here, to observe that some United Churches now, with their robed choirs, their central aisle, and their central Communion table, might pass as Anglican to a careless observer. Central aisles admit of processions, and processions used to be thought of as Romish abominations. But Rome, and the Anglican and Lutheran and Orthodox churches, have not forgotten something that Protestantism has tried to put behind it.

That something is numinosity. It may be disputed that, as Tertullian said, the soul is by nature Christian, but it is very hard to deny that the soul longs for the numinous, and when it cannot find it in religion it may make do with astrology, or spiritualism, or some half-understood version of an Eastern faith. There are plenty of swamies and gurus—some of them home-grown—in Canada today and they are doing well even if they are not doing good. What else accounts for the popularity of science fiction, and movies about space travel, and even the assurance of an eternal life in some eternal Florida, as was offered by the film *Cocoon*? What else accounts for the observable prevalence of superstition, even among people who are ashamed of it and pretend to laugh at it? Science may assert, as was done at the Harvard Medical School in the nineteenth century, that the soul sits on a throne of nucleated cells, but much of mankind, without ever having heard of Leibnitz, agrees with him that the soul is the mirror of an indestructible universe.

Of course there are Canadians who insist, for many reasons which they can support with fluent arguments, that all religion is superstition, and that any notion of the supernatural is weak-minded. But these hard-rock atheists are few. A vastly greater group call themselves agnostics, a name which they have perhaps not examined as carefully as they ought.

They use it to define a cast of mind which asserts that the knowledge of anything beyond the material world—God, an afterlife, any influence on human destiny that lies outside the realm of science—is incapable of proof and may therefore be ignored. The term "agnostic," which gained its popularity after it was used by T.H. Huxley, means at its root to take refuge in ignorance, and since Huxley's day the agnostic position has felt some heavy blows. The weakness of agnosticism is that so many who lay claim to it are religious illiterates; they have not examined what they say they do not believe.

▼ ▼ ▼

If the nineteenth century may be described as the era in which science advanced by giant steps toward a dominating place in human thought, the twentieth century is certainly the age in which a new sort of empirical investigation, initiated by Sigmund Freud, has advanced boldly into the human mind, about which the older science had limited and usually ineffective ideas. Even Freud, who was sometimes said to be an atheist, called the area of his investigation "the psyche" which he used, as Bruno Bettelheim has recently reminded us, as the equivalent of the despised term soul.

It was Freud's rebellious disciple, C.G. Jung, who went further and asserted, on the basis of his extensive experience, that God existed beyond any doubt as a psychological fact, if not a metaphysical being, or such a spirit as defined by the Shorter Catechism.

This is in one sense revolutionary, for it rescues the idea of God from the laboratory scientists and the medical men who asserted that they had never found a soul anywhere in their investigations. In another sense the message of depth psychology is a restatement of an old religious assertion: that God, and the Kingdom of God, is within you, and the enjoyment of God, and entry into His Kingdom, is something you must manage, in the end, for yourself.

Depth psychology gives a new complexion to all religious thinking, though theologians may argue that it brings nothing new in essence. What is important is that these assertions came from outside the organized churches. Some of the churches have resisted them vigorously, but others have welcomed them and done what they can to incorporate them into their own systems. What makes many churchmen nervous is that these words from the pschyoanalyst's consulting room raise the ghost of an ancient heresy. It is Gnosticism.

What you think about Gnosticism depends entirely on where you get your information. Orthodox Christianity condemned it utterly, and attributed the most shocking depravities to its followers. But since the discovery of the scrolls of Nag Hammadi we know more about Gnosticism than we did, and we see why it was hateful to the Church.

The Church was firm on the point that it was the only source of salvation, and that salvation was freely open to all dutiful children of the Church, however unpromising some of them might seem as candidates for any sort of spiritual benefit. Gnosticism was so intolerably elitist as to say that salvation was attainable only through an inner journey, an onward struggle, which would, in the end, if successful, bring enlightenment. This ruled out great numbers of people who had no intellectual equipment or spiritual muscle for such a struggle, and the Gnostics accepted cheerfully the conclusion that such people were best suited to the bondage of a church which would keep them out of mischief, but could not enlighten them. No wonder the Church hates the Gnostics: they had the gall to say that salvation was not free—or at least free to those sufficiently submissive. And they placed Holy Church second to personal enlightenment.

Yet here, in the twentieth century, we have Freud and especially Jung saying in effect what the Gnostics said nineteen centuries ago. Freud and Jung never said that enlightenment was impossible to any except those who had undergone the long and painful discipline of psychoanalysis. They said, as Socrates said long before Christ, that the unexamined life was not worth having, and they went further than Socrates in suggesting means by which life might be profitably examined. Such examination might well, said Jung, bring numinosity back into the life of the seeker; he would discover awe and reverence, and would thereby be enriched.

The hatefulness of such assertions to those (whether churchmen or scientists) who were unwilling to admit the existence of areas of the human mind, or the human spirit, which were not under control and observation by the conscious mind, is readily understood. But the fat is in the fire. The unconscious has been demonstrated by men of impeccable scientific credentials. And thereby a hidden level of being, unknown to conscious being, that was hitherto known chiefly to poets and philosophers, has been added to the life of Everyman.

▼ ▼ ▼

What does this mean in Canada? It is not possible to pretend that Canada's spiritual life exists in total separation from that of the United States. Not because of any conscious desire in the U.S. to dominate Canadian religion, but because of the intellectual and spiritual laziness that is the greatest plague and detriment of our country. A Canadian will work, or fight, or give money to philanthropic causes readily enough, but he will not think if he can possibly, at whatever cost, get someone else to do it for him. The Canadian is, in intellectual matters, a slob. There is a reason for this surrender. Good works are cheap in comparison with solitary pscyhological hard work.

In psychological terms, the U.S. is the most extroverted country in the world. This is not to say that there are no people who are, personally, introverted types in that country, but extroversion is the national attitude, and it has historical roots. The most influential settlers of the American colonies were the Pilgrims, who were people determined to have their own way in every important matter, and ready to make sacrifices to achieve it. The U.S. had its birth in a successful revolution, which lit fires of confidence and determination to succeed that are blazing still. The U.S. meets every external problem head-on, determined to conquer and certain of its rectitude. Of course, there is a price to be paid, and it is the price exacted of the extroverted attitude; numinosity, and the world of the unseen, cannot be conquered by extrovert means. Is it fanciful to suggest that the enthusiasm for space exploration reflects a refusal to face what is nearest to the soul? Has the ultimate in external travel been undertaken to avoid the inner journey and the personal conquest?

The blow sustained by the American people when the Challenger space flight was aborted on January 28, 1986, was a psychological blow, and we were all able to see its consequences on television. What did we see? Rooms full of school-children praying. But to whom or what were they praying? Their heads were bent, but what was in their hearts? They had turned, as they were told to do, to the God invoked on every occasion of national misfortune, but what does God mean to such a people, if not a supernatural problem-solver, an extra thrust of some high-powered fuel, to be invoked to support the national ambition and the national will? God, in fact, not as a spirit, but as a "resource person."

How did Canada behave on this occasion? With our usual cry of "me too." One newscaster even arrayed herself in deep mourning to give us the bad tidings. But did anyone hint that perhaps Challenger was not necessarily the best way to enlarge the spirit of a nation?

Canada might have done so, but Canada is in a psychological mess from which it can extract itself only by taking thought. Canada is not an extrovert country. Its history and its settlement by refugees from various sorts of oppression and betrayal dispose it toward introversion. (Oppression, when the Loyalists came here to escape from the triumphant revolutionaries in the South, who sequestered their lands and made their lives a burden; betrayal, when Scottish and Irish landlords exported their peasants, at so much a head, to the new world in order to seize their lands.) Introvert by inheritance, Canada nevertheless persists in aping the extroversion of the U.S., because to do so requires no thought—only intellectual submission and peonage. But if Canada is to find herself, she must find her own psychological direction, and radical changes in her religious orientation will follow.

Before we can make our introversion work for our national good, however, we must accept it, recognize it, and understand it. We must determine to achieve our ends by subtler means than mere imitation and challenge. We must stop modelling ourselves on Big Brother, for that is wholly unrealistic, and want of realism dooms the introvert who does not work from his true centre. As Jung said, "Who looks outside dreams; who looks inside awakes." Where should we begin looking? There are many good places to start, but we might well try to understand why the native peoples of Canada were pantheists. Something about the land disposed them to encounter the numinous in a special way. We need not ourselves become pantheists because we understand and respect that strong pull, but it could be fruitful in an intelligent approach to the land.

Does a psychological introversion necessitate the abandonment of whatever we have achieved, and a national attitude of mysticism, of inanition, of navel-gazing? Not at all. Introversion is another way of approaching problems of every sort. The extrovert, as the word implies, advances upon the world, and though he gains much he may miss what the world is presenting to him. The introvert, on the other hand, takes careful heed of what the world is offering, or saying to him. He weighs it carefully. Both have their losses and their gains. Until Canada wakes up, uses her excellent head, and adopts her true psychological direction, she will never be herself, but always a shadow of something else. She has nothing to lose, and her soul to gain.

How is it to be done? It cannot be left to government, or to the churches, because they are only aggregations of individuals, and until the individuals change themselves the institutions will remain as they are. To deny a nation's basic psychological attitude is to court every sort of misfortune, and in the world of today too many nations are striving unsuccessfully to imitate the extreme extroversion of the U.S., with results that are bad because the reasons for such action, and the means chosen, are bad. The U.S.S.R. is perhaps the most striking case; it cannot feed itself, but it struggles to keep pace with space exploration and Disneyland conceptions of defence which have no genuine relevance to its nature and its needs. The U.S., which sometimes seems to have lost touch with the realities of life on earth, pursues a course that is at least potentially disastrous for itself and all of us.

So what is Canada to do? As a beginning, some vigorous goading of the national intelligence is essential. Sleazy education and unexamined, patiently accepted government along weary, mixture-as-before lines must go. And as those things go—not after, but concurrently—there will inevitably be an awakening to the numinous, in personal and national life.

▼ ▼ ▼

The time has come to leave St. James's Cathedral, with a brief prayer thanking St. James, an especially determined and resolute saint, for his hospitality and perhaps for his inspiration. I could not have done my meditation in one of Canada's non-sacramental churches because they are locked on weekdays, with an inevitable suggestion that God is not open for business except on Sundays. Visits for private prayer and meditation are not encouraged—a pity because private prayer and meditation are precisely what Canadians need, though not all may wish to undertake them within the bounds of a strict creed. *Relegere*, in fact, rather than *religare*. But whatever the word, the intent should be to glorify and enjoy, to take heed of the numinous as it asserts itself, whenever invited to do so, in the national life because it has illuminated and set free the personal life. Canadians must take heed of what they really are in terms of their past, and their northern land. Only then can they find, through their wholeness, the true path to their future.

From *Saturday Night* 102, 1 (January 1987): 187–92.

GEORGE GRANT (1918–1988), a very widely known philosopher in this country, made his reputation with a distinctly unfashionable philosophy. In a century during which many academic philosophers have ignored fundamental issues affecting people's lives, he always believed that "philosophy must arise from the most immediate and concrete experiences of our lives, both public and private." As a critic of technological progress and modern liberalism too, he has charted his own idiosyncratic path. His pessimistic assessments of the prospects for Canadian nationhood and for the future of western civilization have been crucial in focussing Canadians' ideas on these complex issues.

He was born in Toronto into one of the most distinguished and influential families in Canada. Educated at Upper Canada College, where his father was headmaster, at Queen's University (B.A. History), where his grandfather had been principal, and at Oxford (D.Phil. Philosophy of Religion), he joined the Department of Philosophy at Dalhousie in 1947. He moved to McMaster in 1960 to found a department of Religious Studies. After repeated battles with the administration about what Grant saw as the Americanization of the department, he resigned in 1980, returning to Dalhousie as Professor of Political Science and Classics.

In 1959, Grant published *Philosophy in the Mass Age*, a book that represents the culmination of his intellectual development to that point. It was Grant's attempt to articulate a grand Hegelian synthesis, because he believed that Hegel "had partaken of all that was true and beautiful and good in the Greek world and was able to synthesize it with Christianity and with the freedom of the Enlightenment and modern science." *Lament for a Nation*

(1965) is, as its title suggests, Grant's despairing view of Canada's future, which he saw as compromised by the increasing homogeneity of North American culture, itself accelerated by the twin forces of technology and liberalism. The Vietnam War epitomized for Grant the evil of these forces, and his 1969 collection of essays, *Technology and Empire*, explores this theme. As he says in one of its most important essays, "Canadian Fate and Imperialism,"

> The dominant tendency of the western world has been to divide history from nature and to consider history as dynamic and nature controllable as externality. Therefore, modern men have been extremely violent in their dealings with other men and with other beings. Liberal doctrine does not prepare us for this violence because of its identification of technology with evolution, and the identification of evolution with the movement of the race to higher and higher morality.

In *English Speaking Justice* (1978), he returns to this theme in a new context, speculating about the place of traditional ethical concepts in a world controlled by technological progress. His last book, *Technology and Justice* (1989), was published posthumously. "The Morals of Modern Technology" is a shortened version of an essay from that collection as it first appeared in the *Canadian Forum*.

As an essayist, Grant combines considerable erudition with a disarming, self-effacing quality ("I am lost with the technological and metaphysical questions when they reach a high level," he confessed to one interviewer) which helps give the reader a sense that here is a fellow being, grappling with serious problems because he genuinely cares about them. His willingness to speak frankly about his own religious experience and about moral questions generally has attracted a large audience for his work outside of academia. Against what has been described by Charles Taylor as Grant's "implacable pessimism" must be placed his abiding commitment to the importance of spiritual concerns. The following pronouncement typifies his thought in this regard:

> If faith is the experience that the intelligence is illuminated by love, then how can human beings learn to love if the beginning of love is not love of one's own? It is in this sense that I think love of one's own is connected to love of the good. It is not the element of possession or of extension of self, which makes one's "own" so important, but rather its availability for being known by us, and known as good.

GEORGE GRANT

A Platitude

We can hold in our minds the enormous benefits of technological society, but we cannot so easily hold the ways it may have deprived us, because technique is ourselves. All descriptions or definitions of technique which place it outside ourselves hide from us what it is. This applies to the simplest accounts which describe technological advance as new machines and inventions as well as to the more sophisticated which include within their understanding the whole hierarchy of interdependent organisations and their methods. Technique comes forth from and is sustained in our vision of ourselves as creative freedom, making ourselves, and conquering the chances of an indifferent world.

It is difficult to think whether we are deprived of anything essential to our happiness, just because the coming to be of the technological society has stripped us above all of the very systems of meaning which disclosed the highest purposes of man, and in terms of which, therefore, we could judge whether an absence of something was in fact a deprival. Our vision of ourselves as freedom in an indifferent world could only have arisen in so far as we had analysed to disintegration those systems of meaning, given in myth, philosophy and revelation, which had held sway over our progenitors. For those systems of meaning all mitigated both our freedom and the indifference of the world, and in so doing put limits of one kind or another on our interference with chance and the possibilities of its conquest.

It may be said that to use the language of deprival is to prejudice the issue, because what has gone can more properly be described as illusions, horizons, superstitions, taboos which bound men from taking their fate into their own hands. This may be the case. What we lost may have been bad for men. But this does not change the fact that something has been lost. Call them what you will—superstitions or systems of meaning, taboos or sacred restraints—it is true that most western men have been deprived of them.

It might also be said that the older systems of meanings have simply been replaced by a new one. The enchantment of our souls by myth, philosophy or revelation has been replaced by a more immediate meaning—the building of the society of free and equal men by the overcoming of chance. For it is clear that the systematic interference with chance was not simply undertaken for its own sake but for the realisation of freedom. Indeed it was undertaken partly in the name of that charity which was held as the height in one of those ancient systems of meaning. The fulfillment that many find in the exploration of space is some evidence that the spirit of conquest may now be liberated from any purpose beyond itself, since such exploration bears no relation to the building of freedom and equality here on earth. What we are can be seen in the degree to which the celebration of the accomplishments in space is not so much directed to the value of what has actually been done, but rather to the way this serves as verification of the continuing meaning in the modern drive to the future, and the possibility of noble deeds within that drive. Be that as it may, the building of the universal and homogeneous state is not in itself a system of meaning in the sense that the older ones were. Even in its realisation, people would still be left with a question, unanswerable in its own terms: how do we know what is worth doing with our freedom? In myth, philosophy and revelation, orders were proclaimed in terms of which freedom was measured and defined. As freedom is the highest term in the modern language, it can no longer be so enfolded. There is therefore no possibility of answering the question: freedom for what purposes? Such may indeed be the true account of the human situation: an unlimited freedom to make the world as we want in a universe indifferent to what purposes we choose. But if our situation is such, then we do not have a system of meaning.

All coherent languages beyond those which serve the drive to unlimited freedom through technique have been broken up in the coming to be of what we are. Therefore it is impossible to articulate publicly any suggestion of loss, and perhaps even more frightening, almost impossible to articulate it to ourselves. We have been left with no words which cleave together and summon out of uncertainty the good of which we may sense the dispossession. The drive to the planetary technical future is in any case inevitable; but those who would try to divert, to limit, or even simply to stand in fear before some of its applications find themselves defenceless, because of the disappearance of any speech by which the continual changes involved in that drive could ever be thought as deprivals. Every development of technique is an exercise of freedom by those who develop it, and as the exercise of freedom is the only meaning, the changes can only be publicly known as the unfolding of meaning.

I am not speaking of those temporary deficiencies which we could overcome by better calculations—e.g. cleverer urbanologists—failures of the system which may be corrected in its own terms. Nor do I mean those recognitions of deprivation from the dispossessed—either amongst us or in the southern hemisphere—who are conscious of what they have not got and believe their lack can be overcome by the humane extension of the modern system.

Also, in listening for the intimations of deprival either in ourselves or others we must strain to distinguish between differing notes: those accidental deprivals which tell us only of the distortions of our own psychic and social histories, and those which suggest the loss of some good which is necessary to man as man. As I have said elsewhere, thought is not the servant of psychoanalysis or sociology; but a straining for purification has the authority of the Delphic "know thyself," and of the fact that for Socrates the opposite of knowledge was madness. The darkness of the rational animal requires therapy, and now that "philosophy" sees itself as analysis, men who desire to think must include in their thinking those modern therapies which arose outside any connection with what was once called philosophy. This inclusion of what may be health-giving in psychoanalysis and sociology will be necessary, even within the knowledge that these therapies are going to be used unbridledly as servants of the modern belief that socially useful patterns of behaviour should be inculcated by force. Anything concerning sexuality will serve as an example of the distortions I am trying to describe, because such matters touch every element of fantasy and the unconscious in ourselves, so that judgements about good are there most clouded by idiosyncracy. For example, if a man were to say that the present technical advances were so detaching sexuality from procreation as to deprive women of a maternity necessary to their fullest being, his statement might be suspect as coming from a hatred of women which could not bear to see them free. To take an example from myself, a sophisticated and lucid sociologist has asserted that I was saddened at the disappearance of the Canadian nation into the American empire, not because of my written reasons from political philosophy but because of my biographically determined situation.* I belonged to a class which had its place in the old Canada and could find no place for itself in the new imperial structure. Or again, I know that my thinking about modern liberalism is touched by a certain animus arising from tortured instincts, because of the gynarchy in which I came to know that liberalism. Thought may first arise from the ambiguities of personal history but if it is to stand fairly before the enormous ambiguities of the dynamo, it must attempt to transcend the recurring distortions of personal history. To listen for the intimations of deprival requires attempting a distinction between our individual history and any account which might be possible of what belongs to man as man.

Yet even as one says this, the words fade. The language of what belongs to man as man has long since been disintegrated. Have we not been told that

* R.K. Crook, "Modernization and Nostalgia: A Note on the Sociology of Pessimism," *Queen's Quarterly* (1965).

to speak of what belongs to man as man is to forget that man creates himself in history? How can we speak of excellences which define the height for man, because what one epoch calls an excellence another does not, and we can transcend such historical perspectives only in the quantifiable? Aren't such excellences just a crude way of talking about values, pretending that they have some status in the nature of things beyond our choosing? We are back where we began: all languages of good except the language of the drive to freedom have disintegrated, so it is just to pass some antique wind to speak of goods that belong to man as man. Yet the answer is also the same: if we cannot so speak, then we can either only celebrate or stand in silence before that drive. Only in listening for the intimations of deprival can we live critically in the dynamo.

Whether there are intimations of essential deprivals which are beyond elimination by the calculations of the present spirit is just what must remain ambiguous for us, because the whole of our dominating system of thought denies that there could be such. When we sense their arising, at the same time we doubt that which we sense. But even among some of those who use the language of sheer freedom as protest, there seems to be heard something different than the words allow. Because they have been taught no language but the modern, they use it not only to insist that the promises of the modern be fulfilled, but also to express their anguish at its denials.

Any intimations of authentic deprival are precious, because they are the ways through which intimations of good, unthinkable in the public terms, may yet appear to us. The affirmation stands: how can we think deprivation unless the good which we lack is somehow remembered? To reverse the platitude, we are never more sure that air is good for animals than when we are gasping for breath. Some men who have thought deeply seem to deny this affirmation: but I have never found any who, in my understanding of them, have been able, through the length and breadth of their thought, to make the language of good secondary to freedom. It is for this reason that men find it difficult to take despair as the final stance in most circumstances. Deprivation can indeed become absolute for any of us under torture or pain or in certain madnesses. We can be so immersed in the deprival that we are nothing but deprivation. Be that as it may, if we make the affirmation that the language of good is inescapable under most circumstances, do we not have to think its content? The language of good is not then a dead language, but one that must, even in its present disintegration, be re-collected, even as we publicly let our freedom become ever more increasingly the pure will to will.

We know that this re-collection will take place in a world where only catastrophe can slow the unfolding of the potentialities of technique. We cannot know what those potentialities will be. I do not simply mean specific possibilities—for example, whether housework will be done by robots, how far we can get in space, how long we can extend the life span, how much we can eliminate socially undesirable passions, in what ways we can control the procreation of the race, etc., etc. Some of these possibilities we can predict quite clearly, others we cannot, or not yet. But what is more important, we cannot know what these particular possibilities tell us about the potential in the human and the non-human. We do not know how unlimited are the potentialities of our drive to create ourselves and the world as we want it. For example, how far will the race be able to carry the divided state which characterises individuals in modernity: the plush patina of hectic subjectivity lived out in the iron maiden of an objectified world inhabited by increasingly objectifiable beings? When we are uncertain whether anything can mediate that division, how can we predict what men will do when the majority lives more fully in that division? Is there some force in man which will rage against such division: rage not only against a subjectivity which creates itself, but also against our own lives being so much at the disposal of the powerful objectifications of other freedoms? Neither can we know what this unfolding potentiality tells us of the non-human. As we cannot now know to what extent the non-human can in practice be made malleable to our will, therefore we also do not know what this undetermined degree of malleability will tell us of what the non-human is. Is the non-human simply stuff at our disposal, or will it begin to make its appearance to us as an order the purposes of which somehow resist our malleablizings? Are there already signs of revolts in nature?

Despite the noblest modern thought, which teaches always the exaltation of potentiality above all that is, has anyone been able to show us conclusively throughout a comprehensive account of both the human and non-human things, that we must discard the idea of a presence above which potentiality cannot be exalted? In such a situation of uncertainty, it would be lacking in courage to turn one's face to the wall, even if one can find no fulfillment in working for or celebrating the dynamo. Equally it would be immoderate and uncourageous and perhaps unwise to live in the midst of our present drive, merely working in it and celebrating it, and not also listening or watching or simply waiting for intimations of deprival which might lead us to see the beautiful as the image, in the world, of the good.

From *Technology and Empire: Perspectives on North America* (Toronto: House of Anansi Press, 1969), 137–43. The essay was written in 1968–1969 and has appeared in *Saturday Night*.

The Morals of Modern Technology

GEORGE GRANT

In each moment of our waking and sleeping, we are a technological civilization. Why is it best to characterize what we are now encompassing, and are encompassed by, as technological? The answer can be seen in the very structure of the word. The current use of the word technology in North America lays before us the novelty of our world.

Instead of the English "technology" and "technologies," Europeans have generally used "technique" and "techniques," the former for the whole array of means for making events happen, the latter for the particular means. They have claimed that our usage confuses us by distorting literal meaning. The word technology puts together the Greek word for art and the word for the systematic study of it, as the word biology puts together *bios* and *logos*. Europeans claim our usage parallels a similar imprecision in English in which "history" means both the "study" and "what is studied."

Nevertheless, although the European usage maintains verbal purity, it does not evoke modern reality as directly as our usage does. The American neologism brings before us our novelty. When "technology" is used to describe the means of making events happen, and not simply the systematic study of these means, the word reveals that these new events happen because we westerners willed the development of a new and unique co-penetration of the arts and sciences, a co-penetration that has never before existed. What is given in the neologism—consciously or not—is the idea that modern civilization is distinguished from all previous civilizations because our activities of knowing and making have been brought together in a way that does not allow the once-clear distinguishing of them. In fact, the coining of the word technology catches the novelty of that co-penetration of knowing and making. It also implies that we have brought the sciences and the arts into a new unity in our will to be masters of the earth and beyond.

The use of the word technique for that with which we have encompassed ourselves too easily implies that our understanding of what constitutes knowing and making is not radically different from that of previous civilizations. In fact, the modern "technique" may seem at first to suggest the same kind of meaning as the Greek *techne*, as if we have simply progressed in efficiency of making. We then attribute our greater efficiency to the modern scientists, who guaranteed the progress of knowledge by clarifying its sure methods, and through that objective knowledge achieved greater ability to make things happen. In this account of progressing continuity we assume that our modern western will to be masters of the earth was taken for granted in the *techne* of other civilizations. The time was not accidentally ripe; those peoples were not evolved enough to discover the sure path of science, which would have allowed them to realize the will to mastery.

With such implied histories of the race, we close down on the startling novelty of the modern enterprise and hide the difficulty of thinking about it. We close down on the fact that modern technology is not simply an extension of human making through the power of a perfected science but is a new account of what it is to know and to make in which both activities are changed by their co-penetration. We hide the difficulty of thinking about that novelty, because in our implied histories it is assumed that we can understand the novelty only from within its own account of knowing, which has itself become a kind of making.

Indeed, the English word technology, with its Greek parts and the novelty of what is given in their combination, shows what a transformation has taken place in our sciences, our arts and their interrelation. They have changed from what they were in the civilization from which the parts of the word come. It is very difficult to grasp what is given about art and science in the Greek writings, because we understand previous sciences as preparations for our own sciences and other accounts of nature as stumbling provisions for our objective understanding of them. Nevertheless, at the simple surface of the question it is clear that what was known in the physics of the Greeks was not knowledge of the kind that puts the energies of nature at man's disposal, as does modern western physics. It is only necessary to read Needham's history of Chinese science to see that the same was true there. What is given in the Sanskrit word shows this to be equally true of the civilization founded upon the Vedanta.

When we speak of theoretical and applied science, the distinction contains something different from ancient usage. "Applied" means literally "folded towards." Einstein advised Roosevelt that in the light of the modern discoveries of physics atomic weapons could be built and that the Americans should organize to build them. Physics was being applied not only in deciding that American interests required the making of atomic weapons, but also in the sense that the very discoveries of the science were in their essence folded towards the mastery of the energies of nature, in a way that was absent in the pre-modern sciences. The co-penetration of knowing and making has quite changed what we mean by both the arts and the sciences in the modern era.

Why that foldedness towards potential new makings has been implicit in modern science since its origins is extremely difficult to understand, and indeed has not yet been understood. That it has been so folded is expounded with consummate clarity in such writings as those of Bacon and Descartes. They distinguished modern science's very beginning. The difficulty of understanding how and why it is so folded need not lead us to doubt that the folding is a fact. That fact is given in the neologism technology, and the novelty of that fact declares correct the characterization of our society as technological. There may indeed be some other, more perfect, word to characterize our civilization—some word that will come out of the understanding of what was being revealed when the European peoples brought forth those new sciences and arts. In the meantime, the word technological catches best the uniqueness of our civilization at its surface, and indicates the cause of its worldwide appeal.

In the novelties of our hourly existing, it is easy to recognize how much we have encompassed ourselves within technology. We sweep along superhighways to work in factories, or in the bureaucracy of some corporation; our needs are tended to in supermarkets and health complexes. We can cook, light, heat, refrigerate, and be entertained at home through energy that has been produced and stored in new ways. If we have even a slight knowledge of the past we are aware that we can make happen what has never happened before, and can have done to us what has never before been possible. At a higher level we can recognize that our political and social decisions are interwoven with the pursuit and realization of technological ends.

The technology with which we have surrounded ourselves is not of only superficial or ambiguous benefit. Modern human beings, since their beginnings, have been moved by the faith that the mastery of nature would lead to the overcoming of hunger and labour, disease and war on so widespread a scale that at last we could build a worldwide society of free and equal people. One must never think about technological destiny without looking squarely at the justice in those hopes. Let none of us who live in the well-cushioned West speak with an aesthetic tiredness about our "worldliness."

The more clear-sighted of our ruling classes have recently recognized that progress is a more complex matter than was envisaged by those who believed a better society would arise ineluctably from technology. In the past, human beings have been responsible for the destruction of all the members of some other species. But today, when we watch the osprey's glory in the ocean storm, there is not only awareness that this beauty may be passing away, because the eggs of the bird are being sterilized by our use of chemicals, but also that the source of life itself may become no longer a home of life. Our novelty lies in the fact that where Plato warned clearly against the dirtying of the waters, he did not face their pollution as a possibility in the immediate future. We are now faced with easily calculable crises (concerning population, resources, pollution, etc.) of the drive to mastery. The political response to these interlocking emergencies has been a call for an even greater mobilization of technology, which illustrates the determining power of our technological representation of reality. More technology is needed to meet the emergencies that technology has produced.

▼ ▼ ▼

A computer scientist recently made the following statement about the machines he helps to invent: "The computer does not impose on us the ways it should be used." Obviously, that statement is made by someone who is aware that computers can be used for purposes of which he does not approve—for example, the tyrannous control of human beings. This is given in the word should. The scientist makes a statement in terms of his intimate knowledge of computers that transcends that intimacy, in that it is more than a description of any given computer or of what is technically common to all such machines. Because he wishes to state something about the possible good or evil purposes for which computers can be used, he expresses, albeit in negative form, what computers are in a way that is more than technical description. Computers are instruments, made by human skill for the purpose of achieving certain human goals. They are neutral instruments in the sense that the morality of the goals for which they are used is determined outside them.

Many people who have never seen a computer, and only slightly understand its capacity, have the sense from their daily life that they are being managed by computers and have, perhaps, an undifferentiated fear about the potential extent of this management. Our scientist, who knows about the invention and use of these machines, states what they are in order to put our anxiety into perspective; he states what they are to free us from the terrors of such fantasies as the myth of Doctor Frankenstein. His perspective assumes that the machines are instruments because their capacities have been built into them by human beings and because it is human beings who operate those machines for purposes they have determined. All instruments can obviously be used for bad purposes, and the more complex the capacities of the instrument, the more complex its possible bad uses. But if we apprehend computers for what they are, neutral instruments that we in our freedom are called upon to control, we are better able to come to terms rationally with their potential dangers. The first step in coping with these dangers is to see that they are related to human beings' potential decisions about how to use computers, not to the inherent capacities of the machines themselves. Indeed, the statement above about the computer is the prevalent "liberal" view of the modern situation, a view so rooted in us that it seems to be common sense, even rationality, itself. We have certain technological capacities; it is up to us to use those capacities for decent purposes.

Yet despite the seeming common sense of the statement "the computer does not impose on us the ways it should be used," when we try to think [about] the sentence, it becomes clear that we are not allowing computers to appear before us for what they are. Indeed the statement (like many similar) obscures what computers are. To begin at the surface: the words "the computer does not impose" are concerned with the capacities of these machines, and these capacities are brought before us as if they existed in abstraction from the events that have made possible their existence. Obviously the machines have been made from a vast variety of materials, consummately fashioned by a vast apparatus of fashioners. The machine's existence has required generations of sustained effort by chemists, metallurgists and workers in mines and factories. Beyond these obvious facts, computers have been made within the new science and its mathematics. That science is a particular paradigm of knowledge and, as any paradigm of knowledge, is to be understood as the relation between an aspiration of human thought and the effective conditions for its realization. It is not my purpose here to describe that paradigm in detail, nor would it be within my ability to show its interrelation with mathematics conceived as algebra. Suffice it to say that what is given in the modern use of the word science is the project of reason to gain "objective" knowledge.

Modern "reason" is the summoning of something before a subject and the putting of it to questions [sic], so that something gives us its reasons for being the way it is as an object. A paradigm of knowledge is not something reserved for scientists and scholars. Anybody who is awake in our educational system knows that this paradigm of knowledge stamps the very heart of the institutions and curricula of that system, in what the young are required to know and to be able to do if they are to be called "qualified." That paradigm of knowledge is central to our civilizational destiny and has made possible the existence of computers. I mean by civilizational destiny above all the fundamental presuppositions that the majority of human beings inherit in a civilization and that are so taken for granted as the way things are that they are given an almost absolute status. To describe a destiny is not to judge it. It may indeed be, as many believe, that the development of that paradigm is a great step in the ascent of man, that it is the essence of human liberation, that its development justifies the human experiment itself. Whatever the truth of these beliefs, without this destiny computers would not exist. And like all destinies, it imposes.

What has been said about the computer's existence depending upon the paradigm of knowledge is equally true of the earlier machines of industrialism. The western paradigm of knowledge has not been static but has been realized in a dynamic unfolding. One aspect of that realization has been a great extension of what is given in the conception of "machine." We all know that computers are machines for the transmitting of energy. They require software as well as hardware. Computers have required the development of mathematics as algebra and of algebra as almost identical with logic. The existence of computers has required a fuller realization of the western paradigm of knowledge, an extension of the conception of machine. It may well be said that where the steel press may be taken as the image of Newtonian physics and mathematics, the computer can be taken as the image of contemporary physics and mathematics. Yet in making that distinction, it must also be said that contemporary science and Newtonian science are equal moments in the realization of the same paradigm.

The phrase "the computer does not impose" misleads because it abstracts the computer from the destiny that was required for its making. Common sense may tell us that the computer is an instrument, but it is an instrument from within the destiny that imposes itself upon us. Therefore the computer does impose.

To go further: How are we being asked to take the word ways in the assertion that "the computer does not impose the ways"? Even if the purposes for which the computer's capabilities should be used are determined outside itself, do not these capacities limit the kind of ways for which it can be used? To take a simple example from the modern institutions of learning and training: in most institutions there are cards on which children are assessed as to their "skills" and "behaviour," and this information is retained by computers. It may be granted that such information adds little to the homogenizing vision inculcated throughout society by such means as centrally controlled curricula and teacher training. It may also be granted that as computers and their programming become more sophisticated, the information stored may be able to take more account of differences. Nevertheless, it is clear that the ways computers can be used for storing and transmitting information can only be ways that increase the tempo of the homogenizing processes. Abstracting facts so that they can be stored as information is achieved by classification, and it is the nature of classification to homogenize. Where classification rules, identities and differences can appear only in its terms. Indeed the word information is itself perfectly attuned to the account of knowledge that is homogenizing in its very nature. "Information" is about objects, and comes forth as part of that science that summons objects to give us their reasons.

It is not my purpose to discuss the complex issues of good and evil involved in the modern movement towards homogeneity, nor to discuss the good of heterogeneity, which in its most profound past form was autochthonous. Some modern thinkers state that human beings are beyond the rootlessness characteristic of the present early stages of technological society and are now being called to new ways of being rooted that will be able to accept the benefits of modern homogenization while living out a new form of heterogeneity. These statements are not at issue here. My purpose is to point out that the sentence about computers hides the fact that their ways are always homogenizing. Because this is hidden, the questioning of homogenization is closed down.

To illustrate the matter from another aspect of technological development: the desire of Canadians for the mass-produced car has been a central cause of our political and economic integration and social homogenization with the people of the imperial heartland. This has been not only because of the vast corporate structures necessary for building and keeping in motion such automobiles, and the direct and indirect political power of such corporations, but also because any society with such vehicles tends to become like any other society with the same. Seventy-five years ago somebody might have said "The automobile does not impose on us the ways it should be used," and who would have quarrelled with the statement? Yet it would have been a deluded representation of the automobile.

Human beings may still be able to control the ways that cars are used. Strict administrative measures may prevent the pollution of the atmosphere and keep freeways from destroying central city life. It is to be hoped that cities such as Toronto will maintain themselves as communities by winning popular victories over expressways and airports. But whatever efforts may be made, they will not allow us to represent the automobile to ourselves as a neutral instrument.

The ways automobiles and computers can be used hinge on the fact that these machines are investment-heavy and require large institutions for their production. The potential size of such corporations has been imagined by a reliable economist. He says that if the present growth of IBM is extrapolated, that corporation will in the next thirty years be a larger unit than the economy of any presently constituted national state, including that of IBM's homeland. At the simplest factual level, then, computers can be built only in societies in which there are large corporations. This will be the case whatever ways these institutions are related to the states in which they are incorporated, be that relation some form of capitalism or some form of socialism. Computers have been and will continue to be instruments with effect beyond the confines of particular nation states. They are instruments of the imperialism of certain communities towards other communities. They are instruments in the struggle between competing empires, as the present desire of the Soviet Union for American computers illustrates. It might be that in the long run of progress, humanity will come to the universal and homogeneous state in which individual empires and nations have disappeared. That in itself would be an even larger corporation. But whatever conceivable political and economic alternatives there may be, computers can exist only in societies in which there are large corporate institutions. The ways computers can be used are limited to those situations. In this sense computers are not neutral instruments, but instruments that exclude certain forms of community and permit others.

▼ ▼ ▼

In our era, many believe that the great question about technology is whether the ways it is used will be determined by the standards of justice in one or other of the dominant political philosophies. The rationalism of the West has produced not only modern physical science, but also modern political philosophy. Technology is considered neutral, and its just use will depend upon the victory of true rather than false political philosophy. The appeal of the teachings of political philosophers has been massive in our era, because these teachings have taken the form of ideologies that convince the minds of masses of human beings. The ways that computers should be used can be solved satisfactorily if political regimes are shaped by the true philosophy. The three dominant political alternatives are capitalist liberalism, communist Marxism, and national socialist historicism.

The same account of reason that produced the technologies also produced the accounts of justice given in these modern political philosophies. That account of reason led, moreover, to the public manifestation of those political philosophies as ideologies. The statement "the computer does not impose on us the ways it should be used" abstracts from the fact that "the ways" the computer will be used will be determined by politics, in the broadest sense of that term. Politics in our era is dominated by accounts of society that came forth from the same account of reasoning that produced the new co-penetrated arts and sciences.

It cannot be my purpose to show the nature of that sameness. Such a demonstration would require a detailed history of the modern West, an explanation of the mutual interdependence of the modern physical and moral sciences as they were defined against the account of science in classical philosophy. Much of the enormous enterprise of modern scholarship has been taken up with the detailed mapping of what was done and thought and made by large numbers of inventors, scientists, artists, philosophers, politicians, religious reformers. Beyond scholarship, the demonstration of this interdependence would require the ability to think what was being thought by the greatest scientists and philosophers. By distinguishing the new science from the account of science in the ancient world, scientists and philosophers laid down the modern affirmations of what science is. Concerning the conception of justice, it would be necessary to follow how great philosophers such as Descartes and Locke, Rousseau and Nietzsche, understood the unity between their accounts of justice and the findings of modern science.

Without any of these demonstrations, suffice it to say that the ways computers have been and will be used cannot be detached from modern conceptions of justice, and that these conceptions of justice come forth from the very account of reasoning that led to the building of computers. This is not to say anything about the truth or falsity of modern conceptions of justice, nor is it to prejudge the computer by some reactionary account stemming from a desire to turn our backs on the modern. It is simply to assert that we are not in the position where computers lie before us as neutral instruments, where we use them according to standards of justice reached outside the existence of the computers themselves. The instruments and the standards of justice are bound together; both belong to the same destiny of modern reason. The failure to recognize this hides from us the truth about the "ways" computers can be used.

The force of that destiny is seen in the ambiguity of the word should in the statement "The computer does not impose on us the ways it should be used." Our novel situation is presented as if human beings "should" use computers for certain purposes and not for others. But what has the word should come to mean in advanced technological societies?

"Should" was originally the past tense of "shall." It is still sometimes used in a conditional sense to express greater uncertainty about the future than does the prophetic sense of "shall." ("I shall get a raise this year" is more certain then "I should get a raise this year." The colloquialism "I shouldn't wonder" expresses this.) In its origins, "shall" was concerned with "owing," when used as a transitive verb. Chaucer writes: "And by that feyth I shal to god and yow." But over the centuries "should" took over from "shall" as the word with the connotation of owing, and could be used for that purpose intransitively.

The sentence "The computer does not impose on us the ways it should be used" is concerned with human actions that are owed. If the statement were in positive form—"The computer does impose on us the ways it should be used"—the debt would probably be understood as owed by human beings to machines. We can say of a good car that we owe it to the car to lubricate it properly. If we want the car to do what it is fitted for—which is, in traditional usage, its good—then we must look after it. We would mean the same sense if we were to say we owe it to ourselves to try not to contradict ourselves in trying to think out some matter clearly. But the "should" in the statement about the computer is clearly not being used about what is owed by men to machines. The sentence is concerned with the just use of the machine as instrument. "Should" expresses that we ought to use the machine justly. But what is the nature of the debt? To what or to whom do we owe it? Is that debt conditional? For example, if human beings "should" use computers only in ways that are compatible with constitutional government, and not in ways that promote tyranny, to what or to whom is this support of constitutional government owed? To ourselves? To other human beings? To all, or some of them? To nature? To history? To reasonableness? To God?

Because of the ambiguity that has fallen on all accounts of owing, our era has often been described as a time of nihilism. Many Europeans came to believe over the last three hundred years that their affirmations about goodness could not find foundations in accounts of God or nature, reason or history. The result for many has been a state of mind well described as nihilism. This state of mind has had wide public influence because the mass literacy necessary to technological society made nihilism a situation open not only to the few. In North America, the organization of training in schools and multiversities has produced mass "wised-upness," which is the democratic edition of nihilism.

It is necessary to be careful at this point. Characterizing technological society as essentially nihilistic prejudges the question of what that society is.

A dismayed reaction is as likely as any progressivism to close down thought about its nature. If we use the word good in the simplest way as what we approve, and "bad" as what we deplore, is it not evident that large majorities now give their shared approval to certain activities and that from those activities we can apprehend a positive modern conception of goodness? For example, is it not generally believed that freedom for sexual realization in its varying particularities should be promoted in societies? If one has any knowledge of the modern scientific community, is one not aware of the positive expectations about its accomplishments that permeate the community, from which a positive conception of goodness can be deduced?

A description of the modern era fairer than that of nihilism is that a great change has taken place in the public conception of goodness. The enucleation of that change is best made in terms of what is positive in both the past and the prevalent modern accounts. The original western conception of goodness is of that that meets us with the overriding claim of justice and persuades us that in desiring obedience to that claim we will find what we are fitted for. The modern conception of goodness is of our free creating of richness and greatness of life and all that is advantageous thereto. The presently popular phrase in the modern account of goodness is "quality of life."

The modern conception of goodness does not include the assertion of a claim on us that properly orders our desires in terms of owing, and that is itself the route and fulfilment of desire. In the prevalent modern view, owing is always provisional upon what we desire to create. Obviously we live in the presence of others, and our creating may perforce be limited by what we are currently legally permitted to do to others. However, the limitations, whether national or international, put on creating by claims of others, are understood as contractual; that is, provisional. This exclusion of non-provisory owing from our interpretation of desire means that what is summoned up by the word should is no longer what was summoned up among our ancestors. What moderns hear always includes an "if." The situation is never "beyond all bargains and without an alternative." Moreover, the arrival in the world of this changed interpretation of goodness is related to the arrival of technological civilization. The liberation of human desiring from any supposed excluding claim, so that it is believed we freely create values, is a face of the same liberation in which we overcame chance by technology—gained the liberty to make happen what we want to make happen. We are free, not only in what we want to make happen, but also in choosing the means. Nature becomes more and more at our disposal, as if it were nothing but our raw material.

"The computer does not impose on us the ways it should be used" asserts the essence of the modern view, which is that human ability freely determines what happens. The statement then puts that freedom in the service of the very "should" that that same modern novelty has made provisional. The resolute mastery to which we are summoned in "does not impose" is the very source of difficulty in apprehending goodness as "should." Therefore, the "should" in the statement has only a masquerading resonance in the actions we are summoned to concerning computers. Should is a word carried over from the past to be used in a present that is ours only because the assumptions of that past were criticized out of public existence. The statement therefore cushions us from the full impact of the novelties it asks us to consider. It pads us against wondering about the disappearance of "should" in its ancient resonance and about what this disappearance may portend.

I have written at length about this statement to illustrate how difficult it is to apprehend correctly what is novel in our situation. When we represent technology to ourselves as an array of neutral instruments, invented by human beings and under human control, we are expressing a kind of common sense, but it is a common sense from within the very technology we are attempting to represent. The novelness of our novelties is being minimized. We are led to forget that modern destiny permeates our representations of the world and ourselves. The coming to be of technology has required changes in what we think is good, in what we think good is, in how we conceive sanity and madness, justice and injustice, rationality and irrationality, beauty and ugliness.

From *Canadian Forum* (October 1986), 11–17, an abridged version of "Thinking about Technology," from *Technology and Justice* (Toronto: House of Anansi Press, 1986).

Since the publication of his first book of poems, *The Enchanted Echo* (1944), **AL PURDY** (1918–) has developed one of the most distinctive and thoroughly colloquial voices in Canadian poetry. A poet who has achieved the highly unlikely fusion of wide popular appeal, deceptive simplicity, and high seriousness, he has written poems that have become part of the cultural mindscape of any literate Canadian, such as "The Cariboo Horses," "The Country North of Belleville," "Lament for the Dorsets," "Eskimo Graveyard," "Trees at the Arctic Circle," "Wilderness Gothic," and "The Beavers of Renfrew." He was born near Wooler, Ontario, and though well known for his poetic field trips throughout Canada and the world, he has lived for most of his life in the legendary A-frame that he built in eastern Ontario near Ameliasburgh. In the 1950s, he lived for a time in Vancouver, and has recently moved to Sidney, British Columbia. Some of the highlights of his publishing career include *Poems for All the Annettes* (1962, 1968, 1973); *The Cariboo Horses* (1965), for which he won the Governor General's Award; *North of Summer* (1967); *Being Alive* (1978); *Piling Blood* (1984); *The Collected Poems of Al Purdy* (1986), which also won the Governor General's Award; and the novel *A Splinter in the Heart* (1990).

Purdy's most sustained work in the genre of the essay is contained in *No Other Country* (1977), from which the two essays reprinted here are taken. He expresses his love of Canada throughout the book, while avoiding sentimentality and chauvinism. In the introduction, "The Cartography of Myself," he remarks of his first trip to the Arctic: "In Cuba, England, France, and other countries I'd felt like a stranger: but here, I'd never left home. And I thought what an odd feeling it was in a region that most people think is desolate and alien. But I felt that the Arctic was just a northern extension of southern Canada. . . . I have this same feeling of enjoyment, of being at home, all over Canada." In concluding his introduction, he clearly sets forth a cautionary definition of Canada:

> My own country seems to me not aggressive, nor in search of war or conquest of any kind. It is exploring the broken calm of its domestic affairs. Slowly it investigates its own somewhat backward technology, and sets up committees on how not to do what for whom. My country is trying to resolve the internal contradictions of the Indian and French-Canadian nations it contains. In rather bewildered and stupid fashion it stared myopically at the United States, unable to assess the danger to the south—a danger that continually changes in economic character, and finally confronts us from within our own borders.

For his poems, for his energetic commitment to exploring every nook of his country's geographic and psychological topography, and for his thoughts and feelings as expressed in essays such as those that follow, Al Purdy has accurately been described by George Bowering as "the world's most Canadian poet."

Streetlights on the St. Lawrence

AL PURDY

Canada is a country where the heartland, centres of commerce and population, are almost entirely inland. The Atlantic traveller approaching the United States is suddenly confronted with the whole North American continent—it lifts right out of the sea at New York, and you're surrounded by people with scarcely any transition. But the traveller or immigrant bound for Montreal may enter the great watery jaws between Newfoundland and Cape Breton and be surrounded by five provinces of the new country without even knowing it. Distances in the Gulf of St. Lawrence are so immense that there often could be no land within sight of the marine traveller.

Nineteenth-century immigrants, particularly, must have observed with alarm and sometimes fear the rugged olive-green hills of the North Shore and the mountains of Gaspé drifting past. Some of them may have known that Jacques Cartier called this place of water and stone "the land God gave to Cain"—which seems to me a little extreme, even for an explorer from sunny France. But after voyages sometimes lasting many weeks, cooped-up on ships that must have seemed prisons, the dispossessed Scottish crofters and survivors of the Irish potato famine surely had a right to hope for something better. And to the women and their sometimes half-starved children this new world must have seemed much worse than the old. They were lost in this desolate place, thousands of miles from friends and relatives, without even control of their own bodies and destinies.

In late May, 1974, I reversed the westward track of those nineteenth-century immigrants. Boarding the 8500 ton lake freighter *Golden Hind* at

Thorold on the Welland Canal, Captain Cecil Freeman commanding, I travelled eastward through Lake Ontario and the St. Lawrence Seaway, eventually reaching Baie Comeau on the Quebec North Shore. The ship's cargo was soy beans and corn from Chicago; she carried a crew of thirty-one. At Baie Comeau I left the *Golden Hind* and flew back to Montreal, with the feeling of having added another thousand miles of previously unknown territory to the place in mind that is Canada.

Traversing the seaway was like driving a car, then coming to a whole series of maddening red lights: stop and go, stop and go. We would enter a lock, wait, water pouring out of the concrete playpen with a whoosh, and drop some fifty feet. Then zoom-zoom go the engines and we're on our way to the next traffic light. Moving slowly down the Welland Canal, the whole green country of the Niagara Peninsula is dwarfed—trees, houses, people, everything. The 620-foot-long ship is simply monstrous. And your mind has to handle it somehow. I managed that by saying to myself that lakers like the *Golden Hind*—as well as larger ships—are only boxes made of steel being pushed somewhere by wound-up rubberbands, or some other motive power invented by people. It's less grandiose that way.

The original *Golden Hind* weighed one hundred tons and was probably not more than seventy-five feet long, with a crew of around one hundred. Francis Drake circumnavigated the world with this ship in 1580, an age when many people still thought the Earth was flat and you'd fall off at the other side. Drake was an English pirate and patriot, a religious man who had prayers on shipboard twice a day, and who thought there was nothing irreligious about sacking a Spanish town in the Caribbean Sea between prayers. And yet when Francis Fletcher, his chaplain, criticized him slightly for poor seamanship, Drake padlocked Fletcher to a hatch and excommunicated him in the sight of God and man and the devil. The fair-haired freebooter, sitting cross-legged on a sea chest, ordered that a band be placed around his chaplain's arm that proclaimed the wearer "Francis Fletcher, the falsest knave that liveth." Which seems to indicate that if you don't agree with a captain while at sea you'd better keep the disagreement to yourself.

But Captain Cecil Freeman is nothing like Sir Francis Drake, he's a six-foot-tall, heavily built middle-aged Newfoundlander, and with a nice sense of humour. In the wheelhouse of the *Golden Hind*, between saying to the wheelsman, "Steer between those two buoys," he talks to me about getting a ticket for speeding from the U.S. Coastguard.

"I was master of the S.S. *Thorold* a few years back, and they told me on the radio-telephone that I'd exceeded the fifteen-miles-per-hour speed limit."

"And you hadn't?"

"It's like talking to the cops, they hear only their own side of anything. When you argue you make it worse. But I won this argument."

"How?"

"Well, they measure your speed by the period of time it takes for the distance between the ship's bow and stern to pass a fixed point on land. It's all done mechanically and pretty hard to disagree with. But in this case they had the wrong ship."

"Huh?"

"There happened to be another, earlier S.S. *Thorold*. It was a longer ship than mine, so it took longer to pass their speed-measuring devices. I pointed that out to them, very carefully of course. It's the only time I ever won an argument with the cops."

We have by this time passed through the misty expanse of Lake Ontario overnight; Wolfe Island glimmers grey behind us, the sun burning away early morning mist in the Thousand Islands of the upper St. Lawrence. Then more seaway locks and another set of traffic lights, with gay go up and gay go down, while loudspeakers and computers murmur electronic endearments to each other. An unexpected starling's nest is tucked in the lock wall, where someone must have slipped to allow anything but stone and steel. The mother bird doesn't bat an eyelash as the monster ship gurgles past, home free down the widening river.

On the American side of the seaway, castles of American millionaires are built on green islands, their scores of rooms empty in the late spring season: Heart Island, with battlements and dozens of stone towers, the Boldt Castle, built by a now-dead millionaire. (They die, too, of heart disease and cancer and a great deal of everything, the same way ordinary people do from having too little.) All the limestone and timber components had been hauled in by barge. Farther on, Mary Pickford's castle—she who was America's Sweetheart in the glittering and near-gold heyday of fairyland Hollywood—she who was once a Canadian. And cranes, dozens of the huge birds, rowing through darkening skies to inexpensive tree houses on Ironsides Island.

In many ways the ship is two floating towns, one suburb forward and the other behind. In between are some 450 feet of deck containing the cargo holds. For meals you walk aft to the diningroom, where the crew's cabins and recreation rooms are located, one or two men to each cabin. After dark, streetlights illumine the deck, although I suppose they're called something else. Forward is the officers' quarters, also my own large cabin and bathroom, which fact makes me feel somewhat non-proletarian. There are probably a dozen television sets aboard, and nearly everyone has at least a radio. The meals? Well, the meals are ambrosia and nectar—in fact roast beef, steak, ham, ice cream, the best of everything. Three meat courses for lunch and dinner. Glynn Perry, the First Cook from Roseway, Nova Scotia, could give lessons to a chef at the Queen Elizabeth or Royal York. Leo Riviera, Second Cook, would come first in any culinary contest judged by me.

All these accolades may sound as if I'm being carried away by shipboard luxury. Well, consider this: deckhands are paid between $900 and $1100 a month, and I don't think that they work very hard, daintily touching up rusted paintwork. For three months in the winter they collect unemployment insurance and drink beer. It occurs to me that I should have known about all this sooner, so that I too could have lived like Mary Pickford and that guy in the Boldt Castle, a middle-aged Croesus happily adding up the interest on my paycheques.

But it is not quite so simple. If not deprivation, there definitely is boredom on board a ship. Leo Riviera says, "You can't see your family for months on end. And what if you need a doctor or dentist in the middle of Lake Ontario? What happens then?"

(Of course, if there's something *really* wrong with you they can get a helicopter by radio-telephone.)

And George Rollier, who is French-French, says, "It's not like being on a deep-sea ship, there's not the same sense of brotherhood and good feeling."

And "Peewee," who is seventeen years old, has decided that after another two or three months, "I'm gone!" One youngster who signed on at Thorold jumped ship between locks at the Welland Canal, perhaps in a sudden frenzy of homesickness. Another deckhand, also from Thorold, demanded his pay in Baie Comeau at 4 A.M., but the Second Mate wouldn't wake Captain Freeman at that hour. Whereupon the discontented seaman jumped ship, stole a milk truck, and drove east until he was picked up by the Quebec Provincial Police at Forestville, seventy miles east.

The *Golden Hind* anchors in the St. Lawrence just below Montreal because of a labour slowdown at Baie Comeau. The stevedores' union there is deliberating about whether the men will go on strike or not. An electrician, nicknamed Freddy Kilowatt, has severe pains in his chest. He is sent to a hospital in the city. And Mike McNulty, one of the young deckhands, has love problems. It seems that there was this girl who liked him much, but he (the cad) brushed her off. She took him at his word and would have no more to do with him, despite prolonged pleading on Mike's part after he discerned the girl's true worth (because of her good judgment in males).

"Will you write me a letter to her?" Mike says, me not having made any secret of being a hack writer.

"Would that be honest?" I ask delicately. "Wouldn't it be love under false pretenses or something?"

"Never mind that. If the letter works, our first child will be named Al."

Okay.

Dear Mary:

I thought of you at the Welland locks, I thought of you anchored below Montreal, and I'll be thinking of you at Tadoussac and Baie Comeau if and when we ever get there. Right now there's a yellow cloud from a factory across the river reflecting itself on the water. It made me think of the yellow rose I gave you, before the ship sailed, to win you back. . . .

"Mike, it's no good. Would any self-respecting, honest-to-goodness, red-blooded Canadian gal go for crap like that? She sounds too nice to con her, even if I could. I can't do it."

"Yes, you'll have to do better," Mike says judiciously.

"She won't believe it's you!"

"I'll tell her I had help, and besides, the first child will be named—"

"Yes, I know, after me. But the second and third and fourth, what about them?"

"By that time she'll be cussing you so bad you'll hear it in your grave." We stare at each other a moment, and I can see that it is the moment of truth.

"All right, okay," I say to Mike. "I will, in my own inimitable manner and with all the one-syllable words at my command, flatter the hell outa her. What colour hair and eyes?"

After one day near Montreal the *Golden Hind* raised anchor for Ile du Bic, in the St. Lawrence near Rimouski, and there awaited further orders. It's some thirty degrees colder in this area, with still two feet of snow a few miles inland—and it's the beginning of June. Opposite the ship, several miles distant, a string of cottages on the shore looks like stranded icebergs. And just upriver the huge Saguenay River side-swipes the St. Lawrence, marking its passage into the greater river with a five-mile wavery track of foam. On our right—or I should say "starboard"—the freighter Carol Lake has been anchored since May nineteenth, also waiting orders for proceeding to Baie Comeau.

Everyone feels very pessimistic about the stoppage. Captain Freeman says it's just for a few days. First Mate Jean Perusse says a week. Glen Smith, the Third Mate, thinks longer than that. Glynn Perry, the First Cook, says gloomily, "We may never leave." I say hell, or even stronger words.

There's lots of time to talk, and Leo Riviera tells me about this friend of his, a deckhand on another ship, who died near Rimouski a few weeks ago. The remains of Tom Beckles were flown back to Barbados via Air Canada, his wife going with him on what was apparently his last journey. But the Canadian authorities hadn't filled in the cause of his death on the death certificate, so back came the body to Canada again. After which, armed with the proper information this time, Beckles and his widow again returned to Barbados.

But there's a prior episode which makes Beckles' death even more poignant for Leo Riviera. "Tom Beckles saved my life. It was in 1941, and I was working on the old Canadian National Steamship, *Lady Hawkins*, as a bellboy. The ship was torpedoed by a German sub off Cape Hatteras, and went down very quickly. There were a lot of people, crewmen and passengers, in the sea before lifeboats could be launched. I was one of them. The water was so cold that it must've weakened me, and I couldn't climb into the boat. I hung onto the gunwale and yelled: 'Tom, help me, help me!' Tom Beckles reached down and hauled me into that lifeboat. There were seventy people in the lifeboat, including my two brothers. One of my brothers died of exposure before we were rescued. That's why I remember Tom Beckles."

And the morning and the afternoon were the second day of boredom, anchored near Ile du Bic in the St. Lawrence. Therefore I called a Royal Commission to investigate the Ontario Paper Company—with myself the only sitting member. (I'd brought along some relevant books for just this purpose.) It seems that Ontario Paper Company owns the Quebec and Ontario Transportation Company, which owns the *Golden Hind*, among other ships, and is itself a subsidiary of many-tentacled American interests, which also include the New York *News* and Chicago *Tribune*. The *Tribune* leads directly to Colonel Robert McCormick. The colonel, who died in 1955, controlled wide stretches of Canadian pulpwood territory at Baie Comeau and Heron Bay, in order to supply raw material for his paper mills, which in turn fed newsprint to the Chicago and New York dailies. And the spoon that fed paper to the U.S. mouth was Ontario Paper Company.

Colonel McCormick is said to be a legendary character. He is credited with being the founding father of the North Shore towns of Shelter Bay (now Port Cartier) and Baie Comeau, and probably deserves it. But with the credit for providing employment must go some small opprobrium, since the country around both settlements, as well as around Heron Bay, is stripped of forest, and nothing meets the eye but rather unlovely underbrush. On the outskirts of Baie Comeau (population some 30 000) is a large canoe made of bronze, with the life-sized colonel sitting inside bolt upright, like a real *coureur du bois* instead of a newspaper tycoon—no doubt commissioned and paid for by Ontario Paper Company.

Colonel McCormick was not very popular in Canada during the last global conflict. An officer with General "Black Jack" Pershing in the First World War, he became an isolationist in the Second, apparently quite hostile to England, and *ipso facto* to Canada as well. Thunderous editorials against Britain in the Chicago *Tribune* reflected McCormick's anything-but-neutral views. As a result, a groundswell of public opinion in Canada rose up against his papermaking activities in this country, and newspaper editorials here became quite virulent against the colonel.

Perhaps Napoléon Comeau, for whom the town was named, is somewhat more deserving of transient immortal bronze. Before the century's turn, Comeau was a fabulous hunter, trapper, naturalist, and author, who roamed the North Shore performing marvellous feats, rescuing people trapped on ice, and writing books. One of his rescue exploits is depicted on a crest for the new town of Baie Comeau; it is of course, somewhat less expensive than bronze.

One tid-bit of information about papermaking in the nineteenth century, garnered from being the only sitting member on this RoyCom, is fascinating. Newsprint between 1850 and 1860 was made mostly from rags. Thus some newspapers, because of the expense, had to raise their prices to the thenexorbitant ten cents a copy. "Rags were so valuable that enterprising eastern mill operators (presumably in the U.S.) imported shiploads of mummies from Egypt and used the linen wrappings to make paper." Well!—What would Anwar Sadat or defunct Colonel Nasser say about that? Or Moses, who led the Children of Israel out of Egypt? Some of that rag paper made a hundred years ago—could it have been recycled and used again and again? Are we in Canada, perhaps, reading McClelland and Stewart books printed on shiploads of Egyptian mummies?

And the morning and evening were the third day anchored at Ile du Bic. In dreams at night we sailed from boredom to ennui by way of tedium and monotony. The Scotch was all gone, cigars had to be rationed, and "sleep it is a gentle thing, beloved from pole to pole"—but I couldn't court Morpheus without morphia for more than eight hours. And I'd read all my comic books. Lunch and dinner called for long walks aft to the dining room, but still I wasn't getting enough exercise. Pacing off the distance between cabin areas on the central deck of the 620-foot ship, it came to 325 paces for the full circuit, which ought to be around 975 feet if you're fairly tall like myself. Therefore a dozen circuits of the same deck ought to be at least two miles. So I walked two miles every evening. Observing my laudable attempts to keep in shape from deck chairs aft, the First Cook, the Second Cook, and assorted deckhands made inappropriate comments.

"That crummy writer is off his rocker," said Mike.

"He might be just crazy enough to jump overboard." Peewee remarked. Captain Freeman too looked at me slightly askance. I told him I was investigating the possibility that Canadians could walk faster anchored than Swedes could move on bicycles.

And morning and midnight were the seventh day, after which I rose from my bed and walked ashore at Baie Comeau. Orders had come from above to lift anchor aweigh; the stevedores were placated. The ship finally arrived at Napoléon Comeau's town on June eighth. Long steel-girder conveyors unfolded at the dock like praying mantises, sucking up corn and soy beans from the ship's hold amid a man-created storm of dust. A dozen crew members waited to go ashore at the gangplank, all dressed in good non-working clothes and looking strange to me, with a glow of anticipation on their faces. Anticipation for what?

Beer, and more beer, and more beer. The tables were loaded with it. But I couldn't keep up with them. The last I saw of Mike and Peewee was at the pub in Baie Comeau. They waved to me—on their way to more interesting establishments.

During the flight back to Montreal, I kept thinking of that immense river. The St. Lawrence, more than any other, is the River of Canada. You can't row a boat or swim a stroke there without crossing the paths of Jacques Cartier and Samuel de Champlain. Both are basic to what we were and what we have become.

After the long Atlantic journey, then the immigration station at Grosse Isle, newcomers were ferried with muscle and sweat by *bateau* and shank's mare to Lower and Upper Canada. Where there was no beer waiting for them. It is difficult not to think of those people on the river, the dispossessed from France, England, Scotland, and Ireland; difficult because we are their children, and their children's children.

From *No Other Country* (Toronto: McClelland and Stewart, 1977), 78–88. Published in an earlier form in *Weekend* (1974).

Aklavik on the Mackenzie River

AL PURDY

They came over the land bridge connecting Asia with Alaska, those first men in the Western Hemisphere. The date was between 20 000 and 30 000 years ago. They were short and heavily built people with thick black hair, brown faces, and slightly slanted eyes. They were hunters, dressed in the skins of animals they hunted. Their weapons were stone-tipped spears. All this was long before Homer, before the dynasties of Egypt, before Sumer and the Land of the Two Rivers, and, of course, long before our Christian Bible was written.

At that time the glaciers that had covered Canada and parts of the northeastern United States during the last ice age were melting. They melted first along river valleys, which turned into great misty, fog-haunted corridors between receding walls of ice. One of these river-valley corridors is known today as the Mackenzie River in the Northwest Territories.

The hunters roamed south along melting corridors of ice, pursuing animals for food and clothing. They died eventually, as all people do, and their children came after them in the long stammering repetition of humanity everywhere. The animals they hunted were principally caribou, bear, and mammoth—the latter long since extinct in North America. Camps of some of those early men have been discovered recently. They are the ghostly forbears of modern Indians and Eskimos.

▼ ▼ ▼

"Coffee, sir?" the Pacific Western Airlines stewardess wants to know. She is black-haired and shapely, almost distracting me from my thoughts about those early people. I'm flying north from Edmonton to read poems at libraries of settlements in the Northwest Territories. I decline coffee politely and ask for beer. There is none.

Under me and under the big aeroplane is the Mackenzie River, concealed at this moment by cloud cover. The Mackenzie River drainage system is the biggest in Canada. It rises in the Rocky Mountains with the name of Athabaska, which flows east and then north to its namesake lake. The Slave River flows north from Lake Athabaska to empty into Great Slave Lake; and forty miles from Hay River on this lake, the true Mackenzie begins its thousand-mile journey north to the Beaufort Sea.

At 7:15 P.M. on May 23, we land at Inuvik Airport. Dick Hill, the quiet-mannered director of Inuvik Research Laboratories, drives me to town over a dirt road. High plumes of dust trail behind every car. I register at the Eskimo Inn, which has seventy-nine rooms and colour TV via satellite. Taxis outside are coated with half-inch-thick layers of dust. Taxis and colour TV! Can this be the Arctic of fierce husky dogs and bearded veterans of the north?

The temperature is about 40°F; population is about 5000 people, living and working in buildings resting on piles to make their uneasy peace with the permafrost, which under us is a thousand-foot-thick ice animal crouching. After falling asleep around 11 P.M., I awake briefly at four to find that the day still hasn't stopped or night begun. It is comforting to find that my childhood myths about the land of the midnight sun and its red-mouthed slavering polar bears were not entirely imaginary.

On Saturday, May 24, the sun is shining and the air outside is comfortable for me clad in tweed jacket and sweater. The big question now is how to get to Aklavik, "place of the barren ground grizzly bear," thirty-five miles across the Mackenzie delta. There are no roads. On weekdays, there are commercial flights for paying passengers. But it's Saturday, so I hope to share a charter with someone else.

Aklavik is still a mythic place for me, the big reason why I wanted so badly to come to the western Arctic. Built on sand and sediment thirty feet above the Mackenzie's Peel Channel, threatened by floods every spring (and right now it's spring), inhabited by picturesque trappers and hunters, old codgers breathing history and fire from their own homebrew (I read that somewhere), its existence began in 1915. When the federal government in its wisdom decided in 1954 that Aklavik was unfortunately situated, the town seemed doomed. The new modern Arctic settlement of Inuvik ("the place of man") began to rise on wooden piles in that year, complete with government buildings and schools, fresh water and sewage alike contained in above-ground metal utilidors. The native Indians and Eskimos were supposed to throng to the new town with cries of ecstasy, and some of them did. But it turned out they had to live in the old workers' construction shacks, whereas white workers moved into the newly built houses. Many natives thought they were better off in Aklavik, closer to their traplines, less dependent on white men, and perhaps also closer to their own kind of reality.

So Aklavik refused to lie down and die. Hemmed in by marshes and water, plagued with erosion and haunted by periodic river flooding, it was still a settlement that grew up naturally because of hunting, fishing, and trapping in the delta. There was nothing phony or artificial about it—quite the opposite of the oil-exploration and government town deliberately created at Inuvik; created scientifically and a little cold-bloodedly, a hovering outpost of southern man near the Arctic Sea. Aklavik's character is slightly raffish, a little off-colour—perhaps not quite so respectable. But it's much closer to my own romantic idea of the north, of Eskimos living comfortably amid ice and snow, of arctic explorers and dog teams galloping across the tundra. The Canadian arctic has changed greatly, and no longer are the old and admittedly romantic conceptions possible. Just the same, I cling to them; I like the idea of a town like Aklavik, rejecting the outside world—but, significantly, not its electricity and septic tanks.

I flew to Aklavik on Sunday in a Cessna 180. These tiny aeroplanes resemble an exceptionally large mosquito that climbs up the sky on a cobweb to an altitude of 3000 feet. At that height you get a wide-angle view of the 10 000 square-mile Mackenzie delta, which is over a hundred miles long. The river splits into three channels at Point Separation farther south, then becomes an immense soggy blotting pad containing literally thousands of lakes—or perhaps thousands of islands, because land and water are so interwoven that you can't tell which is which. Seventy miles north of here is the Beaufort Sea, with oil exploration going on in both the delta and arctic waters beyond. West is the Richardson Mountain chain; under us a dozen geese homing to their summer nesting grounds.

We land on a dirt runway and trundle to a bumpy stop. Beside the field is a small log structure, about ten feet by twelve, which is apparently the airport terminal: Aklavik International Airport? I say goodbye to the Cessna pilot, who is scheduled to return for me this evening at eight. It's now 9:15 A.M. so I have nearly eleven hours in which I can talk to people. But there is no one in sight, even though the Cessna landed close to the centre of Aklavik. Dick Hill had given me the name of the settlement-council chairman, Don McWatt, but I don't know where he lives. The whole community seems to be asleep, nothing moves. Only some formidable-looking husky dogs lift their heads as I walk past, and give me a sleepy evil eye: they don't like strangers.

At Aklavik, there are frame houses and trailers here and there, squatting in the mud; mounds of snow and ice, slowly melting in the 60° sun; tin cans and bottles along the boardwalk awaiting spring clean-up; and two graveyards in the town centre, with wooden crosses and markers surrounded by a white picket fence: *Dearly Beloved*s and *RIP*s cradled by water and mud. Mackie's General Store is locked and smokeless. The hotel-cum-restaurant has apparently never had a guest; the pool room is almost noisy with silence. There's a feeling of slight panic: I may walk these dirt streets all day long and never see a human face.

Two blocks away some native kids are walking. I hurry after them, but they disappear like smoke before I can catch up and ask directions to Don McWatt's house. It's like being born again into a world so different from the fat south that your mind works hard to adjust. I intrude past a sign that says "No Admittance" into the electric generating plant, where the man on duty tells me that Don McWatt lives in a white trailer, in a north-south-east-west direction from the river.

Don McWatt's place is completely silent, and I feel embarrassed at knocking and breaking into people's sleep. Some dogs in the willow brush behind make their displeasure known. But Don finally comes to the door sleepily.

Don is a Scotsman, a husky man in a T-shirt. He has a native wife and two children, works for the government, and does a little of everything to make a living. He thinks Aklavik is a great place to live, "At least I did until that thing happened a year ago. I thought this was the ideal place where you settle down and feel at home."

And he told me about the murder: it seems that this Eskimo kid got liquored up last year and killed a priest. Why? There is no certain answer to that question, except that in Aklavik most native people are on social assistance, welfare, call it what you like. The people are split roughly into three divisions, Loucheaux Indians, Eskimos, and whites. Some members of these racial groups mix socially, but many do not. Native teenagers don't know what to do with their time; there is nothing that allows them to keep their self-respect, and most are handicapped by lack of training and education. Hunting, fishing, and trapping are the traditional occupations, but they don't provide a good living any more: not with the oil companies splashing money around lavishly and old native values disappearing quickly in this new world of the white man's north. So Don McWatt is worried over a possible explosion soon, one that will make his "ideal place to live" a battleground of racial warfare.

Neighbour Frank Rivet is sixty-eight, a veteran hunter and trapper with deep lines creasing both cheeks and a greying moustache. Frank won't allow me to use my cassette recorder, says his story is worth lots of money: "I can get thousands of dollars for it from a man in the States!" Well, then, can I make notes? It seems I can, yes. George Kuzzinie, an Indian friend of the family, comes calling. Both Frank and George agree that the Canadian Broadcasting Corporation is "the rottenest thing in the world. All the people here want to see murder, adventure, westerns. What do we get? Culture!" Their voices drip with disgust.

Frank says that 500 caribou were killed and left to rot in the Coppermine country east of here. "There won't be any caribou left if that sort of thing keeps on," he says. George Kuzzinie agrees. A few years ago 275 000 muskrats were taken in the delta: this year, only 40 000. Things are bad all over. "But I have this beautiful agate," Frank says. "My agate has pictures inside it, a lot of pictures, inside the stone itself. I want a million dollars for it."

Frank looks at me. Well, I don't have a million dollars in my pocket, at least not right at this moment. Frank seems to feel that I ought to have that money and it's hard to explain to him that I don't. So I asked about racial tension.

He says, "The country belongs to everybody." Which is a pretty good answer, except that some people generally want more of it than others.

Joe Carnagursky is something else again. He and his wife Dinah are both twenty-nine; their new house is the finest in Aklavik. Joe is of Czech extraction, has been here eight years. Dinah's great-grandfather was John Firth, a Hudson's Bay Company factor called the "King of the North," ruling over a lonely empire on the shores of the Arctic Sea before the century's turn. Dinah is part Loucheaux Indian, and her looks are somewhere between merely pretty and extremely beautiful. I kid her about entering a local beauty contest. She replies pertly that she'd never enter one—"then nobody else would have a chance." Joe and his brother operate Carn Construction, perhaps the biggest such outfit in the Territories.

I happened to have arrived here on the anniversary of Aklavik's murderous night a year ago. The circumstances of that night are still fresh in Joe's and Dinah's minds. One Peter Thrasher, an Alaska Eskimo now living in Aklavik, had received $805 in land settlement money on that date. He put most of it in the bank, bought some clothes and liquor at Inuvik, and gave his son twenty dollars. Whereupon the sixteen-year-old Eugene Lawrence Thrasher got very drunk, whether on his father's whisky or on local homebrew no one seems to know. He broke into the HBC store with an axe and stole a rifle, then made for the Catholic rectory. There he was overheard quarrelling loudly with Father Franche, a much-respected sixty-seven-year-old priest. Father Franche appears to have ejected Thrasher from the rectory. Once outside the young Eskimo fired a bullet through the closed door, wounding the old man seriously. Then he ran.

RCMP Constable Charles Bunting followed the crazed youngster toward some willows beside the river, fired three warning shots over his head, then was shot himself. Frank Rivet, an expert marksman, heard the bombardment, and heard the wounded policeman call, "Shoot him. He shot the priest."

Frank Rivet fired one shot, intending to disable the boy. The slug hit young Thrasher in the chest, killing him. And later that night, another sixteen-year-old, Charles Koe, a friend of Lawrence Thrasher's, got drunk and sprayed bullets into the settlement in all directions. Another constable, rushed in to Aklavik after the earlier shooting, killed Koe. Three people died: Father Franche, Lawrence Thrasher, and Charles Koe.

Terror still haunts Aklavik from that night. Dinah Carnagursky thinks Frank Rivet should have brought down young Thrasher without killing him. Which, of course, is easy to say if you aren't on the scene yourself. Joe Carnagursky says Rivet could only see a small part of the boy's body, and had to bring him down the best way he could.

"And there's still a lot of racial tension here," Joe says. The Indian Brotherhood, the Métis Association, and COPE, the Eskimo organization, are all stirring up trouble. Native kids have nothing to do with themselves, no money or way to get it except by trapping muskrats.

After all this talk of hatred and murder, Dinah says, "I don't like whites!" And yet she is married to a wealthy white man, has many white friends, lives in the settlement's best house.

▼ ▼ ▼

Peter Thrasher, father of the dead boy, is forty-seven, a man built along the lines of an Arctic Hercules run slightly to fat. He weighs 265 pounds, has a bad back, and is a diabetic. He works at Aklavik's fur garment shop. In Peter's kitchen kids scurry back and forth. Soon the whole Thrasher family is going into the bush on a picnic, to take advantage of the warm, sunny weather. I avoid mention of Peter's dead son, thinking that he must have talked about that more than he likes. I do ask him about racial tension. "There is none," he says flatly. More contradictions, a perfect maze of differing opinions.

Peter Thrasher went to mission school as a youngster, but his grandfather, Mingaksek, took him out of school at age fifteen to learn hunting, trapping, and wilderness survival. Mingaksek taught him everything. Once, when the boy nearly drowned in an Arctic river, his grandfather pulled him out and dosed him with homebrew to prevent pneumonia. Mingaksek was father and mother to Peter, since the boy's own mother died spitting blood when he was even younger. Peter followed the old man around everywhere, plainly worshipping him. Man and boy, the two could walk fifteen hours a day on their trapline and keep it up for weeks. As a man come to his full strength, Peter could take 800 pounds on his back and walk with it. Mingaksek died in 1964. Peter dug his grave above the permafrost.

Peter's son is dead, killed by Frank Rivet; Peter's daughter is in a mental hospital at Red Deer, Alberta, because she began to hate all white people after her brother's death; Peter himself is a diabetic with a bad back. Beyond my understanding, he seems to have adjusted to all this tragedy. In the northern world, where nearly everything has changed from the old days, in which roads and pipelines have altered migration patterns of game animals, with oil and gas exploration throughout the Arctic, Peter Thrasher has retained a humanity and warmth I could feel even as a complete stranger.

I walk among willows bordering the river, near the place where young Thrasher was killed. The banks are lined with steel plates against spring break-up, when ice chews at the soft land, sometimes breaking off fifty-foot chunks of it, and carries the dissolving landscape north to the Beaufort Sea. Brown caribou skins rot among bottles and tin cans. Forty miles away the Richardson mountains lift white peaks to the western horizon. It is a country of such mixed squalor and grandeur, of violence and peace, that one comes to terms with it only on *its* terms. But white men have never done that, and the day of the hunter is almost over.

As I fly back to Inuvik in early evening, a solid wall of cloud is rolling in from the Beaufort Sea. Soon everything—man, beast, and mountains—will be covered by that huge overcoat. Glancing down some three hundred feet I see the small Cessna reflected on water, apparently trapped inside a circle of mist in which a rainbow is also trapped. At this moment Peter Thrasher and his family must be gathering up knives and forks and tablecloth and picnic lunch to escape the threatening sky.

Peter is a descendant of those long-ago hunters venturing along glacier-shadowed corridors of northern rivers, hunters of the mammoth and caribou, hunters of the bear. Those prehistoric Asian people moved eastward and the people of Europe moved westward during the long-past millennia, the two finally meeting just a few centuries ago on the eastern seaboard of North America. Westward explorations of Europeans, during the last 500 years, are known and mapped. Eastward migrations of Asians stopped long ago on this continent and turned south. But I have an inexplainable feeling—because of all these eastward and westward movements—that everyone may have been looking for everyone else on the face of the Earth. And that migrations and explorations might have deeper motives than the mere pursuit of food and profit: because humanity has always been searching for itself.

From *No Other Country* (Toronto: McClelland and Stewart, 1977), 142–51. Written in 1976.

MAVIS GALLANT (1922–) is among Canada's best writers of fiction. Known primarily for her short stories, she has also written distinguished essays, novels (*Green Water, Green Sky*, 1960), and a fascinating play, *What Is to Be Done?* (1983). Born in Montreal, she was educated at a variety of Catholic and Protestant schools. She went to work for the National Film Board in 1943, and then took a job with the *Montreal Standard*, for which she wrote feature articles, reviews, and eventually a weekly column. Her work as a reporter was an important apprenticeship for her. As she told an interviewer in 1978, "Writers always imagine it easy to be a reporter, not to speak of a moral philosopher. The latter is simpler. One of the hardest things in the world is to describe what happened next." After a short-lived marriage, she moved to Europe in 1950 to try living on her own and supporting herself through her writing. The *New Yorker* accepted one of her stories in 1951, and has subsequently published over one hundred others. Her first volume of short fiction, *The Other Paris*, was published in 1956, its title referring to the city where she continues to make her home.

Though Gallant's status as an expatriate living in France prevented her from receiving the recognition she deserved in Canada, at least until recently, her sharply observed and intelligent fiction has for a long time now received glowing reviews from an international audience. In characteristically forthright language she insists that living in Paris in no way makes her less Canadian: "I have no identity problem concerning Canada. . . . In fact, I don't believe anyone has. It's something people like to imagine about themselves because it sounds tense and stormy and romantic." Her encyclopedic range of interests and an intimate knowledge of her subjects—the student uprisings in Paris in May 1968, fascism, history, architecture—make her essays particularly informative and stimulating. The one featured here is her introduction to *Home Truths: Selected Canadian Stories* (1981), which won the Governor General's Award.

MAVIS GALLANT

Home Truths

Only personal independence matters.
Boris Pasternak

A Montreal collector once told me that he bought Canadian paintings in order to have a unifying theme in the decoration of his house. It means—if anything so silly can have a meaning—that art is neutral adornment, a slightly superior brand of chintz, and that Canadian painters, because they are Canadian, work from a single vision.

Like most of us, the collector probably has a defined range of taste, and he is drawn to painting that happens to fall within its scope. This will not prevent him from showing visitors art that can be seen in good galleries all over Western Europe, not to speak of in the United States, and calling it "typically" and even "uniquely" Canadian. He has paid for an exclusive point of view; if art is universal, then he has been cheated.

To dissent would lead into hostile territory. It might be considered un-Canadian, an accusation to which the expatriate writer is particularly susceptible, and will go to some lengths to avoid. I have been rebuked by a consular official for remarking that Rome in winter is not as cold as Montreal; and it surely signifies more than lightheadedness about English that "expatriate" is regularly spelled in Canadian newspapers "expatriot." Whether they know it or not, Canadian artists are supposed to "paint Canadian."

Domestic embellishment, though of a slightly different nature, is demanded, too, of Canadian writers, though only when their work is concerned with Canada and Canadians; nobody cares what the Canadian author thinks about Tibet. I often have the feeling with Canadian readers that I am on trial.

The accusation has nothing to do with style or structure or content or imagination or control of subject and form—nothing that has any connection with literature in the usual sense—but with what are taken to be my concealed intentions. I am suspected of using language to screen a deep and disobliging meaning, or to perpetrate a fraud. I am asked if such and such a thing described "really happened," or, apparently more important, though entirely beside the point, "Did it actually happen to you?" The tone of the questioning suggests something more antagonistic than simple curiosity, and I wonder if there is not still somewhere a distrust of imagination. The writer, through whose work imagination speaks, has perhaps committed an act of intellectual deception, evidence of which will turn up in the work itself.

There is another question, asked, in my experience, only by Canadians: "Do you mean what you write?" Often the speaker will quote a passage that had offended him, not for what it says, which is plain, but for some unstated disparagement of Canada and Canadians he feels must be lurking behind it. He thinks there is more than meets the eye, and in a sense he is right: fiction, like painting, consists entirely of more than meets the eye; otherwise it is not worth a second's consideration. The interrogation is a settling of accounts with a Canadian who has failed to "paint Canadian." No division is allowed between the writer's citizenship, with its statutory and emotional ties, and his wider allegiance as an artist.

Unless he has rejected his native origin—and there may be many reasons for doing so—a citizen obviously owes more to his own country than to any other. In a democracy most of his obligations are moral and voluntary, and all the more to be observed on that account. But where his work is concerned, the writer, like any other artist, owes no more and no less to his compatriots than to people at large. This is by no means an original idea; it is an old-fashioned, liberal, and humanist one; but it is worth repeating in the present context of an introduction to Canadian stories.

I take it for granted that "Canadian stories" has a specific meaning. In contradiction to everything said above, I am constantly assured that Canadians no longer know what they are, or what to be Canadian should mean; for want of a satisfactory definition, a national identity has been mislaid. The most polite thing I can say about this is that I don't believe it. A Canadian who did not know what it was to be Canadian would not know anything else: he would have to be told his own name. It is as if a reassuring interpretation, a list of characteristics—the more rigid and confining the better—needed to be drawn up and offered for ratification. But ratified by what? A computer? A parliamentary committee? And what defines you will not define your closest relatives.

I suppose that a Canadian is someone who has a logical reason to think he is one. My logical reason is that I have never been anything else, nor has it occurred to me that I might be. I do not mean that traits that make me different from other people in places where I have lived and travelled are recognizably Canadian. I have lived in Paris for many years; when I travel in other parts of Europe I am often taken to be a Frenchwoman and addressed in French. The finest living writer of French prose, Marguerite Yourcenar, has lived in America for some thirty years. Although she writes only in French and, I would guess, thinks in French, I am sure that if I had never seen her picture and were to meet her in a train I would instinctively speak to her in English; there is a superficial coloration, an acquired surface, that reminds one more of—say—Willa Cather than Colette. And yet the essence of her mind, if one can judge from her writings, is wholly French. Except in rare cases of wilful destruction, the essence always remains undiluted.

I have sometimes felt more at odds in Canada than anywhere else, but I never supposed I was any less Canadian. Feeling at odds is to be expected; no writer calls a truce. If he did, he would probably stop writing. I know I could not suddenly turn myself into a Norwegian or a Pole, or, to be reasonable, since I am English-speaking (and not, please, "Anglophone"), into an Australian or an American or an Englishwoman. (The persistent use of "English" in Quebec to designate me and people like me leaves me wondering if any amount of definitions will ever do. I have constantly to explain that if I were *Anglaise* I would hold a British passport and not a Canadian one.)

When in my American schools I refused to salute the flag, as I've described in *In Youth Is Pleasure*, there was more to it than adolescent mulishness. I most certainly did not resent Americans; it was in New York, at fourteen, that I understood for the first time there was a possibility in life of being happy. It was simply that I was not an American, the Stars and Stripes was not my flag, and that was that. I resisted a change of citizenship when it was offered me because I knew the result would be fake: whatever I was called, I would continue to think of myself as Canadian. I believe it is a wholly respectable thing to be. Yet when I say this, it irritates Canadians. They take me to mean conformist, small-minded. I mean the word in its original sense of worthy of respect, the opposite of shameful and disreputable, and I have always made certain that respect was rendered that part of my identity on the few occasions when it has been slighted.

I am puzzled by those Canadians one occasionally meets abroad who seem reluctant to say what they are. (This, most emphatically, does not apply to French Canadians.) Sometimes they try to pass for British, not too successfully, or for someone vaguely chic and transatlantic. I have wondered, but not wanted to ask, how they replace the national sense of self. Once, in a Swiss hospital, emerging from a long anesthetic, I suffered a brief amnesia. I did not know where I was, why I was there, or what language I would be expected to speak. The first fact that floated to the surface was that I was Canadian and, almost simultaneously, that I was from Quebec. I supposed that I must be in a hospital somewhere in Quebec, and that I had been brought there after an automobile accident. I heard someone rustling pages and thought, They are tampering with my manuscripts: I was a writer. After that, the rest followed quickly.

What I am calling, most clumsily, the national sense of self is quite separate from nationalism, which I distrust and reject absolutely, and even patriotism, so often used as a stick to beat people with. Canada is one of the few countries that confers citizenship by birth, and we are apt to think that a national character automatically attaches itself to a birth certificate. The accident of birth does not give rise to a national consciousness, but I think the first years of schooling are indelible. They provide our center of gravity, our initial view of the world, the seed of our sense of culture. A deeper culture is contained in memory. Memory is something that cannot be subsidized or ordained. It can, however, be destroyed; and it is inseparable from language.

▼ ▼ ▼

As far back as I can remember, I read and spoke English and French, at about the same level. I had very young parents and they found it amusing to give me a simple text in English and have me rattle it off in French; it must have been like playing with a mechanical doll. At my first boarding school, in Montreal, I was the only English-speaking child. Toys were banned in this iron institution, but I had been allowed a few picture books from home. One was called *The Joyous Travellers*: a troupe of merry-looking animals adorned the cover; I do not remember what was inside.

In those days—the nineteen-twenties—it seemed to be mandatory for language teachers in both French and English schools in Canada to understand not a word of the language they set out to teach. The nun who taught English, and who might as well have been speaking Swahili for all I ever understood, held the book up to a class of docile little girls and announced that the title meant *Les Joyeux Travailleurs*, or *The Happy Workers*. My objection was taken to be insolence. Insolence was broken by deprivation of food. It is utterly confusing to a small child to be made to swear that black is white, particularly on a subject so vital as language and meaning. I owned up that "travellers" somehow meant the same thing as "workers," and received a dish of bread-and-milk. Children have fierce feelings about injustice and that is probably why the incident lodged in my mind. What interests me about it now is that a deadlock could develop between a grown woman and a child over a word and its meaning. I knew the meaning; she was led astray by the sound.

A few years after this, when I was ten and at school in Ontario, I was stood before a class of children aged about thirteen and instructed to "say something in French"—an idiot request that plagued my school life until I became old enough to resist. I had just come from Montreal, where "saying something in French" had drawn only approval. If it was not a parlor trick many English-speakers could be bothered to learn, it was thought commendable in the intrepid and the young. And so it was with the confidence that rests on applause that I launched into my set recitation of *La cigale et la fourmi*. From the first words a black wave of hatred hit me; I feel it still. They cannot have hated Jean de La Fontaine, for they had never heard of him; nor can it have been disapproval of the rather nasty and ungenerous philosophy of the fable, for they had no idea what I was saying. It was hatred of an alien sound; and yet how alien those other children seemed to me, with their tiny blue eyes and little pug noses and large front teeth, and their flat, breathy way of "saying something in English."

I have never known anyone perfectly bilingual, and I wonder if such a phenomenon can exist this side of schizophrenia—leaving aside certain cases of genius: Samuel Beckett comes to mind. I wonder, even, if it is desirable: one needs a strong, complete language, fully understood, to anchor one's understanding. The rest is a luxury. What I do not understand is the hatred and fear of another sound, or even the lack of curiosity: how can one *not* want to know what other people think and feel, stated on their own terms?

For more than half my life I have heard and spoken more French than English. In the early nineteen-fifties, when I was moving round Europe, French was still the *lingua franca*. The people I see in Paris are for the most part either French or French-speaking; yet it has never occurred to me to write in French. In fact, I do not write it at all well; I spell it atrociously and deliberately refrain from improvement. I have to keep a strong writing wall in place or move to a different country. I think, write, and usually dream in English, and in thirty years have made only two idiomatic errors, one of which I caught: for "the house on the corner" I wrote "the house that makes the corner," a literal rendering of "*la maison qui fait le coin*." The other came back as a puzzled query on a proof: "Is this French?" I had written "a disaffected factory," which I changed to "an abandoned factory," though that is not the exact meaning of "*une usine désaffectée*," the definition I wanted. There is no precise equivalent for much of anything between English and French, and that is why translations almost inevitably fall short. I cannot imagine any of my fiction in French, for it seems to me inextricably bound to English syntax, to the sound, resonance, and ambiguities of English vocabulary. If I were to write in French, not only would I put things differently, but I would never set out to say the same things. Words have an association that the primary, dictionary definitions cannot provide, and that are all translations usually offer. "It was the *best* butter" means nothing unless you know *Alice in Wonderland*. French conversation is totally different from exchange in English. (I mean by this conversation, not "Pass the salt.") The French taste for abstraction sails close to rhetoric and can sound false or insincere to an English-speaking listener, while a conversation in English, with its succession of illustrative anecdotes that take their departure from a point, rather than lead to one, soon bores a mind trained in French.

Gérard's hatred of English in "Saturday" is not blind and irrational. Deprived of the all-important first language, he is intellectually maimed. The most his mind can do is to hobble along. Like every story in this collection [*Home Truths*], "Saturday" needs to be read against its own time—the Montreal of about 1960. Rereading it, I see that it is not about a family or a society in conflict, but about language; or so it seems to me now. I could not write the same thing today; what loomed as cultural life-and-death a generation ago is now reduced to a much narrower preoccupation. Languages other than French and English are spoken in Montreal. I occasionally hear these referred to as "allophylian," with Greek, German, and Italian singled out for what I take to be arbitrary banishment from the Indo-European family. French and English occupy a stage designed to hold all the Aryan and Semitic tongues. It has the majesty of isolation, all right, but in the long run it may be lonely. The giddy misuse of "allophylian" is a good example of a word wrenched from its meaning to suit a transient need or, rather, transient wishful thinking. A writer stumbling over this and other linguistic taradiddles may feel like a grownup entering a nursery where politicians have been throwing blocks around: "Now then, this won't do at all. Put the alphabet back where you found it and try to be intelligible by suppertime."

▼ ▼ ▼

Except for purely professional reasons, such as the writing of this introduction, I do not read my own work after it is in print. I had remembered "Jorinda and Jorindel" completely differently: I thought it was a story about a summer weekend party of adults and that the children were only incidental. Of "Up North" I recalled a war bride and a train, of "Thank You for the Lovely Tea" that it had something to do with a school. All four were published in *The New Yorker* between 1954 and 1959 but are actually much older. I wrote "Tea" in New York, when I was eighteen, and the others in the forties, when I was working on *The Standard* in Montreal. Except for a few notebooks, I destroyed everything I had written when I left for Europe in 1950. Why I kept anything I do not recall. I did not open the notebooks for a long time. I typed "Up North" about eight years later, almost as I found it. Some pages had the wobbly look of having been written in a train, and I probably started it during a journey very like the one described while on assignment for *The Standard*.

I still fill scribblers and exercise books that remain unread for months and years and decades. Not long ago I came across a short novel I must have written twenty-nine years ago. The handwriting is so small that I had to use a magnifying glass. It is set in Spain: I have read so much twaddle written by foreigners about Spain that I was unable to judge it with the confidence I may have brought to writing it. I put it away for "later." "Later" is the imaginary, unhurried, idle future in which I intend to decipher, sort out, type, finish, save, or destroy "everything." I mention this because I know that readers sometimes believe fiction is composed, written, typed, and rushed into print without loss of time. The writer's preoccupations at the moment of publication—as much of these as may be visible—are thought to throw a light of some kind on the work. I am convinced that there is virtually no connection between mood and composition. "How I've fooled them!" Colette once said of critics who saw in one of her novels the mirror of her own life. The span between the germ of an idea and its maturation can be very long indeed, long enough for a writer's life to go through a good many upheavals and changes, particularly of the invisible and probably more devastating sort—intellectual, political. In my own case, the gap can be lengthened by a publishing delay in *The New Yorker* of anywhere from one to four years. By the time I finally read the work in proof, its origin has sunk out of recollection.

The third group of stories in this volume, set in Montreal, connected through a character named Linnet Muir who speaks in the first person, is an exception. I know exactly how the stories came to be written, and why. (Except for "With a Capital T," which appeared in *Canadian Fiction Magazine*, the stories were published in *The New Yorker* between 1975 and 1977, with unusual promptness, each appearing soon after it was received.)

It happened that by the mid-seventies I had been reading virtually nothing for two years except documents and books about the Dreyfus case. (Captain Alfred Dreyfus was a French Army officer, unjustly court-martialled for high treason in 1894, who spent four and a half years in solitary confinement on Devil's Island before being cleared. He was the first Jewish officer to serve at Staff Headquarters. The campaign to free him split French opinion into bitterly opposing factions; the breach has never quite healed.) If one can fix his personality through his letters and diaries and from the recollections of those who knew him, Dreyfus was a complex person, secretive and reserved. I once dreamed that we met and that he had nothing to say to me, which is probably how it might have been in real life. He was not overly interested in people outside his close family circle, and had next to nothing to say to civilians. He was a born soldier, an emotional nineteenth-century French patriot, identified mind and soul with French military attainments, the French military hierarchy, and the supremacy of French military tradition, none of which he ever questioned.

Nothing could be more remote from me than someone who deliberately could choose a life of rules and restrictions, of living by the book—and such a thin volume—with only a soldier's options: "I obey them" and "They obey me," both of which are to me totally abhorrent. Dreyfus came from a bourgeois and provincial family of cotton manufacturers. It was a background that bred good behaviour but did nothing to foster imagination: there are no Dreyfus poets. His brand of impassioned patriotism was a flame of a kind; he lived to see it become murderous in the First World War, though he undoubtedly did not think of it that way; he lived to see Hitler come to power but died before discovering what the triumph of nationalism meant.

We—Dreyfus and I—were opposites in every sense, and had he been living he probably would have told me to leave his life alone. From beyond the grave he had the right to fairness. In writing about him, I could not say what I thought *might* be true, or would seem plausible if only life were tidy. I had to stand in his shoes, to assume, as best I could, an alien ambition (a soldier's career), an alien intelligence (he trained as an engineer and a mathematician before entering staff college), and to forget that I was a woman out of a twentieth-century North American society where women could vote and had the right to an education, where there was no such thing as peacetime conscription or penal transportation.

I used to wonder about the Paris Dreyfus saw—for instance, on the sunny October morning when he left his apartment near the Place de l'Alma to report to the War Ministry on Boulevard Saint-Germain, obeying a trumped-up order that was really a trap. I walked the route he followed many times, just as I often looked at all the paintings and photographs I could find of that particular Paris. Gradually, as I restored his Paris, his life, I discovered something in common with that taciturn, reserved military figure: we had both resolved upon a way of life at an early age and had pursued our aims with overwhelming singlemindedness. He had been determined to become an officer in the French Army, over his family's advice and objections, just as I had been determined to write as a way of life in the face of an almost unanimous belief that I was foolish, would fail, would be sorry, and would creep back with defeat as a return ticket. ("Do you still have those nutty ideas of yours?" I was asked, not so many years ago.)

Once I had a point in common I moved with greater sureness into the book I wanted to write. I had thought of it sometimes as a river where I was drifting farther and farther from shore. At the same time—I suppose about then—there began to be restored in some underground river of the mind a lost Montreal. An image of Sherbrooke Street, at night, with the soft gaslight and leaf shadows on the sidewalk—so far back in childhood that it is more a sensation than a picture—was the starting point. Behind the image was a fictional structure of several stories, in the order in which they are presented here—three wartime stories, then the rest.

The character I called Linnet Muir is not an exact reflection. I saw her as quite another person, but it would be untrue to say that I invented everything. I can vouch for the city: my Montreal is as accurate as memory can make it. I looked nothing up, feeling that if I made a mistake with a street name it had to stand. Memory can spell a name wrong and still convey the truth. *"Je suis un mensonge qui dit la vérité."* That was Jean Cocteau. It is not the last word about the writing of fiction, because no last word exists; but it says, briefly and plainly, what I might put with less grace.

"An Introduction," from *Home Truths: Selected Canadian Stories* (Toronto: Macmillan of Canada, 1981), xi–xxii.

MARGARET LAURENCE (1926–1986) was born in Neepawa, Manitoba, the small town that inspired the fictional Manawaka of such well-known novels as *The Stone Angel* (1964), *A Jest of God* (1966), and *The Diviners* (1974), and the linked short stories of *A Bird in the House* (1970). The latter is a *künstlerroman* whose heroine, Vanessa MacLeod, shares much with the young Laurence herself. Laurence travelled widely throughout her life, living in Africa and England and different regions of Canada; she gives a typically lively account of her experiences in *The Prophet's Camel Bell* (1963). Some of her fiction—*The Tomorrow-Tamer* (1963) and *This Side Jordan* (1960)—is set in Africa (Somaliland and Ghana), and her appreciation of African culture is attested to both in her one book of literary criticism, *Long Drums and Cannons* (1968), and in her translations of Somali folktales and poetry, *A Tree for Poverty* (1954). After returning to Canada for five years in 1957, Laurence and her children moved to England and lived there until 1974, when she returned to Lakefield, Ontario. In the foreword to her book of essays, *Heart of a Stranger* (1976), she writes of her years as a traveller-cum-expatriate and their effect on her perspective:

> One thing I learned, however, was that my experience of other countries probably taught me more about myself and even my own land than it did about anything else. Living away from home gives a new perspective on home. I began to write out of my own background only after I had lived some years away, and when I finally came back to Canada to stay, nearly ten years after I had returned in my fiction, I knew for certain that it was where I belonged, and I knew why.

Laurence is also a popular children's author, having published *Jason's Quest* (1970), *Six Darn Cows* (1979), *The Olden Days Coat* (1979), and *A Christmas Birthday Story* (1980). Her posthumously published autobiography is entitled *Dance on the Earth* (1989).

Generally Laurence's fiction set in Canada portrays female characters in search of freedom and selfhood, winning battles against patriarchal forces which constrict them. Her essays, on the other hand, are personal accounts of her life in foreign lands and her experiences as a writer, told mostly in straightforward fashion, though often in a subtly ironic voice that delicately balances the wryly perceptive and the self-effacing. Near the end of her life, Margaret Laurence became an energetic campaigner for disarmament, a commitment displayed with characteristic humour and passion in the wise and moving "My Final Hour." Of "Where the World Began," the first essay reproduced here, she writes:

> I wrote this article in 1971, when I was beginning my novel, *The Diviners*. I see now that I used it as one more means of working out a theme that appears in the novel, that is, the question of where one belongs and why, and the meaning to oneself of the ancestors, both the long-ago ones and those in remembered history. . . . I didn't realize I had written so much on this theme before I ever dealt with it fictionally. I didn't realize, either, how compulsively I'd written about the river, the same river that appears in the novel.

Where the MARGARET *World Began* LAURENCE

A strange place it was, that place where the world began. A place of incredible happenings, splendours and revelations, despairs like multitudinous pits of isolated hells. A place of shadow-spookiness, inhabited by the unknowable dead. A place of jubilation and of mourning, horrible and beautiful.

It was, in fact, a small prairie town.

Because that settlement and that land were my first and for many years my only real knowledge of this planet, in some profound way they remain my world, my way of viewing. My eyes were formed there. Towns like ours, set in a sea of land, have been described thousands of times as dull, bleak, flat, uninteresting. I have had it said to me that the railway trip across Canada is spectacular, except for the prairies, when it would be desirable to go to sleep for several days, until the ordeal is over. I am always unable to argue this point effectively. All I can say is—well, you really have to live there to know that country. The town of my childhood could be called bizarre, agonizingly repressive or cruel at times, and the land in which it grew could be called harsh in the violence of its seasonal changes. But never merely flat or uninteresting. Never dull.

In winter, we used to hitch rides on the back of the milk sleigh, our moccasins squeaking and slithering on the hard rutted snow of the roads, our hands in ice-bubbled mitts hanging onto the box edge of the sleigh for dear life, while Bert grinned at us through his great frosted moustache and shouted the horse into speed, daring us to stay put. Those mornings, rising, there would be the perpetual fascination of the frost feathers on windows, the ferns and flowers and eerie faces traced there during the night by unseen artists of the wind. Evenings, coming back from skating, the sky would be black but not dark, for you could see a cold glitter of stars from one side of the earth's rim to the other. And then the sometime astonishment when you saw the Northern Lights flaring across the sky, like the scrawled signature of God. After a blizzard, when the snowploughs hadn't yet got through, school would be closed for the day, the assumption being that the town's young could not possibly flounder through five feet of snow in the pursuit of education. We would then gaily don snowshoes and flounder for miles out into the white dazzling deserts, in pursuit of a different kind of knowing. If you came back too close to night, through the woods at the foot of the town hill, the thin black branches of poplar and chokecherry now meringued with frost, sometimes you heard coyotes. Or maybe the banshee wolf-voices were really only inside your head.

Summers were scorching, and when no rain came and the wheat became bleached and dried before it headed, the faces of farmers and townsfolk would not smile much, and you took for granted, because it never seemed to have been any different, the frequent knocking at the back door and the young men standing there, mumbling or thrusting defiantly their requests for a drink of water and a sandwich if you could spare it. They were riding the freights, and you never knew where they had come from, or where they might end up, if anywhere. The Drought and Depression were like evil deities which had been there always. You understood and did not understand.

Yet the outside world had its continuing marvels. The poplar bluffs and the small river were filled and surrounded with a zillion different grasses, stones, and weed flowers. The meadowlarks sang undaunted from the twanging telephone wires along the gravel highway. Once we found an old flat-bottomed scow, and launched her, poling along the shallow brown waters, mending her with wodges of hastily chewed Spearmint, grounding her among the tangles of yellow marsh marigolds that grew succulently along the banks of the shrunken river, while the sun made our skins smell dusty-warm.

My best friend lived in an apartment above some stores on Main Street (its real name was Mountain Avenue, goodness knows why), an elegant apartment with royal-blue velvet curtains. The back roof, scarcely sloping at all, was corrugated tin, of a furnace-like warmth on a July afternoon, and we would sit there drinking lemonade and looking across the back lane at the Fire Hall. Sometimes our vigil would be rewarded. Oh joy! Somebody's house burning down! We had an almost-perfect callousness in some ways. Then the wooden tower's bronze bell would clonk and toll like a thousand speeded funerals in a time of plague, and in a few minutes the team of giant black horses would cannon forth, pulling the fire wagon like some scarlet chariot of the Goths, while the firemen clung with one hand, adjusting their helmets as they went.

The oddities of the place were endless. An elderly lady used to serve, as her afternoon tea offering to other ladies, soda biscuits spread with peanut butter and topped with a whole marshmallow. Some considered this slightly eccentric, when compared with chopped egg sandwiches, and admittedly talked about her behind her back, but no one ever refused these delicacies or indicated to her that they thought she had slipped a cog. Another lady dyed her hair a bright and cheery orange, by strangers often mistaken at twenty paces for a feather hat. My own beloved stepmother wore a silver fox neckpiece, a whole pelt, *with the embalmed (?) head still on*. My Ontario Irish grandfather said, "sparrow grass," a more interesting term than asparagus. The town dump was known as "the nuisance grounds," a phrase fraught with weird connotations, as thought the effluvia of our lives was beneath contempt but at the same time was subtly threatening to the determined and sometimes hysterical propriety of our ways.

Some oddities were, as idiom had it, "funny ha ha"; others were "funny peculiar." Some were not so very funny at all. An old man lived, deranged, in a shack in the valley. Perhaps he wasn't even all that old, but to us he seemed a wild Methuselah figure, shambling among the underbrush and the tall couchgrass, muttering indecipherable curses or blessings, a prophet who had forgotten his prophesies. Everyone in town knew him, but no one knew him. He lived among us as though only occasionally and momentarily visible. The kids called him Andy Gump, and feared him. Some sought to prove their bravery by tormenting him. They were the mediaeval bear baiters, and he the lumbering bewildered bear, half blind, only rarely turning to snarl. Everything is to be found in a town like mine. Belsen, writ small but with the same ink.

All of us cast stones in one shape or another. In grade school, among the vulnerable and violet girls we were, the feared and despised were those few older girls from what was charmingly termed "the wrong side of the tracks." Tough in talk and tougher in muscle, they were said to be whores already. And may have been, that being about the only profession readily available to them.

The dead lived in that place, too. Not only the grandparents who had, in local parlance, "passed on" and who gloomed, bearded or bonneted, from the sepia photographs in old albums, but also the uncles, forever eighteen or nineteen, whose names were carved on the granite family stones in the cemetery, but whose bones lay in France. My own young mother lay in that graveyard, beside other dead of our kin, and when I was ten, my father, too, only forty, left the living town for the dead dwelling on the hill.

When I was eighteen, I couldn't wait to get out of that town, away from the prairies. I did not know then that I would carry the land and town all my life within my skull, that they would form the mainspring and source of the writing I was to do, wherever and however far away I might live.

This was my territory in the time of my youth, and in a sense my life since then has been an attempt to look at it, to comes to terms with it. Stultifying to the mind it certainly could be, and sometimes was, but not to the imagination. It was many things, but it was never dull.

The same, I now see, could be said for Canada in general. Why on earth did generations of Canadians pretend to believe this country dull? We knew perfectly well it wasn't. Yet for so long we did not proclaim what we knew. If our upsurge of so-called nationalism seems odd or irrelevant to outsiders, and even to some of our own people (*what's all the fuss about?*), they might try to understand that for many years we valued ourselves insufficiently, living as we did under the huge shadows of those two dominating figures, Uncle Sam and Britannia. We have only just begun to value ourselves, our land, our abilities. We have only just begun to recognize our legends and to give shape to our myths.

There are, God knows, enough aspects to deplore about this country. When I see the killing of our lakes and rivers with industrial wastes, I feel rage and despair. When I see our industries and natural resources increasingly taken over by America, I feel an overwhelming discouragement, especially as I cannot simply say "damn Yankees." It should never be forgotten that it is we ourselves who have sold such a large amount of our birthright for a mess of plastic Progress. When I saw the War Measures Act being invoked in 1970, I lost forever the vestigial remains of the naive wish-belief that repression could not happen here, or would not. And yet, of course, I had known all along in the deepest and often hidden caves of the heart that anything can happen anywhere, for the seeds of both man's freedom and his captivity are found everywhere, even in the microcosm of a prairie town. But in raging against our injustices, our stupidities, I do so *as family*, as I did, and still do in writing about those aspects of my town which I hated and which are always in some ways aspects of myself.

The land still draws me more than other lands. I have lived in Africa and in England, but splendid as both can be, they do not have the power to move me in the same way as, for example, that part of southern Ontario where I spent four months last summer in a cedar cabin beside a river. "Scratch a Canadian, and you find a phony pioneer," I used to say to myself in warning. But all the same it is true, I think, that we are not yet totally alienated from physical earth, and let us only pray we do not become so. I once thought that my lifelong fear and mistrust of cities made me a kind of old-fashioned freak; now I see it differently.

The cabin has a long window across its front western wall, and sitting at the oak table there in the mornings, I used to look out at the river and at the tall trees beyond, green-gold in the early light. The river was bronze; the sun caught it strangely, reflecting upon its surface the near-shore sand ripples underneath. Suddenly, the crescenting of a fish, gone before the eye could clearly give image to it. The old man next door said these leaping fish were carp. Himself, he preferred muskie, for he was a real fisherman and the muskie gave him a fight. The wind most often blew from the south, and the river flowed toward the south, so when the water was wind-riffled, and the current was strong, the river seemed to be flowing both ways. I liked this, and interpreted it as an omen, a natural symbol.

A few years ago, when I was back in Winnipeg, I gave a talk at my old college. It was open to the public, and afterward a very old man came up to me and asked me if my maiden name had been Wemyss. I said yes, thinking he might have known my father or my grandfather. But no. "When I was a young lad," he said, "I once worked for your great-grandfather, Robert Wemyss, when he had the sheep ranch at Raeburn." I think that was a moment when I realized all over again something of great importance to me. My long-ago families came from Scotland and Ireland, but in a sense that no longer mattered so much. My true roots were here.

I am not very patriotic, in the usual meaning of that word. I cannot say "My country right or wrong" in any political, social or literary context. But one thing is inalterable, for better or worse, for life.

This is where my world began. A world which includes the ancestors—both my own and other people's ancestors who become mine. A world which formed me, and continues to do so, even while I fought it in some of its aspects, and continue to do so. A world which gave me my own lifework to do, because it was here that I learned the sight of my own particular eyes.

From *Heart of a Stranger* (Toronto: McClelland and Stewart, 1976), 213–19. Published earlier in *Maclean's* (December 1972).

MARGARET LAURENCE

My Final Hour

I am being given a unique opportunity. I will not have to postpone until my last gasp the imparting of the wisdom of my accumulated years to a breathlessly awaiting world. Just as well, as I have never been much of a believer in "famous last words." I suppose this is why King Lear's words, "Prithee, undo this button" seem infinitely more moving to me than any highflown rhetoric purportedly uttered by some well-known person when on the point of departing this vale of tears. Anyway, here I am, faced with the prospect of delivering the message of My Final Hour. I do not promise that it will be My Finest Hour, but I will do my best.

First, I would like to pass on one piece of advice. If, as you grow older, you feel you are also growing stupider, do not worry. This is normal, and usually occurs around the time when your children, now grown, are discovering the opposite—they now see that you aren't nearly as stupid as they had believed when they were young teen-agers. Take heart from that. True, your new-found sense of stupidity will no doubt be partly due to the fact that the technology of the age has far outstripped any feeble knowledge of it that you may once have felt you had. It may, however, also be due to the fact that at last you may be learning a little healthy humility—humility in its true and indeed religious sense, which of course has nothing at all to do with self-effacement but with a recognition of your human limitations. I would not claim that I have learned that kind of humility—that struggle to learn will never cease. But at least I now can accept with some sort of equanimity that many things are beyond my power. I can try to help friends or family or strangers, but I can never "save" another in the profoundest sense. I can do what is within my human power, that is all. Anything else is delusion or spiritual pride, or so I believe. My limitations extend to many fields. I know now that I will never know an enormous amount about music or painting. My knowledge of science is likely to remain minuscule. I will never know as much as I would like to about the planets and their patterned courses. Even in my own area of so-called expertise, I will never read all the novels I would like to read, even though I read great numbers of them yearly. I will also never write a novel with which I am really satisfied. There is so much to do, so much to learn and experience, and one lifetime, however long it may be, is so short. I think of the verse from Psalms 39: "Here my prayer, O Lord, and give ear unto my cry; hold not thy peace at my tears; for I am a stranger with thee, and a sojourner, as all my fathers were." Mothers, too, I feel compelled to add. Sojourner, yes, but this need not mean "tourist." My lifetime here is a short span, but I am not here as a visitor. Earth is my home. I have tried to read as widely as I can; I have always believed I had to live as well as write, to be a citizen and a person and a mother and a friend as well as a writer. But basically, I have spent a great part of my adult life in learning a profession—or, as I prefer to call it, a trade—that can never be mastered in its complexity and richness. I am fond of the story about the brain surgeon, who, meeting a novelist at a party, says, "Oh . . . you're a novelist, eh? When I retire, I plan to take up novel writing." "How interesting," the novelist replies. "When *I* retire, I plan to take up brain surgery."

Well, an acceptance of limitations does not mean that one is not constantly trying to extend the boundaries of knowledge and accomplishment. And it certainly does not mean an acceptance of defeat, in whatever fields our endeavours take place. It is my feeling that as we grow older we should become not *less* radical but *more* so. I do not, of course, mean this in any political-party sense, but in a willingness to struggle for those things in which we passionately believe. Social activism and the struggle for social justice are often thought of as natural activities of the young but not of the middle-aged or elderly. In fact, I don't think this was ever true, and certainly in our own era we are seeing an enormous upsurge of people of all ages who are deeply and committedly concerned about the state of our hurting and endangered world. There is a line from the old Anglo-Saxon poem, "The Battle of Maldon," that I think of frequently. It is this: "Mind must be the firmer, heart the more fierce, courage the greater, as our strength diminishes."

So the basic message of My Final Hour would have to be—do not despair. Act. Speak out. In the words of one of my heroines, Catharine Parr Traill, "In cases of emergency, it is folly to fold one's hands and sit down to bewail in abject terror. It is better to be up and doing."

▾ ▾ ▾

We are faced now with an emergency that concerns not only our own personal lives, but the lives of all people and all creatures on earth. Ours is a terrifying world. Injustice, suffering, and fear are everywhere to be found. It is difficult to maintain hope in such a world, and yet I believe there must be hope. I want to proclaim my belief in the social gospel, as a Christian, a woman, a writer, a mother, and a member of humanity, a sharer in a life that I believe in some way to be informed by the holy spirit. I do not think it is enough to hope and pray that our own lives and souls will know grace, even though my entire life as a writer has been concerned with my belief that all individual human beings matter, that no one is ordinary. The new commandment of the man of Nazareth speaks very clearly. "Thou shalt love thy neighbour as thyself."

The social gospel is no easier now than it ever was. My generation was the first in human history to come into young adulthood knowing that the human race now had the dreadful ability to destroy all life on earth and possibly the earth itself. Only later did we realize the full extent of the destruction of life, a continuing destruction passed on to the then-unborn children of the survivors, but we *did* know that after Hiroshima, August 6, 1945, the world would never be the same again. The annihilation caused by the first atomic bombs was unthinkable, but it had happened. Also, we had taken it for granted that through wars, through disasters, yet would the earth endure forever. It was clear to many of us in 1945 that this was no longer to be taken for granted. We have lived with that thought ever since, and have yet borne our children, lived our lives, done our work. The will to survive and to pass on important caring to future generations is very strong. But today we have to realize that the bombs used at Hiroshima and Nagasaki were *small* bombs, compared to today's nuclear weapons.

I ask you to think of the Holocaust in Europe, when the Nazis murdered a very great part of all the Jewish communities. That horror, surely, must *never* be forgotten. No amount of mourning will *ever* be enough for those millions of children, women, and men whose lives were torn from them by a group of de-humanized humans who had taken power in Hitler's Germany. Are we to remember the Holocaust and the horrors of Hiroshima and Nagasaki and yet remain silent when we hear today about a "winnable" nuclear war or a "limited" nuclear war? I think not.

Our lives and the lives of all generations as yet unborn are being threatened, as never before, by the increasing possibility of a nuclear war. I believe that the question of disarmament is the most pressing practical, moral, and spiritual issue of our times. I'm not talking about abstractions. I'm talking about my life and your life and my kids' lives and the lives of people everywhere. If we value our own lives, and the lives of our children and all children everywhere, if we honour both the past and the future, then we must do everything in our power to work non-violently for peace. These beliefs are not only an integral part of my social and moral stance but of my religious faith as well. Human society now possesses the terrible ability to destroy all life on earth, and our planet itself. Can anyone who as ever marvelled at the miracle of creation—who has ever borne or fathered a beloved child, who has even looked closely at a tree or a plant or a river—fail to feel concerned and indeed anguished, every single day, at this thought?

A central disagreement, of course, exists between those who think that more and yet more nuclear arms will ensure that nuclear arms will never be used, and those of us who believe that the proliferation of nuclear weapons brings us closer all the time to the actuality of nuclear war—a war that no side could possibly win; a war that would be so devastating that we cannot begin to imagine that horror. Whatever we are being told about a "limited" or a "winnable" nuclear war, the fact remains that such a war could destroy the future, not only of the world's peoples but of all creatures that share our planet with us.

As America and Russia develop more and more nuclear arms, so the other will inevitably respond in kind. Nuclear arms have long since ceased to be a "deterrent," if indeed they were ever so, and have become by their very existence a monstrous threat. Daily, the chances are increasing for a nuclear war to break out by accident, by a failure of the intricate and not totally reliable control and warning systems on either side, or simply by human panic and a mutual mistrust between the superpowers.

Dr. Helen Caldicott, that courageous woman who has done so much in the struggle against nuclear arms, has said that both America and Russia have now enough nuclear weapons to "overkill every person on earth 16 times." Think of that. Do the world's leaders really suppose that it is all just an act on TV and that the dead would get up again and take on a different role in another TV series so they might be killed again and again? I fear greatly that many of the world's leaders have so little imagination and so little real caring that they cannot visualize at all what a nuclear holocaust would mean. Do they really think that they and their families and executive staffs would survive in deep-buried bunkers? And if, by any unlikely chance they did, what kind of a world do they think they would emerge back into? It would be a dead and a putrefying world. Dr. Helen Caldicott says, "If we look behind the headlines and understand the historical perspective, we realize that America is preparing to fight a nuclear war. Now, that should make us all distinctly uncomfortable. In fact, we should be screaming in the streets, if we really care about ourselves, our children, and if we really love this planet." With well-researched figures, Dr. Caldicott also says, "In the event of a nuclear war, we predict that within 30 days after an exchange, 90% of Americans will be dead. So will Canadians, probably Mexicans, certainly Russians, certainly Europeans, the British, and probably the Chinese."

Roger Molander, a former White House nuclear strategist for the National Security Council, in an article in the *Guardian* in April of 1982, tells of one of the many things that made him decide to give up that job. He is now Executive Director of Ground Zero, an anti-nuclear weapons project. He says, "The final chance event that confirmed my determination to help correct our flaws involved another military officer. It happened at a meeting in the Pentagon when a Navy Captain offered the view that in America and Europe people were getting too excited over nuclear war. He argued that people were talking as if nuclear war would be the end of the world, when in fact only 500 million people would be killed. Only 500 million. I remember repeating it to myself... only 500 million...." Exactly. These are cold figures, statistics. It takes no time at all to say 500 million. But it all looks different, as it did to Roger Molander, if we think of each one of those people as our own children, ourselves, our parents, and friends.

▼ ▼ ▼

It is precisely this failure of the imagination on the part of militarists and leaders that is so dangerous today, the failure to visualize what a nuclear holocaust would mean, the apparent inability to imagine the scorched and charred bodies of children... our children or children of Russian parents or parents anywhere, and to know, by an extension of imagination that *all* children are our children. The jargon of the militarists is a distortion and a twisting of language, of our human ability to communicate. Language itself becomes the vehicle of concealment and deception. Such words as "overkill" and "megadeath" do not convey in any sense at all what would really happen—the dead, mutilated, and dying people clogging the ruined cities and towns like so much unvalued discarded rubbish, the suffering humans screaming for help with no medical help available, no water, no relief at all for the unbearable pain of millions of humans except finally the dark relief of death for all. Any shelters that the few might reach would in time turn into tombs. Civil defence plans are a sham. In a nuclear war there would be nowhere to hide, and nowhere except a dead and contaminated world to emerge back into.

I profoundly believe that we must proclaim that *this must not happen*.

Yes, but what about the Russians? If we try to persuade our government to refuse Cruise missile testing, aren't we playing into the hands of the bad guys? Won't the Soviet Union, as soon as they have clear superiority in nuclear arms, blow us all to hell without a second's thought? I do not think so. Isn't it necessary to have more and ever more nuclear weapons in the hands of the Americans so that we can feel *safe*? I do not think so. Let me make it clear that I hold no brief for the present Russian system of government. I hold no brief for *any* system of government that is repressive and cruel, and this includes those far-right regimes in countries such as El Salvador, to whom the U.S.A. is determinedly giving so much military aid. The U.S.A. and Russia, the two superpowers, must, I believe, co-exist in this world, even if there are some terrible things wrong in *both* systems, and *there are*. Russia suffered horribly in World War II, whereas war has not been fought on American soil since the Civil War. I cannot believe that the Russian leaders are all that anxious to begin nuclear war in which the Soviet Union would be, if not totally annihilated, then certainly decimated beyond any hope of recovery. George Kennan, formerly U.S. ambassador to Russia, who has been awarded both the Pulitzer Prize and the Albert Einstein Peace Prize, and who is a distinguished diplomat, academic, and writer, says in his book *The Nuclear Delusion*,

> Aren't we then . . . being unrealistic in the amount of attention we devote to protecting ourselves from the Russians who, God knows, are not ten feet tall, who have all sorts of troubles of their own, who can't run an agricultural system that really works, who can't adequately house their population, who are rapidly losing their prestige and leadership in the world Communist movement, and have to reckon with China on their long frontier in the East? Isn't it grotesque to spend so much of our energy on opposing such a Russia in order to save a West which is honeycombed with bewilderment and a profound sense of internal decay?

Quite frankly, I can't believe that Russia any longer has hopes of a world revolution. I can believe, though, that the Russian people, the ordinary people who love their children just as much as I love mine, are frightened, just as I am frightened, just as a very large proportion of the American people are frightened and are expressing that fear and outrage. The American people are indeed our cousins, and a very great many of them, young and old, are saying virtually the same things as I am saying here.

No American president has as yet declared himself willing to embrace a policy of "no first strike" in terms of nuclear weapons. President Reagan recently made the statement that America must reduce Marxism-Leninism "to the ash heap of history." If he proposed to do this by making his country such a true and fine example of social justice, of caring for the poor, of equal rights for women, of peace-making on the international scene, and of a refusal to support corrupt and violent regimes in, say, Central and South America, so that people the world over would look to America, as indeed once they did, as the home of the free, then I would say—*Great*. But I do not think that is what he had in mind. The president also, not long ago, addressed a group of fundamentalist Christians and told them that good and evil exist in the world and that the good must utterly destroy the evil. By evil, he was not referring to organized crime in his own land, or unemployment or poverty in the richest nation in the world. He was talking about America as wearing the white cowboy hat (to use a metaphor from his Hollywood days) and Russia wearing the black one. Good guys and bad guys. George Kennan says,

> I do not have, and have never had, any sympathy for the ideology of the Soviet leadership. I know that this is a regime with which it is not possible for us to have a fully satisfactory relationship. I know that there are many important matters on which no collaboration between us is possible, just as there are other matters on which we can collaborate. There are a number of Soviet habits and practices that I deeply deplore. . . .

He goes on to say,

> All this being said, I must... say that I find the view of the Soviet Union that prevails today in large portions of our governmental and journalistic establishments so extreme, so subjective, so far removed from what any sober scrutiny of external reality would reveal, that it is not only ineffective but dangerous as a guide to political action.

He concludes this portion of an essay written in 1981 by saying,

> And we shall not be able to turn these things around as they should be turned, in the plane of military and nuclear rivalry, until we learn to correct these childish distortions... until we correct our tendency to see in the Soviet Union only a mirror in which we look for the reflection of our own virtue—until we consent to see there another great people, one of the world's greatest, in all its complexity and variety, embracing the good with the bad, a people whose life, whose views, whose habits, whose fears and aspirations, whose successes and failures, are the products, just as ours are the products, not of any inherent iniquity but of the relentless discipline of history, tradition and national experience. Above all, we must learn to see the behaviour of the leadership of that country as partly the reflection of our own treatment of it. If we insist on demonizing these Soviet leaders... on viewing them as total and incorrigible enemies, consumed only with their fear or hatred of us and dedicated to nothing other than our destruction—that, in the end, is the way we shall assuredly have them, if for no other reason than that our view of them allows for nothing else, either for them or for us.

In a moving essay written in 1982, entitled "A Christian's View of the Arms Race," Kennan also says, "utterly unacceptable, from the Christian viewpoint as I see it, is the holding of innocent people hostage to the policies of their government, and the readiness, or the threat, to punish them as a means of punishing their government."

Our Prime Minister recently asked the NDP leader, Ed Broadbent, who was seeking to have the whole issue of the Cruise missile testing debated in the Commons, if he, Broadbent, had written to Soviet leader Andropov to tell *him* to stop testing, too. This snide remark was, of course, beside the point. Our federal government, at the present time talking out of both sides of its collective mouth, says that on the one hand the actual testing of the Cruise hasn't yet been agreed upon and on the other hand Canada must honour its commitment to NATO. According to Pauline Jewett, NDP defence critic, who has done much research on this matter, Canada's commitment to NATO does *not* include the necessity of our allowing *America*—America, not NATO—to test nuclear weapons here. My point is that Canada could have... and must have, in my view... considerable impact as a mediator in nuclear arms talks, as a non-nuclear nation, as a country that might conceivably be helpful in lowering the present climate of hysteria between the two superpowers, and in bringing about world disarmament.

This is why I think we must keep on trying to make our government hear us. Why would I write to Andropov or Reagan? I don't have a vote or a voice in those countries. I have both vote and voice here, though.

I believe that our land should be declared a nuclear-weapons-free zone, with absolutely no testing of nuclear arms or production of parts for those arms allowed in our country. I think that Canada could do a great deal to bring about a gradual and verifiable reduction of nuclear arms by both sides, monitored by neutral countries such as the Scandinavian countries, and to bring about a freeze on the production and testing of nuclear weapons. Canada could be a strong influence for a "no-first-strike" agreement among nations, for multilateral disarmament and for world peace.

Canada is not powerless nor are we insignificant in a world sense. Yet our present government appears to be quite willing to allow the Cruise missile to be tested over our land, in Alberta. The Cruise missile, an American nuclear weapon, was not designed as a deterrent weapon—it was designed as a "first-strike weapon." Its presence in the nuclear arsenal will not be verifiable, thus making any kind of nuclear-weapons control virtually impossible. The Litton plant in Ontario is producing, with the aid of millions of *our* tax dollars, guidance systems for the Cruise missile. Canada has sold nuclear reactors to such repressive regimes as Argentina, and is delivering fuel for those reactors, despite the fact that our government is aware that nuclear weapons could soon be within Argentina's capability. These are only a few of the many examples of Canada's complicity in the nuclear arms race.

Do we care so little about our children? Do we honour life so little that we will not speak out? I believe we do care, passionately and profoundly. Indeed, one thing that gives me hope is that so many of our churches and synagogues, so many people of all faiths, of all professions and trades, of all ages, are speaking out against the arms race and the descent into total madness. *Physicians for Social Responsibility*, active in this country as well as in America and elsewhere, are telling us what human damage would be done, and how impossible any thought of medical aid would be in a nuclear war. Inter-church groups such as *Project Ploughshares* are making strong representations to our government, as are labour unions, academics, and indeed and perhaps most importantly, women and men everywhere, in every walk of life. This is true in so very many places in the world today. When I speak of lobbying our government, that is because we must begin where we are. But we join our voices with those everywhere who believe as we do.

The money spent on arms, including nuclear arms, continues to mount. Recently I read that $550 billion dollars are being spent, world-wide, yearly, on arms. An even more recent estimate puts it at $600 billion dollars. That sum is so great we cannot really comprehend it. But we *can* comprehend that for the cost of *one* Trident nuclear submarine, malaria could be wiped out from the world. Think of that for one minute. I think of the people in the world who are suffering from thirst, from starvation, from preventable diseases, from ceaseless fighting, and the brutality of oppressive regimes. I think, too, of the growing number of unemployed people in our own land. I think of the Reagan program in America—more and yet more money spent on nuclear arms; less and less spent on social programs and help to the poor and the disabled.

▼ ▼ ▼

I have to speak about how I feel as a writer. I don't like calling myself "an artist," but I guess I am, and would join with my tribal sisters and brothers in many ways. I believe that as a writer . . . an artist, if you will . . . I have a responsibility, a moral responsibility, to work against the nuclear arms race, to work for a recognition on the part of governments and military leaders that nuclear weapons must never be used and must systematically be reduced. Throughout human history, artists have affirmed and celebrated life. Whether we work in words, in music, in painting, in film, in bronze or stone or whatever our medium may be, the artist affirms the value of life itself and of our only home, the planet Earth. Art mirrors and ponders the pain and joy of our experience as human beings. In many parts of the world, and over many centuries, artists have risked and even given their own lives to portray the society around them as they perceived it, and to speak out against injustices. Since the most ancient times, artists have passed on to succeeding generations the tales, the histories, the songs, the sagas, the skills of their trade. Can we conceive of a world in which there would be no succeeding generations? A world in which all the powerful works of the human imagination would be destroyed, would never again be seen or listened to or experienced? We must conceive that this is now a possibility, and one not too far in our uncertain future, either. We must not, as artists, or so I feel, stand by and passively allow this to happen. The death of the individual is the end which we will all one day meet, but in the knowledge that our children and their children will live, that *someone's* children will go on, that the great works of humankind will endure in art, in recorded history, in medicine, in the sciences and philosophies and technologies that our species has developed with devotion and a sense of vocation throughout the ages. The individual is the leaf on the tree. The leaves fall but the tree endures. New leaves are born. This concept has been the mainstay of our species from time immemorial. Now the tree itself is threatened. All art is a product of the human imagination. It is, deeply, an honouring of the past, a perception of the present in one way or another, and a looking towards the future. Whatever the medium of any particular artist, art is reaching out, an attempt to communicate those things which most concern us seriously in our sojourn here on earth. Artists, the real ones, the committed ones, have always sought, sometimes in ways prophetic and beyond their own times, to clarify and proclaim and enhance life, not to obscure and demean and destroy it. Even the so-called literature of despair is not really that at all. Despair is total silence, total withdrawal. Art, by its very nature of necessary expression, is an act of faith, an acknowledgement of the profound mystery at the core of life.

As a writer, therefore, I feel I have a responsibility. Not to write pamphlets, not to write didactic fiction. That would be, in many ways, a betrayal of how I feel about my work. But my responsibility seems to me to be to write as truthfully as I can, about human individuals and their dilemmas, to honour them as living, suffering, and sometimes joyful people. My responsibility also must extend into my life as a citizen of my own land and ultimately of the world.

I do not claim to have done this well. There are no personal victories in those areas. The individual, here, becomes part of a community and only as a part of that community can one person ever be effective and true to herself or himself. There has to be the resolve not to give up, and to join with all others who believe that life itself is more important than our own individual lives, important though these certainly are.

Dr. Helen Caldicott speaks of "psychic numbing," the temptation to shut out from our minds and hearts all the terrifying things in our world. To think that the problems may just possibly go away if we ignore them. To feel that we are totally helpless, and so . . . why bother trying to do anything? What Dr. Caldicott calls "psychic numbing" I would call "despair," and although I would take issue with the early Church Fathers on many things, I would agree that despair is rightly placed as one of the deadly sins. The problems of our world will not go away if we ignore them. It is not all happening on TV. It is happening in our earth, and we, humankind, are the custodians of that earth. We cannot afford passivity. We must take on responsibility for our lives and our world and we must be prepared to make our government listen to and hear us. Our aim must be no less than human and caring justice, and peace . . . *for all people that on earth do dwell.*

So, if this were indeed my Final Hour, these would be my words to you. I would not claim to pass on any secret of life, for there is none, or any wisdom except the passionate plea of caring. In your dedication to your own life's work, whatever it may be, live as though you had forever, for no amount of careful and devoted doing is too great in carrying out that work to which you have set your hands. Cultivate in your work and your life the art of patience, and come to terms with your inevitable human limitations, while striving also to extend the boundaries of your understanding, your knowledge, and your compassion. These words are easily said; they are not easily lived. Learn from those who are older than you are; learn from your contemporaries; and never cease to learn from children. Try to feel, in your heart's core, the reality of others. This is the most painful thing in the world, probably, and the most necessary. In times of personal adversity, know that you are not alone. Know that although in the eternal scheme of things you are small, you are also unique and irreplaceable, as are all your fellow humans everywhere in the world. Know that your commitment is above all to life itself. Your own life and work and friendships and loves will come to an end, because one day you will die, and whatever happens after that, or if anything happens at all, it will not be on this earth. But life and work and friendship and love will go on, in others, your inheritors. The struggle for peace and for social justice will go on—provided that our earth survives and that caring humans still live. It is up to you, now, to do all that you can, and that means a commitment, at this perilous moment in our human history, to ensure that life itself *will* go on.

In closing, I want to quote one verse from that mighty book ... more like a vast library ... that Dr. Northrop Frye calls "The Great Code," and which has so shaped, sometimes so ambiguously, the imagination, the art, and the many facets of faith in our world. This verse is from Deuteronomy, Chapter 30: "I have set before you life and death, blessing and cursing; therefore choose life, that both thou and thy seed may live."

An address first delivered to the Trent University Philosophy Society, 29 March 1983, and published in *Canadian Literature* 100 (Spring 1984): 187–97.

ROBERT KROETSCH (1927–) was born in Heisler, Alberta, received his B.A. from the University of Alberta (1948), his M.A. from Middlebury College in Vermont (1956), and his Ph.D. from the University of Iowa (1961). He taught for a number of years at the State University of New York at Binghamton before assuming a professorship in the Department of English at the University of Manitoba, where he continues to exert a shaping influence on a new generation of western Canadian writers. Kroetsch has long been regarded as Canada's leading practitioner of post-modernist poetics and as one of the strongest proponents of post-structuralist literary theories inspired by French writers such as Jacques Derrida, Michel Foucault, and Roland Barthes.

Kroetsch's interest in self-reflexive (or metafictional) fiction, demythologizing, and deconstruction, is exemplified by both his novel, *What the Crow Said* (1978), and the non-fictional *The Crow Journals* (1980), which details the process of writing that novel. His first novel, *But We Are Exiles* (1966), though in the tradition of conventional social and psychological realism, already displays the talents of a writer very much interested in writing into existence the stories of his western Canadian experience. In it, the author finds for his and his community's experiences the appropriate parallels and prototypes in ancient myth and other literatures, and then plays literarily with those myths and references to show their ultimate inappropriateness to the life of western Canadians. He followed this with three novels that constitute a trilogy—Kroetsch calls them a "triptych"—linked thematically and stylistically: *The Words of My Roaring* (1966), *The Studhorse Man* (1969), and *Gone Indian* (1973). The second of these, which won the Governor General's Award, is representative of Kroetsch's post-modern techniques and metafictional concerns. Its anti-hero, the significantly named Hazard Lepage, is nobody's white-hatted cowboy. He is the subject of another's—Demeter Proudfoot's—biography, a subject who resists at every twist and turn of the picaresque plot his "author's" attempt to force him into an inappropriate literary mould. The models at hand in Proudfoot's literary baggage are those of classical mythology, Hollywood, and classical literatures, and provide the unsuitable slots into which the writer Proudfoot fails to cram the unruly Lepage.

Kroetsch has continued his search for what he calls "the fiction [that] makes us real" in such novels as *Badlands* (1975) and *Alibi* (1983), in poetry collections such as *The Stone Hammer Poems* (1975) and *Sketches of a Lemon* (1981), and the autobiographical triptych, or "life poem," *Field Notes* (1981), composed of *The Ledger* (1975), *Seed Catalogue* (1977), and *The Sad Phoenician* (1979). He remarks of this kind of poem, which unfolds in step with the poet's life: "The continuing poem: not the having written, but the writing. The poem as long as a life. The lifelost poem."

Kroetsch was a co-founder of *Boundary 2: A Journal of Post-Modern Literature*, one of the first North American periodicals devoted to the new theories and practices. He is the editor of *Creation* (1970) and co-editor of *Gaining Ground* (1985), and the subject of a book-length interview-cum-conversation with Shirley Neuman and Robert Wilson entitled *Labyrinths of Voice: Conversations with Robert Kroetsch* (1983). His essays, which he describes as "very much the consequence of extended conversation," have been featured in a special issue of the journal *Open Letter* (Spring 1983) and collected in *The Lovely Treachery of Words* (1989). In the essay that follows, Kroetsch muses on one of his favourite subjects, "how do you write a new country," by discussing the potential virtue in the problematical status of the Canadian identity.

No Name Is My Name

ROBERT KROETSCH

In a new place, and in its literature, the Adamic impulse to give name asserts itself, as it did in the New England of Emerson and Thoreau and Hawthorne. Writers in a new place conceive of themselves profoundly as namers. They name in order to give focus and definition. They name to create boundaries. They name to establish identity.

Canadian writing is the writing down of a new place. Indeed, Northrop Frye tells us in his now famous statement that the Canadian sensibility "is less perplexed by the question 'Who am I?' than by some such riddle as 'Where is here?' "*

Frye's insight is basic to the unriddling of whatever it is to be a Canadian. Yet it slights a question that is at least manifest, if not central. The interest in the question of identity speaks its presence in a curious way. That presence announces itself as an absence. Or, more specifically, one of the peculiarities of this new literature is the recurrence of major fictional characters who have no names.

This resistance to a speakable name occurs early in Canadian writing. Thomas Haliburton, in a series of newspaper pieces begun in 1835 in Nova Scotia and published together in 1836 under the title *The Clockmaker*, invented the wilful and eloquent character to whom he gave the name Sam Slick. That same Sam Slick, that first great Canadian literary character, is not a Bluenose at all but, rather, a New Englander, a Yankee clockmaker. The

* Northrop Frye, *The Bush Garden: Essays on the Canadian Imagination* (Toronto: Anansi, 1971), 220.

narrator of the story, the incipient Canadian (this is before Confederation), refuses to name himself.

The two men travel together on horseback as they ride circuit, one a clock peddler, the other a lawyer. (And travel itself, is, of course, a form of escape from name; Canadian writing is obsessively about travel.) On this ride, Sam Slick does most of the talking. The other man tells about the talking; he is at once at a remove from the action and its mediator. And he is, by fascinating design, anonymous.

We are in Episode XI before the matter of his anonymity is confronted. It is suppertime. The narrator is approached by the hostess of Pugwash's inn: "Approaching me, she said, with an irresistible smile, 'Would you like, Mr—' Here there was a pause, a hiatus, evidently intended for me to fill up with my name. . . . "*

The irresistible smile of the hostess is, it turns out, resistible. And the narrator gives us a longish paragraph on why. He says of his name:

> but that no person knows, nor do I intend they shall; at Medley's Hotel, in Halifax, I was known as the Stranger in No. 1. The attention that incognito procured for me, the importance it gave me in the eyes of the master of the house, its lodgers and servants, is indescribable. It is only great people who travel incog (p. 43).

He names himself by giving a name that leaves him nameless. He is, or was, the Stranger in No. 1. But even that was somewhere else, not here in Pugwash's inn. This narrator has discovered a version of privilege in anonymity. He is not above a little deceit. His delight is almost naïve. But the lawyer-impulse in the narrator makes him attempt at least a partial description of the indescribable: "State travelling is inconvenient and slow; the constant weight of form and etiquette oppresses at once the strength and the spirits. It is pleasant to travel unobserved, to stand at ease, or exchange the full suit for the undress coat and fatigue jacket" (p. 43).

The man who wants to be recognized for his importance wants also to go unobserved. This comes close to contradiction. We see here an early manifestation of the Canadian personality. The man who exploits social hierarchy by being falsely named into it wants also to be free of it. He wants to have a system that gives him identity and stature, but he wants to be free of that system. This man is surely ready to enter into the Canadian Confederation. Having created his own coffin and climbed into it, he now manages, by some wonderful sleight of hand, to nail it shut:

> Wherever, too, there is mystery there is importance; there is no knowing for whom I may be mistaken; but let me once give my humble

* Thomas Haliburton, *The Clockmaker* (1836; edited rpt Toronto: McClelland and Stewart, 1958 [New Canadian Library]), 43. Further references will appear in the text.

cognomen and occupation, and I sink immediately to my own level, to a plebeian station, and a vulgar name; not even my beautiful hostess, nor my inquisitive friend, the Clockmaker, who calls me "Squire," shall extract that secret! (p. 43)

This remarkable and sort-of anonymous man fears that by naming himself accurately he will, in a mind-boggling paradox, sink immediately to his own level. Perhaps this is at the heart of the enduring Canadian crisis about the federal state: I would never join a country that would have me as a member.

It is better, much more desirable, the narrator insists, to be *mistaken*. And yet this same narrator is fascinated by—captivated by—the person who admits to and even proclaims for himself a plebeian station and a vulgar name.

Sam Slick is the double and opposite of Haliburton's narrator. He is the named man who fearlessly and proudly, and with his own kind of shrewdness, speaks his own name. For all his "soft sawder," Sam speaks direct truths. He is, in a certain way, the carnivalesque destroyer of the hierarchy that the narrator both admires and wishes to escape. He deals in actual clocks and profane time and the randomness and the chance and the poetry at the edge of *law*. The nameless narrator meets his alter ego and both hankers for the freedom of Sam's sly directness and clings to the legalistic indirectness of his own being "incog." Not even his beautiful hostess, he says (and her charms, he lets us know, in an extravagant fit of naming, are like an Italian sky, unclouded, unrivalled), nor the inquisitive Clockmaker, who, with soft sawder that is usually effective, calls him Squire, "shall extract that secret!"

That secret remains a recurring theme in Canadian writing. Haliburton announces it and complicates it. His narrator, who is the Stranger in No. 1 and the mystery and the Squire, is also Haliburton. That trace of the autobiographical is to persist in later renderings of the nameless figure. Haliburton is himself, astonishingly, the man of law—lawyer and judge—creating at once the carnivalesque energy of Sam Slick and the contained lawlessness of his status-seeking narrator. Haliburton himself, when he could no longer live with his own contradiction, his own tension, his own dialogic involvement, went to England and became a member of Parliament and opposed the movement of the British North American colonies toward independence. And in his later writings, in a further bizarre paradox, he turned against his own character, Sam Slick, as if that character must be a real person and not his creation.

But Haliburton, in his first "refusing to name" scene, was brilliantly aware of the ironies of his posture. "Would you like, Mr—" the narrator quotes again, after his own longish digression. And then he continues to narrate the incident:

> "Indeed, I would," said I, "Mrs. Pugwash; pray be seated, and tell me what it is."
>
> "Would you like a dish of superior Shittyacks for supper?"
>
> "Indeed I would," said I, again, laughing: "but pray tell me what it is?"

"Laws me!" said she with a stare. "Where have you been all your days, that you never heerd of our Shittyack oysters? I thought everybody had heerd of them" (pp. 43–44).

The man who withholds his name himself comes to a name that for him names nothing. Haliburton sees, comically, the necessary and absurd implications both of naming and of his own refusal to name. He is, there in 1835, the writer, the namer, in the new world, come to the old genesis problem, the old genesis moment. Where Melville's narrator could speak so richly and powerfully, "Call me Ishmael," Haliburton's narrator could only insist, with ambiguous laughter, on having no name.

If we look to the invisible characters in American writing, the invisible man, or the voice that says "nobody knows my name," those are the voices of people who feel they are being made nameless by others. The Canadian narrator makes him- or herself invisible. And that Canadian is often, as was Haliburton's narrator, from the dominant force or class in society.

The paradigmatic text in Canadian writing may be Sinclair Ross's 1941 novel *As for Me and My House*. The prairie world of Ross's novel is without boundaries—instead of a boundary it is crossed by a railway that suggests a meaningless infinity. The name of the town, Horizon, suggests a no-place that is tantalizingly visible but always out of reach: a version of namelessness.

Mr and Mrs Bentley move into a nondescript house of their own, and are hardly ever seen in the house next door where God seems to be either too often absent or too often ignored—and seldom named. The minister, Mr Bentley, in his inadequacies as a carpenter, is announced as a near-nameless Joseph-figure.

The novel is presented in the form of Mrs Bentley's diary. This fascinating woman, while keeping something as intimate as a diary, never reveals to us her first name, her maiden name, or her family background. We know at best that she once entertained thoughts of a career in music—and hers is a version of European music that does not transport a lot of personal information. It serves almost to elaborate her disguise or her fate, her condition of namelessness.

This same "nameless" Mrs Bentley—and that is our name for her; she toys with the stereotype of "minister's wife" but won't name herself as such—is quite possibly the most discussed fictional character in Canadian writing. She, in a sense, writes about an unwritten novel which we as readers must imagine or reconstruct while reading her diary entries about the missing text; the novel itself as a larger act of naming is called into doubt.

Mrs Bentley, while carefully not naming herself, with equal care explores and records the names of all the people and even the animals around her. A major figure in Mrs Bentley's diary, the schoolteacher Paul Kirby, is an amateur etymologist and philologist so caught up in the meaning of names that he cannot get beyond them to people. Her husband Philip, the minister, after taking in a stray dog, bathes it in a mock-baptism (naming), and Mrs Bentley reports carefully that the "drowned-looking Philip named him [the dog] El Greco—because El Greco was an artist who had a way of painting people long and lean as if they'd all been put on the rack."* While on a potentially Edenic vacation on a ranch she notices a picture of a Hereford over her bed and writes in her diary:

> I looked at him [that is the Hereford, not the husband; he is absent] closer when I got up today, and found that his name was Gallant Lad the Third. His son, Annie tells me, is here now on the ranch and carrying on. As a calf, though, he belonged to Paul, and instead of Gallant Lad the Fourth he's Priapus the First (p. 99).

This might be a clue to the paternity of the fatherless son who is born to a dying mother, Judith West, and adopted by the Bentleys. But it also reduces naming to a kind of absurdity. And the novel ends with still another ambiguous naming act, when Mrs Bentley names the adopted baby boy Philip. "Another Philip?" her husband, Philip, protests. "That's right, Philip," she thinks to herself. "I want it so" (p. 165).

Mrs Bentley will settle for either too little or too much naming. But she won't herself be named. Like Haliburton's narrator, she engages in vast and devious verbal design to give herself at least margins of freedom, while finding herself tagged as the minister's helpmate in a claustrophobic small town on a limitless prairie. She names her world in great detail in order to keep herself nameless. She is the taboo-keeper, not of God's name, but of her own. Perhaps she is first of all a nameless figure in her husband's world, but she wins through that preserved and nurtured namelessness a complex humanity.

That rural or small-town setting—not the wilderness, but its edge—somehow remains the basic place of Canadian fiction, as if there must be a doubt even about where the place is. Place threatens to become mere space. From Susanna Moodie's *Roughing It in the Bush* to Ernest Buckler's *The Mountain and the Valley*, from Sheila Watson's *The Double Hook* to Margaret Laurence's *The Diviners* and Jack Hodgins' *The Invention of the World*, there is a resistance to centres. The rural or small-town setting remains the test place, the energy source, for those sophisticated writers. They are all tempted to set their stories in "Horizon." Nature itself becomes an undeciphered text as the old names fall away or prove to be inadequate or false. And with that emptiness at the centre of sign comes the feeling of guilt about our innocence that is so characteristic of Canadian writing.

We do, of course, have in our canon urban novels. Quite possibly the best of these is A.M. Klein's *The Second Scroll* (1951). Klein was a Montreal writer who had a distinguished career as a poet, as a political activist, as a student of Joyce, and as a lawyer. The narrator of his only novel is a Jewish-Canadian writer-journalist who goes to Europe on a double quest. And that narrator is nameless.

* Sinclair Ross, *As for Me and My House* (1941; rpt Toronto: McClelland and Stewart, 1970 [New Canadian Library]), 81.

He is sent to Israel by a publisher to produce "a volume of translations of the poems and songs of Israel's latest nest of singing birds." That is, he is to investigate the emergence of a literature newer even than Canada's; and again, as in Canada, there is a vast prior literature to confront. But the nameless narrator is also in search of an uncle, Uncle Melech, a great but mysterious Hebrew scholar.

The novel begins (and the first chapter is called "Genesis"): "For many years my father—may he dwell in bright Eden!—refused to permit in his presence even the mention of that person's name." The narrator realizes that in order to seek his uncle he must engage in a naming act that assumes the proportions of a taboo-breaking. Again, the old names must somehow be made new, and the person assigned the task, the person assigned to mediate the transformation (as in Ross's novel), never reveals his own name, almost as if he has none to reveal.

Against this potentially tragic assignment, Klein plays his sense of the new-naming and the mis-naming that are a part of the contemporary urban world. In the process of finding a Catholic monsignor in Rome who knows something of Uncle Melech, Klein's narrator meets Settano, a "polylingual autodidact." The narrator reports:

> When after several Scotch and sodas I had ordered—out of pure thirst and nostalgia—a Coke . . . , he had scoffed at me, styled me a typical emissary of the new religion, a sound, orthodox Cocacolian. I had spitefully accepted the compliment and . . . had expatiated upon the beauty of the Coca-Cola bottle, curved and dusky like some Gauguin painting of a South Sea maiden, upon the purity of its contents, its ubiquity in space, its symbolic evocations—a little torchless Statue of Liberty.*

He continues in that parody of his own quest:

> . . . and the evening had ended with a quasi-friendship, both of us at last quaffing it down with Canadian V.O. As an abbreviation, he said, for vodka. He then bade me good night, *Americano*.
>
> "I am not an American. I'm a Canadian."
>
> "Is there a difference? Isn't Canada the forty-ninth state?"
>
> "On the contrary. The States are our eleventh province."
>
> His laughter—the gall of the Canuck! the utter absurdity—rang through the corridor (p. 46).

Klein has an overwhelming sense of the sacred and the profane, of the political and the personal implications of namelessness. His long silence at the end of his life is a painful statement of that awareness. On the one hand he could imagine, through renaming, wide ecumenical possibilities, as he does in

* A.M. Klein, *The Second Scroll* (1951; rpt Toronto: McClelland and Stewart, 1969 [New Canadian Library]), 45. Further references will appear in the text.

the glosses at the end of his novel. On the other hand he saw that we cannot name our brands of booze with any sense of conviction. He could imagine the English and the French and the Jewish communities of Montreal living in harmony, yet he entertained profound doubts about the notion of the self as something whole and realizable in the urban world. He anticipates contemporary anxieties about the very notion of self, and he grounds that anxiety in a nameless narrator who goes in quest of a figure whose name is not be mentioned. In the course of conducting that search, both Klein and his narrator move through varieties of discourse, including within the one short novel varieties of the poem, of the play, of the essay, of the gloss—not to mention a variety of languages. When the narrator finally finds at least a snapshot of his missing uncle, it turns out to be "a double, a multiple exposure" (p. 61). There is no longer, in Klein's world, the possibility of a simple and definitive naming.

In that same Montreal, fourteen years after the appearance of *The Second Scroll*, Hubert Aquin was to publish in French his novel *Prochain Episode*. And again, it is a novel whose narrator-hero has no name.

Where Klein's hero was on a double quest, the nameless narrator in *Prochain Episode* is at least a double agent in his own story. He is in a Montreal prison, but has been transferred to a clinic where he is to be, as he puts it, "submitted to psychiatric expertise before being sent to trial." * In this condition of enforced stasis he writes a story of a frantic trip through Switzerland where he was attempting to serve Quebec's revolutionary cause by killing another double agent, a well-to-do historian who is the narrator's own double.

This book, along with being about time and history and Quebec and revolution, is about the writing act itself. We read on the first page:

> At heart, only one problem occupies me: how should I set about writing a story of espionage? And I complicate the problem with my dream of doing something original in a field encumbered by a great many written and unwritten rules. Fortunately, laziness immediately persuades me to give up any thought of reshaping the espionage format. I also feel great security, I confess, in gently yielding to the demands of a literary style already so well defined. So I decide to slip my novel into the mainstream of the spy-story tradition (p. 9).

He lays claim even to the anonymity of authorship that is offered by an adherence to convention. He grounds that anonymity in a philosophic claim that originality is no longer possible and, in any case, only barely desirable. He says, later in the story, "It's no longer a matter of how to be original in literature: suddenly I am disillusioned by the question of the individual existence!" (p. 69).

* Hubert Aquin, *Prochain Episode*, translated from the French by Penny Williams (1967; Toronto: McClelland and Stewart, 1972), 15. Further references will appear in the text.

Process has replaced end in a radical way, as the title of Aquin's book would suggest. The narrator says: "The meaning of this novel will not be the shattering novelty of its final format. I am this book from hour to hour and day to day; as long as I don't commit suicide, I have no intention of stopping. This disorderly book and I, we are the same" (p. 69).

The narrator and the book are one in a process that borders on dissolution. Aquin has written a successful description of a total failure—his book becomes the synonym for a character who is not only nameless but who finds himself unnameable.

Yet this version of anonymity generates story. There can only be the next episode, and this is possible because every character or event divides, turns against itself, doubles back on itself—Switzerland becomes a double and a contrary to Quebec; Quebec becomes its Eastern Townships and its St Lawrence River; the victim gives the same account of his life as did the would-be murderer; the blonde woman K (or Québec) sought after and longed for by the narrator might be the blonde woman K (for Québec) sought after and longed for by the historian and scholar H. de Heutz, who might be the banker Carl von Ryndt.

Writing, the narrator says, wins time: "dead time which I cover with erasures and phonemes, which I embellish with syllables and bravado, which I shower with all my atoms, fragments of a whole they will never equal. I write automatically, concentrating on spelling to avoid the compelling logic of homicide."

Aquin's hero finds in his namelessness a prison and a destiny, a defeat and a cause, a way of writing and a reason not to write. Aquin himself took his own life in 1977—he postponed his suicide by a day when his wife said the day he had chosen would be inconvenient for her. Aquin was true to his fictional vision. The intertext of suicide is in his books. He blurred the distinction between book and life. He entered into his own narrative of unnameability.

It remained for Margaret Atwood, in her 1972 novel *Surfacing*, to test urban Canadian characters in a rural Canadian setting. Atwood's heroine and narrator in *Surfacing* is an Everywoman figure come to an archetypal confrontation with parental figures, with garden and forest, with the city of the present and the totemic creatures of the past. The nameless narrator begins her story: "I can't believe I'm on this road again, twisting along past the lake where the white birches are dying, the disease is spreading from the south, and I notice they now have sea-planes for hire. But this is still near the city limits; we didn't go through, it's swelled enough to have a bypass, that's success." *

This woman harks back to Haliburton's narrator: she is like him a city person gone into the country; she is aware of a stronger sense of definition that comes up from the south and, like Haliburton's narrator, she is attracted to and suspicious of one of those defining characteristics—success.

* Margaret Atwood, *Surfacing* (Toronto: McClelland and Stewart, 1972), 7. Further references will appear in the text.

Atwood's character enters into a labyrinth where she has not even the reassurance of her own name. Instead of a quest for a fixed and knowable and bounded identity in the labyrinth of the world, we have the idea of identity itself as the labyrinth. Like Aquin's hero, Atwood's narrator risks being destroyed and has experienced the desire to kill. Like Ross's heroine, she finds in the (now imagined) paternity of a child a locus for her obsession: an awareness of the possibility and impossibility of connecting name and object, of putting a name on things.

Atwood's four travellers in their car enter into Quebec. The narrator says, "Now we're on my home ground, foreign territory" (p. 11). There is not even the consolation of home as a safe place for this narrator. She returns home and sees the familiar signs in a language she cannot quite read. She meets the people she has "known" for a long time and cannot quite speak with. In Québec, on "my home ground, foreign territory," she is, like Aquin's narrator, only made aware of a larger failure of language to name, to signify.

"Nothing," she says, "is the same, I don't know the way any more" (p. 12). And yet she is, like Aquin's narrator, the figure of the artist. The artist is supposed to know the way. She too, like Aquin's narrator, is the artist at the edge of dissolution. "I can't believe . . . " is the cry of her beginning. At the end of the book she frees herself of history, of clothing, of artifacts like scrapbooks and photographs and wedding rings. Only when she has made herself unnameable in any traditional terms can she begin what might be a rebirth, a renaming into a valid vision or version of the world.

One comes reluctantly, uneasily, to the question: What is this anonymity all about? What is the name for what is not named?

Perhaps Atwood's heroine is a new Eve, freeing herself from Adam's named world. It may well be that Canadian writing owes its first debt to the model of Eve, and not to that of Adam. Eve is created into the world after Adam has been created—and after the naming has been done.

The Canadian writer in English must speak a new culture not with new names but with an abundance of names inherited from Britain and the United States. And that predicament is in turn doubled—by the writing done in the French language in Canada.

The problem then is not so much that of knowing one's identity as it is that of how to relate that newly evolving identity to its inherited or "given" names. And the first technique might be simply to hold those names in suspension, to let the identity speak itself out of a willed namelessness.

The experience of feeling powerless might also be a factor in the Canadian sense of being nameless. American literature is powerfully grounded in its nineteenth-century greatness, in the implications and assumptions of American Romanticism. Canadian literature is very much a literature of the later twentieth century. The nineteenth century gave American literature special interests in and definitions of self, freedom, heroism, society, nature, happiness. The twentieth century, as the basis of Canadian writing, puts special pressure on all those concepts. It would be illuminating to contrast the "I" of Whitman that can encompass the world with the "I" of bp Nichol's long poem *The Martyrology*, an "I" that yields itself to the encompassing world.

In Canadian writing, and perhaps in Canadian life, there is an exceptional pressure placed on the individual and the self by the community or society. The self is not in any way Romantic or privileged. The small town remains the ruling paradigm, with its laws of familiarity and conformity. Self and community almost fight to a draw. There seems to be little literature in Canada that tells of the small-town person going to the city—a tradition that is strong in European and American literature. The principal character in Sheila Watson's *The Double Hook* kills his mother, goes into town to a place where he might catch a train and leave—and then he turns around and rides back to the community in which he committed the murder. David Canaan in Ernest Buckler's *The Mountain and the Valley* gets into the car that would take him away from his small town and into the city—then gets out of the car and stays. The pressure of community at its strongest—or worst—is towards erasure.

But at its best, the threat of anonymity generates story. Aquin makes a labyrinthine novel of his hero's inability to fix on a name. Sinclair Ross's narrator writes a commentary on a novel that we don't have (her husband's silence) and in the process writes the basic Canadian story. Morag Gunn, that busy, troubled, interrupted, procrastinating woman in Margaret Laurence's *The Diviners*, raised as an orphan and threatened with that version of namelessness, insists over and over that she can't get her work done, isn't getting her novel written, can't in effect put a name to her experience—and we end up having finished reading the novel just as she finishes writing it.

It may be that the villain (namelessness) turns out to be the hero in the story of the Canadian story. The nameless figure who seems to threaten us may in fact be leading us to high ground. To avoid a name does not (as Haliburton's narrator so well realized) deprive one of an identity; indeed, it may offer a plurality of identities. Like the epic hero of old, we might even lay claim to a certain virtue in our ability to withhold and deceive. In a wilful misremembering of Homer's Odysseus we might say, ambiguously, proudly, tauntingly, no name is *my* name!

From *The Lovely Treachery of Words: Essays Selected and New* (Toronto: Oxford University Press, 1989), 41–52.

MORDECAI RICHLER

(1931–), as essayist and journalist, has secured a role as one of the most sought-after interpreters of Canada to the United States and England. As with all privileged insiders who reveal family secrets to the neighbours, he has met with harsh criticism at home. But Richler's attitude towards his native land is more complex than can be conveyed in the simplifications and dismissive phrases of his critics. The sardonic title of his book of essays, *Home Sweet Home: My Canadian Album* (1984), nicely points up this difficulty. The essays frequently reveal a depth of feeling for things Canadian—Montreal, the Montreal Canadians, Yellowknife—that the book title belies. In a recent *Quill & Quire* interview (July 1989), Richler confesses, "I have a lot of feeling for this country, [though] it's not necessarily what the nationalists consider feeling," leaving the reader to puzzle over the qualification, and the use of "necessarily," even "feeling." Yet there is no such equivocating when in the same interview he remarks scathingly on the cultural dangers of Canadian (or any) nationalism: "In the real world . . . there are only two kinds of writing: good writing and bad writing. Nationalism has protected a number of second-rate reputations." This is the judgment of a professional writer who has worked long and hard to earn an international reputation. What the literary critic Malcolm Ross observed of Stephen Leacock's attitude towards Mariposa is as true of Richler's ambivalent stand vis-à-vis Canada: "He loves what he hates." Such may well be a precondition of the humorist-satirist or the comic novelist. In "The Fall of the Montreal Canadians," Richler reveals the source of his own mixed feelings for Canada and Montreal which drive his critics to accuse him of everything from cultural treason to anti-Semitism:

> An earlier generation, not mine, was raised to manhood on a British standard. *The Boy's Own Annual.* "Fear God, Honour the Crown, Shoot Straight, and Keep Clean." But those of us who were kids during World War II (flipping the diddle as the battles raged elsewhere) and went on to become teenagers in the late Forties were a thoroughly American bunch. We endured Montreal and blackheads, but New York, New York, was our heart's desire. The real world, the big time.

Richler was born in Montreal and attended Sir George Williams University (now Concordia University). Since 1959, with the publication of *The Apprenticeship of Duddy Kravitz*, he has earned his living as a writer of screenplays, as a journalist, and as a novelist. If he has in the last two decades become an interpreter of Canada to the English-speaking world, he has always been in his fiction one of the most perceptive and entertaining interpreters of Canadians to themselves. He has written some of the funniest comic novels in recent times, including *St. Urbain's Horseman* (1971), for which he won his second Governor General's Award, and *Joshua Then and Now* (1980). He published his first novel, *The Acrobats* (1954), at the age of twenty-three, and followed it with *Son of a Smaller Hero* (1955), *A Choice of Enemies* (1957), *The Incomparable Atuk* (1963), and *Cocksure* (1968). He is also a children's author of such well-known books as *Jacob Two-Two Meets the Hooded Fang* (1975). His books of journalism and essays include *Hunting Tigers under Glass* (1968), *The Street* (1969), *Shovelling Trouble* (1972), *Notes on an Endangered Species* (1974), and *Broadsides* (1990). His most recent novel is *Solomon Gursky Was Here* (1989).

In "My Father's Life," Richler displays his talent for detailed description and his skill at capturing a particular time and place, in this instance Montreal in the 1930s and 40s. Characteristic of much of his work, this essay is elegiac in tone, conveying what must be seen as an enduring regret at the heart of Richler's writing: regret for the loss of a more colourful world, for missed opportunities, for the simple passage of time, for change. In "Why I Write," taking off from a similarly entitled essay by George Orwell, Richler engagingly discusses what compels him to put pen to paper, revealing a range of reasons both intellectual and emotional, and, in the process, telling us much about what motivates Canada's finest comic novelist.

MORDECAI RICHLER

My Father's Life

After the funeral, I was given my father's *talis*, his prayer shawl, and (oh my God) a file containing all the letters I had written to him while I was living abroad, as well as carbon copies he had kept of the letters he had sent to me.

> December 28, 1959: "Dear Son, Last week I won a big Kosher Turkey, by bowling, when I made the high triple for the week. How I did it I do not know, I guess I was lucky for once, or was it that the others were too sure of themselves, being much better at the game than I am."

> February 28, 1963: "This month has been a cold one, making it difficult, almost impossible to work outside. Yes! it's been tough. Have you found a title for your last novel? What can you do with a title like this? 'UNTIL *DEBT* DO US PART'? "

His letter of February 28, 1963, like so many others written that year, begins, "Thanks for the cheque." For by that time we had come full circle. In the beginning it was my father who had sent checks to me. Included in the file I inherited were canceled checks, circa 1945, for $28 monthly child support, following the annulment of my parents' marriage. A bill dated January 15, 1948, for a Royal portable, my first typewriter, a birthday gift. Another bill, from Bond Clothes, dated August 21, 1950, on the eve of my departure for Europe, for "1 Sta. Wag. Coat, $46.49."

My own early letters to my father, horrendously embarrassing for me to read now, usually begin with appeals for money. No, *demands*. There is also a telegram I'd rather forget. March 11, 1951. IMPERATIVE CHECK SENT PRONTO MADRID C O COOKS WAGON LITS ALCALA NR 23 MADRID. BROKE. MORDECAI.

Imperative, indeed.

▼ ▼ ▼

I was also left a foot-long chisel, his chisel, which I now keep on a shelf of honor in my workroom. Written with a certain flourish in orange chalk on the oak shaft is my father's inscription:

Used by M.I. Richler
Richler Artificial Stone Works
1922
De La Roche Street
NO SUCCESS.

My father was twenty years old then, younger than my eldest son is now. He was the firstborn of fourteen children. Surely that year, as every year of his life, on Passover, he sat in his finery at a dining-room table and recited, "We were once the slaves of Pharaoh in Egypt, but the Lord our God brought us forth from there with a mighty hand and an outstretched arm." But, come 1922, out there in the muck of his father's freezing backyard on De La Roche Street in Montreal—yet to absorb the news of his liberation—my father was still trying to make bricks with insufficient straw.

Moses Isaac Richler.

Insufficient straw, *NO* SUCCESS, was the story of his life. Neither of his marriages really worked. There were searing quarrels with my older brother. As a boy, I made life difficult for him. I had no respect. Later, officious strangers would rebuke him in the synagogue for the novels I had written. Heaping calumny on the Jews, they said. If there was such a thing as a reverse Midas touch, he had it. Not one of my father's penny mining stocks ever went into orbit. He lost regularly at gin rummy. As younger, more intrepid brothers and cousins began to prosper, he assured my mother, "The bigger they come, the harder they fall."

My mother, her eyes charged with scorn, laughed in his face. "You're the eldest and what are you?"

Nothing.

After his marriage to my mother blew apart, he moved into a rented room. Stunned, humiliated. St. Urbain's cuckold. He bought a natty straw hat. A sports jacket. He began to use aftershave lotion. It was then I discovered that he had a bottle of rye whiskey stashed in the glove compartment of his Chevy. My father. Rye whiskey. "What's that for?" I asked, astonished.

"For the femmes," he replied, wiggling his eyebrows at me. "It makes them want it."

I remember him as a short man, squat, with a shiny bald head and big floppy ears. Richler ears. My ears. Seated at the kitchen table at night in his Penman's long winter underwear, wetting his finger before turning a page of the *New York Daily Mirror*, reading Walter Winchell first. Winchell, who knew what's what. He also devoured *Popular Mechanics*, *Doc Savage*, and *Black Mask*. And, for educational purposes, *Reader's Digest*. My mother, on the other hand, read Keats and Shelley. *King's Row*. *The Good Earth*. My father's pranks did not enchant her. A metal ink spot on her new chenille bedspread. A felt mouse to surprise her in the larder. A knish secretly filled with absorbent cotton. Neither did his jokes appeal to her. "Hey, do you know why we eat hard-boiled eggs dipped in salt water just before the Passover meal?"

"No, Daddy. Why?"

"To remind us that when the Jews crossed the Red Sea they certainly got their balls soaked."

Saturday mornings my brother and I accompanied him to the Young Israel synagogue on Park Avenue near St. Viateur. As I was the youngest, under bar-mitzvah age, and therefore still allowed to carry on the Sabbath, I was the one who held the prayer shawls in a little purple velvet bag. My father, who couldn't stomach the rabbi's windy speeches, would slip into the back room to gossip with the other men before the rabbi set sail. "In Japan," my father once said, "there is a custom, time-honored, that before he begins, a speaker's hands are filled with ice cubes. He can shoot his mouth off for as long as he can hold the ice cubes in his hands. I wouldn't mind it if the rabbi had to do that."

He was stout, he was fleshy. But in the wedding photographs that I never saw until after his death the young man who was to become my father is as skinny as I once was, his startled brown eyes unsmiling behind horn-rimmed glasses. Harold Lloyd. Allowed a quick no-promises peek at the world and what it had to offer, but clearly not entitled to a place at the table.

My father never saw Paris. Never read Yeats. Never stayed out with the boys drinking too much. Never flew to New York on a whim. Nor turned over in bed and slept in, rather than report to work. Never knew a reckless love. What did he hope for? What did he want? Beyond peace and quiet, which he seldom achieved, I have no idea. So far as I know he never took a risk or was disobedient. At his angriest, I once heard him silence one of his cousins, a cousin bragging about his burgeoning real estate investments, saying, "You know how much land a man needs? Six feet. And one day that's all you'll have. Ha, ha!"

Anticipating Bunker Hunt, my father began to hoard American silver in his rented room. A blue steamer trunk filling with neatly stacked piles of silver dollars, quarters, dimes. But decades before their worth began to soar, he had to redeem them at face value. "I'm getting hitched again," he told me, blushing. He began to speculate in postage stamps. When he died at the age of sixty-five I also found out that he had bought a city backlot somewhere for $1200 during the Forties. In 1967, however—riding a bloated market, every fool raking it in—the estimated value of my father's property had shrunk to $900. All things considered, that called for a real touch of class.

I was charged with appetite, my father had none. I dreamed of winning prizes, he never competed. But, like me, my father was a writer. A keeper of records. His diary, wherein he catalogued injuries and insults, betrayals, family quarrels, bad debts, was written in a code of his own invention. His brothers and sisters used to tease him about it. "Boy, are we ever afraid! Look, I'm shaking!" But as cancer began to consume him, they took notice, fluttering about, concerned. "What about Moishe's diary?"

I wanted it. Oh, how I wanted it. I felt the diary was my proper inheritance. I hoped it would tell me things about him that he had always been too reticent to reveal. But his widow, an obdurate lady, refused to let me into the locked room in their apartment where he kept his personal papers. All she would allow was, "I'm returning your mother's love letters to her. The ones he found that time. You know, from the refugee."

That would have been during the early Forties, when my mother began to rent to refugees, putting them up in our spare bedroom. The refugees, German and Austrian Jews, had been interned as enemy aliens in England shortly after war was declared in 1939. A year later they were transported to Canada on a ship along with the first German and Italian prisoners of war. On arrival at the dock in Quebec City, the army major who turned them over to their Canadian guards said, "You have some German officers here, very good fellows, and some Italians, they'll be no trouble. And over there," he added, indicating the refugees, "the scum of Europe."

The refugees were interned in camps, but in 1941 they began to be released one by one. My father, who had never had anybody to condescend to in his life, was expecting real *greeners* with sidecurls. Timorous innocents out of the *shtetl*, who would look to him as a master of magic. Canadian magic. Instead, they patronized him. A mere junk dealer, a dolt. The refugees turned out to speak better English than any of us did, as well as German and French. After all they had been through over there, they were still fond of quoting a German son of a bitch called Goethe. "Imagine that," my father said. They also sang opera arias in the bathtub. They didn't guffaw over the antics of Fibber McGee 'n' Molly on the radio; neither were they interested in the strippers who shook their nookies right at you from the stage of the Gayety Theatre, nor in learning how to play gin rummy for a quarter of a cent a point. My mother was enthralled.

▼ ▼ ▼

My father was afraid of his father. He was afraid of my unhappy mother, who arranged to have their marriage annulled when I was thirteen and my brother eighteen. He was also afraid of his second wife. Alas, he was even afraid of me when I was a boy. I rode streetcars on the Sabbath. I ate bacon. But nobody was ever afraid of Moses Isaac Richler. He was far too gentle.

The Richler family was, and remains, resolutely Orthodox, followers of the Lubavitcher rabbi. So when my mother threatened divorce, an all but unheard-of scandal in those days, a flock of grim rabbis in flapping black gabardine coats descended on our cold-water flat on St. Urbain Street to plead with her. But my mother, dissatisfied for years with her arranged marriage, in love at last, was adamant. She had had enough. The rabbis sighed when my father, snapping his suspenders, rocking on his heels—*speaking out*—stated his most deeply felt marital grievance. When he awakened from his Saturday afternoon nap there was no tea. "Me, I like a cup of hot tea with lemon when I wake up."

In the end, there was no divorce. Instead, there was an annulment. I should explain that in the Province of Quebec at that time each divorce called for parliamentary approval. A long, costly process. A lawyer, a family friend, found a loophole. He pleaded for an annulment. My mother, he told the court, had married without her father's consent when she had still been a minor. He won. Technically speaking, as I used to brag at college, I'm a bastard.

▼ ▼ ▼

Weekdays my father awakened every morning at six, put on his phylacteries, said his morning prayers, and drove his truck through the wintry dark to the family scrapyard near the waterfront. He worked there for my fierce, hot-tempered grandfather and a pompous younger brother. Uncle Solly, who had been to high school, had been made a partner in the yard, but not my father, his firstborn. He was a mere employee, working for a salary, which fed my mother's wrath. Younger brothers, determined to escape an overbearing father, had slipped free to form their own business, but my father was too timid to join them. "When times are bad they'll be back. I remember the Depression. Oh, boy!"

"Tell me about it," I pleaded.

But my father never talked to me about anything. Not his own boyhood. His feelings. Or his dreams. He never even mentioned sex to me until I was nineteen years old, bound for Paris to try to become a writer. Clutching my Royal portable, wearing my Sta. Wag. coat. "You know what safes are. If you have to do it—*and I know you*—use 'em. Don't get married over there. They'd do anything for a pair of nylon stockings or a Canadian passport."

Hot damn, I hoped he was right. But my father thought I was crazy to sail for Europe. A graveyard for the Jews. A continent where everything was broken or old. Even so, he lent me his blue steamer trunk and sent me $50 a month support. When I went broke two years later, he mailed me my boat fare without reproach. I told him that the novel I had written over there was called *The Acrobats* and he immediately suggested that I begin the title of my second novel with a B, the third with a C, and so on, which would make a nifty trademark for me. Writing, he felt, might not be such a nutty idea after all. He had read in *Life* that this guy Mickey Spillane, a mere *goy*, was making a fortune. Insulted, I explained hotly that I wasn't that kind of writer. I was a serious man.

"So?"

"I only write out of my obsessions."

"Ah, ha," he said, sighing, warming to me for once, recognizing another generation of family failure.

▼ ▼ ▼

Even when I was a boy his admonitions were few. "Don't embarrass me. Don't get into trouble."

I embarrassed him. I got into trouble.

In the early Forties, my father's father rented a house directly across the street from us on St. Urbain, ten of his fourteen children still single and rooted at home. The youngest, my Uncle Yankel, was only three years older than I was and at the time we were close friends. But no matter what after-school mischief we were up to, we were obliged to join my grandfather at sunset in the poky little Gallicianer *shul* around the corner for the evening prayers, a ritual I didn't care for. One evening, absorbed in a chemistry experiment in our "lab" in my grandfather's basement, we failed to appear. On his return from *shul*, my grandfather descended on us, seething, his face bleeding red. One by one he smashed our test tubes and our retorts and even our cherished water distiller against the stone wall. Yankel begged forgiveness, but not me. A few days later I contrived to get into a scrap with Yankel, leaping at him, blackening his eye. Oh boy, did that ever feel good. But Yankel squealed on me. My grandfather summoned me into his study, pulled his belt free of his trousers, and thrashed me.

Vengeance was mine.

I caught my grandfather giving short weight on his scrapyard scales to a drunken Irish peddler. My grandfather, Jehovah's enforcer. Scornful, triumphant, I ran to my father and told him his father was no better than a cheat and a hypocrite.

"What do you know?" my father demanded.

"Nothing."

"They're anti-Semites, every one of them."

My grandfather moved to Jeanne Mance Street, only a few blocks away, and on Sunday afternoons he welcomed all the family there. Children, grandchildren. Come Hanukkah, the most intimidating of my aunts was posted in the hall, seated behind a bridge table piled high with Parcheesi games one year, Snakes and Ladders another. As each grandchild filed past the table he was issued a game. "Happy Hanukkah."

My grandfather was best with babies, rubbing his spade beard into their cheeks until they squealed. Bouncing them on his lap. But I was twelve years old now and I had taken to strutting down St. Urbain without a hat, and riding streetcars on the Sabbath. The next time my father and I started out for the house on Jeanne Mance on a Sunday afternoon, he pleaded with me not to disgrace him yet again, to behave myself for once, and then he thrust a *yarmulke* at me. "You can't go in there bareheaded. Put it on."

"It's against my principles. I'm an atheist."

"What are you talking about?"

"Charles Darwin," I said, having just read a feature article on him in *Coronet*, "or haven't you ever heard of him?"

"You put on that *yarmulke*," he said, "or I cut your allowance right now."

"O.K., O.K."

"And Jewish children are not descended from monkeys, in case you think you know everything."

"When I have children of my own I'll be better to them."

I had said that, testing. Sneaking a sidelong glance at my father. The thing is I had been born with an undescended testicle and my brother, catching me naked in the bathroom, had burst out laughing and assured me that I would never be able to have children or even screw. "With only one ball," he said, "you'll never be able to shoot jism."

My father didn't rise to the bait. He had worries of his own. My mother. The refugee in the spare bedroom. His father. "When you step in the door," he said, "the *zeyda* will ask you which portion of the Torah they read in *shul* yesterday." He told me the name of the chapter. "Got it?"

"I'm not afraid of him."

My grandfather, his eyes hot, was lying in wait for me in the living room. Before a court composed of just about the entire family, he denounced me as a violator of the Sabbath. A *shabus goy*. Yankel smirked. My grandfather grabbed me by the ear, beat me about the face, and literally threw me out of the house. I lingered across the street, waiting for my father to seek me out, but when he finally appeared, having endured a bruising lecture of his own, all he said was, "You deserved what you got."

"Some father you are."

Which was when I earned another belt on the cheek.

"I want you to go back in there like a man and apologize to the *zeyda*."

"Like hell."

I never spoke to my grandfather again.

But when he died, less than a year after the annulment of my parents' marriage, my mother insisted it was only proper that I attend his funeral. I arrived at the house on Jeanne Mance to find the coffin set out in the living room, uncles and aunts gathered round. My Uncle Solly drove me into a corner. "So here you are," he said.

"So?"

"You hastened his death; you never even spoke to him even though he was sick all those months."

"I didn't bring on his death."

"Well, smart guy, you're the one who is mentioned first in his will."

"Oh."

"You are not a good Jew and you are not to touch his coffin. It says that in his will. Don't you dare touch his coffin."

I turned to my father. Help me, help me. But he retreated, wiggling his eyebrows.

▼ ▼ ▼

So many things about my father's nature still exasperate or mystify me. All those years he was being crushed by his own father, nagged by my mother, teased (albeit affectionately) by his increasingly affluent brothers and cousins, was he seething inside, plotting a vengeance in his diary? Or was he really so sweet-natured as not to give a damn? Finally, there is a possibility I'd rather not ponder. Was he not sweet-natured at all, but a coward? Like me. Who would travel miles to avoid a quarrel. Who tends to remember slights—recording them in my mind's eye—transmogrifying them—finally publishing them in a code more accessible than my father's. Making them the stuff of fiction.

Riddles within riddles.

My father came to Montreal as an infant, his father fleeing Galicia. Pogroms. Rampaging Cossacks. But, striptease shows aside, the only theatre my father relished, an annual outing for the two of us, was the appearance of the Don Cossack Choir at the St. Denis Theatre. My father would stamp his feet to their lusty marching and drinking songs; his eyes would light up to see those behemoths, his own father's tormentors, prance and tumble on stage. Moses Isaac Richler, who never marched, nor drank, nor pranced.

Obviously, he didn't enjoy his family. My mother, my brother, me. Sundays he would usually escape our cold-water flat early and alone and start out for the first-run downtown cinemas, beginning with the Princess, which opened earliest, continuing from there to the Capitol or the Palace, and maybe moving on to the Loew's, returning to us bleary-eyed, but satiated, after dark. Astonishingly, he kept a sharp eye out for little production errors. Discovering them filled him with joy. Once, for instance, he told us, "Listen to this, Clark Gable is sitting there in this newspaper office and he tells Claudette Colbert he will be finished typing his story in an hour. But when she comes back and we are supposed to believe an hour has passed, *the hands on the clock on the wall haven't moved. Not an inch.*" Another time it was, "Franchot Tone is in this tank in the desert, you're not going to believe this, and he says 'O.K., men, let's go. Attack!' And they attack. But if you look closely inside the tank just before they push off, the fuel gauge is indicating EMPTY. No gas. Get it?"

The Best Years of Our Lives overwhelmed him.

"There's a scene in there where Fredric March burps. He's hung over, he drinks an Alka-Seltzer or something, and he lets out a good one. Right there on screen. Imagine."

My mother was fond of reminding me that the night I was born, my father had not waited at the hospital to find out how she was, or whether it was a boy or a girl, but had gone to the movies instead. What was playing, I wondered.

My father didn't dream of Italy, where the lemon trees bloomed. He never went for a walk in the country or read a novel, unless he had to, because it was one of mine and he might be blamed for it. Bliss for him was the Gayety Theatre on a Saturday night. My father and a couple of younger brothers, still bachelors, seated front row center. On stage, Peaches, Anne Curie, or the legendary Lili St. Cyr. My father rapt, his throat dry, watching the unattainable Lili simulating intercourse with a swan as the stage lights throbbed, then trudging home through the snow to sit alone at the kitchen table, drinking hot milk with matzohs before going to sleep.

We endured some rough passages together. Shortly after the marriage annulment, I fought with my father. Fists flew. We didn't speak for two years. Then, when we came together again, meeting once a week, it wasn't to talk, but to play gin rummy for a quarter of a cent a point. My father, I began to suspect, wasn't reticent. He didn't understand life. He had nothing to say to anybody.

▼ ▼ ▼

In 1954, some time after my return to Europe, where I was to remain rooted for almost two decades, I married a *shiksa* in London. My father wrote me an indignant letter. Once more, we were estranged. But no sooner did the marriage end in divorce than he pounced: "You see, mixed marriages never work."

"But, Daddy, your first marriage didn't work either and Maw was a rabbi's daughter."

"What do you know?"

"Nothing," I replied, hugging him.

When I married again, this time for good, but to another *shiksa*, he was not overcome with delight, yet neither did he complain. For after all the wasting years, we had finally become friends. My father became my son. Once, he had sent money to me in Paris. Now, as the scrapyard foundered, I mailed monthly checks to him in Montreal. On visits home, I took him to restaurants. I bought him treats. If he took me to a gathering of the Richler clan on a Sunday afternoon, he would bring along a corked bottle of 7-Up for me, filled with scotch whisky. "There'll be nothing for you to drink there, and I know you."

"Hey, Daddy, that's really very thoughtful."

During the Sixties, on a flying trip to Montreal, my publishers put me up at the Ritz-Carlton Hotel, and I asked my father to meet me for a drink there.

"You know," he said, joining me at the table, "I'm sixty-two years old and I've never been here before. Inside, I mean. So this is the Ritz."

"It's just a bar," I said, embarrassed.

"What should I order?"

"Whatever you want, Daddy."

"A rye and ginger ale. Would that be all right here?"

"Certainly."

▼ ▼ ▼

What I'm left with are unresolved mysteries. A sense of regret. Anecdotes for burnishing.

My wife, a proud lady, showing him our firstborn son, his week-old howling grandchild, saying, "Don't you think he looks like Mordecai?"

"Babies are babies," he responded, seemingly indifferent.

Some years later my father coming to our house, pressing chocolate bars on the kids. "Who do you like better," he asked them, "your father or your mother?"

In the mid-Sixties, I flew my father to London. He came with his wife. Instead of slipping away with him to the Windmill Theatre or Raymond's Revue Bar, another strip joint, like a fool I acquired theatre tickets. We took the two of them to *Beyond the Fringe*. "What did you think?" I asked as we left the theatre.

"There was no chorus line," he said.

Following his last operation for cancer, I flew to Montreal, promising to take him on a trip as soon as he was out of bed. The Catskills. Grossinger's. With a stopover in New York to take in some shows. Back in London, each time I phoned, his doctor advised me to wait a bit longer. I waited. He died. The next time I flew to Montreal it was to bury him.

From *Home Sweet Home: My Canadian Album* (Toronto: McClelland and Stewart, 1984), 56–69.

MORDECAI RICHLER

Why I Write

As I write, October 1970, I have just finished a novel of intimidating length, a fiction begun five years ago, on the other side of the moon, so I am, understandably enough, concerned by the state of the novel in general. Is it dead? Dead *again*. Like God or MGM. Father McLuhan says so (writing, "The Age of Writing has passed") and Dylan Thomas's daughter recently pronounced stingingly from Rome, "Nobody reads novels any more."

I'm soon going to be forty. Too old to learn how to teach. Or play the guitar. Stuck, like the blacksmith, with the only craft I know. But brooding about the novel, and its present unmodishness, it's not the established practitioner I'm grieving for, it's the novice, that otherwise effervescent young man stricken with the wasting disease whose earliest symptom is the first novel. These are far from halcyon days for the fledgling novelist.

Look at it this way. Most publishers, confronted with a rectal polyp, hold on to hope, tempting the surgeon with a bigger advance. They know the score. What's truly terminal. Offered a first novel or worse news—*infamy*—a short story collection, they call for the ledgers which commemorate last season's calamities. The bright new talents nobody wanted to read. Now more to be remaindered than remembered, as *Time* once observed.

I know. Carting off my cumbersome manuscript to be xeroxed, it was my first novel that was uppermost in my mind, *The Acrobat*, published in 1954, when I was twenty-three years old. At the time, I was living in Montreal, and my British publisher, André Deutsch, urged me to visit his Canadian distributor before sailing for England. So I caught the overnight Greyhound bus to Toronto, arriving at 7 A.M. in a city where I knew nobody and walking the sweltering summer streets until 9:30, when offices would open.

The Canadian distributor, bracingly realistic, did not detain me overlong with *recherché* chitchat about style, content or influences. "Have you written a thick book or a thin book?" he demanded.

A thin one, I allowed.

"Thick books sell better than thin ones here."

A slow learner, I published five more before I at last surfaced with a thick one, *St. Urbain's Horseman*, which was all of 180 000 words. And retrieving my seven xeroxed copies, I couldn't help but reflect that the £80 I forked out for them was only slightly less than the British advance against royalties I was paid for my first novel sixteen years ago. The American publisher, G.P. Putnam's Sons, was more generous; they sent me 750 dollars. But I was disheartened when I received their catalogue. Putnam's was, at the time, trying a new experiment in book selling. If you didn't enjoy one of their books, your bookseller would return you the money, no questions asked. Only two books listed in the autumn catalogue conspicuously failed to carry this guarantee, mine, and another young writer's.

The Acrobats ultimately sold some 2000 copies in England and less than a 1000 in the U.S., but it was—as I pointed out to my aunt, on a visit to Montreal—translated into five foreign languages.

"There must," she said, smoothing out her skirt, "be a shortage of books."

My uncle, also a critic, was astonished when he computed my earnings against the time I had invested. I would have earned more mowing his lawn, and, furthermore, it would have been healthier for me.

The novel, the novel.

Write a study of the pre-Columbian butterfly, compose an account of colonial administration in Tongo, and Nigel Dennis, that most perspicacious and witty of British reviewers, might perversely enshrine it in a 1000 word essay in the *Sunday Telegraph*. Or Malcolm Muggeridge might take it as the text for a lengthy sermon, excoriating once more that generation of younger vipers who will continue to enjoy, enjoy, after he has passed on to his much-advertised rest. But novels, coming in batches of twenty weekly, seldom rate a notice of their own in England. Sixteen are instant losers. Or, looked at another way, payola from the literary editor. Badly-paid reviewers' perks. The reviewer is not even expected to read them, but it is understood he can flog them for half-price to a buyer from Fleet Street. Of the four that remain, comprising the typical novel column, one is made especially for skewering in the last deadly paragraph, and two are destined for the scales of critical balance. On the one hand, somewhat promising, on the other, ho-hum. Only one makes the lead. But it must lead in four of the five influential newspapers, say, the *Sunday Times, Observer, Times* and *Guardian*, if anybody's to take notice. Some even buying.

"Basically," a concerned New York editor told me, "the trouble is we are trying to market something nobody wants. Or needs."

The novel has had its day, we are assured, and in the Age of Aquarius, film, man, film's the stuff that will do more than fiction can to justify God's way to man. Given any rainy afternoon who wants to read Doris Lessing fully-clothed for forty bob when, for only ten, you can actually see Jane Fonda starkers, shaking it for you and art, and leaving you with sufficient change for a half-bottle of gin?

To be fair, everything has (and continues) to be tried. Novels like decks of playing cards. Shuffle, and read it anyway it comes up. Novels like jokes or mutual funds. You cut your potential time-investment loss by inviting everybody in the office to pound out a chapter. *Naked Came The Stranger. I Knew Daisy Smutten.* Or instead-of-sex. Why weary yourself, performing badly perhaps when, if only you lose yourself in *The Adventurers*, you can have better-hung Dax come for you? And, sooner or later, somebody's bound to turn to the cassette. No need to bruise your thumbs turning pages. You slip the thing into a machine and listen to Racquel Welch read it. "The latest Amis as read by. . . . "

On a recent visit to Canadian university campuses, I found myself a creature to be pitied, still writing novels when anybody could tell you that's no longer "where it's at." But I've tried the logical alternative, screen writing, and though I still write for the films from time to time, it's not really for me.

The trouble is, like most novelists, I am conditioned to working for years on material I discuss with nobody. To adjust from that to script writing is too much like what Truman Capote once described as group sports. Even so, five years in a room with a novel-in-progress can be more than gruelling. If getting up to it some mornings is a pleasure, it is, just as often, a punishment. A self-inflicted punishment. There have been false starts, wrong turns, and weeks with nothing to show except sharpened pencils and bookshelves re-arranged. I have rewritten chapters ten times that in the end simply didn't belong and had to be cut. Ironically, even unforgivably, it usually seems to be those passages over which I have laboured most arduously, nurtured in the hot-house, as it were, that never really spring to life, and the pages that came too quickly, with utterly suspect ease, that read most felicitously.

Riding into my second year on *St. Urbain's Horseman*, disheartened by proliferating school bills, diminished savings, and only fitful progress, I finally got stuck so badly that there was nothing for it but to shove the manuscript aside. I started in on another novel, a year's heat, which yielded *Cocksure*. Anthony Burgess clapped hands in *Life*, *Time* approved, *Newsweek* cheered, and the British notices were almost uniformly fulsome. Encouraged and somewhat solvent again, I resolved to resume work on *Horseman*. After twelve years in London, I was to return to Montreal for a year with my wife and five children, to report for duty as writer-in-residence at Sir George Williams University, my *alma mater*. Or, put plainly, in return for taking a "creative writing" seminar one afternoon a week, I could get on with my novel, comparatively free of financial worry.

Ostensibly, conditions were ideal, winds couldn't be more favourable, and so I started in for the ninth time on page one of *St. Urbain's Horseman*. I didn't get much further before, my stomach crawling with fear, I began to feel I'd lost something somewhere.

I got stuck. Morning after morning, I'd switch to an article or a book review, already long overdue. Or compose self-pitying letters to friends. Or dawdle until eleven A.M., when it was too late to make a decent start on anything, and I was at last free to quit my room and stroll downtown. St. Catherine Street. Montreal's Main Stem, as the doyen of our gossip columnists has it. Pretending to browse for books by lesser novelists, I could surreptitiously check out the shops on stacks of the paperback edition of *Cocksure*.

Or take in a movie maybe.

Ego dividends. I could pick a movie that I had been asked to write myself, but declined. Whatever the movie, it was quite likely I would know the director or the script writer, maybe even one of the stars.

So there you have it. Cat's out of the bag. In London, I skitter on the periphery of festooned circles, know plenty of inside stories. Bomb-shells. Like which cabinet minister is an insatiable pederast. What best-selling novel was really stitched together by a cunning editor. Which wrinkled Hollywood glamour queen is predisposed toward gang shags with hirsute Neapolitan waiters from the Mirabelle. Yes, yes, I'll own up to it. I am, after eighteen years as a writer, not utterly unconnected or unknown, as witness the entry in the indispensable *Oxford Companion to Canadian Literature*.

> Richler, Mordecai (1931–) Born in Montreal, he was educated at Sir George Williams College and spent two years abroad. Returning to Canada in 1952, he joined the staff of the Canadian Broadcasting Corporation. He now lives in England, where he writes film scripts, novels, and short stories. The key to Richler's novels is. . . .

After eighteen years and six novels there is nothing I cherish so much as the first and most vulnerable book, *The Acrobats*, not only because it marked the first time my name appeared in a Canadian newspaper, a prescient Toronto columnist writing from London, "You've not heard of Mordecai Richler, yet, but, look out, she's a name to watch for"; but also because it was the one book I could write as a totally private act, with the deep, inner assurance that nobody would be such a damn fool as to publish it. That any editor would boot it back to me, a condescending rejection note enclosed, enabling me to quit Paris for Montreal, an honourable failure, and get down to the serious business of looking for a job. A real job.

I did in fact return to Montreal, broke, while my manuscript made the rounds. My father, who hadn't seen me for two years, took me out for a drive.

"I hear you wrote a novel in Europe," he said.

"Yes."

"What's it called?"

"The Acrobats."

"What in the hell do you know about the circus?"

I explained the title was a symbolic one.

"Is it about Jews or ordinary people?" my father asked.

To my astonishment, André Deutsch offered to publish the novel. Now, when somebody asked me what I did, I could reply, without seeming fraudulent to myself, that I was indeed a writer. If, returned to Hampstead once more, I still tended to doubt it in the early morning hours, now *The Acrobats*, in shop windows here and there, was the proof I needed. My novel on display side by side with real ones. There is no publication as agonizing or charged with elation as the first.

Gradually, you assume that what you write will be published. After the first book, composing a novel is no longer self-indulgent, a conceit. It becomes, among other things, a living. Though to this day reviews can still sting or delight, it's sales that buy you the time to get on with the next. Mind you, there are a number of critics whose esteem I prize, whose opprobrium can sear, but, for the most part, I, in common with other writers, have learned to read reviews like a market report. This one will help move the novel, that one not.

Writing a novel, as George Orwell has observed, is a horrible, exhausting struggle. "One would never undertake such a thing if one were not driven by some demon whom one can neither resist nor understand." Something else. Each novel is a failure, or there would be no compulsion to begin afresh. Critics don't help. Speaking as someone who fills that office on occasion, I must say that the critic's essential relationship is with the reader, not the writer. It is his duty to celebrate good books, eviscerate bad ones, lying ones.

When I first published, in 1954, it was commonly assumed that to commit a film script was to sell out (Daniel Fuchs, Christopher Isherwood, Irwin Shaw), and that the good and dedicated life was in academe. Now, the inverse seems to be the Canadian and, I daresay, American case. The creative young yearn to be in films, journeymen retire to the universities: *seems* to be the case, because, happily, there are exceptions.

All of us tend to romanticize the world we nearly chose. In my case, academe, where instead of having to bring home the meat, I would only be obliged to stamp it, rejecting this shoulder of beef as Hank James derivative, or that side of pork as sub-Jimmy Joyce. I saw myself no longer a perplexed free-lancer with an unpredictable income, balancing this magazine assignment, that film job, against the time it would buy me. No sir. Sipping Tio Pepe in the faculty club, snug in my leather winged-back armchair and the company of other disinterested scholars, I would not, given the assurance of a monthly cheque, chat about anything so coarse as money.

– Why don't you, um, write a novel yourself this summer, Professor Richler?

– Well, Dr. Lemming, like you, I have too much respect for the tradition to sully it with my own feeble scribblings.

– Quite.

– Just so.

Alas, academe, like girls, whisky, and literature, promised better than it paid. I now realize, after having ridden the academic gravy train for a season, that vaudeville hasn't disappeared or been killed by TV, but merely retired to small circuits, among them, the universities. Take the Canadian poets, for instance. Applying for Canadian Council grants today, they no longer catalogue their publications (the obsolete accomplishments of linear man) but, instead, like TV actors on the make, they list their personal appearances, the campuses where they read aloud. Wowsy at Simon Fraser U., hotsy at Carleton. Working wrinkles out of the act in the stix, with a headliner coming up in the veritable Palace of the Canadian campus circuit, the University of Toronto.

If stand-up comics now employ batteries of gag writers because national TV exposure means they can only use their material once, then professors, playing to a new house every season, can peddle the same oneliners year after year, improving only on timing and delivery. For promos, they publish. Bringing out journals necessary to no known audience, but essential to their advancement.

Put plainly, these days everybody's in show business, all trades are riddled with impurities. And so, after a most enjoyable (and salaried) year in academe—a reverse sabbatical, if you like—I returned to the uncertain world of the free-lance writer, where nobody, as James Thurber once wrote, sits at anybody's feet unless he's been knocked there. I returned with my family to London, no deeper into *St. Urbain's Horseman* than when I had left.

Why do you write?

Doctors are seldom asked why they practise, shoemakers how come they cobble, or baseball players why they don't drive a coal truck instead, but again and again writers, like housebreakers, are asked why they do it.

Orwell, as might be expected, supplies the most honest answer in his essay, "Why I Write."

"1. Sheer egoism. Desire to seem clever, to be talked about, to be remembered after death, to get your own back on grownups who snubbed you in childhood, etc., etc." To this I would add egoism informed by imagination, style, and a desire to be known, yes, *but only on your own conditions*.

Nobody is more embittered than the neglected writer and, obviously, allowed a certain recognition, I am a happier and more generous man than I would otherwise be. But nothing I have done to win this recognition appals me, has gone against my nature. I fervently believe that all a writer should send into the marketplace to be judged is his own work; the rest should remain private. I deplore the writer as a personality, however large and undoubted the talent, as is the case with Norman Mailer. I also do not believe in special licence for so-called artistic temperament. After all, my problems, as I grudgingly come within spitting distance of middle age, are the same as anybody else's. Easier maybe. I can bend my anxieties to subversive uses. Making stories of them. When I'm not writing, I'm a husband and a father of five. Worried about pollution. The population explosion. My sons' report cards.

"2. Aesthetic enthusiasm. Perception of beauty in the external world, or, on the other hand, in words and their right arrangement." The agonies involved in creating a novel, the unsatisfying draft, the scenes you never get right, are redeemed by those rare and memorable days when, seemingly without reason, everything falls right. Bonus days. Blessed days when, drawing on resources unsuspected, you pluck ideas and prose out of your skull that you never dreamt yourself capable of.

Such, such are the real joys.

Unfortunately, I don't feel that I've ever been able to sustain such flights for a novel's length. So the passages that flow are balanced with those which were forced in the hothouse. Of all the novels I've written, it is *The Apprenticeship of Duddy Kravitz* and *Cocksure* which come closest to my intentions and, therefore, give me the most pleasure. I should add that I'm still lumbered with the characters and ideas, the social concerns I first attempted in *The Acrobats*. Every serious writer has, I think, one theme, many variations to play on it.

Like any serious writer, I want to write one novel that will last, something that will make me remembered after death, and so I'm compelled to keep trying.

"3. Historical impulse. Desire to see things as they are. . . ."

No matter how long I continue to live abroad, I do feel forever rooted in Montreal's St. Urbain Street. That was my time, my place, and I have elected myself to get it right.

"4. Political purpose—using the word 'political' in the widest possible sense. Desire to push the world in a certain direction, to alter other people's idea of the kind of society that they should strive after."

Not an overlarge consideration in my work, though I would say that any serious writer is a moralist and only incidently an entertainer.

▼ ▼ ▼

After a year on the academic payroll, I returned to London in August 1969, abysmally depressed, because after four years *St. Urbain's Horseman* was no nearer to completion and, once more, my savings were running down. I retired to my room each morning, ostensibly to work, but actually to prepare highly impressive schedules. Starting next Monday, without fail, I would write three pages a day. Meanwhile, I would train for this ordeal by taking a nap every afternoon, followed by trips to the movies I simply had to see, thereby steeling myself against future fatigue and distractions. Next Monday, however, nothing came. Instead, taking the sports pages of the *International Herald-Tribune* as my text, I calculated, based on present standings and won-lost ratios, where each team in both major baseball leagues would end the season. Monday, falling on the eighth of the month, was a bad date, anyway. Neither here nor there. I would seriously begin work, I decided, on the 15th of the month, writing *six* pages daily. After all, if Simenon could write a novel in a week, surely.... When I failed to write even a paragraph on the 15th, I was not upset. Finally, I grasped the real nature of my problem. Wrong typewriter. Wrong colour ribbon. Wrong texture paper. I traded in my machine for one with a new type face, bought six blue ribbons, and three boxes of heavy bond paper, but still nothing came. Absolutely nothing.

Then, suddenly, in September, I began to put in long hours in my room, writing with ease, one day's work more gratifying than the next, and within a year the novel was done, all 550 typewritten pages.

The first person to read the manuscript, my wife, was, like all writers' wives, in an invidious position. I depend on my wife's taste and honesty. It is she, unenviably, who must tell me if I've gone wrong. If she disapproved, however diplomatically, there would be angry words, some things I would have to say about her own deficiencies, say her choice of clothes, her cooking, and the mess she was making of raising our children. I would also point out that it was gratuitously cruel of her to laugh aloud in bed, reading *Portnoy's Complaint*, when I was having such a struggle with my own novel. All the same, I would not submit the manuscript. If she found it wanting, I would put it aside for six months to be considered afresh. Another year, another draft. And yet—and yet—even if she proclaimed the manuscript a masterpiece, radiating delight, I would immediately discount her praise, thinking she's only my wife, loyal and loving, and therefore dangerously prejudiced. Maybe a liar. Certainly beyond the critical pale.

After my wife had pronounced, foolishly saying *St. Urbain's Horseman* was the best novel I'd written by far (making me resentful, because this obviously meant she hadn't enjoyed my earlier work as much as she should have done) I submitted the manuscript to my editors. Another hurdle, another intricate relationship. I deal with editors who are commonly taken to be among the most prescient in publishing—Robert Gottlieb at Knopf and, in England, Tony Godwin at Weidenfeld & Nicolson—but once I had sent them my manuscript, and they had obviously not dropped everything to read it overnight, wakening me with fulsome cables, long distance calls, champagne and caviar, I began to arm myself with fancied resentments and the case that could be made against their much-advertised (but as I had reason to suspect) over-rated acumen. As each morning's mail failed to yield a letter, and the telephone didn't ring, I lay seething on the living room sofa, ticking off, in my mind's eye, all the lesser novelists on their lists, those they flattered with larger ads, bigger first prints, more generous advances, more expensive lunches, than they had ever allowed me. In fact I had all but decided it was time to move on to other, more appreciative publishers when, only a week after I had submitted the manuscript, both editors wrote me enthusiastic letters. Enthusiastic letters, that is, until you have scrutinized them for the ninth time, reading between the lines, and grasp that the compliments are forced, the praise false, and that the sour truth hidden beneath the clichés is that they don't really like the novel. Or even if they did, their taste is demonstrably fallible, and corrupted by the fact that they are personal friends, especially fond of my wife.

Put plainly, nothing helps.

From *The Great Comic Book Heroes and Other Essays*, ed. Robert Fulford (Toronto: McClelland and Stewart, 1978), 80–91. First appeared in *Works in Progress* (The Literary Guild of America Inc., 1971) and then in *Shovelling Trouble*, by Mordecai Richler (McClelland and Stewart, 1972).

ROBERT FULFORD (1932–) is the third child of Albert Fulford, a newspaper reporter, and Frances Blount, the daughter of an Ottawa bookseller. He was, as he notes in his autobiographical account of his career, *Best Seat in the House* (1988), one of those students for whom "school simply never acquires meaning." Journalism offered an escape from school's penal servitude and he dropped out in grade twelve to become a sportswriter with the *Globe and Mail* in 1950. During the next eighteen years, he was to hold eight different full-time positions, including jobs with *Canadian Homes*, the *Toronto Star*, *Maclean's*, and *Mayfair*. In addition, he did a great deal of freelancing, some of it the "hack work" that is an important part of any reporter's apprenticeship: an article for *Canadian Bride* in which he ghosted a young wife's account of decorating her apartment, profiles of people he had never met, descriptions for a travel magazine of places that he had never been to. He also honed his skills as a reviewer during this time:

> The core of my work was discovery—searching though the books and art galleries for what was interesting and possibly important, then describing what I found accurately and engagingly. I also understood that, no matter how carefully I honed my standards, the most compelling artists would set their own standards—and sometimes would produce art that was significant even though it didn't please me.

His dedication and his talent for self-effacement made Fulford a penetrating and prescient reviewer, as a glance at what he wrote about the early McLuhan, Davies, or Atwood reveals. The crucial role he played in helping to make Stephen Vizinczey's *In Praise of Older Women* an international best-seller attests to his influence. During his nineteen-year tenure as editor of *Saturday Night*, from 1968 to 1987, it became the most widely read journal of its kind. Fulford made his regular column, "Notebook," which he described as "the best pulpit in Canada," essential reading for students of Canadian culture. Characteristically, he criticizes himself for not making *Saturday Night* profitable; but Fulford, while he has been critical of the starry-eyed who dream grandiose dreams of the financial viability of a fiercely nationalistic Canadian publishing industry, knows better than most that in the modern age culture operates not at a loss, but at a cost.

His books include *Crisis at the Victory Burlesque: Culture, Politics and Other Diversions* (1968), *This Was Expo* (1968), *An Introduction to the Arts in Canada* (1977), and *The Journalists* (1981). His career in radio and television extends from his hosting of CHUM "Teentime" in 1948, to "This is Robert Fulford" and "Realities," interview programs on the CBC and TV Ontario. Fulford's versatility as an interviewer is at least as impressive as his skills as a writer. He has interviewed figures as diverse as Duke Ellington, Jerzy Kosinski, Neil Young, Hugh MacDiarmid, Susan Sontag, W.H. Auden, Alice Munro, Mavis Gallant, Robertson Davies, David Hockney, Joy Kogawa, Jonathan Miller, and Allan Bloom. He can ask penetrating questions on subjects as varied as day-care for single mothers, Churchill's conduct of domestic affairs during the Second World War, and a moral philosophy of human sexuality. One of Fulford's great subjects is what he calls "cultural politics," and he has helped in the transformation of Canadian literary art in the last twenty-five years. This development has made people such as Atwood, Richler, and Frye important not only because they now attract a larger readership but because their work has a genuine impact: it shapes our lives. His *Best Seat in the House* is a crisply annotated Who's Who of Canadian arts and publishing, and his lucid analysis in the same book of Canadian culture's obsession with its own death should be tacked to the bulletin board of every newspaper editor and network executive in the country. In the following essays, he recounts the events of a year that brought great changes to the Canadian West and discusses the role that geography has played in the making of Canadian art.

ROBERT FULFORD

How the West Was Lost

They may never have seen each other's faces, but the two most famous non-whites in the late nineteenth-century Canada—Louis Riel and Big Bear—were linked by history and by the events of the crisis year 1885. They were dissimilar in many ways—Riel a Montreal-educated Métis who travelled widely and was three times elected to the Canadian parliament. Big Bear a Plains Cree who knew no world beyond the Prairies. But they were also alike: both were mystics and prophets and both were charismatic leaders of peoples doomed by the westward thrust of the Canadian empire. At the beginning of 1885 Riel was a towering figure in the West, feared as well as respected, and Big Bear was a chief of considerable reputation. By the end of the year Riel was dead, hanged for high treason; and Big Bear was in prison, an object of hatred to the whites and of contempt to the Indians. They were defeated by a process they only dimly understood and could do nothing to resist.

This year Canada is marking the hundredth anniversary of the North-West Rebellion with a TV documentary, radio programmes, books, a large exhibition of Métis crafts in Calgary, and half a dozen academic conferences. These events can't be construed as a celebration, because not even the most blissfully unaware Canadian white can regard the destruction of the Métis and Indian societies as an accomplishment. But it isn't exactly an occasion for mourning either; only total hypocrites would pretend to mourn a series of events by which we have all handsomely profited. Perhaps the centenary of the rebellion can serve us best if it broadens our understanding of how we came to be what we are, and of the human price that was paid for modern Canada.

Both Louis Riel and Big Bear were products as well as victims of the Europeanization of North America. Descendants of fur traders who married Indian women, the Métis built the brief prosperity of their society (it lasted about seven decades) by feeding the European and white North American markets with buffalo hides and other skins. Big Bear led an Indian community that was heavily influenced by Europe: in the middle of the nineteenth century he and his followers were hunting buffalo on horses brought by the Europeans and shooting them with European guns. In many ways, the Europeans were a curse to the Indians—they brought smallpox (which Big Bear survived in childhood while many of his contemporaries died)—but at times they must also have seemed a blessing. In the short term, Europeans made possible the greatest mobility and freedom the Plains Cree had ever enjoyed.

The events of the 1885 brought that period of intense and sometimes happy collaboration to an end. By the beginning of that year, Riel was already a legend. He had behind him the abortive rebellion of 1869–70, which failed to establish a Métis political jurisdiction but nevertheless led to the creation of Manitoba. He had survived his years of exile in Montana and been called back, to the leadership of his people. But what the Métis in general had in mind, and what Riel dreamed, were different. They wanted their land rights; he wanted not only land rights but a new Roman Catholicism in which everyone would be a priest, the pope would be a Canadian, the Métis would be the chosen people, and he himself would be the "Prophet of the New World." Riel's eighteen months in a mental hospital were now years behind him, but his old illness—a kind of megalomania—was upon him again. The man who was about to become one of the central myths of our history was (the evidence seems clear) in the throes of madness.

Riel interpreted the Gospels in a way that made violence acceptable and necessary. "Justice commands us to take up arms," he told his followers. On March 18, at Batoche, in what is now Saskatchewan, he and about sixty supporters ransacked the stores and seized a number of people, including the Indian agent. The next day he formed a provisional government and a few days later took part in a battle in which twelve Mounties and five Métis were killed. It was only a matter of time before the soldiers arrived from the East, defeated the Métis (in early May), and arrested Riel. The war seemed to be over almost before it began. Soon the soldiers were returning to the East, and—as Bob Beal and Rod Macleod write in their absorbing new book, *Prairie Fire: The 1885 North-West Rebellion* (Hurtig)—it was a time of national triumph for the young Dominion of Canada: "Every city and town that had sent a unit greeted their return with ecstatic crowds, and an orgy of banquets, church services, speeches, and plans for memorials followed. By the end of July all the troops were home and the last military operation in which Canadians shot and killed each other was over."

It could be argued that in pursuing their grievances the Métis were blindly impetuous. In 1885 only fools could have imagined that violent action by a tiny, isolated community would win an argument with the government of Canada. And perhaps Riel knew this all along. George Woodcock, in his 1975 book on Riel's general, *Gabriel Dumont*, suggested that Riel was courting martyrdom, consciously or not: "He belonged to a people against whose characteristic culture almost all the forces of the nineteenth century were aligned; even if he had survived, the way of life he defended could hardly have done so, and perhaps that was one of the reasons . . . he decided to die and even made sure of doing so by disputing his defence lawyer's plea of insanity when he was tried at Regina." But if the Riel rebellion was a kind of madness, the course of patient and peaceful negotiation was no more profitable. The experience of Big Bear was proving that point forcefully.

▼ ▼ ▼

The year 1885 is mainly remembered for Riel's defeat, but it was also the year the Plains Cree finally collapsed into the arms of white civilization and began their long decades of servitude as wards of the Canadian state. The end of their free civilization on the Prairies was at least as melancholy as the destruction of the Métis.

Big Bear's life—described recently in Hugh A. Dempsey's richly informative *Big Bear: The End of Freedom* (Douglas & McIntyre)—encompassed the whole story of nineteenth-century prairie Indians, from triumph on the open plains to humiliation on the reserves. A chief's son, Big Bear won his own reputation in adolescence as a buffalo hunter and a warrior. Like the Métis, the Plains Cree built their lives around the buffalo, which provided most of what they needed—not only food but skins that could be made into clothes and tents, even bones to be made into implements. But the buffalo, while plentiful enough to serve the Indians who hunted them with bow and arrow, didn't last long when attacked by Indians, Métis, and whites with fast horses and repeater rifles. It was said that in the peak years 160 000 buffalo were killed every season, and by the late 1870s they had all but disappeared.

The Cree knew no other way to live, and in 1878 Big Bear explained to Lieutenant Governor David Baird: "The Great Spirit has supplied us with plenty of buffalo for food until the white man came. Now as that means of support is about to fail us, the government ought to take the place of the Great Spirit, and provide us with the means of living in some other way." His statement sounded absurd at the time, but it turned out to be a summary of government policies for native peoples for at least the next century.

It was commonly said of Big Bear that if he had been white he would have been a great statesman. He approached the whites in a spirit of friendliness and brotherhood, but he was the last major chief in the West to sign a treaty with the government. Other chiefs, promised a few dollars and some provisions, signed away their rights to the land without knowing what their acquiescence meant for the future. Big Bear somehow knew. He never understood the complexities of white power—he seems always to have thought that "government" was the name of a man in Ottawa who controlled everything—but he realized that the whites were taking away all that the Indians had. His dreams often guided the Plains Cree; in his youth, shortly after the smallpox attack, a vision had told him that eventually the whites would come in great number, bearing gifts, and take away the Indian land. That process was set in motion in 1869 when the Hudson's Bay Company sold the West to the new Dominion of Canada for £300 000. The news of this transaction baffled and distressed the Indians, who had believed until then that no-one owned the land.

Their reaction illustrated the mutual incomprehension that made a reconciliation between Indians and whites impossible. The whites were bound by their view of the world as something to be owned and conquered. The Indians, as pre-agrarians, knew the world only as something to live with. In the nineteenth century no white man could understand a view so fundamentally alien to his own—or even admit that it existed. Given this profound difference, there was nothing for the whites to do except convert the Indians to Christianity, British justice, and farming.

Big Bear never imagined that a war against the whites would be profitable; he counselled peace while he practised the tactics of delay. His followers were not so patient, and in the 1880s his authority began to slip away. Younger men, more attracted to violent action, pushed him aside. In the spring of 1885, when Big Bear and his people were camped near the Frog Lake settlement—north of the North Saskatchewan River, in what is now Alberta—the younger men were in control. When word came that Louis Riel and the Métis had taken control of Batoche, the Plains Cree were ready to join.

▼ ▼ ▼

At this point, the history of my own family intersected with Canadian history in a way that has always made 1885 a compelling date for me. The Canadian government had decided that the Indians should be taught to farm. In 1879, John Delaney, until then an Ottawa Valley lumberman, went to work as a farm instructor in the North-West. He settled at Frog Lake and built a house. In 1882 he went back to the Ottawa Valley to marry his fiancée, Theresa Fulford, my great-aunt. The journey to Frog Lake, the last 400 miles by buckboard, was their wedding trip.

As my great-aunt later told the story, her husband was an exemplary figure, "generous to a fault. He was liked by all the bands." But then, she took that view of the whites in general. "*The Indians have no grievances and no complaints to make*," she reported, emphasizing her opinion with italics in *Two Months in the Camp of Big Bear*, the book she wrote with another Frog Lake survivor, Theresa Gowanlock. "Their treatment is of the best and most generous kind. The government spares no pains to attempt to make them adopt an agricultural life. . . ." Hugh Dempsey's book describes Indians starving within sight of white settlements, where food was doled out to them in minuscule amounts; Dempsey believes the government consciously used starvation to subdue the Indians. Aunt Theresa didn't see that, or didn't care to recall it.

Before they left the Ottawa Valley, John Delaney must have told her a great deal about Frog Lake. But there was one part of his life in the West that he almost certainly didn't mention to her. Writing some sixty-five years after the events of 1885, an Anglican clergyman, the Reverend Edward Ahenakew, set down a cryptic remark about Frog Lake: "The reason for the bad feeling entertained by some of these individual Indians I need not mention at this late date, though I can do so. It is enough to say that there was some slight reason for trouble at this particular place." Ahenakew was probably referring, in his discreet way, to John Delaney's sexual relations with Indian women.

In 1885, two months after the massacre, an article in the Stratford *Beacon* described Delaney as one of those government employees "who prostituted their authority to the debauchery of young Indian women." In the archives Hugh Dempsey has found a letter written in 1881 from one government official to another. According to the letter, Delaney was accused of stealing the wife of an Indian named Sand Fly. When Sand Fly protested, Delaney charged him with assault. When this didn't lead to a jail sentence, Delaney brought a theft charge and had him sent to jail for two-and-a-half years. The letter says that there was a general feeling that "Mr. Delaney had the man arrested in order to accomplish his designs." He lived with the prisoner's wife all that winter. For these and other reasons, such as his sternness, Delaney was disliked in the Frog Lake settlement.

On the night of April 1, the Indians at Frog Lake—made bitter by hunger, possibly enraged by Delaney's behaviour, certainly emboldened by the news of Riel's uprising—put on war paint and gathered for a dance. Wandering Spirit, the most militant of them all and now in effect Big Bear's successor, announced, "Tomorrow I am going to eat two-legged meat"—an expression that meant killing someone. During the night and the early morning, Wandering Spirit and others broke into the stores and seized the whites' guns. They apparently drank two cases of Perry Davis's Pain Killer, which was ninety percent alcohol. In the morning they took the twelve whites in the community prisoner and went with them to the Roman Catholic Church for Holy Thursday services. In church, the Indians shouted and otherwise made evident their newfound confidence. Outside, after the service, they began shooting. Big Bear, some distance away, cried, "Stop! Stop! Don't do it!" But they went on shooting, and in a few minutes killed nine men, including two Oblate priests. John Delaney fell dead at his wife's side. The only whites who escaped were a Hudson's Bay Company clerk and the two women—Theresa Delaney and Theresa Gowanlock, the wife of a man who was constructing a mill nearby. She too was widowed.

The Indians took the women hostage but apparently treated them with considerable kindness. Finally the women escaped, at about the time the Indians' brief armed struggle against the whites was ending in defeat. They then went east and wrote their book, published the same year by the Parkdale Times in Toronto (and republished in 1976 in Stuart Hughes's compilation, *The Frog Lake "Massacre"*). My great-aunt settled again in the Ottawa Valley, never remarried, taught school for a while, and lived well into the twentieth century.

Six Indians, including Wandering Spirit, were hanged for the killings. The jury that heard Big Bear's trial recommended mercy and he was sentenced to three years in Stony Mountain Penitentiary; after two years he was released on grounds of sickness. Back among his people, he was a failure and an outcast. His visions, his preaching, his leadership, his moderation had done no-one good. Another chief visited him one day and Big Bear, after a long silence, said, "You must wonder why I don't speak. My heart is broken. All I can think of are my past deeds and the misfortunes which have happened to me. . . . " He died in January, 1888. Hugh Dempsey, in the last sentence of his biography, provides an epitaph for both Big Bear and the policies of the Canadian government: "Big Bear had tried to sow the seeds of communication and cooperation between Indians and whites, but the seeds had fallen on barren ground."

▼ ▼ ▼

A century ago, Canada was imposing a grid of European rationalism on the West, carefully dividing up the land and preparing it for farming. Hunting and trapping were no longer to be important, were even to be discouraged—Aunt Theresa probably reflected official opinion when she declared her hatred of the Hudson's Bay Company, whose continued presence encouraged Indians to hunt when (in her view) they should have been farming. The force that struck down both Louis Riel and Big Bear was western civilization, with its urgent need to expand and develop. The landscape, created over millions of years by natural forces, was now to yield in a couple of generations to surveyors and government agents. Neither Riel's violence nor Big Bear's hopeful arguments could face down a power as tragic as it was splendid.

In the early days of Indian–white contact, Indian skills were essential to explorers and fur traders. But in 1885 no-one needed them any more, and no-one needed the Métis either. This story of acceptance followed by rejection was enacted again and again throughout North America, as Ramsay Cook remarked a few years ago in *The Frontier in History*: "As the fur trade was succeeded by agricultural settlement and industry, the American Indian was gradually pressed to the margins of North American society. His way of life was an obstacle to agricultural production organized through private land ownership. His technology and skills, so important in the fur trade, were no longer in demand in the more diversified society. He rarely fitted into the new capitalist economy, even at the lowest level."

Mad Louis Riel, the most hated man in the West a century ago, is now a kind of hero: westerners who resent the power of the East join their grievances with his and see him as a pioneer spokesman for western alienation (some even want a posthumous pardon bestowed on him by the government). But there's something perverse in our tendency to idolize him (as we also increasingly idolize Big Bear). It requires us to stand history on its head. Riel and Big Bear remain the natural enemies of those who now populate the West and indeed of all prosperous modern Canadians; it was only after the defeat of the Métis and the Indians that easterners could move west and begin the settlements that laid the foundations of Saskatchewan and Alberta.

But of course Riel has lived on in another way, his story woven into the larger story of Canadian politics. Sir John A. Macdonald's decision to let him hang (when there were good grounds to commute his sentence) profoundly alienated Quebec and helped Sir Wilfrid Laurier's Liberals seize that province in a grip so powerful it would not be broken until 1958. Riel had his posthumous revenge, if not on all Canadians then at least on the Conservatives.

The criminal trials of the Indians and the Métis in the autumn of 1885 seem, in retrospect, outrageously illogical—the rebels were convicted of treason against an empire that had conscripted them as citizens without consulting them. But the North-West Rebellion also produced a trial that was merely bizarre. Shortly after the rebellion ended, an article in the Toronto *News* said that Montreal's Sixty-fifth Battalion had conducted itself during the hostilities in a way that was mutinous, reckless, disorderly, and drunken. Officers of the battalion sued, and eventually the editor of the *News*—a notorious enemy of French Canadians and the French langauge—was summoned to Montreal to stand trial for criminal libel. Convicted and fined $200, he emerged from the courtroom, barely escaped with his life from a howling mob of outraged Montrealers, and went home to be greeted by a torchlight parade of 4000 cheering supporters in Toronto. Two years later, fed up with the stresses of daily newspaper work, the editor, Edmund E. Sheppard, founded a new periodical, *Saturday Night.*

From *Saturday Night* 100, 7 (July 1985): 5–8.

The Lesson of Canadian Geography

ROBERT FULFORD

History strives earnestly to teach us its enduring lessons, but in Canada geography is our real teacher, the one to which we must listen with the greatest care. It is geography which sets the tone of Canadian life just as it sets the rules of our working lives and governs our economic relations with other countries. Perhaps the Japanese can mostly ignore their own terrain; possibly Austrians can shove the geography of Austria to the margin of their national consciousness. But Canadians have no such choice. The history of our culture is the history of our attempt to come to terms imaginatively with the variety and vastness of the Canadian landscape—a process which even now may be only in its preliminary stages. In Canada it is of course possible to live a mainly urban life, and in this generation most of us do so. It is also possible to ignore, in one's daily work and recreation, the size of Canada. But inside the unconscious of even the most citified Canadian sits the vast and almost unimaginable empire that we govern. Its presence colours all that we do and feel; it shapes our politics, our public philosophy, our poetry, our very selves. In 1946 Wyndham Lewis, the English novelist and painter, wrote: "Canada will always be so infinitely bigger physically than the small nation that lives in it, even if its population is doubled, that this monstrous, empty habitat must continue to dominate this nation psychologically, and so culturally." A visitor with the sensitive nerve-ends of an artist, Lewis grasped the central point of the country in which he spent the Second World War. But few foreigners ever quite understand the force of Canadian geography. Canadians, for our part, have it in our bones, yet find difficulty articulating our feelings about it.

The most impressive work of Canadian art I have ever seen is an official map of Canada I once encountered in a government boardroom in Ottawa. It was about nine feet high and thirty or so feet across. As I stood before it at mid-point, with my nose almost touching it, my eyes met what most of us would call "the North"—indeed, a place much farther north than most Canadians have ever been. But the real north still went on and on, above my head, towards the ceiling of the room. Southern Ontario, where I have spent most of my life, was a tiny corner at my right foot; the heavily settled part of British Columbia was another tiny corner far to my left. The cities in which most Canadians live, right up to Edmonton, made only a small strip near the floor.

The map had no specific relationship to the purposes of the room in which I found it, and I assume it was put there simply to remind the bureaucrats who used the room of the lengths to which their imaginations must stretch to encompass the reality of Canada. Try as we may, Canadians cannot ignore this reality, but so far we have reached only a dim understanding of how it conditions us.

For generations the study of Canadian history consisted mainly of showing how our country was shaped from the outside—how France and Britain and then the United States manipulated the conditions of our existence. The story of that historical dependency, and of our glacial movement towards independence, is important, but as we told and re-told it we failed to understand the internal reality, the mythic power of the land itself. We came to believe (as many of us believe yet) that if only we could understand the foreigners dominating us, and perhaps understand our own failure to resist them, we would somehow come to a realization of our own identity. We made the common mistake of believing that we could define ourselves exclusively by our relation to others. Only a handful of white Canadians—some explorers, later some entrepreneurs, later still some artists—understood what the natives knew all along, that we were at the mercy of our geography and for good or ill we would be moulded by it. A.R.M. Lower stated the conventional theme of his classic history of Canada in the political terms of his title, *Colony to Nation*; but he concluded by pointing towards a future in which Canadians would come to terms with the Canadian land-mass:

> Canada with its division of races presents no common denominator in those profundities which normally unite, in race, language, religion, history and culture. If a common focus is to be found, it must come out of the common homeland itself. If the Canadian people are to find their soul, they must seek for it not in the English language, or the French, but in the little ports of the Atlantic provinces, in the flaming autumn maples of the St. Lawrence Valley, in the portages and lakes of the Canadian Shield, in the sunsets and relentless cold of the prairies, in the foothill, mountain and sea of the west and in

the unconquerable vastness of the north. From the land, Canada, must come the soul of Canada.

If that was true when Lower wrote it in 1946, it is far more true today. Canada has developed in the last three decades perhaps the most liberal immigration policies in the world. Unlike other democracies of the West, Canada does not temporarily import "guest workers," use their talents, and then send them home when they are not wanted. Instead it offers the gift of full citizenship—and many, from all over the world, eagerly accept that gift. The result is that the growing population lacks a shared pre-Canadian background; all that Canadians have in common (and it is, I argue, a great deal) is the physical fact of Canada and the opportunities that fact offers.

Since Lower wrote, Canadians have spent some considerable time in search of the soul he imagined; what we have found has so far surprised us, and in some cases alarmed us. Slowly we are beginning to understand what a Canadian is, but that turns out to be different from what we expected. We are a "nation," but not in the sense that history (mostly European history) taught us to use that word. Conditioned by our experience of and our reading about nineteenth-century nations, we expected that a mature Canada would resemble those earlier nations in certain essential ways. Canadians would, for instance, develop a patriotism more or less binding on all citizens; we would develop a point of view, perhaps an ideology. We would have an identity. But maturity for Canada has turned out to be something new under the sun, something for which the history of others could not prepare us.

Public policy, in everything from railway construction to broadcasting regulation, has urged us in the direction of unity; instead we have grown more diverse. Public policy has tried to elicit agreement on methods of national development; instead we have tended to disagree more and more, and to make our disagreements more vocal. Public policy in Ottawa has pushed for centralization of power; instead the regions of Canada have become more self-consciously separate. Our most characteristic public forum is the First Ministers Conference, at which provincial premiers become television stars, each with a performance to give, each with a set of regional or provincial grievances to state, each with an audience back home to please. And the focus of our national public life is not the improvement of our general condition but rather the appropriate method of dividing the revenues from our natural resources. The issues dictated by geography overcome all other issues, moving back and forth across party lines, so that socialists and conservatives from one region, while disagreeing on all else, find themselves in agreement on their region's entitlement to the fruits of the earth. All the calculations of political scientists and historians are defeated by the brute facts of the Canadian terrain. Michael Bliss, the historian, recognized this when he described the federal Geological Survey as "that little band of explorers who have done as much to map our national identity as all our writers and artists combined." The identity the geologists map is the same identity we see displayed at the First Ministers Conference.

What is at work here is not the frustration of a benign national purpose by fractious regionalists; it is the inevitable development of a pluralistic society coming to terms with the proprietorship of an empire. The force of our geography has not been diminished by modern communications, as many once thought it would be. Mass communications have instead made us all more conscious of our rights and our separate identities; they have reinforced rather than dissolved our demands by providing us with the means to express our feelings. At the same time, they have helped us to find pleasure in our diversity. In an earlier time many a theorist of mass media guessed that television would smooth out regional differences and create a bland sameness across society. But something like the opposite has happened. While television has taught us to know each other better, it has heightened our awareness of one another. And jet aircraft, while they take us swiftly from place to place, don't make us want to eliminate the distinctions between regions. A Torontonian and a Newfoundlander can now visit each other with some ease, but each in the end will probably decide that what makes the other valuable is his separate and different existence. It is only in the age of mass communications that genuine pluralism can flourish, because it is only in this age that we have the means to learn about each other.

The size of our country and its physical variety, combined with democratic traditions, have created a unique political and social atmosphere. A dozen years ago, when I was counselling American draft dodgers on their future in this country, I caught a glimpse of Canada as it must seem to outsiders who have personal reasons to be concerned about the openness of Canadian life. The draft dodgers were escaping from forced military service, of course, but I discovered among them a good many who had other concerns; there were even some who were physically ineligible for the army but who had declared themselves "draft dodgers" anyway and had crossed the border. What they were fleeing, no matter their politics (and some were far more conservative than I had expected), was the pressure of American political opinion. In the United States they had felt called upon to commit themselves to political factions, whether they wanted to or not, because American public life demanded commitment to this or that point of view. What they noticed first about Canada was the absence of a compulsion to conform. They discovered to their surprise that patriotism is not a prerequisite of Canadian citizenship. What the draft dodgers found in Canada was a unique kind of psychic freedom, a rather different matter from political freedom. It is this freedom, expressed in ethnic, linguistic, and regional terms, that forms the real basis of Canadian life.

The curious fact is that in order to qualify as Canadians we are not required to be loyal, even in theory, to the idea of Canada. At an editorial meeting at *Maclean's* early in the 1960s, the then-new subject of Quebec separatism was introduced. One editor declared firmly that separatists should be prosecuted for treason. He was an English immigrant, still innocent in Canadian ways, and his suggestion was greeted with derisive laughter, but it occurred to me at the time that if one looked at his views from a global perspective they were not altogether preposterous. In a very few countries would the idea of national dismemberment be greeted with such insouciance. But in fact, by unspoken agreement, Canadian citizenship carries the ultimate freedom: the freedom to declare that one doesn't want to be a Canadian, to urge that one's region should cease to be part of Canada, and yet to go on being a Canadian and receiving the appropriate benefits. No Quebec or Alberta separatist, so far as I know, has been denied a federal welfare payment or even a Canada Council grant because of his or her desire to separate.

This is the openness which the draft dodgers found at first rather baffling and then engaging. It is an openness which some Canadians find vexing, and which makes our public life unpredictable. It even makes it possible for the leader of the allegedly federalist party in Quebec, the provincial Liberals, to explain constantly that his loyalty to Canada is contingent and may be withdrawn at any moment. This relaxed and almost casual style of public discourse has always created difficulties and always will. Nevertheless, we should cherish it: nothing is closer to the essence of Canada, and nothing makes a greater contribution to the freedom of the Canadian citizen.

Out of the immense problems created by our geography, we have made a political system based on severely limiting the power of each level of government. It is commonly assumed in Canada that the individual is more important than the state, no matter how powerful the state becomes, and that one's private life is more important than one's public life. These assumptions flow directly from the troublesome but finally beneficial contest between the centralizing force of Ottawa and the disparate forces which stubbornly resist the central government. We understand, without having to articulate it, that it is as Canadian to resist Ottawa as to support it. This struggle is so all-encompassing that it touches every aspect of our lives: it affects the individual because it cripples the psychological power of government. When a country's government is so clearly split, so obviously at war with itself, it is unable to impose conformity on the citizens. In these terms, federal–provincial conflict can be seen as one of the keys to individual liberty. To a foreigner it may seem odd—even perverse—that Canadians so often vote for one party provincially and another party federally, but this is no more than the Canadian way of keeping government in its place.

The vastness of Canada has made this federal–provincial balance both possible and necessary: Canada as a unitary state would be a nightmare of bureaucracy. But while our size effectively brakes most of the excesses of government, it has an even more striking effect on political ideas. When they arrive in Canada, political ideas change. The harsh demand and the urgent appeal are dissipated by the size of the country; radicalism of left or right turns up in one region or another from time to time, but no truly radical idea has ever seized the country as a whole. Neither of the two great malevolent myths of the twentieth century, communism and fascism, has developed a sizeable following in Canada. Political movements which set out to swallow the country are instead swallowed up themselves, lost somewhere over the prairies. A neat, compact European country can generate among its citizens enough agreement to bring even the most terrifyingly brutal idea to power, but in Canada too many countervailing forces are at work. In this, as in so many other ways, Canadians are more fortunate than most of their fellow citizens of the globe.

This is true even of specific and apparently manageable issues, and even among people one might expect to agree easily. In Vancouver today liberal, enlightened opinion believes that the Newfoundland harp seal hunt is barbarous and should be outlawed; in St. John's, liberal, enlightened opinion believes precisely the opposite. What the people of one area regard as wise, the people of another may see as ridiculous. Once, when I tried to explain Canadian cultural nationalism of the 1970s to an art college seminar in Halifax, I found that the whole nationalist movement—developed by dozens of artists across the country over several years—was dismissed as "Ontario politics." A political generality which seems strikingly true in Prince George may appear shaky when it reaches Thunder Bay, rather dubious when it gets to Chicoutimi, and outlandish when it is heard in Cornerbrook.

This means that in Canada no proposition can be finally binding, no argument settled, no plan totally agreed upon. For that reason Canada offers an especially frustrating life to intellectuals, whose training is usually based on European or American models. At some point in their careers, having absorbed foreign experience, they turn to their own country and attempt to impose on it patterns and ideologies developed elsewhere.

They almost always break their swords. They discover that Canadians can't or won't make hard decisions; that every idea approved in one part of Canada is cancelled out by another part. Canada, because of its size and diversity, is not a country of *either/or* but a country of *maybe* and *I hope perhaps*. This is a basic fact of our nature, but to intellectuals it appears as nothing more than a form of spinelessness. Intellectuals want clear definitions, and Canada can't provide them. Leslie Armour, professor of philosophy at the University of Ottawa, is just such an intellectual. Armed with his Ph.D. from the University of London, he brings the full weight of the western philosophical tradition to bear on the problems currently besetting Canadian life. In his *The Idea of Canada and the Crisis of Community* (1981), he examines our life as a nation and (no surprise!) finds us wanting. Canada is disintegrating, he says, because we haven't evolved a common view of ourselves and our future. He notes that we come together—sometimes—when faced with a threat from outside, but "this is not enough to make a nation. To have a nation there must be a tendency toward a common strategy." Intellectuals adopt this theme when commenting on every area of our national life, from secondary manufacturing to mass culture. An economist seeking to revive our sickly manufacturing sector will talk endlessly of "industrial strategy" (which means emphasizing one industry at the expense of another, and usually one region at the expense of another). A cultural bureaucrat trying to make sense of, say, Canadian television will write papers about long-range planning and the political will required to support it. Canadians will hear these views, nod in apparent agreement, then ignore what has been said—and the politicians, sensing the national attitude, will do the same. In place of the central planning and ruthless decision-making favoured by the Japanese and the West Germans, Canadians put their faith in luck and improvisation. A common strategy—even a tendency towards a common strategy—is precisely what Canadians, collectively, do not want and never have wanted, except perhaps in wartime. This has been the case for so long that it must be a part of our national character, and to ignore it when considering the fate of Canada is to miss the essence.

On the last page of his rather melancholy book, Leslie Armour declares: "We must, indeed, eventually decide what we want." *Au contraire*, it is just by declining to make that sort of decision that we have so far survived. Even those institutions which have endured in Canada for centuries—the Crown, for example—have rarely been subjected to careful examination or defined with care. No one can say what the Crown means to Canadians in 1982, anymore than anyone could say what it meant in 1922; we avoid deciding upon that definition precisely because to do so would be divisive. Were we to make a national decision (abolish the monarchy, say, or, on the other hand, place it squarely at the symbolic core of the country), we would require assent from all the regions of Canada, and not all the regions would be able to give assent. Ergo, the Crown is allowed to float free above Canada, neither quite rejected nor quite embraced; every Canadian is thus permitted his own view of the Crown, as of so many other things.

One of the few intellectuals who understood this, almost from the beginning of his career, was Mackenzie King. He drove the most thoughtful of his fellow citizens almost mad with rage by adamantly refusing to make the decisions that they thought needed to be made. When King died, the socialist poet F.R. Scott wrote a bitter memorial tribute:

> He blunted us.
>
> We had no shape
> Because he never took sides,
> And no sides
> Because he never allowed them to take shape.

A cruel indictment, and not altogether inaccurate, yet King governed Canada during some of its most painful years, and left it intact. It was King's party, not Scott's CCF, that successfully (if rather surreptitiously) brought the welfare state to Canada. And King's most persistent and brilliant critic during his career, the historian Frank H. Underhill, acknowledged at the end of the day that it was King, not Underhill, who understood how to govern Canada.

That aspect of life that intellectuals most enjoy and admire—the sharp clash of ideas, the articulation of fully developed ideologies—was precisely what King laboured to avoid. No wonder we hated him, and hate his memory still. Someday a thorough search of King's diaries—that vast ocean of insight, gossip, and malice, cumulatively the most important work of literature in our history—may finally reveal his secret. How did he see so deeply into the nature of his country? Perhaps he himself never consciously grasped the quality of his own genius. Perhaps King's ascension to power and his ability to hold it were produced by the fortuitous conjunction—so rare in history—of an unshaped, inarticulate people and a leader who perfectly embodied his nation's character.

▼ ▼ ▼

Plutarch says of the geographers of the ancient world that they would "crowd into the edges of their maps parts of the world which they do not know about, adding notes in the margin to the effect that beyond this lies nothing but sandy deserts full of wild beasts, and unapproachable bogs." In the mind of the modern Canadian, the map of his own country has many such edges, each of them filled with images (accumulated since childhood) of vast empty wastelands beyond the horizon, uninhabited and therefore uninhabitable. The maps prepared by our cartographers are accurate and detailed, but our spiritual maps have much in common with those of Plutarch's time. Now and then word comes back to us—from an artist or an explorer—that some empty space on our map is in fact filled with life, and mentally we adjust our conception of that one place. But the process is necessarily slow. A Canadian comes into the world with a spatial imagination no larger than that of a Belgian or a Greek, but to understand his own country he must stretch that imagination to its limits. He may find it easier simply to ignore or belittle most of the country, and in this the Europeans long ago set an example for us: it was Voltaire in *Candide* (1759) who had a shrewd, cynical character describe Canada as "a few acres of snow." But those of us who have inherited those acres of snow, or who have adopted them by moving here from somewhere else, cannot so casually dismiss our surroundings. If we wish truly to inhabit Canada, rather than simply to live in some circumscribed area of it, then we need to fill those empty acres imaginatively. We can do this only through art, and art of a particular kind. Landscape painting and photography, nature poetry, novels like W.O. Mitchell's that set down on paper the style of a terrain—these are the means by which human beings take spiritual possession of territory. Before we can finally take Canada into our minds we need to experience it through art; in effect, artists must invent it for us.

This was the central insight of the Group of Seven, who made it their business to display the landscape of Canada to the people who controlled it. In this the Group was not entirely original: there had been landscape painters in

Canada for centuries, and one artist after another had tried to set down with oil paint or watercolour the essence of the country. In most cases they had brought to Canada the manners of European art; the Canadian landscape as they recorded it had a gentle, romantic air. While the members of the Group of Seven also drew a great deal from the European tradition, they set for themselves a sterner artistic task. They shaped their style to fit the material, producing a rugged and even (by the standards of their time) brutal art. Working together, exchanging ideas constantly, they moved forward like mountain climbers linked by rope, developing what would become almost a religion. In their view, the Canadian landscape deserved no less. Tom Thomson (who died in 1917, three years before the Group was officially formed), Lawren Harris, A.Y. Jackson, and the others eventually produced a challenging visual account of the physical fact of Canada. In their hands, central and northern Ontario, the Rockies, and the Arctic became the setting for a great and vigorous artistic drama.

Their paintings shocked some of the first to see them, but before many years had passed the Group received an astonishing reward for their labours. Though they never achieved more than fleeting recognition outside Canada, within it they became the most remarkable success in the history of our culture. No other artists—in music or literature or any other medium—have had such an impact. No others have appealed simultaneously to rich patrons, school-children, their fellow artists, and the public in general. No others have maintained their status over the decades. The Group of Seven captured the imagination of Canada in a way that it has never otherwise been captured, before or since.

This success was not an accident produced by publicity or the machinations of art dealers; had it been, it would have slipped away when the early Group of Seven paintings grew old and the painters, one by one, died. But the popularity of the Group has instead grown with every passing decade; by the time Harris and Jackson died in the 1970s, they were treated as national heroes, their obituaries running as long as those of generals or statesmen. The Group had become part of the cultural myth of a whole people.

When Canadians looked at the Group of Seven's paintings they experienced a rare moment of self-recognition, and they continued to have this experience whenever they returned to the art. They saw in those hundreds of paintings and sketches a vision of the Canadian spirit as formed by the Canadian landscape. As a result, the Group has inspired generations of artists—not only painters but also film-makers, photographers, and illustrators. It is even arguable that their influence has moved into literature; certainly Canadian literature continues to exhibit an exceptionally close relationship with Canadian geography. "Everything that is central in Canadian writing," Northrop Frye tells us, "seems to be marked by the imminence of the natural world." Even though Canada in the twentieth century became more and more a country of city-dwellers, art and literature continued to find their focus in natural settings. This was not nostalgia for the audience's or the artists' rural backgrounds; it was part of a continuing attempt to come to terms with the country.

From the beginning, Canadian artists have at the same time reacted against the use of the landscape in Canadian art. "Every damned tree in the country has now been painted," a young rebel on the Toronto art scene commented in the 1950s, and in doing so spoke for a whole generation that at first had found the Group of Seven oppressive. For these artists the Group's tradition, far from opening up new frontiers to art, seemed on the contrary to foreclose possibilities by dictating a narrow view of artistic possibilities in Canada. In the 1950s and 1960s, abstractionism was fuelled by international sources of inspiration and reflected mainly the newer urban reality—or seemed to do so for a time. But even the most urbanized of artists ended up by returning in his or her own fashion to the landscape and its continuing impact on Canadians. The generation that started out by reacting against the Group ended up by embracing it. In Toronto an artist like Gordon Rayner, after drawing on all the techniques of abstraction developed in New York, and using them brilliantly, returned—just like the Group of Seven—to the central Ontario bush for the background to his most impressive canvases. Michael Snow is above all other things an urban intellectual, but when he took a major exhibition to Paris he included in it a re-interpretation of the Group of Seven's insights. Harold Town, who in his early career saw little value in the Group's heritage, eventually wrote a compelling and important book on Tom Thomson. Joyce Wieland, whose first canvases were as far from the Group as it was possible for them to be, later turned to film-making and used the myth of Tom Thomson—as well as his physical surroundings—as the basis for her feature film, *The Far Shore*.

Meanwhile, the painters who consistently appealed to a large public—for instance, Toni Onley in Vancouver and the late William Kurelek in Toronto—were those who found fresh ways to interpret the Canadian landscape; Onley through the lovely haze of a gentle, English-influenced manner, Kurelek in the rough but expressive terms of the self-taught primitive.

Each of these artists encountered the land in personal terms. Kurelek, who grew up in deprived circumstances on a prairie farm in the Depression, was telling the public his own story as much as the land's; in the process he became perhaps the most universally admired artist of his generation as well as the most successful book illustrator in Canada. Kurelek reflected in his work a quality that eastern city-dwellers have often noted in westerners: they are closer to the land, not so much in space as in time. Even that majority which has no direct experience of rural life carries a folk memory of breaking the plains: an accountant in Calgary, say, is the grandson of a pioneer, and his childhood memories include stories of the heroic age of western development. Even in the 1980s, the remembered vision of the prairie as virginal and untouched—menacing in its way, and yet conveying enormous promise—is always just on the edge of the conversation.

For an artist like Joyce Wieland, who grew up in Toronto, the experience is different but no less profound. In her case the encounter with the landscape is a matter of consciously seeking out the background to Canadian life. Her work may in some ways reflect a more romantic view of the landscape, but it remains a view that places the natural world at the core of Canadian consciousness.

The function of art is to make life comprehensible and bearable, but the function of these particular artists is to resolve the tension within us between the enormity of Canada and our urgent need to encompass it. The size of Canada, and the emptiness of it, George Woodcock has noted, are two facts that are often present in the mind of every Canadian. To make art out of that emptiness, to humanize nature—to deny, in fact, that the country is empty—is a supremely human act, an act which is required of the Canadian imagination if the country is to realize its own artistic possibilities.

In the end the need to know Canada's physical nature is crucial to our future because it is in the land that we can find the grounds for genuine optimism. Native mythology, to which few of us pay sufficient attention, has always insisted that life will be governed by the natural world; it has always drawn its symbols from the immediate landscape, and carried the powerful implication that an understanding of human conduct can be drawn from that landscape. And from the moment when the earliest explorers were swallowed up by the apparently endless St. Lawrence River, the land has been the basis for hope. In later generations it was always the astonishing gift of our geography that stimulated the ambitions of Canadians—in one era the abundance of fish in the waters, in another the opening of the west to agriculture, in another John Diefenbaker's northern vision, in still another the slow unfolding of the Arctic's infinite promises of resource development.

The incredible space on earth which history absent-mindedly gave us has laid down the rules of Canada's existence: it determines the content of parliamentary debates as much as it determines the content of our art galleries; it has protected our freedom and made us, in comparison with almost any other peoples in the world, enviably wealthy. It is our heritage and our problem and the source of our future happiness. Perhaps we shall never come to terms with it intimately; but it is the task and privilege of the present generation, in the midst of our self-generated tensions and conflicts, to move still closer to an understanding of what this geographic empire means to us and to our descendants. James Reaney, that remarkable poet who has written so often and so well on Canada, has given us a brief account of a childhood memory; it might be called The Birth of a Canadian Imagination:

> I can remember as a child looking at a map of Canada at school and wolfing down the whole thing as *my* country. The shape of Hudson

Bay, the Northern Arctic islands, the coast of Labrador and the shapes of the Great Lakes were particularly lovable. Quebec always seemed like the profile of—someone—the Duchess in *Alice in Wonderland* with the Ottawa River defining her chin and jaws, Cape Jones as her nose, Labrador as her head-dress and some unknown river (the Nottaway) as the outline of her rather pursed mouth. Ontario seems like someone in a rather grotesque rocking chair. The Arctic Islands had the fascinating fretted shapes of mackerel clouds in a sunset. Naturally I have never since known Canada as well as I did then.

Written as the "Foreword" to *Canada: A Landscape Portrait*, by Janis Kraulis (Edmonton: Hurtig, 1982), 5–11.

MARGARET ATWOOD (1939–) spent much of her childhood in Northern Ontario, where her father was doing entomological research. (She attributes her fascination with the theme of metamorphosis to these early experiences during which she watched insects "go through some mysterious process and emerge as something else.") She was educated at Victoria College, where she studied with Northrop Frye and Kathleen Coburn, receiving her B.A. in 1961. The following year she went to Radcliffe, where she obtained an M.A. in Victorian literature. From that point her progress as a writer was meteoric.

Atwood's *The Circle Game* won the Governor General's Award for poetry in 1966, and since then she has published an average of more than a book a year—poetry, novels, criticism, short stories, history, children's books. Her volumes of poetry include *Double Persephone* (1961), *The Animals in That Country* (1968), *Procedures for Underground* (1970), *The Journals of Susanna Moodie* (1970), *Power Politics* (1971), *You are Happy* (1974), *Two-Headed Poems* (1978), *True Stories* (1981), and *Interlunar* (1984). *Survival: A Thematic Guide to Canadian Literature* (1972) was a landmark in Canadian literary criticism, and novels such as *The Edible Woman* (1969), *Surfacing* (1970), *Lady Oracle* (1976), *Life before Man* (1979), *The Handmaid's Tale* (1985, another Governor General's Award winner), and *Cat's Eye* (1988) have made her one of Canada's best known and most acclaimed writers.

Ambitious and multi-talented, Atwood has succeeded in inscribing her name, her personality, and her opinions on the issues that have swirled around the writing of books in Canada. She is also one of our most articulate and outspoken cultural nationalists, and has worked tirelessly to defend the literature she has helped create. And not just the literature. Amid the drone of abstract arguments for and against free trade with the United States, her comparison of Canada–U.S. relations to connubial ones sounded a welcome note of sardonic sanity: "About the only position they've ever adopted toward us, country to country, has been the missionary position, and we were not on the top." But like anyone who willingly embroils herself in controversy, she has been the object of a number of attacks, from both right and left. This is no doubt why she told one interviewer, "I don't particularly like being a public figure": the creator of Canadian myths has not always been able to control the myths created about her.

The essay is a particularly congenial format for Margaret Atwood, simply because she has something new to say, she wants to communicate it, and her prose conveys an entire personality, a style that combines courage and bravado, the aphoristic and the confessional, the incisive and the outrageous. Whether she is providing the reader with notes towards a definition of the male character or of the Canadian north, she is always displaying something of that intangible quality that makes Atwood's writing so distinctive.

Writing the Male Character

MARGARET ATWOOD

I'm more than delighted that you've invited a token woman to give the Hagey lectures this year, and though you might have chosen one more respectable than myself, I realize that the supply is limited.

My lack of respectability I have on good authority: the authority, in fact, of the male academics at the University of Victoria, in British Columbia, where I was being interviewed on radio not long ago. "I did a little survey," said the rather pleasant male interviewer, "among the professors here. I asked them what they thought of your work. The women were all very positive, but the men said that they weren't sure whether or not you were respectable." So I'm giving you advance warning that everything you are about to hear is not academically respectable. The point of view I'm presenting is that of a practising novelist, inhabitant of New Grub Street for many years, not that of the Victorianist I spent four years at Harvard learning to be; though the Victorianism does creep in, as you can already see. So I will not even mention metonymy and synecdoche, except right now, just to impress you and let you know that I know they exist.

All of the above, of course, is by way of letting the male members of the audience know that, despite the title of this lecture, they don't need to feel threatened. I believe we have now reached, as a culture, the point at which we need a little positive reinforcement for men. I'm starting my own private project along these lines tonight. I have with me some gold stars, some silver stars and some blue stars, fictional ones of course. You get a blue star, if you want one, just for being unthreatened enough to have actually turned up tonight. You get a silver star if you are unthreatened enough to laugh at the jokes, and you get a gold star if you don't feel threatened at all. On the other hand, you get a black mark if you say, "My *wife* just *loves* your books." You get two black marks if you say, as a male CBC producer said to me not long ago, "A number of us are upset because we feel women are taking over the Canadian literary scene."

"Why do men feel threatened by women?" I asked a male friend of mine. (I love that wonderful rhetorical device, "a male friend of mine." It's often used by female journalists when they want to say something particularly bitchy but don't want to be held responsible for it themselves. It also lets people know that you *do* have male friends, that you aren't one of those fire-breathing mythical monsters, The Radical Feminists, who walk around with little pairs of scissors and kick men in the shins if they open doors for you. "A male friend of mine" also gives—let us admit it—a certain weight to the opinions expressed.) So this male friend of mine, who does by the way exist, conveniently entered into the following dialogue. "I mean," I said, "men are bigger, most of the time, they can run faster, strangle better, and they have on the average a lot more money and power." "They're afraid women will laugh at them," he said. "Undercut their world view." Then I asked some women students in a quickie poetry seminar I was giving, "Why do women feel threatened by men?" "They're afraid of being killed," they said.

From this I concluded that men and women are indeed different, if only in the range and scope of their threatenability. A man is not just a woman in funny clothes and a jock strap. *They don't think the same*, except about things like higher math. But neither are they an alien or inferior form of life. From the point of view of the novelist, this discovery has wide-ranging implications; and you can see that we are approaching this evening's topic, albeit in a crabwise, scuttling, devious and feminine manner; nevertheless, approaching. But first, a small digression, partly to demonstrate that when people ask you if you hate men, the proper reply is, "which ones?"—because, of course, the other big revelation of the evening is that *not all men are the same*. Some of them have beards. Apart from that, I have never been among those who would speak slightingly of men by lumping them all together; I would never say, for instance—as some have—"Put a paper bag over their bodies and they're all the same." I give you Albert Schweitzer in one corner, Hitler in another.

But think of what civilization would be today without the contributions of men. No electric floor polishers, no neutron bomb, no Freudian psychology, no heavy metal rock groups, no pornography, no repatriated Canadian Constitution . . . the list could go on and on. And they're fun to play Scrabble with and handy for eating up leftovers. I have heard some rather tired women express the opinion that the only good man is a dead man, but this is far from correct. They may be hard to find, but think of it this way: like diamonds, in the rough or not, their rarity makes them all the more appreciated. Treat them like human beings! This may surprise them at first, but sooner or later their good qualities will emerge, most of the time. Well, in view of the statistics . . . some of the time.

That wasn't the digression . . . this is the digression. I grew up in a family of scientists. My father was a forest entomologist and fond of children, and incidentally not threatened by women, and many were the happy hours we spent listening to his explanations of the ways of the wood-boring beetle, or picking forest tent caterpillars out of the soup because he had forgotten to feed them and they had gone crawling all over the house in search of leaves. One of the results of my upbringing was that I had a big advantage in the schoolyard when little boys tried to frighten me with worms, snakes and the like; the other was that I developed, slightly later, an affection for the writings of the great nineteenth century naturalist and father of modern entomology, Henri Fabre. Fabre was, like Charles Darwin, one of those gifted and obsessive amateur naturalists which the nineteenth century produced in such abundance. He pursued his investigations for the love of the subject, and unlike many biologists today, whose language tends to be composed of numbers rather than words, he was an enthusiastic and delightful writer. I read with pleasure his account of the life of the spider, and of his experiments with ant-lions, by which he tried to prove that they could reason. But it was not only Fabre's subject matter that intrigued me; it was the character of the man himself, so full of energy, so pleased with everything, so resourceful, so willing to follow his line of study wherever it might lead. Received opinion he would take into account, but would believe nothing until he had put it to the test himself. It pleases me to think of him, spade in hand, setting forth to a field full of sheep droppings, in search of the Sacred Dung Beetle and the secrets of her egg-laying ritual. "I am all eyes," he exclaimed, as he brought to light a little object, not round like the Sacred Beetle's usual edible dung-ball, but cunningly pear-shaped! "Oh blessed joys of truth suddenly shining forth," he wrote. "What others are there to compare with you!"

And it is in this spirit, it seems to me, that we should approach all subjects. If a dung-beetle is worthy of it, why not that somewhat more complex object, the human male? Admittedly the analogy has certain drawbacks. For instance, one dung-beetle is much like another, whereas, as we've noted, there's quite a range in men. Also, we are supposed to be talking about novels here, and, to belabour the obvious, a novel is not a scientific treatise; that is, it can make no claim to present the kind of factual truth which can be demonstrated by repeatable experiments. Although the novelist presents observations and reaches conclusions, they are not of the same order as the observations of Fabre on the behaviour of the mating practices of the female scorpion, although some critics react as though they are.

Note that we have landed in the middle of a swamp, that is, at the crux of the problem: if a novel is not a scientific treatise, what is it? Our evaluation of the role of the male character within the novel will of course depend on what kind of beast we think we're dealing with. I'm sure you've all heard the one about the four blind philosophers and the elephant. Substitute "critics" for "philosophers" and "Novel" for "elephant" and you'll have the picture. One critic gets hold of the novelist's life and decides that novels are disguised spiritual autobiographies, or disguised personal sexual phobias, or something of the kind. Another gets hold of the *Zeitgeist* (or Spirit of the Times, for those unlucky enough never to have had to pass a Ph.D. language exam in German) and writes about the Restoration Novel or the Novel of Sensibility or The Rise of the Political Novel or The Novel of Twentieth Century Alienation; another figures out that the limitations of the language have something to do with what can be said, or that certain pieces of writing display similar patterns, and the air fills with mythopoeia, structuralism and similar delights; another goes to Harvard and gets hold of the Human Condition, a favourite of mine, and very handy to fall back on when you can't think of anything else to say. The elephant however remains an elephant, and sooner or later gets tired of having the blind philosophers feelings its parts, whereupon it stretches itself, rises to its feet and ambles away in another direction altogether. This is not to say that critical exercises are futile or trivial. From what I have said about dung-beetles—which also preserve their innermost secrets—you will know that I think the description of elephants is a worthwhile activity. But describing an elephant and giving birth to one are two different things, and the novelist and the critic approach the novel with quite different sets of preconceptions, problems and emotions.

"Whence comest thou?" says a well-known male character in a multi-faceted prose narrative with which I am sure you are all familiar. "From going to and fro in the earth, and from walking up and down in it," answers his adversary. Thus the novelist. One would of course not want to continue with this analogy—a critic is not God, contrary to some opinions, and a novelist is not the Devil, although one could remark, with Blake, that creative energies are more likely to emerge from the underworld than from the upper world of rational order. Let us say only that the going to and fro and the walking up and down in the earth are things that all novelists seem to have done in some way or another, and that the novel proper, as distinguished from the romance and its variants, is one of the points in human civilization at which the human world as it is collides with language and imagination. This is not to limit the novel to a Zola-like naturalism (though Zola himself was not a narrow Zola-like naturalist, as anyone who has read the triumphant final passage of *Germinal* will testify); but it is to state that some of the things that get into novels get into them because they are there in the world. There would have been no flogging scene in *Moby Dick* if there had been none on nineteenth century whaling ships, and its inclusion is not mere sado-masochism on the part of Melville. However, if the book consisted of nothing but, one might have cause to wonder.

Thus one must conclude that the less than commendable behaviour of male characters in certain novels by women is not necessarily due to a warped view of the opposite sex on behalf of the authors. Could it be... I say it hesitantly, in a whisper, since like most women I cringe at the very thought of being called—how can I even say it—a *man hater*... could it be that the behaviour of some men in what we are fond of considering real life... could it be that not every man always behaves well? Could it be that some emperors have no clothes on?

This may seem to you an obvious point to make. But not so. Among the going to and fro that novelists do these days is the going to and fro across Canada during the McClelland & Stewart Wreck-an-Author tour, talking to media denizens, and some of the walking up and down they do happens after reading the reviews of their books. Let's pretend for the sake of argument that media denizens and newspaper critics bear at least some relation, if not to the average reader, at least to the officially promoted climate of opinion; that is, what it is considered, at the moment, fashionable and therefore safe to state publicly. If so, the officially promoted climate of opinion these days shows a noteworthy shift towards male whining.

Let me take you back a few years, to the days of Kate Millett's *Sexual Politics*, which was preceded ancestrally by Leslie Fiedler's *Love and Death in the American Novel*. Both were criticisms based on an analysis of the relations, within novels, of men and women, and both gave black marks to certain male authors for simplistic and stereotyped negative depictions of women. Well, that was interesting, but the worm has turned. Now we're handing out black marks for what male critics (and, to be fair, some female ones) consider to be unfavourable depictions of men by female authors. I base this conclusion mainly on reviews of my own books, naturally, since that's what I see most of, but I've noted it elsewhere too.

Now, we know there's no such thing as value-free novel writing. Creation does not happen in a vacuum, and a novelist is either depicting or exposing some of the values of the society in which he or she lives. Novelists from Defoe through Dickens and Faulkner have always done that. But it sometimes escapes us that the same is true of criticism. We are all organisms within environments, and we interpret what we read in the light of how we live and how we would like to live, which are almost never the same thing, at least for most novel readers. I think that political interpretations of novels have a place in the body of criticism, as long as we recognize them for what they are; but total polarization can only be a disservice to literature. For instance, a male friend of mine—just to let you know I have more than one—wrote a novel which has a scene in it in which men are depicted urinating outdoors standing up. Now, so far as I know, this is something men have been doing for many years, and they are still doing it, judging from the handwriting in the snow; it is merely one of those things that happens. But a female poet took my friend to task in print. She found this piece of writing not only unforgivably Central Canadian—you can tell she was from British Columbia—she also found it unforgivably *macho*. I'm not sure what novelistic solution she had in mind.

Possibly she wanted my friend to leave out the subject of urination altogether, thus avoiding the upsetting problem of physiological differences; maybe she wanted the men to demonstrate equality of attitude by sitting on toilets to perform this function. Or maybe she wanted them to urinate outdoors standing up but also to feel guilty about it. Or maybe it would have been all right if they had been urinating into the Pacific Ocean, regionalism being what it is today. You may think this kind of criticism is silly, but it happens all the time on New Grub Street, which is where I live.

For the female novelist, it means that certain men will find it objectionable if she depicts men behaving the way they do behave a lot of the time. Not enough that she may avoid making them rapists and murderers, child molesters, warmongers, sadists, power-hungry, callous, domineering, pompous, foolish or immoral, though I'm sure we will all agree that such men do exist. Even if she makes them sensitive and kind she's open to the charge of having depicted them as "weak." What this kind of critic wants is Captain Marvel, without the Billy Batson *alter ego*; nothing less will do.

Excuse me for underlining the obvious, but it seems to me that a good, that is, a successfully-written, character in a novel is not at all the same as a "good," that is, a morally good, character in real life. In fact, a character in a book who is consistently well-behaved probably spells disaster for the book. There's a lot of public pressure on the novelist to write such characters, however, and it isn't new. I take you back to Samuel Richardson, author of such running-away-from-rape classics as *Pamela and Clarissa*. Both contain relatively virtuous women and relatively lecherous and nasty-minded men, who also happen to be English gentlemen. No one accused Richardson of being mean to men, but some English gentlemen felt that dirt had been done to them; in other words, the insecurities were primarily class ones rather than sex ones. Obligingly, Richardson came up with *Sir Charles Grandison*, a novel in which he set out to do right by the image of the English gentleman. It starts out promisingly enough, with an abduction with intent to rape by a villain after that priceless pot of gold, the heroine's virginity. Unfortunately Sir Charles Grandison enters the picture, saves the heroine from a fate worse than death, and invites her to his country residence; after which most readers kiss the novel goodbye. I however always sit to the end, even of bad movies, and since I'm the only person I've ever met who has actually made it through to page 900 of this novel I can tell you what happens. Sir Charles Grandison displays his virtues; the heroine admires them. That's it. Oh, and then there's a proposal. Feel like reading it? You bet you don't, and neither do all those male critics who complain about the image of men in books by women. A friend of mine—not a male one this time, but a perceptive reader and critic—says that her essential criterion for evaluating literature is, "Does it live or does it die?" A novel based on other people's needs for having their egos stroked, their images shored up, or their sensitivities pandered to is unlikely to live.

Let us take a brief look at what literature has actually done. Is *Hamlet*, for instance, a slur on men? Is *Macbeth*? Is *Faust*, in any version? How about the behaviour of the men in *Moll Flanders*? Or *Tom Jones*? Is *A Sentimental Journey* about the quintessential wimp? Because Dickens created Orlick, Gradgrind, Dotheboys Hall, Fagin, Uriah Heep, Steerforth, and Bill Sykes, must we conclude that he's a man-hater? Meredith was unrelentingly critical of men and quite admiring of women in such novels as *Richard Feverel* and *The Egoist*. Does that mean he's the equivalent of a class traitor? How about the fascinating Isabel Archer's failure to match herself with a man who's up to her, in James' *Portrait of a Lady?* Then there's *Tess of the D'Urbervilles*, with sweet gentle victimized Tess, and the two male protagonists, one of whom is a cad, the other a pig. I give you *Anna Karenina* and *Madame Bovary*, just to do a little culture-hopping; and while we're at it, we might mention that Captain Ahab, although a forceful literary creation, is hardly anybody's idea of an acceptable role model. Please note that all these characters and novels were the creations of men, not women; but nobody, to my knowledge, has accused these male authors of being mean to men, although they've been accused of all sorts of other things. Possibly the principle involved is the same one involved in the telling of ethnic jokes: it's all right within the group, but coming from the outside it's racism, though the joke may be exactly the same. If a man depicts a male character unfavourably, it's The Human Condition; if a woman does it, she's being mean to men. I think you can to a certain extent reverse this and apply it to women's reactions to books by women. I, for instance, was expecting to be denounced by at least a few feminists for having written my characters Elizabeth and Auntie Muriel in *Life Before Man*, both of whom would be less than desirable as roommates. But not a bit of it. By the time the book appeared, even feminist critics had tired somewhat of their own expectations; they no longer required all female protagonists to be warm but tough, wise and experienced but sensitive and open, competent, earth-motherly and passionate but chock full of dignity and integrity; they were willing to admit that women too might have blemishes, and that universal sisterhood, though desirable, had not yet been fully instituted upon this earth. Nevertheless, women have traditionally been harder on women's image issues in connection with books by women than men have. Maybe it's time to do away with judgement by role-model and bring back The Human Condition, this time acknowledging that there may in fact be more than one of them.

Incidentally, you could make a case—if you wanted to—for concluding that women authors have historically been easier on men in their books than male authors have. Nowhere in major English novels by women do we find anything approaching that fallen angel and monster of depravity, Mister Kurtz, of *Heart of Darkness* fame; about the closest you could come, I think, would be the infamous Simon Legree (but I said *major* novels). The norm is more likely to range between Heathcliff and Mr Darcy, both of them flawed but sympathetically depicted; or, to invoke the greatest single English novel of the nineteenth century, George Eliot's *Middlemarch*, between dried-up envious Mr Casaubon and idealistic but misguided Dr Lydgate. The wonder of this book is that George Eliot can make us understand not only how awful it is to be married to Mr Casaubon, but how awful it is to *be* Mr Casaubon. This seems to me a worthy model to emulate. George Orwell said that every man's life viewed from within is a failure. If I said it, would it be sexist?

The Victorians, of course, has certain advantages that we lack. For one thing, they were not as self-conscious about the kind of thing we're discussing this evening as we have been forced to become. Though under constant pressure from the Mr and Mrs Grundies of their world never to write a line that might bring a blush to the cheek of a maiden of eighteen, which would in fact give you quite a lot of latitude today, they were not hesitant about depicting evil and calling it evil, or parading in front of their readers whole menageries of comic and grotesque figures, without worrying that such portraits might be interpreted as a slur upon one sex or the other. Female Victorian novelists had a couple of other advantages. Sex was out, so if they were creating a male character they could get away without trying to depict what sex felt like from a male point of view. Not only that, novels were assumed to be female-oriented, which meant that it took them a while to be viewed as a serious art form. Some of the first English novels were by women, the readership was preponderantly female, and even male novelists slanted their work accordingly. There are of course lots of exceptions, but on the whole we can say that the novel for almost two centuries had a decidedly female bias, which may account for the fact that many more male writers depicted female characters as central protagonists than the other way around. The advantage to the female novelist (as opposed to the Walter Scott romancer) was obvious. If novels were aimed at women, women had inside information.

The novel as a form has changed and expanded a good deal since then. Still, one of the questions people have been asking me most frequently is, "Do you write women's novels?" You have to watch this question, since, like many other questions, its meaning varies according to who's asking it and of whom. "Women's novels" can mean pop *genre* novels, such as the kind with nurses and doctors on the covers or the kind with rolling-eyed heroines in period costumes and windblown hair in front of gothic castles or Southern mansions or other locales where villainy may threaten and Heathcliff is still lurking around in the Spanish moss. Or it may mean novels for whom the main audience is assumed to be women, which would take in quite a lot, since the main audience for novels of all kinds, with the exception of Louis L'amour western romances and certain kinds of porn, is also women. Or it can mean feminist propaganda novels. Or it can mean novels depicting male–female relationships, which again covers quite a lot of ground. Is *War and Peace* a women's novel? Is *Gone With the Wind*, even though it's got a war in it? Is *Middlemarch*, even though it's got The Human Condition in it? Could it be that women aren't afraid to be caught reading books that might be considered "men's novels," whereas men still think something they need will fall off them if they look too hard at certain supposedly malevolent combinations of words put together by women? Judging from my recent walking to and fro in the earth and going up and down in bookstores for the purpose of signing my name on a lot of fly-leafs, I can tell you that this attitude is on the fade. More and more men are willing to stand in line and *be seen*; fewer and fewer of them say, "It's for my wife's birthday."

But I almost put the boots to my old friend and cohort, the redoubtable Pierre Berton, when he asked me on television why all the men in my recent book *Bodily Harm* were wimps. Displaying the celebrated female compassion, not to be confused with feeble-mindedness, I merely dribbled aimlessly for a few minutes. "Pierre," I should have said, "who do you think is likely to have had more experience of men in sexual relationships: you, or me?" This is not quite so mean as it sounds, and there's even something to it. Women as people have a relatively large pool of experiences from which to draw. They have their own experiences with men, of course, but they also have their friends', since, yes, girls do discuss men more than men—beyond the dirty anecdotes syndrome—discuss women. Women are willing to talk about their weaknesses and fears to other women; men are not willing to talk about theirs to men, since it's still a dog-eat-dog world out there for them and no man wants to reveal his underbelly to a pack of fang-toothed potential rivals. If men are going to talk about their problems with women to anybody, it's usually either to a shrink or—guess what? to another woman. In both reading and writing, women are likely to know more about how men actually behave with women than men are; so that what a man finds a slur on his self-image, a woman may find merely realistic or indeed unduly soft.

But to go back to Pierre Berton's assertion, I thought quite carefully about my male characters in *Bodily Harm*. There are three of them with whom the heroine actually sleeps, and the fourth main male character with whom she doesn't. A female novelist and critic noted that there is one good man in the book and no good women, and she's quite right. The other men are not "bad"—in fact they are quite nice and attractive as male characters in literature go, a sight better than Mr Kurtz and Iago—but the *good* man is *black*, which is perhaps why the "mean-to-menners" overlooked him. When playing the role-model game, you have to read carefully; otherwise you may be caught in an embarrassing position, like that one.

Now, back to the practical concerns of New Grub Street. Let us suppose that I am writing a novel. First: how many points of view will this novel have? If it has only one point of view, will it be that of a man, a woman or a seagull? Let us suppose that my novel will have one point of view and that the eyes through which we see the world of the novel unfolding will be those of a woman. Immediately it follows that the perceptions of all male characters in the book will have to pass through the perceiving apparatus of this central character.

Nor will the central character necessarily be accurate or just. It also follows that all the other characters will be, of necessity, secondary. If I'm skilful I will be able to bounce another set of perceptions off those of the central character, through dialogue and between-the-lines innuendo, but there will be a strong bias toward A as truth-teller and we will never get to hear what Characters B and C really think when they're by themselves, urinating outdoors perhaps or doing other male things. However, the picture changes if I use a multiple point of view. Now I can have Characters B and C think for themselves, and what they think won't always be what Character A thinks of *them*. If I like, I can add in yet another point of view, that of the omniscient author (who is of course not "me," the same me that had bran muffins for breakfast this morning and is right now giving this speech) but yet another voice within the novel. The omniscient author can claim to know things about the characters that even they don't know, thus letting the reader know these things as well.

The next thing I have to decide is what tone I'm taking, what mode I'm writing in. A careful study of *Wuthering Heights* will reveal that Heathcliff is never to be observed picking his nose, or indeed even blowing it, and you can search through Walter Scott in vain for any mention of bathrooms. Leopold Bloom on the other hand is preoccupied with the mundane wants of the body on almost every page, and we find him sympathetic, yes, and comic and also pathetic, but he is not exactly love's young dream. Leopold Bloom climbing in through Cathy's window would probably slip. Which is the more accurate portrayal of Man with a capital M? Or, like Walter Mitty, does each man contain within him both an ordinary, limited and trivial self and a heroic concept, and if so, which should we be writing about? I carry no brief for either, except to remark that serious novelists in the twentieth century usually opt for Leopold, and poor Heathcliff has been relegated to the Gothic romance. If a given serious novelist of the twentieth century is female, she too will probably go for Leopold, with all his habits, daydreams and wants. This doesn't mean she hates men; merely that she's interested in what they look like without a cloak.

All right. Suppose I've chosen to have in my novel at least one male character as a narrator or protagonist (not necessarily the same thing). I do not want to make my male character unnaturally evil, like Mr Hyde; instead I'm trying Dr Jekyll, an essentially good man with certain flaws. That's a problem right there; because, as Stevenson knew, evil is a lot easier to write about and make interesting than goodness. What, these days, is a believable notion of a good man? Let us suppose that I'm talking about a man who is merely unbad; that is, one who obeys the major laws, pays his bills, helps with the dishes, doesn't beat up his wife or molest his kids, and so forth. Let's suppose that I want him to have some actual good qualities, good in the active, positive sense. What is he to do? And how can I make him—unlike Sir Charles Grandison—interesting in a novel?

This I suspect is the point at which the concerns of the novelist coincide with those of society. Once upon a time, when we defined people—much more than we do now—by how far they lived up or failed to live up to certain pre-defined sexual role models, it was a lot easier to tell what was meant by "a good man" or "a good woman." "A good woman" was one that fulfilled our notions of what a woman should be and how she should behave. Likewise "a good man." There were certain concepts about what constituted manliness and how you got it—most authorities agreed that you weren't just born with it, you somehow had to earn, acquire or be initiated into it; acts of courage and heroism counted for something, ability to endure pain without flinching, or drink a lot without passing out, or whatever. In any case there were rules, and you could cross a line that separated the men from the boys.

It's true that the male sexual role model had a lot of drawbacks, even for men—not everybody could be Superman, many were stuck with Clark Kent—but there were certain positive and, at that time, useful features. What have we replaced this package with? We know that women have been in a state of upheaval and ferment for some time now, and movement generates energy; many things can be said by women now that were once not possible, many things can be thought that were once unthinkable. But what are we offering men? Their territory, though still large, is shrinking. The confusion and desperation and anger and conflicts that we find in male characters in novels don't exist only in novels. They're out there in the real world. "Be a person, my son," doesn't yet have the same ring to it as "Be a man," though it is indeed a worthy goal. The novelist *qua* novelist, as opposed to the utopian romancer, takes *what is there* as a point of departure. What is there, when we're talking about men, is a state of change, new attitudes overlapping with old ones, no simple rules any more. Some exciting form of life may emerge from all this.

Meanwhile, I think women have to take the concerns of men as seriously as they expect men to take theirs, both as novelists and as inhabitants of this earth. One encounters, too often, the attitude that only the pain felt by persons of the female sex is real pain, that only female fears are real fears. That for me is the equivalent of the notion that only working-class people are real, that middle-class people are not, and so forth. Of course there's a distinction between earned pain and mere childish self-pity, and yes, women's fear of being killed by men is grounded in authenticity, not to mention statistics, to a greater extent than men's fear of being laughed at. Damage to one's self-image is not quite the same as damage to one's neck, though not to be underestimated: men have been known to murder and kill themselves because of it.

I'm not advocating a return to door-mat status for women, or even to the arrangement whereby women prop up and nurture and stroke and feed the egos of men without having men do at least some of the same for them. To understand is not necessarily to condone; and it could be pointed out that women have been "understanding" men for centuries, partly because it was necessary for survival. If the other fellow has the heavy artillery, it's best to be able to anticipate his probable moves. Women, like guerrilla fighters, developed infiltration rather than frontal attack as their favoured strategy.

But "understanding" as a manipulative tool—which is really a form of contempt for the thing understood—isn't the kind I would like to see. However, some women are not in the mood to dish out any more understanding, of any kind; they're feeling a lot like René Lévesque: the time for that is over, they want power instead. But one cannot deprive any part of humanity of the definition "human" without grievous risk to one's own soul. And for women to define themselves as powerless and men as all-powerful is to fall into an ancient trap, to shirk responsibility as well as to warp reality. The opposite also is true; to depict a world in which women are already equal to men, in power, opportunities and freedom of movement, is a similar abdication.

I know I haven't given any specific directions for writing the male character; how can I? They're all different, remember. All I've given are a few warnings, an indication of what you're up against from the real world and from critics. But just because it's difficult is no reason not to try.

When I was young and reading a lot of comic books and fairy tales, I used to wish for two things: the cloak of invisibility, so I could follow people around and listen to what they were saying when I wasn't there, and the ability to teleport my mind into somebody else's mind, still retaining my own perceptions and memory. You can see that I was cut out to be a novelist, because these are the two fantasies novelists act out every time they write a page. Throwing your mind is easier to do if you're throwing it into a character who has a few things in common with you, which may be why I've written more pages from a female character's point of view than from a male's. But male characters are more of a challenge, and now that I'm middle-aged and less lazy I'll undoubtedly try a few more of them. If writing novels—and reading them—have any redeeming social value, it's probably that they force you to imagine what it's like to be somebody else.

Which, increasingly, is something we all need to know.

From *Second Words: Selected Critical Prose* (Toronto: House of Anansi Press, 1982), 412–30. A somewhat different version of this paper was delivered as a Hagey Lecture at the University of Waterloo, February 1982. That version was published in *This Magazine* 16, 4 (September 1982): 4–10.

MARGARET ATWOOD

True North

Land of the silver birch,
Home of the beaver,
Where still the mighty moose
Wanders at will,
Blue lake and rocky shore,
I will return once more;
Boom-diddy-boom-boom
Boom-diddy-boom-boom
Boo-OO-oo-oo-oom.

Archaic Song

We sang this once, squatting around the papier-mâché Magic Mushroom in the Brownie pack, while pretending to be wolves in Cub Scouts, or while watching our marshmallows turn to melted Styrofoam on the ends of our sticks at some well-run, fairly safe summer camp in the wilds of Muskoka, Haliburton, or Algonquin Park. Then we grew up and found it corny. By that time we were into Jean-Paul Sartre and the lure of the nauseous. Finally, having reached the age of nostalgia, we rediscovered it on a cassette in The Children's Book Store, in a haunting version that invested it with all the emotional resonance we once thought it possessed, and bought it, under the pretence of giving our children a little ethnic musical background.

It brought tears to our eyes, not for simple reasons. Whales get to us that way too, and whooping cranes, and other things hovering on the verge of extinction but still maintaining a tenuous foothold in the world of the actual. The beavers are doing all right—we know this because they just decimated our poplars—but the mighty moose is having a slimmer time of it. As for the blueness of the lakes, we worry about it: too blue and you've got acid rain.

Will we return once more, or will we go to Portugal instead? It depends, we have to admit, partly on the exchange rate, and this makes us feel disloyal. I am, rather quixotically, in Alabama, teaching, even more quixotically, a course in Canadian literature. Right now we're considering Marian Engel's novel *Bear*. Since everything in Canada, outside Toronto, begins with geography, I've unfolded a large map of Ontario and traced the heroine's route north; I've located the mythical house of the book somewhere on the actual shore of Georgian Bay, northern edge. I've superimposed a same-scale map of Alabama on this scheme, to give the students an idea of the distances. In the north, space is larger than you think, because the points of reference are farther apart.

"Are there any words you came across that puzzled you?" I ask.

Blackfly comes up. A large black fly is proposed. I explain blackflies, their smallness, their multitude, their evil habits. It gives me a certain kick to do this: I'm competing with the local water moccasins.

Mackinaw. A raincoat? Not quite. *Loon. Tamarack. Reindeer moss. Portage. Moose. Wendigo.*

"Why does she make Lucy the old Indian woman talk so funny?" they ask. Lucy, I point out, is not merely Indian but a *French-speaking* Indian. This, to them, is a weird concept.

The north is another country. It's also another language. Or languages.

▼ ▼ ▼

Where is the north, exactly? It's not only a place but a direction, and as such its location is relative: to the Mexicans, the United States is the north, to Americans, Toronto is, even though it's on roughly the same latitude as Boston.

Wherever it is for us, there's a lot of it. You stand in Windsor and imagine a line going north, all the way to the pole. The same line going south would end up in South America. That's the sort of map we grew up with, at the front of the classroom in Mercator projection, which made it look even bigger than it was, all that pink stretching on forever, with a few cities sprinkled along the bottom edge. It's not only geographical space, it's space related to body image. When we face south, as we often do, our conscious mind may be directed down there, towards crowds, bright lights, some Hollywood version of fame and fortune, but the north is at the back of our minds, always. There's something, not someone, looking over our shoulders; there's a chill at the nape of the neck.

The north focuses our anxieties. Turning to face north, face the north, we enter our own unconscious. Always, in retrospect, the journey north has the quality of dream.

▼ ▼ ▼

Where does the north begin?

Every province, every city, has its own road north. From Toronto you go up the 400. Where you cross the border, from here to there, is a matter of opinion. Is it the Severn River, where the Shield granite appears suddenly out of the earth? Is it the sign announcing that you're halfway between the equator and the North Pole? Is it the first gift shop shaped like a wigwam, the first town—there are several—that proclaims itself The Gateway to the North?

As we proceed, the farms become fewer, rockier, more desperate-looking, the trees change their ratios, coniferous moving in on deciduous. More lakes appear, their shorelines scraggier. Our eyes narrow and we look at the clouds: the weather is important again.

▼ ▼ ▼

One of us used to spend summers in a cottage in Muskoka, before the road went in, when you took the train, when there were big cruise ships there, and matronly motor launches, and tea dances at the hotels, and men in white flannels on the lawns, which there may still be. This was not just a cottage but a Muskoka cottage, with boathouse and maid's quarters. Rich people went north in the summers then, away from cities and crowds; that was before the cure for polio, which has made a difference. In this sort of north, they tried to duplicate the south, or perhaps some dream of country life in England. In the living room there were armchairs, glass-fronted bookcases, family photos in silver frames, stuffed birds under glass bells. The north, as I said, is relative.

▼ ▼ ▼

For me, the north used to be completely in force by the Trout Creek planing mill. Those stacks of fresh-cut lumber were the true gateway to the north, and north of that was North Bay, which used to be, to be blunt, a bit of an armpit. It was beef-sandwich-on-white-bread-with-gravy-and-canned-peas country. But no more. North Bay now has shopping malls, and baskets of flowers hanging from lampposts above paving-stone sidewalks, downtown. It has a Granite Club. It has the new, swish, carpeted buildings of Laurentian University. It has gourmet restaurants. And in the airport, where southbound DC-9s dock side by side with northbound Twin Otters, there's a book rack in the coffee shop that features Graham Greene and Kierkegaard, hardly standard airport fare.

The south is moving north.

▼ ▼ ▼

We bypass North Bay, which now has a bypass, creeping southerliness, and do not go, this time, to the Dionne Quints Museum, where five little silhouettes in black play forever beside an old log cabin, complete with the basket where they were packed in cotton wool, the oven where they were warmed, the five prams, the five Communion dresses.

Beyond North Bay there is a brief flurry of eccentricity—lawns populated with whole flocks of wooden-goose windmills—and then we go for miles and miles past nothing but trees, meeting nothing but the occasional truck loaded with lumber. This area didn't used to be called anything. Now it's the Near North Travel Area. You can see signs telling you that. Near what, we wonder uneasily? We don't want to be near. We want to be far.

At last we see the Ottawa River, which is the border. There's a dam across it, two dams, and an island between them. If there were a customs house it would be here. A sign faces us saying *Bienvenue*; out the back window there's one saying *Welcome*. This was my first lesson in points of view.

And there, across the border in Québec, in Témiscaming, is an image straight from my childhood: a huge mountain made of sawdust. I always wanted to slide down this sawdust mountain until I finally did, and discovered it was not like sand, dry and slippery, but damp and sticky and hard to get out of your clothes. This was my first lesson in the nature of illusion.

Continue past the sawdust mountain, past the baseball diamond, up the hill, and you're in the centre of town, which is remarkable for at least three things: a blocks-long public rock garden, still flourishing after more than forty-five years; a pair of statues, one a fountain, that look as if they've come straight from Europe, which I think they did; and the excellent, amazingly low-priced hamburgers you can get at the Boulevard Restaurant, where the décor, featuring last year's cardboard Santa Claus and a stuffed twenty-three pound pike, is decidedly northern. Ask the owner about the pike and he'll tell you about one twice as big, forty-five pounds in fact, that a fellow showed him strapped to the tailgate of his van, and that long, too.

You can have this conversation in either French or English: Témiscaming is a border town and a northern one, and the distinctions made here are as likely to be north–south as French–English. Up in these parts you'll hear as much grumbling, or more, about Québec City as you will about Ottawa, which is, after all, closer. Spit in the river and it gets to Ottawa, eh?

For the north, Témiscaming is old, settled, tidy, even a little prosperous-looking. But it's had its crises. Témiscaming is the resource economy personified. Not long ago it was a company town, and when the company shut down the mill, which would have shut down the town too, the workers took the unprecedented step of trying to buy it. With some help they succeeded, and the result was Tembec, still going strong. But Témiscaming is still a one-industry town, like many northern towns, and its existence is thus precarious.

Not so long ago, logging was a different sort of business. The men went into the woods in winter, across the ice, using horse-drawn sledges, and set up camp. (You still come across these logging camps now and then in your travels through the lakes, abandoned, already looking as ancient as Roman aqueducts; more ancient, since there's been no upkeep.) They'd cut selectively, tree by tree, using axes and saws and the skills that were necessary to avoid being squashed or hacked. They'd skid the trees to the ice; in the spring, after the ice went out, there would be a run down the nearest fast river to the nearest sawmill.

Now it's done with bulldozers and trucks, and the result is too often a blitzed shambles; cut everything, leave a wreck of dead and, incidentally, easily flammable branches behind. Time is money. Don't touch the shoreline though, we need that for tourists. In some places, the forest is merely a scrim along the water. In behind it's been hollowed out.

Those who look on the positive side say it's good for the blueberries.

▼ ▼ ▼

Sometimes we went the other way, across to Sudbury, the trees getting smaller and smaller and finally disappearing as you approached. Sudbury was another magic place of my childhood. It was like interplanetary travel, which we liked to imagine, which was still just imagination in those days. With its heaps of slag and its barren shoulders of stone, it looked like the moon. Back then, we tell the children, before there were washer-dryers and you used something called a wringer washer and hung the sheets out on something called a clothesline, when there weren't even coloured sheets but all sheets were white, when Rinso white and its happy little washday song were an item, and Whiter than White was a catch phrase and female status really did have something to do with your laundry, Sudbury was a housewife's nightmare. We knew people there; the windowsills in their houses were always grey.

Now the trees are beginning to come back because they built higher smokestacks. But where is all that stuff going now?

▼ ▼ ▼

The Acid Rain Dinner, in Toronto's Sheraton Centre, in 1985. The first of these fund-raising events was fairly small. But the movement has grown, and this dinner is huge. The leaders of all three provincial parties are here. So is the minister of the environment from the federal government. So are several labour leaders, and several high-ranking capitalists, and representatives of numerous northerly chambers of commerce, summer residents' associations, tourist-camp runners, outfitters. Wishy-washy urban professionals who say "frankly" a lot bend elbows with huntin', shootin', fishin', and cussin' burnt-necks who wouldn't be caught dead saying "frankly." This is not a good place to be overheard saying that actually acid rain isn't such a bad thing because it gets rid of all that brown scum and leeches in the lake, or who cares because you can water-ski anyway. Teddy Kennedy, looking like a bulky sweater, is the guest speaker. Everyone wears a little gold pin in the shape of a rain drop. It looks like a tear.

Why has acid rain become the collective Canadian nightmare? Why is it—as a good cause—bigger than baby-seal bashing? The reasons aren't just economic, although there are lots of those, as the fishing-camp people and foresters will tell you. It's more than that, and cognate with the outrage aroused by the uninvited voyage of the American icebreaker *Polar Sea* through the Northwest Passage, where almost none of us ever goes. It's territorial, partly; partly a felt violation of some area in us that we hardly ever think about unless it's invaded or tampered with. It's the neighbours throwing guck in our yard. It's our childhood dying.

On location, in summer and far from the glass and brass of the Sheraton Centre, we nervously check our lakes. Leeches still in place? Have the crayfish, among the first to go, gone yet? (We think in terms of "yet.") Are the loons reproducing, have you seen any young? Any minnows? How about the lichen on the rocks? These inventories have now become routine, and that is why we're willing to fork out a hundred dollars a plate to support our acid-rain lobbyists in Washington. A summer without loons is unthinkable, but how do you tell that to people who don't know it because they've never had any to begin with?

▼ ▼ ▼

We're driving through Glencoe, in the Highlands of Scotland. It's imposing, as a landscape: bleak, large, bald, apparently empty. We can see why the Scots took so well to Canada. Yet we know that the glens and crags round about are crawling with at least a thousand campers, rock climbers, and other seekers after nature; we also know that, at one end of this glen, the Campbells butchered the MacDonalds in the seventeenth century, thus propelling both of them into memorable history. Go walking here and you'll find things human: outlines of stone fences now overgrown, shards of abandoned crofts.

In Europe, every scrap of land has been claimed, owned, re-owned, fought over, captured, bled on. The roads are the only no-man's-land. In northern Canada, the roads are civilization, owned by the collective human *we*. Off the road is *other*. Try walking in it, and you'll soon find out why all the early traffic here was by water. "Impenetrable wilderness" is not just verbal.

And suppose you get off the road. Suppose you get lost. Getting lost, elsewhere and closer to town, is not knowing exactly where you are. You can always ask, even in a foreign country. In the north, getting lost is not knowing how to get out.

You can get lost on a lake, of course, but getting lost in the forest is worse. It's tangly in there, and dim, and one tree does begin to look remarkably like another. The leaves and needles blot up sound, and you begin to feel watched: not by anyone, not by an animal even, or anything you can put a name to, just watched. You begin to feel judged. It's as if something is keeping an eye on you just to see what you will do.

What will you do? Which side of the tree does moss grow on, and here, where there are ferns and the earth is damp, or where it's dry as tinder, it seems that moss grows everywhere, or does not grow at all. Snippets of Boy Scout lore or truisms learned at summer camp come back to you, but scrambled. You tell yourself not to panic: you can always live off the land.

Easier said than done, you'd soon find. The Canadian Shield is a relatively foodless area, which is why even the Indians tended to pass through it, did not form large settlements except where there was arable land, and remained limited in numbers. This is not the Mekong delta. If you had a gun you could shoot something, maybe, a red squirrel perhaps; but if you're lost you probably don't have a gun, or a fishing rod either. You could eat blueberries, or cattail stems, or crayfish, or other delicacies dimly remembered from stories about people who got lost in the woods and were found later in good health although somewhat thinner. You could cook some reindeer moss, if you had matches.

Thus you pass on to fantasies about how to start a fire with a magnifying glass—you don't have one—or by rubbing two bits of stick together, a feat at which you suspect you would prove remarkably inept.

The fact is that not very many of us know how to survive in the north. Rumour has it that only one German prisoner of war ever made it out, although many made it out of the actual prisoner-of-war camps. The best piece of northern survival advice is: *Don't get lost.*

▼ ▼ ▼

One way of looking at a landscape is to consider the typical ways of dying in it. Given the worst, what's the worst it could do? Will it be delirium from drinking salty water on the high seas, shrivelling in the desert, snakebite in the jungle, tidal waves on a Pacific Isle, volcanic fumes? In the north, there are several hazards. Although you're probably a lot safer there than you are on the highway at rush hour, given the odds, you still have to be a little wary.

Like most lessons of this sort, those about the north are taught by precept and example, but also, more enjoyably, by cautionary nasty tale. There is death by blackfly, the one about the fellow who didn't have his shirt cuffs tight enough in the spring and undressed at night only find he was running with blood, the ones about the lost travellers who bloated up from too many bites and who, when found, were twice the size, unrecognizable, and dead. There is death from starvation, death by animal, death by forest fire; there is death from something called "exposure," which used to confuse me when I heard about men who exposed themselves: why would they intentionally do anything that fatal? There's death by thunderstorm, not to be sneered at: on the open lake, in one of the excessive northern midsummer thunderstorms, a canoe or a bush plane is a vulnerable target. The north is full of Struwwelpeter-like stories about people who didn't do as they were told and got struck by lightning. Above all, there are death by freezing and death by drowning. Your body's heat-loss rate in the water is twenty times that in air, and northern lakes are cold. Even in a life jacket, even holding on to the tipped canoe, you're at risk. Every summer the numbers pile up.

Every culture has its exemplary dead people, its hagiography of landscape martyrs, those unfortunates who, by their bad ends, seem to sum up in one grisly episode what may be lurking behind the next rock for all of us, all of us who enter the territory they once claimed as theirs. I'd say that two of the top northern landscape martyrs are Tom Thomson, the painter who was found mysteriously drowned near his overturned canoe with no provable cause in sight, and the Mad Trapper of Rat River, also mysterious, who became so thoroughly bushed that he killed a Mountie and shot two others during an amazing wintertime chase before being finally mowed down. In our retelling of these stories, mystery is a key element. So, strangely enough, is a presumed oneness with the landscape in question. The Mad Trapper knew his landscape so well he survived in it for weeks, living off the land and his own bootlaces, eluding capture. One of the hidden motifs in these stories is a warning: maybe it's not so good to get *too* close to Nature.

I remember a documentary on Tom Thomson that ended, rather ominously, with the statement that the north had taken him to herself. This was, of course, pathetic fallacy gone to seed, but it was also a comment on our distrust of the natural world, a distrust that remains despite our protests, our studies in the ethics of ecology, our elevation of "the environment" to a numinous noun, our save-the-trees campaigns. The question is, would the trees save us, given the chance? Would the water, would the birds, would the rocks? In the north, we have our doubts.

▼ ▼ ▼

A bunch of us are sitting around the table, at what is now a summer cottage in Georgian Bay. Once it was a house, built by a local man for his family, which finally totalled eleven children, after they'd outgrown this particular house and moved on to another. The original Findlay wood-burning cook stove is still in the house, but so also are some electric lights and a propane cooker, which have come since the end of the old days. In the old days, this man somehow managed to scrape a living from the land: a little of this, a little of that, some fishing here, some lumbering there, some hunting in the fall. That was back when you shot to eat. "Scrape" is an appropriate word: there's not much here between the topsoil and the rock.

We sit around the table and eat, fish among other things, caught by the children. Someone mentions the clams: there are still a lot of them, but who knows what's in them any more? Mercury, lead, things like that. We pick at the fish. Someone tells me not to drink the tap water. I already have. "What will happen?" I ask. "Probably nothing," they reply. "Probably nothing" is a relatively recent phrase around here. In the old days, you ate what looked edible.

We are talking about the old days, as people often do once they're outside the cities. When exactly did the old days end? Because we know they did. The old days ended when the youngest of us was ten, fifteen, or twenty; the old days ended when the oldest of us was five, or twelve, or thirty. Plastic-hulled superboats are not old days, but ten-horse-power outboard motors, circa 1945, are. There's an icebox in the back porch, unused now, a simple utilitarian model from Eaton's, ice chamber in the top section, metal shelves in the bottom one. We all go and admire it. "I remember ice boxes," I say, and indeed I can dimly remember them, I must have been five. What bits of our daily junk—our toasters, our pocket computers—will soon become obsolete and therefore poignant? Who will stand around, peering at them and admiring their design and the work that went into them, as we do with this icebox? "So this was a *toilet seat*," we think, rehearsing the future. "Ah! A *light bulb*," the ancient syllables thick in our mouths.

The kids have decided some time ago that all this chat is boring, and have asked if they can go swimming off the dock. They can, though they have to watch it, as this is a narrow place and speedboats tend to swoosh through, not always slowing down. Waste of gas, in the old days. Nobody then went anywhere just for pleasure, it was the war and gas was rationed.

"Oh, *that* old days," says someone.

There goes a speedboat now, towing a man strapped in a kneeling position to some kind of board, looking as if he's had a terrible accident, or is about to have one. This must be some newfangled variety of water-skiing.

"Remember Klim?" I say. The children come through, trailing towels. "What's Klim?" one asks, caught by the space-age sound of the word.

"Klim was 'milk' spelled backwards," I say. "It was powdered milk."

"Yuk," they say.

"Not the same as now," I say. "It was whole milk, not skim; it wasn't instant. You had to beat it with an eggbeater." And even then some of it wouldn't dissolve. One of the treats of childhood was the little nodules of pure dry Klim that floated on top of your milk.

"There was also Pream," says someone. How revolutionary it seemed.

The children go down to take their chances in the risky motorized water. Maybe, much later, they will remember us sitting around the table, eating fish they themselves had caught, back when you could still (what? Catch a fish? See a tree? What desolations lie in store, beyond the plasticized hulls and the knee-skiers?). By then we will be the old days, for them. Almost we are already.

▼ ▼ ▼

A different part of the north. We're sitting around the table; by lamplight—it's still the old days here, no electricity—talking about bad hunters. Bad hunters, bad fishers, everyone has a story. You come upon a campsite, way in the back of beyond, no roads into the lake, they must have come in by float plane, and there it is, garbage all over the place, beer cans, blobs of human poop flagged by melting toilet paper, and twenty-two fine pickerel left rotting on a rock. Business executives who get themselves flown in during hunting season with their high-powered rifles, shoot a buck, cut off the head, fill their quota, see another one with a bigger spread of antlers, drop the first head, cut off the second. The woods are littered with discarded heads, and who cares about the bodies?

New way to shoot polar bear: you have the natives on the ground finding them for you, then they radio the location in to the base camp, the base camp phones New York, fellow gets on the plane, gets himself flown in, they've got the rifle and the clothing all ready for him, fly him to the bear, he pulls the trigger from the plane, doesn't even get out of the g.d. *plane*, they fly him back, cut off the head, skin it, send the lot down to New York.

These are the horror stories of the north, one brand. They've replaced the ones in which you got pounced upon by a wolverine or had your arm chewed off by a she-bear with cubs or got chased into the lake by a moose in rut, or even the ones in which your dog got porcupine quills or rolled in poison ivy and gave it to you. In the new stories, the enemies and the victims of old have done a switch. Nature is no longer implacable, dangerous, ready to jump you; it is on the run, pursued by a number of unfair bullies with the latest technology.

One of the key nouns in these stories is "float plane." These outrages, this banditry, would not be possible without them, for the bad hunters are notoriously weak-muscled and are deemed incapable of portaging a canoe, much less paddling one. Among their other badnesses, they are sissies. Another key motif is money. What money buys these days, among other things, is the privilege of no-risk slaughter.

As for us, the ones telling the stories, tsk-tsking by lamplight, we are the good hunters, or so we think. We've given up saying we only kill to eat; Kraft dinner and freeze-dried food have put paid to that one. Really there's no excuse for us. However, we do have some virtues left. We can still cast a fly. We don't cut off heads and hang them stuffed on the wall. We would never buy an ocelot coat. We paddle our own canoes.

▼ ▼ ▼

We're sitting on the dock at night, shivering despite our sweaters, in mid-August, watching the sky. There are a few shooting stars, as there always are at this time in August, as the earth passes through the Perseids. We pride ourselves on knowing a few things like that, about the sky; we find the Dipper, the North Star, Cassiopeia's Chair, and talk about consulting a star chart, which we know we won't actually do. But this is the only place you can really *see* the stars, we tell each other. Cities are hopeless.

Suddenly, an odd light appears, going very fast. It spirals around like a newly dead firecracker, and then bursts, leaving a cloud of luminous dust, caught perhaps in the light from the sun, still up there somewhere. What could this be? Several days later, we hear that it was part of an extinct Soviet satellite, or that's what they say. That's what they would say, wouldn't they? It strikes us that we don't really know very much about the night sky at all any more. There's all kinds of junk up there: spy planes, old satellites, tin cans, man-made matter gone out of control. It also strikes us that we are totally dependent for knowledge of these things on a few people who don't tell us very much.

Once, we thought that if the balloon ever went up we'd head for the bush and hide out up there, living—we naively supposed—off the land. Now we know that if the two superpowers begin hurling things at each other through the sky, they're likely to do it across the Arctic, with big bangs and fallout all over the north. The wind blows everywhere. Survival gear and knowing which moss you can eat is not going to be a large help. The north is no longer a refuge.

▼ ▼ ▼

Driving back towards Toronto from the Near North, a small reprise runs through my head:

Land of the septic tank,
Home of the speedboat,
Where still the four-wheel-drive
Wanders at will,
Blue lake and tacky shore,
I will return once more:
Vroom-diddy-vroom-vroom
Vroom-diddy-vroom-vroom
Vroo-OO-oo-oom

Somehow, just as the drive north inspires saga and tragedy, the drive south inspires parody. And here it comes: the gift shops shaped like teepees, the maple-syrup emporiums that get themselves up like olde-tyme sugaring-off huts; and, farther south, the restaurants that pretend to offer wholesome farm fare, the stores that pretend to be general stores, selling quilts, soap shaped like hearts, high-priced fancy conserves done up in frilly cloth caps, the way Grandma (whoever she might be) was fondly supposed to have made them.

And then come the housing developments, acres of prime farmland turning overnight into Quality All-Brick Family Homes; and then come the Industrial Parks; and there, in full anti-bloom, is the city itself, looming like a mirage or a chemical warfare zone on the horizon. A browny-grey scuzz hovers above it, and we think, as we always do when facing re-entry, we're going into *that*? We're going to breathe *that*?

But we go forward, as we always do, into what is now to us the unknown. And once inside, we breathe the air, not much bad happens to us, we hardly notice. It's as if we've never been anywhere else. But that's what we think, too, when we're in the north.

From *Saturday Night* 102, 1 (January 1987): 141–48.

D. M. R. BENTLEY

(1947–) was born in Kenya, and his family moved to Victoria, British Columbia, in 1960. He received his B.A. from the University of Victoria in 1969, and in the same year was awarded a Certificat de Langue Française from the Sorbonne and a Graduate Fellowship to Dalhousie University, where he then obtained an M.A. (1970). With the assistance of a Canada Council Doctoral Fellowship, he went to King's College, University of London, to write his Ph.D. thesis on the Victorian poet Dante Gabriel Rossetti (1974). He then completed an interdisciplinary M.A. in Canadian Studies at Carleton University in Ottawa (1975). Since 1975, he has taught in the Department of English at the University of Western Ontario. He has been a director since 1985 of the Canadian Institute for Historical Microreproductions, serving as its president since 1988. With Michael Gnarowski, he founded the influential journal *Canadian Poetry: Studies, Documents, Reviews* in 1977, and continues as its sole editor. More recently, with the establishment of Canadian Poetry Press, he has been publishing a series of critical and scholarly editions of early Canadian long poems which has changed the way teachers and students of Canadian literature perceive the continuum of Canadian poetry.

Bentley's writings express his ongoing concern with the history of Canadian poetry from the Conquest of Quebec to the Second World War, with particular emphasis on the relationships among technique, form, landscape, and region. Combining to distinctive advantage his expertise in the complementary fields of Victorian and nineteenth-century Canadian poetry, he has emerged over the past fifteen years as the foremost authority on early Canadian poetry, and regularly publishes critical-scholarly essays that express his original approach to the criticism of Canadian poetry. He is guided by a model which holds that the poetry is neither slavishly derivative nor original but has instead adapted poetics originating elsewhere to a uniquely Canadian environment. Informed by wide learning and lively intelligence, Bentley's essays express the workings of the eclectic mind of the humanist critic-scholar at its best.

The essay that follows focusses on those aspects of mind and culture considered of fundamental importance to a conservative and humanist such as Bentley: individual memory and communal history. He views the essay as a "response to the homogenization of culture that has been taking place in Canada and elsewhere in recent years as a result of various factors, including the spread of multi-national consumer civilization and its various languages—advertising, post-modernism, literary theory, etc."

Forgetful of Former Care: Notes on the Past and Present State of Canadian Memory

D. M. R. BENTLEY

In February 1948, Communist leader Klement Gottwald stepped out on the balcony of a Baroque palace in Prague to address the hundreds of thousands of his fellow citizens packed into Old Town Square. It was a crucial moment in Czech history—a fateful moment of the kind that occurs once or twice in a millennium.

Gottwald was flanked by his comrades, with Clementis standing next to him. There were snow flurries, it was cold, and Gottwald was bareheaded. The solicitous Clementis took off his own fur cap and set it on Gottwald's head.

The Party propaganda section put out hundreds of thousands of copies of a photograph of that balcony with Gottwald, a fur cap on his head and comrades at his side, speaking to the nation. On that balcony the history of Communist Czechoslovakia was born. Every child knew the photograph from posters, school-books, and museums. Four years later Clementis was charged with treason and hanged. The propaganda section immediately airbrushed him out of history and, obviously, out of all the photographs as well. Ever since, Gottwald has stood on that balcony alone. Where Clementis once stood, there is only bare palace wall. All that remains of Clementis is the cap on Gottwald's head.

Milan Kundera
The Book of Laughter and Forgetting

The struggle of remembering against forgetting which in Kundera's Czechoslovakia is the "struggle of man against power" is a struggle that is discernible, albeit less dramatically, throughout the history of Canadian culture. The provincial motto of Quebec, "Je me souviens," is enough to remind us of the importance of memory in securing the survival of cultural and individual identity. Without the memories of the past that are constitutive of cultural and intellectual continuity, there can be no fully comprehended present either for a collectivity or for an individual, and with no remembered past to define and direct the present there can be no planned or idealized future. As the Archmage Ged tells Arren in Ursula Le Guin's *Earthsea Trilogy*, "To deny the past is to deny the future. . . . If the rowan's roots are shallow, it bears no crown." Or as Cicero put it: "To know nothing of what happened before you were born is to remain forever a child." A key element for the realization of our individual destiny, memory is also a means by which relatively powerless clusters of cultural and personal identity such as Czechoslovakia and Canada are able to resist the coercions of larger powers whose economic or ideological futurism can convince them that even their own history, let alone the history of other places and peoples, can be treated either selectively or as "bunk." In view of the possibly enormous stakes involved, a concerned look at the state of Canadian memory, at what is remembered and forgotten in this country and its culture, could prove as intriguing and telling in its own way as Kundera's chilling account of those wintry photographs of Clementis and his cap.

That the same man who proclaimed history "bunk" also invented the assembly line and the monochrome car will surprise no one who has recognized that a hostility to history and a dehumanizing drive towards uniformity are by no means unrelated aspects of consumer capitalism, a system which has every economic reason for coercing people into living a present-participle existence (drinking, eating, sailing, having fun . . .) in a perpetual present that, even as it happens, is obsolete by design. Some people may be immune to such coercion but, if so, it will not be by grace of today's educational system, which, under the pressure of the liberal ethos that governs consumer capitalism, has allowed itself at nearly every level to be predicated on a belief in process, on the notion that *thinking* and *writing* about issues and problems is more important than *what* is thought or written *about*. The idea of memorizing something—a great poem, an historically important speech, a piece of purple prose from a novel (the Bible, needless to say, cannot be mentioned, even for its style)—seems to modern educators and students as pointless as studying Latin or some other "dead language" (though some of these languages are, of course, essential to the apprehension of the memories implicit in English words). It has become for many people sufficient to know a few sentences and slogans and, not surprisingly (since, after school, the greatest influences on most children are the media) most of the sentences and slogans that people find in their minds are from advertisements: "Harvey's makes a hamburger a beautiful thing," "Just for the taste of it—Diet Coke," "Come to where the flavor is". . . . Neither is it surprising that most people can remember the punch-lines of television commercials but not the plots and events of the programmes that they ostensibly interrupt. ("Readers who have watched a number of episodes of say, *Three's Company* or *Hangin' In* might try to recollect them," wrote

Patrick Flaherty in a recent issue of the *Globe and Mail*; "Bet you can't.") The plots and events of such programmes have to be as forgettable as the commercials that support them are memorable or—much to the detriment of consumer capitalism—the North American media networks would not survive.

Perhaps the most devastating consequence of our perpetual bombardment by the messages of consumer capitalism is that, as Mikhail Bakhtin long ago theorized and as Martin Amis has recently shown (in *Money*: a frightening novel; read it, especially if you are a feminist or a chauvinist), we are all of us being thought by the consumerism that surrounds us: most of our ideas and memories are not in any meaningful way our own. By no means fortuitously, a principal characteristic of Amis's protagonist as he wanders soporifically between and around London and New York is amnesia, a forgetfulness of the events of his own life that is an evident consequence of his absorption by the voices of consumer culture (pornography, the weather, the cult of youth . . .). The Nobel-Prize-winning poet Czeslaw Milosz has observed that "a refusal to remember" is a primary characteristic of the latter part of the twentieth century. Could it be that an *inability* to remember is gradually becoming a characteristic of our age, alienating us as it does so from ourselves and from our traditional culture? Could it even be that Alzheimer's is as much a social as a personal disease? A glance at some early Canadian literature, at a few of those "documents of little glory" (Michel Foucault), and some of great glory, which can shed so much light on both our past and our present, will place the movement from remembering to forgetting in Canadian culture in literary and historical perspective, while also preparing the way for a discussion of the roles of Modernism (and to an extent post-Modernism) in the manipulation of Canadian memory.

▼ ▼ ▼

In Romantic and post-Romantic English and Canadian poetry the most obvious catalysts for memory (Memory: Mnemosyne: the Mother of the Muses) are places—familiar places that, when revisited, call forth from the poet a flood of valuable reminiscences. In William Wordsworth's "Tintern Abbey" and Matthew Arnold's "Terrace at Berne," for example, the poet's return to a familiar place engenders memories of times past that are not pursued as a nostalgic end in themselves but as an illumination of the present and a guide to the future. This pattern is followed towards the end of the century by Charles G.D. Roberts in "Tantramar Revisited" (1886), the poem that he wrote after returning from Goldwin Smith's Toronto to the New Brunswick landscape of his childhood. (In Canada's metaphysical geography, it may be noted, the direction of remembering is from West to East and that of forgetting from East to West or North.) "Well I remember it all," Roberts says twice in "Tantramar Revisited," and he concludes the poem by rejecting a possibly disillusioning descent into his cherished landscape and choosing instead to remember it in his mind's eye and in his elegiac poem:

Muse and recall far off, rather remember than see
Lest on too close sight I miss the darling illusion,
Spy at their task even here the hands of chance and change.

Recognizing the illusory nature of stability (and, eventually, opting for life in the fast lanes of New York), Roberts nevertheless resolves in this instance to accept the traditional role of the Canadian poet as the chronicler and celebrator less of "chance and change" than of peace, order and good government, particularly as manifested in the life of the Euro-Canadian farm or village. Roberts' interest in memory makes him as sensitive as Marcel Proust to the particular power of the senses of smell and taste in the calling-up of remembrances: "Oh . . . the nose," he has a character exclaim in *A Sister to Evangeline,* "How subtle and undestructable are its memories! They know the swiftest ways to the source of joy and tears."

An awareness of both the personal pleasures and the social benefits of memory is not confined to Canadian poetry of the Romantic tradition. Almost a century earlier than Roberts, Thomas Cary in *Abram's Plains* (1789) had held "blest converse with the learned dead" (the great writers and philosophers of the classical and neoclassical traditions) on the "green sod" outside Quebec City and, in true Tory form, affirmed in the very year of the French Revolution the importance of remembering forward the achievements of the past. As Edmund Burke said at the time "Society is . . . a contract . . . , a partnership not only between those who are living, but between those who are living, those who are dead, and those who are to be born." In *The Rising Village* (1825), the Canadian Oliver Goldsmith links "forgetful[ness]" with the onset of social malaise and, concomitantly, he sees virtue and health in the shared memory of the hardships and dangers encountered in the settlement of the land:

When . . . in peace are met a happy few,
Sweet are the social pleasures that ensue.
What lively joy each honest bosom feels,
As o'er . . . past events his memory steals. . . .

Not until the present century, with the Modernist myth of discontinuity with the past and the post-Modernist determination to ignore large portions of the nation's literature and history, does there appear in Canada the programmatic forgetfulness of roots that, in conjunction with the educational and social phenomena briefly outlined earlier, leaves any culture open to a betrayal from within or without of its essential character.

▼ ▼ ▼

Natural locales made special or resonant by personal experiences or historical events are not the only catalysts or repositories of memory in Canada. In *The Stones of Venice*, John Ruskin ascribes to old buildings the power to sustain memory in an urban environment: "We may live without [ancient architecture], and worship without her," he writes, "but we cannot remember without her." If it be granted that this is true, then it follows that the converse is also true: new buildings and new architecture (the correlative for the second-generation British Modernist W.H. Auden of a desirable "change of heart") may provide spaces in which people can live and worship but they will also obliterate personal and collective memories. As if to confirm the truth of Ruskin's argument and its correlative, Stephen Leacock gives us the following description in *Sunshine Sketches of a Little Town* (the little town being, of course, Mariposa, Leacock's synthesis of "seventy or eighty" "little towns in Ontario," primarily Orillia):

> First of all they . . . demolished the little stone church to make way for the newer [one]. It seemed almost a sacrilege, as the Dean himself said, to lay hands on it. Indeed it was first proposed to take the stone of it and build it into a Sunday School. . . . Then, when that proved impracticable, it was suggested that the stone be reverently fashioned into a wall that should stand as a token. And when even that could not be managed, the stone of the little church was laid reverently into a stone pile; afterwards it was devoutly sold to a building contractor, and, like so much else in life, was forgotten.

"*Like so much else in life, was forgotten*": the elegiac association of the absent church with other unmentioned (because unrecallable?) absences indicates that more is at stake here than a mere building, that the destruction of a familiar and historied edifice amounts to the creation of a memory hole into which psychic energies and entities are irretrievably drawn, to the considerable impoverishment of what remains behind.

Where old buildings remain intact in Canadian towns and cities they function very much in the manner predicted by Ruskin. A vivid illustration of this is "Autobiographical" where A.M. Klein, a Modern poet whose Jewish background lent him an unusually acute awareness of tradition, "chronicles" the way in which the architectural forms and human presences in the "streets" and "slums" of the "jargoning city" of Montreal give rise to "memories" that are at once nostalgic and sustaining. Literary memories in the form of allusions to Wordsworth's "emotion recollected in tranquillity" (the source of poetry) and T.S. Eliot's "Gerontion" (an "old man" who envisages "History" as an old whore) help "Autobiographical" to chart its course among less visionary uses of memory than that which Klein claims for himself"

> I am no old man fatuously intent
> On memories, but in memory, I seek
> The strength and vividness of nonage days,
> Not tranquil recollection of event.
> It is a fabled city that I seek . . . .

Almost paradoxically, the "fabled" cities of the imagination are contingent upon the presence (and, therefore, preservation) of the real cities and buildings of the past. In memory and old architecture lie the foundations of dreams and imaginary cities. That town planners in many parts of Canada have failed to understand this will be evident to anyone who, to their psychic impoverishment, has attempted to visit a childhood home in, say, Calgary or Edmonton, cities where most of the old houses have been destroyed, taking with them the memories of countless individuals and a large part of the provincial culture. No Heritage Fund, however huge, can compensate now or ever for the destruction of real heritage and tangible history that has been carried out in Alberta in the name of progress and prosperity. Nor is it necessary to go to Alberta to witness the destruction of architectural memory. In London, Ontario, there is now a temporary memory hole on Richmond Street where the Adam Beck house recently stood and before long there will be a permanent one on Talbot Street opposite the Market.

The first Canadian poet to recognize the devastating effect on memory and identity of the new architecture of modern materialism was Archibald Lampman. In "The City of the End of Things," first published in 1894 amid heated discussion in the United States and Canada about the plight and future of modern industrial cities, Lampman envisages a city in the international factory-town style whose "roofs and towers have grown/None knoweth how high within the night . . . "—an infernal realm in which robotic creatures with "clanking hands" move to "unheard commands" and obey a "hideous routine." As its very title suggests, "The City of the End of *Things*" depicts the horrible and dehumanized outcome of the material emphases of industrial civilization. To glimpse "The City of the End of Things" is to glimpse death; to be caught in its "terrific spell" is to suffer the spiritual obliteration that is contingent upon the destruction of memory:

> And whoso of our mortal race
> Should find that city unaware,
> Lean death would smite him face to face
> And blanch him with its venomed air:
> Or caught by the terrific spell,
> Each thread of memory snapt and cut,
> His soul would shrivel and its shell
> Go rattling like an empty nut.

Sensing the connection between materialism, memory loss, and spiritual vacuity, Lampman goes on to envisage the ruler of his deadly city (in part, no doubt, the Ottawa of then and now) as an "idiot" who sits "looking towards the lightless north, / Beyond the reach of memories." Built in "days that no man thinks on," "The City of the End of Things" has "no rounded name," no identifying word to conjure up in its inhabitants such feelings of nostalgia, affection and pride as they are still capable of experiencing. With the destruction of memory comes the destruction of thought, feeling, tradition, identity, spirit—in short, the destruction of humanity.

Worth remarking is the fact that two of the most memorable poetic treatments of memory that are associated with Canada and Canadians have also come into close association with backward-looking architectural forms. The first and earlier of these is the famous "Lone Shieling" stanza of "The Canadian Boat-Song" (1829). It is engraved on a plaque near a re-creation of a Scottish crofter's hut on Cape Breton Island:

From the lone shieling of the misty island
Mountains divide us, and the waste of seas—
Yet still the blood is strong, the heart is Highland
And we in dreams behold the Hebrides.

The second and later of the two poems is, as may already have been guessed, "In Flanders Fields," a work almost ineluctably associated in most people's minds either with a high-school reader (it used to be, in British Columbia at least, that students had to memorize it), or with the Remembrance Day ceremonies centred on the National War Monument in Ottawa (one of the few genuinely national repositories of Canada's collective memory). Whereas memory in the "Lone Shieling" stanza promises sustaining dreams for the living, remembrance in Colonel MacRae's poem promises peaceful sleep for the dead: "If ye break faith with us who die / We shall not sleep, though poppies grow / In Flanders fields." Here, indeed, is a social contract between "those who are living, those who are dead, and those who are to be born." Both the "Lone Shieling" and "In Flanders Fields" urge in different ways that if the struggle of remembering against forgetting is won the result will be an achievement of the continuity in which individual and cultural identity is founded.

▼ ▼ ▼

It is not fortuitous that all but one of the works so far placed on view were written before or during the First World War or—to put the matter another way—that almost none of them was written after the arrival in Canada of Anglo-American Modernism. At least a partial explanation of this resides in the fact that Modernism, a movement energized by the big cities of Western Europe and North America (Paris, London, and, in Canada, Montreal), has at its heart a myth of discontinuity with the immediate past that denies a part of history (in Canada an especially important part since all our easily accessible history is relatively recent) and, in so doing, threatens personal and cultural identity. Also at the heart of Modernism is another threat to distinct identities, whether personal or cultural: a structuralist belief in the existence of a monomyth that is merely elaborated in local and idiosyncratic ways which are of vastly less importance than the pattern that underlies them. As a result of these and other tendencies, Canadian Modernism has been as programmatically hostile to early (pre-World War I) Canadian literature and culture as it has been receptive in all areas to the reductive (international, mythopoeic) assumptions and styles of the "great" European and American Modernists. A.J.M. Smith championed "cosmopolitan" (high Modern) over "native" poetry, and followed T.S. Eliot in espousing the notion of the impersonal poet. F.R. Scott rejected "old myths" in favour of "new names," and forgot on principle that his father, Canon F.G. Scott, had been a second-generation Confederation poet. Both looked in the direction of "forgetfulness"—towards what Lampman calls the "lightless north"—for the stuff of a poetry that would be uncontaminatedly fresh in its newness. As Scott would candidly recall later: "I in my innocence was feeling that we could start afresh in Canada . . . and [was] deeply impressed by the northland . . . and its sense of something waiting to be made. I forgot that we had already imported from Europe our language, our laws, our religion, and most of the factors that make up a social community." That the very nature of language as a vehicle of cultural memory doomed from the start the attempt of these Modern poets to articulate the pristine quality of the "northland" is less interesting to the present discussion than the consequences for historical continuity, social community and individual identity of the Modernist denial of the existing, "native" culture.

The classical statement of the Modern Canadian poet's rejection of that culture is Scott's "The Canadian Authors Meet," first published in 1927. Trendily incorporating into its texture snatches of an English nursery rhyme ("Shall we go round the mulberry bush?"), an American gospel song ("Shall/We gather at the river?"), and the then unofficial national anthem ("O Canada, O Canada"), Scott's poem employs irony and sarcasm to put distance between Modernism and Canadian Romanticism, "cosmopolitan" and "native," Canada present and Canada past. Attendant upon this rupture of continuity is, as Lampman and others predict, the loss of the self that is constituted by the memory of one's past, both individual and collective. When "The Canadian Authors Meet" was first published it contained a stanza in which the poet identifies and defines himself:

> Far in the corner sits (though none would know it)
> The very picture of disconsolation
> A rather lewd and most ungodly poet
> Writing these verses, for his soul's salvation.

In subsequent printings of "The Canadian Authors Meet," this stanza was deleted, and with it the poet's and the reader's sense of the identity of the poem's creator—an identity that is tellingly Modern in its marked privileging of the male (female poets are lewdly caricatured earlier as "Miss Crotchet") and its concern with the "soul's salvation." (In a central text for Canadian Modernism, *Modern Man in Search of a Soul*, Carl Jung describes the "modern man" as "the man of the immediate present," the man who "break[s] with tradition" and "renounce[s] . . . history" in order to be "fully conscious of the present.") No doubt, Scott moved away in time from the scathing rejection of the pre-Modern and the personal that is evident in the final version of "The Canadian Authors Meet." But his rejection of tradition is evident in his own poems (to their cost) in the arbitrary and poetically uninteresting use of such traditional forms as the sonnet (which, willy-nilly, carry the signature of Petrarch's Italy and Shakespeare's England) and, more generally, in the failure of even his best-known poems to take sufficient account of the resonances and associations of their linguistic and formal mediums.

▼ ▼ ▼

The truncated view of the Canadian poetic continuity that results from the rejection by the early Modernists of preceding and competing literary voices has unfortunately become institutionalized in the classrooms of Canada and commonplace in the country's literary histories, academic journals, and newspaper reviews, thus contributing to the assaults on Canadian memory outlined earlier. The major reason for this institutionalization of a form of amnesia is that, even today, the teaching and criticism of Canadian literature is dominated by people whose assumptions are essentially Modernist, people like George Woodcock, the founder of *Canadian Literature*, who seems tireless in his assertion that Canadian poetry "really" began with the arrival in Canada of early or classic Modernism. Little wonder that, under Woodcock's editorship, *Canadian Literature* largely forgot the Confederation poets but lavished very considerable attention on two writers who, though impeccably Modern, were only tangentially Canadian: Malcolm Lowry and Wyndham Lewis. A therapeutic (psychoanalytical) interest in memory as a means to self-awareness (individuation) has been a major concern of several Canadian novelists in the Modern tradition (think, for example, of Hagar "rampant with memory" in Margaret Laurence's *The Stone Angel*), and, in the years since Expo 67 especially, the past has frequently been put at the service of attempts to define the Canadian identity (think here of Margaret Atwood's *Journals of Susanna Moodie* with its conception of Canada as a nation of "paranoid schizophren[ics]"). But in the same time-period Canadian criticism has all too often failed to institute the sort of meaningful dialogue with the pre-Modern past and post-Modern present that could sustain (perhaps even create) a sense of the depth and diversity of Canadian culture. Repeatedly Canadian critics of the Modernist line treat the distant past (if they treat it at all) as a mere anticipation of Modernism and the recent past (which, being men of the present, they must treat) as either a happy extension or unfortunate betrayal of the movement that they admire above all others. The effect of what amounts to a critical inability to appreciate and accept the wide spectrum of Canadian culture is twofold: a fixation on selective aspects of Canadian literature and—to elaborate a metaphor from Kundera—an intellectual "airbrushing" of certain components of the Canadian tradition. Three examples will suffice to illustrate these effects.

▼ ▼ ▼

In the first of his enormously influential Conclusions to the *Literary History of Canada* (1965), Northrop Frye offers a number of notions such as the "garrison mentality" which have served to fix the attention of numerous Canadian critics on a small and not necessarily typical range of Canadian works, from John Richardson's *Wacousta* (1832) to Earle Birney's "Bushed." While this feature of the Conclusion of the *Literary History of Canada* has become widely recognized, little cognisance has been taken of the fact that in his Conclusion Frye (who did not, significantly, research one of the historical portions of the *Literary History*) frequently uses verbal wit to dismiss a topic about which he quite evidently knows very little. A case in point is his comment that the "writings . . . of many of the early explorers are as innocent of intention as a mating loon," where the amusing figure of the "mating loon" serves to direct attention away from the vagueness of the pronouncement that precedes it. What exactly is meant by "many"? As a category, whom does it exclude and whom does it include? Samuel Hearne spent years revising and editing his journals for publication; Alexander Mackenzie employed a ghost writer to help him with his; and David Thompson never did succeed in subduing his diaries to a narrative. Were these people "innocent of intention"? More important for present purposes than the answers to these questions is the recognition that, in wittily burying the writings of the explorers under the figure of the "mating loon," Frye employs a typical liberal or progressivist formula: he characterizes his distant predecessors in the Canadian continuity as comical in their artlessness and, in so doing, asserts his own intellectual and artistic power over them. By combining the dismissive force of ridicule with a simile's ability to obliterate what it purports to illuminate, Frye's "mating loon" is dismayingly effective in encouraging the reader of the *Literary History of Canada* to ignore a portion of Canada's past. One is left, as it were, with Clementis's cap—the "mating loon"—but Clementis himself—the explorers and their writings—have been airbrushed out of the picture.

A more recent example of airbrushing by a Modernist critic can be found in W. J. Keith's contribution to the Longman Literature in English series: *Canadian Literature in English* (1985). Here the formula used to dismiss selected writers is not ridicule and concealment but complete omission—the absolute silence that negates absolutely. Arguing from the typically Modern conviction that the best writing combines an avoidance of verbal ornateness with a fidelity to real experience, Keith also asserts that the "quintessentially Canadian" artistic stance is one that exhibits a "poised balance between British and American models"—a "poised balance," that is, between "the sanctioned methods of the Old World and the fresh approaches of the New." To these two criteria for separating the central from the peripheral in Canadian literature, Keith adds a third: only writers who seem to possess "a strong sense of cultural continuity" can be considered truly a part of that "cultural continuity." Although this looks promising from an historical perspective, its narrowly Modernist and Nationalist biases combine (strange bedfellows indeed) to produce some unhappy skewings and disturbing omissions in *Canadian Literature in English*. In the light of Keith's assumptions, Lampman, for example, is at his best when he catches "the engaging sharpness of the Canadian landscape that will later impress poets like A.J.M. Smith and F.R. Scott," and Lampman's fellow Confederation poet, Duncan Campbell Scott, though "less admired in his time" establishes by virtue of his realism "the most effective lines of poetic continuity between nineteenth- and twentieth-century Canadian verse." (The slippery phrases in these two comments are, of course, "engaging sharpness" and "most effective.") The real victims of Keith's book, however, are writers who fall afoul of his valorization of "balance" and an explicit awareness of cultural "continuity." Among the poets from the recent past, several—Frank Davey, Daphne Marlatt, and Gwendolyn MacEwen, for example—are mentioned only once in passing in *Canadian Literature in English*. The list of those consigned entirely to oblivion without so much as a mention in the volume's text, chronology or bibliography could go on for many lines; it includes Christopher Dewdney, bill bissett, Joe Rosenblatt, Andrew Suknaski, Robert Bringhurst, Steve McCaffery and bp Nichol. In Keith's case, the Clementis's hats are the recent Canadian writers who are mentioned only in passing in *Canadian Literature in English* and the Clementises are those whose experimental bias and eccentric failure to make evident their engagement with Canadian culture have marked them as fit subjects for the airbrush.

A third and final example of airbrushing in Canadian literature of the Modernist line is drawn from a more journalistic source. In an appreciation of F.R. Scott in a recent issue of *Poetry Canada Review*, David O'Rourke reveals the extent to which popular and semi-academic reviewing accepts even in the mid-to-late eighties the Modernist myth that little or nothing of value precedes the arrival of Modernism in Canada. The opening paragraph of O'Rourke's appreciation of Scott is an entirely gratuitous swipe at late-nineteenth-century Canadian poetry. Its first (and repeated) piece of sleight-of-hand is a fatuous—some would say colonial--appeal to an hypothetical authority outside Canada:

> Let's face it. Although nineteenth-century Canadian poetry is a growth industry, there's not a hell of a lot that an outsider would call good. Despite all the Canada Council make-work projects, the steady stream of archaeological finds being heaped on our cultural heritage, how many nineteenth-century Canadian poets would you read if you didn't have to? One? Two? Say you're going on an ocean cruise, or intend to lie for a week in the sun. Would you take: Charles G.D. Roberts or Bliss Carman? Even Lampman and Crawford. The point is not that this poetry is old, but that it just cannot—nor could it ever—compete internationally because so much of it is so bad.

This is a particularly hortatory, but not in its assumptions untypical, example of recent journalistic criticism of Canadian writing. In addition to an appeal to "international" (read Modernist) standards that are never defined, it contains two manoeuvres that place rhetoric over fact.

(1) *"Say you were going on an ocean cruise.... Would you take: Charles G.D. Roberts or Bliss Carman? Even Lampman or Crawford."* This is Cruisoism (neologism intended)—the use of the "if-you-were-on-a-desert-island-or-ocean-cruise-and-had-only-one-book" formula to force a choice which, in this instance, is limited by the exclusion of all other possibilities. Why not ask: "Who would you take: Bliss Carman or F.R. Scott?" Probably because the answer might conceivably be Bliss Carman, and this—albeit only from a very narrow perspective on literary periods—would go against O'Rourke's Modernist assumption that nearly all nineteenth-century Canadian poetry is bad.

(2) O'Rourke's second manoeuvre is to assert without demonstration, and, as it happens, contrary to fact, that Confederation poetry *"cannot—nor could it ever—compete internationally"*—the implication being, needless to say, that Modern Canadian poetry can and has competed in this way. In fact, the precise contrary is true: Bliss Carman was a significant Canadian and American poet in his day who exerted a palpable influence on Ezra Pound, Wallace Stevens, Carl Sandberg and possibly Robert Frost, and D.C. Scott was responsible for inspiring John Masefield to take up the writing of poetry. That Carman and Scott were more competitive in the manner and forum admired by O'Rourke than any Modern Canadian poet (with the possible exception of Klein) makes especially ironical O'Rourke's subsequent and essential assertion that "Canadian poetry properly begins with A.J.M. Smith and F.R. Scott, but we often forget how important they were." ("Properly"?) In addition to Canada's "old" poets, it is the "cultural heritage" which O'Rourke professes to champion that is the casualty of his bias towards the Montreal Modernism of the McGill Movement writers.

▼ ▼ ▼

Up until about twenty years ago, the history that was valued by those with an interest in Canada's past was primarily that of European settlement. The two most obvious consequences of this were a nostalgic emphasis on the history, however brief, of the small town (*The Rising Village* and *Sunshine Sketches* are examples already encountered; Laurence's Manawaka, Robertson Davies' Deptford and Alice Munro's Jubilee are others) and a less palatable amnesia regarding what, from the perspective of the dominant Euro-Canadian culture, becomes the negligible pre-history of the native peoples and the land itself. For Goldsmith the "savage beasts" and the "savage tribes" are aspects of a wilderness that, to all intents and purposes, is deserted ("desolate") until the arrival of European settlers. Leacock speaks eloquently but unintentionally of the memory hole into which the European orientation consigns the pre-settlement past of the Indians and the land when in *Sunshine Sketches* he has "old Dr. Gallagher" bring "his latest Indian relics" to show to Rural Dean Drone:

> As soon as the doctor laid his tomahawk on the table, the Dean would reach for his Theocritus. I remember that on the day when Dr. Gallagher brought over the Indian skull that they had dug out of the railway embankment, and placed it on the rustic table, the Dean read to him so long from Theocritus that the doctor, I truly believe, dozed off in his chair.

In efforts aimed partly at countering an amnesiac attitude to any past that lies outside the history of Canada's settlement by Europeans, many recent writers of the late- and post-Modern persuasion—the John Newlove of "The Pride," for example, and the Christopher Dewdney of a *Palaeozoic Geology of London, Ontario*—have effectively drawn into consciousness the submerged history of the Indians and the land. In the "Author's Preface" to his *Palaeozoic Geology* Dewdney offers one of his alternatives to the official record (the history constituted by great men and events and its literary equivalents: the psychological and social novels): "A man's entire experiential memory exists only unto himself, is fractionally communicable and chronologically ephemeral. . . . There do exist, however, certain three-dimensional, universally perceptible memories. . . . THE FOSSIL IS PURE MEMORY." Using the resources of imaginative memory and deconstructive logic, Dewdney and others (particularly in the West) have attempted to liberate and articulate themselves and their culture by uncreating what is generally remembered of the Canadian past and recreating what is generally forgotten. These expansive efforts are attractive and welcome but, as Robert Kroetsch points out in *Seed Catalogue* (1977), "forgetfulness" in any guise is a "strange muse" whose gift may be mindlessness and silence:

> no memory then
> no meditation
> no song (shit
> we're up against it).

Being "up against it," making of unmaking and absence the stuff of fresh writing, has, almost paradoxically, permitted Kroetsch to avoid the mindlessness (and, by extension, silence) which, it was argued at the beginning of this essay, are ever-present possibilities for the inhabitants of our almost all-encompassing consumer culture. But in fleeing to the margins both geographically and in their writing, Kroetsch and others of the post-Modern orientation run the risk of promoting the advance of a system that has everything to gain and nothing to lose by fostering any and all forms of forgetfulness, any and all regressions from a comprehensive memory of the past into an infantile being in the present. Could it be that in the post-Modern insistence on process, on writing as activity rather than artefact, there is a willingness to exist in the present tense that bodes as ill for the realization of our full human potential and the maintenance of our independence, both as individuals and as a culture, as the curiously parallel emphasis on process in our educational system?

The recent revelation that one of the foremost practitioners of deconstructive criticism, the late Paul de Man, was during the Second World War the author of numerous anti-Semitic and pro-Nazi articles, has called into question the Yale Professor's motives for insisting on the "pastness of the past," for wanting "to paralyse the move to history." De Man died in 1983, leaving a brilliant and complex contribution to a theory of literary criticism which is certainly ahistorical and arguably totalitarian in its insistence that everywhere and at all times words obey the same rules, that the meaning of any individual utterance *(parole)* depends on its place in a total system (*langue*). In the post-Saussurean realm of deconstruction, you can have any colour you like as long as it is black (or/and white). By one of those odd coincidences that Jung might have ascribed to the workings of syncronicity (made famous of late by Sting), de Man was given a memorial service at Yale in January, 1984, a year recalling inevitably (?) George Orwell's warning that an erasure of the past is one of the conditions that allows a totalitarian *régime* to manipulate the future. First to begin this essay with a quotation from Kundera and then to end it with a reference to Orwell would be to frame its comments on Canadian memory in perhaps too apocalyptic a light. Yet the passage from Kundera and the glance towards Orwell are useful, it seems to me, if only to throw into relief the very real differences between the situation in Canada today and the situations in Kundera's Czechoslovakia and Orwell's *1984*. The point is not that the events lying behind that photograph on the balcony in Prague or leading up to the totalitarian state in *1984* could never happen in Canada. It is that with their freedom and ability to remember still largely intact, Canadians—particularly those fortunate enough to be working or studying in one of the major custodians of the country's memory such as the University of Western Ontario is today—have the ability and the responsibility to exercise one of the most formidable defences against the many forces that encourage amnesia and threaten the basis of our personal and cultural awareness and identity.

From *Western Today* 1 (March 1988): 18–25. In addition to the authors and works mentioned in the course of the essay, the following have contributed to the ideas expressed here: Mary Douglas, *Edward Evans-Pritchard* (1980); M. Halbwachs, *The Social Framework of Memory* (1975); Lynne V. Cheney, *American Memory* (1987); Jon Wiener, "Deconstructing de Man," *The Nation*, January 9, 1988, 22–24; and an anonymous and intriguing speculation on the "aphoristic habit" and the "impairment of memory": "The Price of Emersonism," *The Week*, May 1, 1891, 346. For other comments on Canadian memory and related matters, see "Remembering and Forgetting in Canadian Literature and Criticism, *What* 4 (April/May, 1986): 15–17 and "Keeping the Past Present: The Work of the Canadian Institute for Historical Microreproductions," *Facsimile*, 5. Thanks to Susan Bentley, Richard Green, Michael Groden, Michael Williams and J.M. Zezulka for valuable suggestions and discussions.

LINDA HUTCHEON

(1947–) was born in Toronto. She received her M.A. from Cornell University in 1971, and both her B.A. (1969) and Ph.D. (1975) from the University of Toronto. From 1976 to 1988 she was an English Professor at McMaster University; since 1988, she has been Professor of English and Comparative Literature at the University of Toronto, spending 1988–1989 as John P. Robarts Professor of Canadian Studies at York University. Among her numerous other appointments are sessions as Instructor at the Italian Association for Canadian Studies at the University of Turin (1986) and at the International Summer Institute for Semiotics and Structural Studies at the University of Victoria (1984–1990).

As teacher, critic, and editor, Hutcheon has emerged in recent years as a highly perceptive practitioner of post-structuralist criticism. The author of some fifty literary essays and seven books, her range of interests includes the politicizing of gender and representation, the problematizing of history and literary history, the semiotics of irony, modes of literary narcissism, the limits of genre, and the theory of intertextuality. She brings to the study of Canadian literature an eclectic mind familiar with the world's literatures and new developments in critical theory, often finding surprising parallels and juxtapositions among various post-modern art forms. These convergences can startle readers into new ways of contextualizing the seemingly random expressions of contemporary culture. She sees no fundamental opposition between formalist and "impressionist" approaches to literary criticism, since in both "interpretation is carried out according to some chosen orthodoxy, some set of ideas that provides an authority, tacit or acknowledged. In this sense, all criticism is deductive." Her interest in metafiction and parody derives from what she sees as one of contemporary fiction's central preoccupations. Thus at the end of *The Canadian Postmodern* (1988), her study of the contemporary novel in Canada, Hutcheon notes,

> To write self-reflexively and often parodically of fantasy and imagination, of games and of play, of history as process in progress (instead of as completed product)—all of these were ways to break down the finality of narrative closure that was a legacy of the realist novel.... None of these modes denied the mimetic connection between art and life; they merely relocated its site of operation—from the products of fiction to the processes.

The following essay on the kinds of irony in Canadian literature and art is typical of Hutcheon's writing in its daunting range of reference, its exhaustive treatment of the subject which nonetheless encourages readers to ponder further, and, in post-modern fashion, its own ironic humour. Finally, it might be observed that in concluding *The Canadian Essay* with Hutcheon's "As Canadian as... Possible... under the Circumstances!" the editors bring full circle the discussion of one of the book's recurrent themes—the character of Canadians—introduced by Sara Jeannette Duncan in "An Eminently Unliterary People."

As Canadian as... Possible... under the Circumstances!

LINDA HUTCHEON

The rather strange title for this essay came from a report in the *Canadian Forum*[1] in which the reader was asked to consider the phrase: "As American as. . . ." The author felt that most Canadians would be able to fill in that blank with little difficulty but that, when confronted with "As Canadian as . . . ," they would falter. Part of the reason would be that they would have to specify if they were French- or English-Canadian—or neither. The article goes on to suggest that perhaps the most Canadian of answers would be that of a woman responding to a recent survey with the words of my title: "As Canadian as possible under the circumstances." The self-deprecating irony that underlies such a response has been considered typical of the inhabitants of Canada, that strange country which, according to one historian, rests "on paradoxes and anomalies, governed only by compromise and kept strong only by moderation."[2]

That Canada is an odd national entity is likely clear to the rest of the world, if not to Canadians, if only because what other nation has—as its combined national hero and colourful symbol—a policeman in a funny costume? That the language we speak, "Canadian," is in itself an odd beast was underlined by Ted Blodgett when he called it "a mixed language, by law ambiguous, and always offering possible escape routes . . . without ever leaving home."[3] It is also, I think, either "by law" or by preference, frequently *ironic*. Obsessed (still) with articulating its identity, Canada's voice is often a doubled one, that of the forked tongue of irony. Although usually seen as either a defensive or an offensive rhetorical weapon, irony (even in the simple sense of saying one thing and meaning another) is also a mode of "speech" (in any medium) which allows speakers to address and at the same time slyly confront an "official" discourse, that is, to work *within* a dominant tradition but also to challenge it—without being utterly co-opted by it. This is the irony we hear in the voice of Al Purdy speaking to those Canadians who want him to explain what "being Canadian" means today in a North American and post-colonial context: "But you want heroes, you want history, you want, you want, etc. Lindbergh you want; George Patton you want, or guys like Churchill and Wellington maybe? Would you settle for Norman Bethune, John A. and J.S. Woodsworth?"[4] The obvious verbal markers of irony here—the repeated "you want" and the understatement implied in "would you settle for . . . ? "—make what might be taken as a straight nationalistic defence into a more powerful attack on the very need to ask what "being Canadian" might mean. Irony here is not the double-talking evasion of fence-sitting: it involves taking a position, however open to divergent interpretations that position might appear to be. Its power depends on the twin conditions of context and community of belief.

Context and community: together these two issues give rise to a problem right from the start. To whom do I refer when I speak of either the ironies of being Canadian or the ironies used by Canadians? To begin with, I shall here mean the pluricultural entity known (somewhat reductively) as English Canada: the historical and political complexities of Quebec would necessitate an entire other study. I want to try to avoid what Philip Stratford has called the double danger of Canadian comparative studies: unification or division.[5] Both of these models for the relations between English Canadian and Québécois culture present obvious problems, and until I have made a fuller study of the political, historical and cultural background of Quebec, I would prefer to resist the temptations of generalization, to retain the duality (without necessarily suggesting total difference), and to limit my focus to English Canadian culture. As bp Nichol taught us, in Book III of *The Martyrology*, there is no "we" that encompasses all.

When then is the basis of the relationship I *am* positing between irony and Canadian culture? I would not want to say *all* Canadian culture is bathed in what someone once called the cold douches of irony; that would manifestly be wrong. Nor would I want to say that *only* Canadian culture has dipped its toes into those ironic waters; that too is patently false. I merely want to suggest that irony is *one* mode of self-defining discourse used by English Canadians, and I want to look in particular at the forms of and motives behind that usage. I am not the only one, by a long shot, to have suggested this connection, but most who have done so have been content to state the relationship and leave it more or less at that. They have all noticed that Canadians often direct their ironies as much against themselves as against others. Northrop Frye has declared that they "have a highly developed sense of irony."[6] And Eleanor Cook has suggested that irony, satire, self-mockery are all "strategies for survival, and even for a kind of celebration" for Canadians.[7] The study that has gone furthest beyond this kind of provocative statement to actual analysis of irony in Canadian culture is Gaile McGregor's *The Wacousta Syndrome: Explorations in the Canadian Langscape*[8] where, though quite late in the book, the point is made that "the single adjective most often applied to Canadian literature by critics is probably 'ironic'" (p. 419). McGregor is careful to distinguish between the irony *of* a work and irony *in* a work, as most theorists of irony have before her,[9] and concentrates on the latter, outlining ironies of situation, narrative, theme, or structure. She claims that "a book may contain any or all of these kinds of ironies without communicating an essentially ironic vision" (p. 419). She laments the "misapprehension" that

> *whenever* a meaning is left inexplicit or a situation ambiguous or a character ambivalent, especially if either the condition itself or the character's response is such as conventionally invited ironic treatment in contemporary American or European fiction, that the circumstance is inevitably ironic. Not so. Irony involves discrepancy, but not every discrepancy involves irony. The thing that makes the difference is perspective (p. 419).

The definition of that perspective that McGregor goes on to give is one that has a long history in literature, dating back at least to eighteenth-century theories of wit and satire and those nineteenth-century developments that led to what we now call Romantic Irony. She asserts: "The fact is, nothing is ironic unless it is juxtaposed with a countering ideal or at least set against a *relatively* preferable state of affairs" which does not have to be explicit but "does have to be accessible *in terms of the work itself*" (p. 419). The implicit paradigm for irony that McGregor uses is a combination of the satirical (in terms of distance and normativity) and the romantic (in terms of self-consciousness), and its locus of operation in her analysis is in relation to romance. This she sees as characteristic of American, not Canadian, literature. Given her model of irony, I would likely agree. But there are other, perhaps more historically appropriate, paradigms for irony that *do* fit the Canadian context.

Theorists of the trope have noted that there has been a change in its usage and motivation, so that "[o]ne apparently needs to insist nowadays that the term 'irony' need not always be taken with a strongly emotive and moral accent," but can be seen as a more general "cognitive principle of metaphor and metaphoric structure."[10] What we now call American New Criticism was largely responsible for this change, and the subsequent postmodern re-valuing of irony as a mode of indirection and deferral of meaning has completed the shift in the meaning of the trope. A look at the variety of motives for irony in contemporary Canadian writing, in fact, shows much more than the satiric and normative impulse at work. And even that corrective[11] motive, with its ideal at base (that McGregor rejects in Canadian literature) is surely not totally absent from Libby Scheier's "Why Poems Should Not Be Fictions: A Polemic" in which the list of reasons why poems should not be fictions includes: "because Revlon has a higher profit margin / than McClelland & Stewart /

because Revlon has a profit margin."[12] It has been suggested that it is the northern life of Canadians, the moral and puritanical life, that "affords the substance and creates the disposition for satire."[13] But that would not account for all the *other* motives and dispositions of irony.

For instance, there is the *Irony Rhetorical*—used primarily for emphasis—or the simple *Irony Humorous*. Sigmund Freud, however, said that no joke is without its tendentious aspect, its barb against someone.[14] The affectionate, gently ironic, feminist poems to the penis by Lorna Crozier might be a good example of this. But Canadian are often said to specialize in the *Irony Self-deprecating*. More ingratiating than aggressive, such self-deprecation is said to "acknowledge the opinion of the dominant culture—even appear to confirm it—and [allow] the speaker or writer to participate in the humorous process without alienating the members of the majority."[15] Of course it also allows one to suggest that what is being presented as ironically inferior has its own implied superiority. This *Irony Self-deprecating* can also achieve diffidence through self-aggrandising: there exists a very clever television spoof called *The Canadian Conspiracy* which purports to "expose" how Canadians have infiltrated all major American institutions. Such irony often uses stereotypes and clichés to turn them against their perpetrators as much as against their victims.

Related to the *Irony Self-deprecating* is the *Irony Self-protective*, a way of appearing to accommodate oneself to convention while still standing apart—critical, distanced, in control, and perhaps not a little defensive. There is a relation here, perhaps, to the *Irony Evasive:* the irony of hypocrisy, equivocation, duplicity, deception, or at its most benign, the non-committal irony of fence-sitting. Novelist Susan Swan recently told me that she saw irony as a "nice form of dishonesty" and that was why polite Canadians excelled at it. And, after all, she may be right: the difference between lying and irony is merely a matter of intent: a lie intends the second meaning of words to remain hidden; irony intends it to be perceived—at least by part of the audience.

This last point brings us to the *Irony Elitist*—though some would say *all* irony is elitist in its exclusions, in its assumption of superior (or at least additional) knowledge. The extreme of this is what Wayne Booth calls the "Snotty Sublime."[16] While there is no doubt that some ironies are intended to separate the initiate from the rabble, the comprehension of irony assumes no more than a set of shared values and a shared cultural context. Not that that isn't enough. That alone could account for those myriad missed ironies that litter the history of any culture.

There are many other motives for irony than these, however. There is the *Irony Demystifying*—the critical, debunking, judging irony of the work of Bandanna Zack's neo-Dadaist sculptures that tackle conventional attitudes and forms. *A Trio of Great Canadians* (1976–1977) is one such example. Three life-sized horses' rumps that protrude from a wall are clearly a broad visual pun on the idea of a "horse's ass" with the threat of a kick never far away. Such are the "great Canadians."[17] This is clearly related to the *Irony Destabilizing* that postmodernism seems to revel in, the accepting of paradox and provisionality as inevitable. This is close to what Wayne Booth has called "unstable irony" and what deconstructive literary critics call "aporia." What-ever we call it, its function is to undo certainties, even its own. Often this kind of irony is coupled with the *Irony Oppositional*, the subversive doubling within and against the dominant that can be seen especially in the work of those artists concerned with issues of class, race, gender, sexual preference, and post-colonial identity.

The ironies I have been listing have obviously been in a certain ascending order of virulence or force. The *Irony Corrective* of satire that is McGregor's model would fit in at this point, followed by the even more potent *Irony Corrosive*—the aggressive, cutting, cruel, derisive, disdainful, sneering irony of negation. I have gone through this long list of ironies in order to show that the model or paradigm we use to discuss irony in Canadian culture should perhaps be broadened beyond McGregor's "romantic/ironic axis" and beyond too the eighteenth-century theories of wit and satire that see irony only as seeking to diminish by ridicule, obviously clear and confident about the normative standard by which such judgements can be made. As a prominent ironologist has put it: "The word 'irony' does not now mean only what it meant in earlier centuries, it does not mean in one country all it may mean in another, nor in the street what it may mean in the study, nor to one scholar what it may mean to another."[18] His first point, the historical argument, is important here, because my interest is primarily in contemporary culture where the postmodern thrives, and irony may have different functions than those McGregor delineates primarily for earlier periods. Irony is a slippery concept and an upsetting one for many commentators who seek certainties and master narratives, rather than provisional possibilities. As Booth has put it: "irony is usually seen as something that undermines clarities, opens up vistas of chaos, and either liberates by destroying all dogma or destroys by revealing the inescapable canker of negation at the heart of every affirmation."[19]

But this is nothing new. There are scores of books and articles on the growth of irony as a world vision in the dystopic twentieth century. One writer even claims that "[i]rony, ambiguity, skepticism—these aren't attitudes any more which come and go like moods, but parts of our anatomy."[20] From Northrop Frye to Ortega y Gasset to Kenneth Burke, irony has been proclaimed as the trope of our century.[21] And what is also evident is that the clear distinction McGregor wants to make between irony and discrepancy probably will not hold any longer. A protean form, irony has been associated with things Sophoclean, Socratic, Romantic, Modernist, New Critical, and now Postmodern. As Alan Wilde has argued, it is "a characteristic response to the polysemic world we inhabit."[22] What I am calling postmodern irony, in all its many motivations and modes, recognizes that all communicational codes, especially language, are—in practice—ambiguous, doubled, even duplicitous, that they are what Mary Jacobus calls "a kind of impropriety or oxymoronic otherness."[23] The gap between meanings that irony highlights explains its attraction to theorists of difference and deferral in literary language, such as Jacques Derrida and Paul de Man.[24] The postmodern view of irony is one that William Spanos has contrasted to the "balanced and resolving irony of modernism" as a *refusal* "to fulfill the expectation of closure or to provide the distancing certainty the literary tradition . . . has inscribed in the collective consciousness of Western readers."[25] McGregor may be correct in saying that there is little of the *Irony Corrective* of satire in Canadian culture, but today the reason for this might be a deep postmodern suspicion of the certainties, the master narratives, upon which depend the judgments and norms that underpin satire's exposition of (and desire to correct) vanity, folly or hypocrisy.[26]

Postmodern irony is tricky business. The most puzzling trick it plays is an ideological one: how is it that irony can be both subversive and authorizing, but undercutting and excluding? Indeed it includes as it excludes. Irony is also a semantically slippery beast. Its very doubleness—the need to keep both literal and ironic meaning afloat together—disrupts any notions of meaning as single, stable, decidable, complete, closed, innocent, or transparent. The double, complex meaning of irony is only graspable in context and with the acceptance and understanding of simultaneous double-voicing. To use a famous visual analogy, it is not a case of seeing, in that well known, ambiguous form, either a duck or a rabbit; we must see both at once or we are not dealing with irony. We may alternate rapidly between two semantic poles, more rapidly than our eye will move from duck to rabbit and back, but this vibration or oscillation refuses resolution into either pole; the doubleness is held in tension always. This is not the New Critical use of irony as a way to recuperate contradiction; the contradictions remain in postmodern irony, and they delight in each other and in their mutual provisionality.

Some ironologists fear that the terms "irony" and "ironic" have become "little more than all-purpose, flexible, slot-fillers, vogue words useful whenever one does not want to choose stronger terms—or dares not do so because they will be too clear—or whenever one simply has nothing to say and wants to sound educated."[27] Others fear that the reign of deconstruction in North American criticism, with its challenges to notions of intention and authority, will mean the end of "irony" as a useful critical term.[28] But, if Irving Layton is right in defining a Canadian as "a born sucker for anything that will tie [her] up in knots,"[29] meet a born sucker—who is in good company in Canada in being willing to let herself be tied up in knots by irony. I am sure I am not the only one ever to speculate that irony is a wonderfully covert way for repressed Canadians to express either aggression or enthusiasm: think of the political radio satire of the Royal Canadian Air Farce or Vancouver's Double Exposure. After all, irony is often effective because of the impression of restraint it offers.

No doubt this all has something to do with Canadian attempts to define a distinctly Canadian identity in the face of a colonial past and perhaps a different, if equally colonial, future. This would certainly seem to be the case in this poem by John Robert Colombo called "A Canadian Is Somebody Who":

Thinks he knows how to make love in a canoe
Bets on the Toronto Maple Leafs
Enjoys Air Canada dinners, desserts and all
Distinguishes between Wayne and Shuster
Attends the concerts of Anne Murray and Liona Boyd
Boasts Donald Sutherland was born in New Brunswick
Possesses "a sound sense of the possible"
Is sesquilingual (speaks one and a half languages)
Has become North American without becoming
Either American or Mexican
Knows what the references in this poem are all about.[30]

The *Irony Self-deprecating* meets the *Irony Self-mocking.*

Yet, is any of this at all surprising for a people who have to live out the last decade of this century trying to live down Sir Wilfrid Laurier's "The Twentieth Century belongs to Canada"? Daily, Canadians ask: *when* can they take possession? Canadian literature is replete with ironic voices of many tonalities: the genial ironies of Tom Wayman or Frank Davey; the droll and dry ironies of Margaret Atwood, Alice Munro, Mavis Gallant, Michael Ondaatje, or Leonard Cohen; the clever and funny ironies of Miriam Waddington, Leon Rooke, or George Bowering; the arch tone of Robertson Davies or John Metcalf; the pointed one of Susan Swan, Libby Scheier, Lorna Crozier, Claire Harris and Marlene Philip. And we must not forget the rambunctious ironies of Robert Kroetsch and Al Purdy or the more scathing ones of Irving Layton.

Doug Barbour and Stephen Scobie introduced their 1981 anthology of comic Canadian poetry, *The Maple Laugh Forever*, with these lines from Earle Birney: "our forefathers literary/had little laugh or quippery." The poem goes on to state that "Grove was grave & Mair still more." The editors here felt that until this century, Canadian poetry had been "colonial and Romantic, and neither of these attributes are conducive to humour."[31] Their book reveals that Canada has turned out, *pace* McGregor, a lot of able and effective satire, from the ironic use of structure and diction by F.R. Scott to the devastating deployment of anticlimax by Francis Sparshott. Barbour and Scobie note that Canadian poets have used comedy—and I would add, irony—"for entirely serious poetic purposes." They have also used both for political purposes, particularly in relation to a series of self-defining Canadian self-positionings: that is, Canada's positions in response to her colonial past and to her present, American-dominated as it increasingly seems to be. Internal self-positionings are also relevant here: what is the relation of irony to the positions taken up by the regional in relation to the central, and by those perceived as marginalized (by things like gender, ethnicity, race, sexual orientation, or class) within the majority culture? Whether it is accurate or not, the perception of English Canada's dominant culture is that it is Euro- and Amero-centric, male, white, heterosexual, capitalist, and centrist (geographically and politically). In the light of the general postmodern questioning of any notion of coherent, stable, autonomous identity (be it individual or national),[32] these positions are, almost by definition, provisional and tentative—not because they are weak, but because they stand ideologically opposed to the mastery and presumption of dominant and dominating cultures. In its postmodern paradigm, irony becomes a potential mode of addressing those cultures from within, while simultaneously signalling a position of difference and even opposition.

From another angle, though, while we may question the validity, stability and sureness of notions of the self—or the nation—we may also still yearn for them, our philosophical convictions to the contrary. In the age of Derridean deconstruction, Al Purdy's words become very postmodern: "Certainty of nationality and personality is an illusion, since there is no permanence in anything, anything at all. And yet we cling to this shifting and uncertain self, this rag of aging bone, this handful of dust to which we've given a loved name."[33] Irony has become one way of working within prevailing discourses, while still finding a way to articulate doubts, insecurities, questionings, and perhaps even alternatives. I suppose it is, in a sense, a way to have your cake and eat it too, to launch a challenge but also to admit a loss.

While Canadian culture is not alone in deploying the creative tension between differences that I am calling postmodern irony, it does seem to be particularly fertile ground for the cultivating of doubleness. In a recent article addressed to an American audience,[34] Bill Kilbourn says: "The Canadian identity—the phrase is both a chimera and an oxymoron—is full of odd conjunctions, split visions, and unresolved tension" (p. 1). Kilbourn writes with affection and irony of "that particularly Canadian catatonic state of being caught between two or more higher authorities and on both sides of every debate" (p. 3), and recounts the New York City joke: "Why does a Canadian cross the road?" "To get to the middle." There certainly seems little in Canada that is not (or has not been) inherently doubled and therefore at least structurally ripe for ironizing. Its history offers many a binary opposition: Native/colonial, federal/provincial, not to mention English/French. As one wag has put it: "In any world menu, Canada must be considered the vichyssoise of nations—it's cold, half-French, and difficult to stir."[35] But the oppositions are more than historical: the very geography of the country sets up others—east/west, empty northern tundra/dense southern urbanization. And the climate sets up still others—balmy B.C. and frigid Newfoundland winters.

Other examples of inherent doubleness in Canada would be its identity as a *bi*lingual yet *multi*cultural nation. Within the latter is another set of oppositions: Canada, like all the Americas, is a country of immigration, where (at least for a time) all its inhabitants have felt dual allegiances. Perhaps the greatest doubleness for writers, however, is the fact that English Canada shares a language with many other nations, two of which are particularly problematic: Britain, as a past political force, and the United States, as a current economic and cultural power. Where is the "Canadian" in this "English"? For Frye, the influence of these two larger and more powerful cultures sharing the language has been "practically beneficial" to English Canadians but "theoretically confusing." He goes on to inject his own irony into this distinction: "It is often suggested that Canada's identity is to be found in some *via media*, or *via mediocris*, between the other two."[36] To this we can add Miriam Waddington's query and answer:

> What is a Canadian
> anyway? . . .
> a yes-no somehow-or-other maybe
> might-be should-be could-be.[37]

Elsewhere, Waddington called Canadians

> sensitive
> to double-talk double-take
> (and double-cross)
> in a country
> too wide
> to be single in.[38]

Doubleness pervades Canadian politics too: think of the difference between the responses in French and English to questions in the House of Commons by linguistically adept parliamentarians—and prime ministers. Even Canada's national reputation is one of negotiation and compromise, and the country's very evolution into nationhood, unlike that of the United States, occurred *within* British institutions. Is this how Canadians came to learn the subversive double-voicing that speaks the language of tradition but implies a second level of meaning that can alter that tradition from within? But this subversion is not the only function of irony in Canadian culture.

In fact, irony would appear to have at least two possible functions: deconstructive and constructive. The first, the deconstructive, is a kind of critical ironic stance that works to distance, undermine, unmask, relativize, destabilize—and all those other postmodern verbs we hear so often today. This is primarily a form of critique which can at times border on the defensive, but which is always concerned with internally oppositional positions. Here *marginality* becomes the model or metaphor for internal subversion of that which presumes to be central. The other, the constructive kind of irony, is distinct from this insofar as it works to assert difference as a positive and does so through double-talking, doubled discourses. Instead of marginality, this irony's metaphor is perhaps *liminality*, a term used by anthropologist Victor Turner to refer to the open space "whence novel configurations of ideas and relations may arise."[39] Irony opens up new space, literally between opposing meanings, where new things can happen. As poet Claire Harris puts it: "Liminality, the space between two worlds, is a place of paradox."[40] It is also a place of irony. And in both cases, this is where the action is.

Irony as *deconstructive* critique can range in tone and motivation from the lightly humorous to the savagely sarcastic. As Walter Benjamin stated in regard to Bertolt Brecht's epic theatre: "there is no better starting-point for thought than laughter; speaking more precisely, spasms of the diaphragm generally offer better chances for thought than spasms of the soul."[41] The complexity of this kind of irony can range from its relatively clear voicing (its saying one thing and meaning another as well) in a political cartoon to the intricate interplay of the visual and verbal codes in photography like that of Geoff Miles, but it always asserts otherness and difference, as the poetry of Lilian Allan or Himani Bannerji underlines. And it makes this assertion in opposition to such things as perceived power and authority, sure and established (or unexamined) values, or sometimes just pretension. To speak from the margins, figuratively or literally, is to decentre centrisms, be they ethno-, phallo-, or hetero-centrisms, and irony has a role to play in this, both within Canadian culture and in Canada's relation to other cultures.

Less oppositional than transgressive, what I am calling the *constructive* kind of irony is that sort of ironic paradox that pushes our notions of the accepted and acceptable into new, liminal spaces, the spaces between meanings. What some feminist and postmodern writers do ironically with the myths of both gender and national identity has little to do with nostalgia or a search for order, and much to do with a distancing from the old and a making room for the new. Furthermore, given the history of irony as it developed into Romantic Irony, it is not surprising that irony today might still be tied to self-reflexivity, and self-reflexivity happens to be an attribute rampant in postmodern discourses. A good example of this linkage would be Tim Zuck's *Performance Piece No. 1* (1971), a mixing of performance and conceptual art. Zuck spent a day in a gallery in a wooden box with a plexiglass front. Over the day, he painted the inside of the box black, gradually concealing himself entirely behind the paint, which then literally stood between artist and audience: "In this way Zuck commented ironically on the assumptions that we see the artist through his work, and that the artist conceals himself behind his work."[42]

The same kind of play with conventions can be done in literature too. Witness Robert Zend's ironizing of the Japanese Haiku form in "A Chain of Haik":

Japanese people
think it is quite boring to
finish their senten

I agree with them
we can guess anyway what
should come after the

We go to bed when
we are sleepy and not when
we finished what we

We die the same way
there are many unfinished
things to do when sud

Western reader, I
hope you will understand me,
and if not, you can [43]

Sometimes, context is not only important for the comprehension of irony; it can literally *make* ironies, even outside the will of the text's creator. My favourite example of this is from the Personal column in the *Globe and Mail*[44] where, sandwiched between "Mrs. Jace—Palm, cards, crystal ball reader. Dependable & helpful advice" and "Psychic can help you obtain love, health and wealth," we find: "Ownership of copywrite [sic] is sought for fragments of Malcolm's Katie [not italicized, to add sexually possessive ambiguity for the non-Canlit-specialists] by Isabella Valancy Crawford to be published in edition of that poem. Reply to: Cdn. Poetry Press, Dept. of English, UWO, London, Ont. N6A 3K7." This kind of perceived incongruity is one of the major markers of irony, a trope which, unlike metaphor or allegory, depends on some significant difference: a disparity, contrast, opposition, contradiction, or incompatibility. Irony is fundamentally diacritical, for it results in the knowledge of difference, taking its full meaning from the difference between the two meanings of a single sign. It is often also comic because of this incongruity. But as historian Reinhold Niebuhr once noted, the comic becomes ironic when a "hidden relation is discovered in the incongruity."[45] This is the secret that addressee and addresser share, the knowing smile. That hidden sameness that makes the comic incongruity into the ironic one, the chuckle of recognition of relation, can be felt in Gary Hyland's poems about adolescents, written in their idiom. "Deke and Dante" is one such poem in which Deke tells how he went to the library and started to read Dante's *Divine Comedy*. He found it an odd, unfunny kind of comedy, to say the least, but he got hooked on "that snazzy lingo" and kept reading:

All the time I just kept imaginin Beatrice
was Elaine Wells and I was this Dante guy
and I sailed through that whopper of a book
in I'd say only about two or three months.[46]

Media which use verbal and visual codes together can often get the most effective mileage out of ironic juxtapositions. Donald Brittain's film *The King Chronicle* (1988) is an excellent example. At one point the camera moves from a shot of the man who was Canada's Prime Minister for twenty-two years coming to a sexual climax in the arms of a prostitute to a shot of King and his friends singing "Safe in the Arms of Jesus." Brittain's script and own sardonic tone of voice underline and create other ironies: William Lyon Mackenzie King "didn't know what the Depression was all about and he didn't seem to care.... His mind was encrusted with nineteenth-century platitudes and his compassion was confined to friends and acquaintances. He was very kind to dogs." Brittain deploys what could be called both verbal and structural ironies here, and both rely on incongruous juxtaposition of meanings.

Many of the examples I have been citing suggest that irony seems to have a particularly *political* function in much art today. This is perhaps most noticeable in the visual arts, but the larger structural possibilities that the novel and dramatic genres allow also make for fertile ground for irony, as any novel by Margaret Atwood reveals. However, poetry seems to present problems for some ironologists. One claims that the lyric is "by and large, [the] least ironical" of all the literary forms.[47] And yet surely the lyric, with its compression of language and its play of tropes, is the perfect vehicle for verbal—and even structural—ironies. In fact, Frye's definition of irony is also a fine definition of lyric poetry: "a technique of saying as little and meaning as much as possible, or, in a more general way, a pattern of words that turns away from direct statement or its own obvious meaning."[48] Today it is the multiplicities and duplicities of the shiftings of language that attract poets to ironies. Many of them "have at" the most worn out of linguistic elements—clichés—in order to reactivate, through irony, their hidden power and yet also to foreground their degradation through overuse. The most infamous example is Christopher Dewdney's two-page tour-de-force of narrativized clichés: "The Dialectical Criminal: Hand in Glove with an Old Hat." "Dialectical criminal" is a good designation for irony in a poem that begins—and continues—in this vein:

> When it's raining cats and dogs you've got to cut corners because
> you could get your eyes peeled. You must come to grips with
> yourself until you fly off the handle & then if you're not fit as a
> fiddle you'll spill the beans. That's hitting below the belt with
> the short end of the stick, if I can bring the point home, ladies.[49]

Visual artists also play with language, of course, mostly in their titles and almost always to ironic effect. Joanne Tod's *Reds on Green*, a title that suggests some colour-field painting, is actually a verbal/visual punning: a painting of Chinese communists shaking hands against a green background. Many other artists, such as the group General Idea, also use irony as a primary linguistic and structural device to point beyond the slippery nature of language to the incongruities of our culture and our society at large. In this light, many would claim that Margaret Atwood is therefore the paradigmatic Canadian ironist, not only because of her flat, understated tone, but for how her works' titles are ironically undercut by their politicized contents: think of *True Stories*, a collection of poems about the impossibility of any true stories, on the one hand, and about the pain and torture of the real stories beneath the "true" ones of contemporary politics—"The true story is vicious/and multiple and untrue."[50]

The political stand of much of this kind of irony in visual media has been put down by one critic as "basically an amalgam of Marxism and women's lib with a few extra tid-bits like Canadian nationalism on the side for good measure."[51] And if one thinks of the work of Joyce Wieland, Fastwurms, Carole Conde and Karl Beveridge, this seems more or less accurate—minus the negative connotations. But, in the visual arts, even to posit—much less do—political art is *in itself* to go against the major tenets of modernism: its formalist emphasis and its view of art's autonomy from politics—or life. The dominance of modernism has meant that visual art's main *valued* goal has been to define and explore the specificity of its own medium. Much postmodern art does this, but so self-consciously that the self-reflexivity turns against the isolationism of modernism and out to the world at large. In using irony to point to the artifice, the un-natural and constructed status of the "natural," this politicized art raises issues of power and knowledge that have been suppressed—or at least ignored—by the dominant modernist aesthetic of the century.

I do not mean to suggest that irony is only a weapon for political protest; it *can* have that function, but it can also be used to co-opt, to compromise, to authorize, to exclude. After all, irony always operates in somebody's interests. But in much Canadian art today, it is the deconstructing rather than the co-opting that seems to dominate. In allowing alternative meanings to be suggested, irony neutralizes the impulse to believe only one side of the story, any story. I suggested earlier that deconstructive ironies are those that have become the particular province of groups that perceive themselves as marginalized: Canadians in general, and within Canada, those who are not made to feel part of the dominant culture by reason of race, ethnicity, class, gender or sexual orientation. Certainly irony appears to be used by those who are concerned about the incongruities and discrepancies of power structures. And with such disparities come the possibilities of using irony as a demystifying and exposing weapon. Witness Dionne Brand's multi-barbed irony of repetition and anticlimax in this poem:

> so we spent hours and hours
> learning Marx.
> so we picketed embassies and stood
> at rallies,
> so it's been 13 years agitating
> for the liberation of Africa,

so they still think, I should be in charge
of the refreshments.[52]

What irony allows writers like Brand, Rienzi Crucz, Andrew Suknaski, Mary di Michele and others to do is to break the link between the unrepresent*ed* and the unrepresent*able*. Beyond even deconstruction, in the liminal interstices of ironic doubleness, the other finds a way to represent itself—as black, South Asian, ethnic, female, or gay.

The issue of class also receives powerful ironic articulation in the poetry of Milton Acorn, Alden Nowlan, Al Purdy, Patrick Lane, and Tom Wayman, as it did in John Scott's installation at the WaterWorks exhibition at Toronto's Harris Water Filtration Plant in the summer of 1988. Working with art and labour historian Rosemary Donegan and others, Scott filled over 150 feet of underground tunnel space between the alum tower and the filtration plant proper with a memorial and an ironic testimony to workers killed in industrial accidents in Toronto since the turn of the century. The repeated poster-size images are of a skull or a hand or a rose, sometimes spattered with red. The skulls underline both the theme of the work and the historical echo of the tunnel as catacombs.[53] Beneath each picture are simply the name, date, and details of the death of a worker—minus the media thrill or sensationalism of press accounts. There are many layers of class-related irony operating in this work, and they are similar to those articulated in Michael Ondaatje's novel *In the Skin of a Lion*, part of which is about the very building of this filtration plant by Harris, the city official who commissioned and designed it. The beautiful building hides many harsh realties: the price to pay for Harris's baronial, grandiose dream was the death of many workers; the price to pay for Toronto's clean water—and by extension many other industrial advances and advantages today—is also death for some. Just as the tunnel is hidden beneath the buildings themselves, so the social cost is hidden.

Works of and about marginalization like this tend to use irony as a deconstructive device because it allows them to address a dominant culture from within its own structures of understanding, while still contesting and offering resistance to those structures. Because marginality tends to be "imaged" in terms of doubleness (centre/margin; voice/silence; visibility/invisibility), irony is often an attractive trope to turn doubleness in on itself to reveal hidden hierarchies and polarizations. This might explain the current postmodern re-valuing of irony as a subversive, anti-authoritarian rhetorical device—rather than as the weapon of elitist, exclusionary put-down. The double-talk of irony blurs the borders between what it is permitted to say and what is chosen. The spoken and the unspoken change their usual hierarchical places in irony: the spoken is to be discounted in favour of the unspoken—which now counts.

The politicized possibilities of Canadian irony might best be seen in the critique of ideology operative in the ironic treatment by Canadian artists of what is now the dominant culture against and within which Canada operates: that of the United States of America. As many have pointed out, Canada's history is not the stuff of which romance or tragedy are made: "peace, order and good government" do not quite have the same ring as "life, liberty and the pursuit of happiness."[54] Over the years, Canada has had to get used to being called, in Fredric Jameson's latest phrasing, "the semi-periphery of the American core."[55] This is why many Canadian artists feel the need to articulate difference from the American cultural monolith. Photographer Geoff Miles's brief catalogue accompanying the aptly named work, *Foreign Relations: Re-W/riting a Narrative in Parts* offers an instructive ironic political fable:

> There was once a country which existed to the north of a much stronger nation. Its southern neighbour considered itself to be beyond any other the seat of all that was good in both politics and culture and it believed that its influence over the course of human events would stretch to many millennia. The southern nation looked upon this northern territory somewhat with contempt, viewing its inhabitants as barbaric and its land as their own. Although there was trade between the two it was not often free due to the strength and wealth of the southern country. Such was the power of the southern country that it could at any moment wage war of many different kinds. And yet the little northern territory still managed to ward off the might of the other and even occasionally produced exports which had a greater impact on its stronger neighbour than was ever fully realized. One such moment occurred when the practices of a certain artist became widespread amongst the peoples of the south—his name was Orpheus and he entered Athens from Thrace sometime during the 6th century B.C.[56]

Canadians can be forgiven for falling into Miles's trap, but the lesson is an interesting and ironic one.

When it comes to U.S./Canada topics, the *Irony Critical* or *Corrosive* often overlaps with the *Irony Self-deprecating* or even *Self-critical.* Margaret Atwood, speaking to Susanne Becker,[57] has claimed: "It is possible if you live in the United States to take a real megalomaniac view of yourself but that's not possible in Canada—which may be why parody and satire and political cartooning have been developed so widely among us. We're likely to think of things as ironic." The familiar *Irony Self-deprecating* is also never far away in this kind of American/Canadian confrontation; but neither is the *Irony Demystifying*, deflating and criticizing its American target. This mix can be seen in Susan Swan's *The Biggest Modern Woman of the World*,[58] where nineteenth-century Canadian giantess, Anna Swan, goes to the United States (in a section entitled "The American Dream") and becomes very aware of the differences between the two nations' ideologies. And these differences provoke double-edged ironies. A parenthetical remark may hit home: "(We are from the

Canadas, are we not? where compromise is an art form.)" (p. 140). But Anna also uses her gift for irony against America, playing into the stereotypes of their perceptions of Canada. Here she is, trying to sell a Canadian cough drop idea to the very American P.T. Barnum:

> 'The Canadian cough drop is unequalled as an oesophageal elixir, and if administered in regular doses, along with maple leaves, our pills produce a calming side effect. In time, the user will exhibit an agreeable tendency to avoid confrontation and seek consensus instead.
>
> 'A desire to avoid war-like behaviour, a failure to sustain violent controversy such as the calamitous war you are fighting with your southern brothers—what more can a scientist ask of a drug?' (p. 69)

When asked: "Are Canadians infectious?" Anna replies in her best deadpan manner: "The cold mummifies agents of disease, rendering the majority of people in the Canadas harmless" (p. 69). That these ironies are also self-directed ironies is not hard to see.

I have deliberately left to the end one of the best examples of the complex ironies of and about Canadian culture: the work of Joyce Wieland, especially her nationalistic, ecological and feminist work of the early seventies that culminated in her 1971 retrospective at the National Gallery in Ottawa, called *True Patriot Love / Veritable Amour Patriotique*. In this context, let me only focus on one set of works from that show, the twin quilts, *Reason over Passion* and *La raison avant la passion*. These obviously take their point of departure from Pierre Elliott Trudeau's personal (Canadian?) motto, but the male power slogan here becomes re-coded into a feminist ironic subversion. This strong rationalist statement is both undercut and ironically humanized by its presentation as a soft, warm bed-covering. This suggests not only the strange bedfellow that politics is said to make, but an unavoidable sexual element that suggests more the passion over the reason. But these political or national ironies are intensified by gendered ones: the medium of quilting has associations that are almost entirely female. It has been seen as a metaphor for women's networks and collaboration,[59] but quilting also suggests domesticity, in the sense of women's work as well as comfort, hominess, and warmth—set against both the Canadian and the rationalist male cold. But there are further ironies: its stuffing suggests both the cliché of the stuffed shirt and a possible response to Trudeau's text—"Stuff it!" Men's words literally *on* women's work also recall the sampler form with its instructive motto; here, however, that motto and its instruction both get ironized. While some critics have felt that the use of the quilt medium with its nurturing, domestic connotations subdues and undercuts the political statements,[60] most see that it, in fact, underlines and ironizes the politics. It may (literally) cushion her message, but there are hidden needles in that cushion. Nevertheless Wieland is not often viewed as a political artist. According to one analyst, the reasons may be multiple: "because she is not an ideologue, or because her content is such a seamless part of her art, or because she is Canadian."[61] Perhaps *that* final irony requires no further commentary.

Irony today has become one of the major strategic rhetorical practices of postmodern art in general, of course. Perhaps it is not surprising, then, that in the visual arts this has meant that Canadian art has flourished in a politicized postmodern context—with its problematized ironic confrontations with both history and representation. I think the same is true of literature in Canada, as it too relates to the social and aesthetic histories out of which it comes with "irony, parody, mimetism, allegory, collage, appropriation"—to use Chantal Pontbriand's list.[62] The individual ironic voice of the artist—be it Timothy Findley's or Marlene Philip's—is no longer separable, perhaps, from both the collectivity and the history in which that voice is rooted. In the visual arts, the ironies of the overtly political work of Carole Conde and Karl Beveridge on the history of the Canadian labour movement are examples which readily come to mind. These are some of the liminal spaces in between, the double meanings that double-talking ironies are making room for. The tactics used to bring these spaces into being, as I have tried to show, are common enough: those familiar rhetorical devices of understatement, hyperbole, anticlimax, and repetition, as well as those modes of strategic positioning that provoke counter-expectation: incongruity, re-contextualizing, defamiliarizing clichés, or parody. Whatever the medium and whatever the function, irony seems to be at least one of the ways English Canadians have chosen to articulate their problematic identities. They are not alone in this postmodern world, of course, but as expatriate Canadian filmmaker and critic, Laura Mulvey, has put it: "Canadian culture is not yet a closed book. The historical anomalies that Canada has grown from make contradictions [and thus, I would add, ironies] visible. Uniform national identity is challenged by a pride in heterogeneity and difference."[63] *Vive la différence!*

An abridged version of the Robarts Lecture, John P. Robarts Centre for Canadian Studies, published under the same title in booklet form (ECW Press in association with York University, 1990).

NOTES

1. David Howes, "We, the Other People: Two Views on Identity," *Canadian Forum* (January 1988), 11.

2. W.L. Morton, *The Canadian Identity*, 2nd ed. (Toronto: University of Toronto Press, 1961, 1972), 51.

3. E.D. Blodgett, "After Pierre Berton What? In Search of a Canadian Literature," *Essays on Canadian Writing* 30 (1984–1985): 60.

4. Al Purdy, "Permanently Canadian," *Globe and Mail,* 14 November 1987, D6.

5. Philip Stratford, "Canada's Two Literatures: A Search for Emblems," *Canadian Review of Comparative Literature* 6 (1979): 138: "Blinded by proximity to their subject, swayed by politics and history, hamstrung by an inevitable, natural, linguistic and cultural affiliation to one of the two camps, [comparatists of Canadian subjects] must neither unify, nor divide."

6. In *Divisions on a Ground: Essays on Canadian Culture*, ed. James Polk (Toronto: Anansi, 1982), 73.

7. Eleanor Cook, "'A Seeing and Unseeing in the Eye': Canadian Literature and the Sense of Place," *Daedalus* 117, 4 (1988): 222.

8. Gaile McGregor, *The Wacousta Syndrome: Explorations in the Canadian Langscape* (Toronto: University of Toronto Press, 1985). All page numbers will appear in the text following citations.

9. See D.C. Muecke, *Irony and the Ironic* (London and New York: Methuen, 1970, 1982), 22 on "being ironic" (Instrumental Irony) and "it is ironic that . . . " (Observable Irony). See too Wayne C. Booth, *A Rhetoric of Irony* (Chicago: University of Chicago Press, 1974), *xiv*.

10. William K. Wimsatt, Jr. and Cleanth Brooks, *Literary Criticism: A Short History* (New York: Knopf, 1959), 747.

11. The term is Muecke's in *Irony and the Ironic*, 4.

12. Libby Scheier, *The Larger Life* (Windsor: Black Moss Press, 1983), 25.

13. Morton, *The Canadian Identity*, 109.

14. See Sigmund Freud, *Jokes and their Relation to the Unconscious* in *The Standard Edition of the Complete Psychological Works of Sigmund Freud*, ed. James Strachey (London: Hogarth Press and Institute of Psycho-analysis, 1960).

15. Nancy Walker, *A Very Serious Thing: Women's Humor and American Culture* (Minneapolis: University of Minnesota Press, 1988), 123.

16. Booth, *A Rhetoric of Irony*, 211.

17. For a different view of this, see Penelope Glasser, "Two Toronto Artists: Bandanna Zack and Joyce Wieland," *Artmagazine* 9, 38/39 (1978): 68–73.

18. Muecke, *Irony and the Ironic*, 7.

19. Booth, *A Rhetoric of Irony*, *ix*.

20. William Gass, *The World within the Word* (New York: Knopf, 1978), 144–45.

21. See Northrop Frye, "The Road to Excess" in *Myth and Symbol*, ed. Bernice Slote (Lincoln: University of Nebraska Press, 1963), 11; Ortega y Gasset, *The Dehumanization of Art,* trans. Willard R. Trask (Garden City, NY: Doubleday, 1956), 13; Kenneth Burke, *Counter Statement*, 2nd ed. (Los Altos, California: Hemes Publications, 1953), 104–5.

22. Alan Wilde, *Horizons of Assent: Modernism, Postmodernism, and the Ironic Imagination* (Baltimore: Johns Hopkins University Press, 1981), 1.

23. Mary Jacobus, "The Question of Language: Men of Maxims and *The Mill on the Floss*," *Critical Inquiry* 8, 2 (1981), 218.

24. See Paul de Man, "The Rhetoric of Temporality," in *Interpretation: Theory and Practice*, ed. C.S. Singleton (Baltimore: Johns Hopkins University Press, 1969), 192: irony occurs where "the sign points to something that differs from its literal meaning and has for its function the thematization of this difference."

25. William V. Spanos, *Repetitions: The Postmodern Occasion in Literature and Culture* (Baton Rouge: Louisiana State University Press, 1987), 216.

26. For a different interpretation of non-satiric, non-corrective irony from a more phenomenological point of view, see Alan Wilde, *Horizons of Assent*, 55, 58. The argument here is that, "unmoored from satire," irony becomes an autonomous vision of the universe as disparate and incongruous and therefore uncorrectable.

27. Wayne C. Booth, "The Empire of Irony," *Georgia Review* 37, 4, (1983): 721.

28. Muecke, *Irony and the Ironic*, 101.

29. Irving Layton, "What Canadians Don't Know about Love," in his edition of *Love Where the Nights Are Long* (Toronto: McClelland and Stewart, 1962), 12.

30. In Douglas Barbour and Stephen Scobie, eds., *The Maple Laugh Forever: An Anthology of Comic Canadian Poetry* (Edmonton: Hurtig, 1981), 31.

31. Ibid., 11.

32. See Linda Hutcheon, *A Poetics of Postmodernism: Theory, History, Fiction* (New York and London: Routledge, 1988) and *The Canadian Postmodern* (Toronto: Oxford University Press, 1988).

33. Purdy, "Permanently Canadian," D6.

34. William Kilbourn, "The Peaceable Kingdom Still," *Daedalus* 117, 4 (1988): 1–29. Page references will appear in parentheses in the text.

35. Stuart Keate, cited by Margaret Atwood in *The Canlit Foodbook* (Toronto: Totem, 1987), 7.

36. Northrop Frye, *The Bush Garden: Essays on the Canadian Imagination* (Toronto: Anansi, 1971), 218.

37. Miriam Waddington, "What is a Canadian," *Collected Poems* (Toronto: Oxford University Press, 1986), 125.

38. Miriam Waddington, "Canadians," *Collected Poems*, 149.

39. Victor Turner, *The Forest of Symbols: Aspects of Ndembu Ritual* (Ithaca, NY: Cornell University Press, 1967), 97.

40. Claire Harris, "Poets in Limbo," in *A Mazing Space: Writing Canadian / Women Writing*, ed. Shirley Neuman and Smaro Kamboureli (Edmonton: Longspoon/NeWest Presses, 1986), 125.

41. Walter Benjamin, "The Author as Producer," in *Thinking Photography*, ed. Victor Burgin (London: Macmillan, 1982), 29.

42. David Burnett and Marilyn Schiff, *Contemporary Canadian Art* (Edmonton: Hurtig; Toronto: Art Gallery of Ontario, 1983), 279.

43. Robert Zend, in *The Maple Laugh Forever*, 49.

44. *Globe and Mail*, 8 September 1987.

45. Reinhold Niebuhr, *The Irony of American History* (New York: Scribner's Son, 1952), *viii*. My thanks to Tom Traves for bringing this work to my attention.

46. Gary Hyland in *The New Canadian Poets 1970–1985*, ed. Dennis Lee (Toronto: McClelland and Stewart, 1985), 308.

47. Muecke, *Irony and the Ironic*, 5.

48. Northrop Frye, *Anatomy of Criticism* (Princeton, NJ: Princeton University Press, 1957), 40.

49. Christopher Dewdney, "The Dialectical Criminal: Hand in Glove with an Old Hat," in *The New Canadian Poets 1970–1985*, 72.

50. Margaret Atwood, *True Stories* (Toronto: Oxford University Press, 1981), 11.

51. Eric Cameron, review of AGO show of Carole Conde and Karl Beveridge, *It's Still Privileged Art*, in *Vie des Arts* 21, 84 (1976): 94.

52. Dionne Brand, *Winter Epigrams & Epigrams to Ernesto Cardenal in Defense of Claudia* (Toronto: Williams-Wallace, 1983), p. 24.

53. For a discussion of this work, see *Art-Views* (Spring–Summer 1989), 64.

54. See Morton, *The Canadian Identity*, 111.

55. Fredric Jameson, in Anders Stephanson, "Regarding Postmodernism—A Conversation with Fredric Jameson," *Social Text* 17 (1987): 46.

56. Geoff Miles, *Foreign Relations: Re-W/riting a Narrative in Parts*, catalogue, Gallery 44.

57. Susanne Becker interviewed Atwood on 24 October 1988; unpublished transcription.

58. Susan Swan, *The Biggest Modern Woman of the World* (Toronto: Lester and Orpen Dennys, 1983). Page references will appear in parentheses in the text.

59. See Lucy Lippard, "Watershed: Contradiction, Communication and Canada in Joyce Wieland's Work" in *Joyce Wieland* (Toronto: AGO; Key Porter Books, 1987), 10.

60. See Lauren Rabinovitz, "Issues of Feminist Aesthetics: Judy Chicago and Joyce Wieland," *Women's Art Journal* 1, 2 (1980–1981): 40.

61. Lippard, "Watershed," 3.

62. Chantal Pontbriand, "The Historical Factor: A Fundamental Theme in Canadian Contemporary Art," *Parachute* 47 (1987): 51.

63. Laura Mulvey, "Magnificent Obsession," *Parachute* 42 (1986): 11.

ESSAY CREDITS

An honest attempt has been made to secure permission for all material used, and if there are errors or omissions, these are wholly unintentional and the Publisher will be grateful to learn of them.

Hugh MacLennan, "Prologue: The Writer and His Audience," in The Other Side of Hugh MacLennan: Selected Essays Old and New, *ed. Elspeth Cameron (Toronto: Macmillan of Canada, 1978), 1–5. Reprinted by permission of Macmillan of Canada, A Division of Canada Publishing Corporation.*

Stephen Leacock, "The Devil and the Deep Sea: A Discussion of Modern Morality." From Essays and Literary Studies *by Stephen Leacock. Used by permission of the Canadian Publishers, McClelland and Stewart, Toronto.*

Stephen Leacock, "Common Sense and the Universe." From Last Leaves *by Stephen Leacock. Used by permission of the Canadian Publishers, McClelland and Stewart, Toronto.*

Frederick Philip Grove, "A Call for Speed." From Over Prairie Trails *by Frederick Philip Grove. Used by permission of the Canadian Publishers, McClelland and Stewart, Toronto.*

Frederick Philip Grove, "Apologia pro Vita et Opere Suo," in A Stranger to My Time: Essays by and about Frederick Philip Grove, *ed. Paul Hjartarson (Edmonton: NeWest Press, 1986), 192–97. Reprinted with permission.*

Ethel Wilson, "A Cat among the Falcons." From Ethel Wilson: Stories, Essays and Letters *by Ethel Wilson, ed. David Stouck. Reprinted by permission of UBC Library and Macmillan of Canada, A Division of Canada Publishing Corporation.*

Hugh MacLennan, "Confessions of a Wood-chopping Man," in The Other Side of Hugh MacLennan: Selected Essays Old and New, *ed. Elspeth Cameron (Toronto: Macmillan of Canada, 1978), 116–21. Reprinted by permission of Macmillan of Canada, A Division of Canada Publishing Corporation.*

Hugh MacLennan, "The Rivers that Made a Nation," in Seven Rivers of Canada: The Mackenzie, the St. Lawrence, The Ottawa, The Red, The Saskatchewan, The Fraser, The St. John *(Toronto: Macmillan of Canada, 1961), 9–29. First appeared as "By Canoe to Empire,"* American Heritage *(October, 1961). Reprinted by permission of Russell & Volkening as agents for the author. Copyright ©1961 by Hugh MacLennan, renewed in 1989 by Hugh MacLennan.*

W. L. Morton, "Seeing an Unliterary Landscape." This article originally appeared in MOSAIC, *Manitoba Centennial Issue, 3/3 (Spring 1970), p. 1–10. Reprinted with the permission of the journal.*

W. L. Morton, "The 'North' in Canadian Historiography," Transactions of the Royal Society of Canada *series 4, vol. 8 (1970): 31–40. Delivered to a symposium on "The Influence of Climate on Canadian Culture." Reprinted with the permission of the Royal Society of Canada.*

Marshall McLuhan, "The Role of New Media in Social Change," Antigonish Review *74–75 (Summer–Autumn 1988), 43–49. Reprinted with the permission of Corinne McLuhan and the Herbert Marshall McLuhan Foundation.*

Northrop Frye, "Canada: New World without Revolution." From Divisions on a Ground: Essays on Canadian Culture *(Toronto: House of Anansi Press, 1982). Reprinted with the permission of Stoddart Publishing, Don Mills, Ontario.*

Northrop Frye, "Speculation and Concern," in The Stubborn Structure: Essays on Criticism and Society *(London: Methuen, 1970), 38–55. Reprinted with the permission of the author.*

George Woodcock, "The Tyranny of the Clock," in The Rejection of Politics, and other Essays on Canada, Canadians, Anarchism and the World *(Toronto: New Press, 1972), 46–50. Reprinted by permission of the author.*

George Woodcock, "Gabriel Dumont, the Forgotten Hero," in A George Woodcock Reader, *ed. Douglas Fetherling (Ottawa: Deneau and Greenberg, 1980), 120–27. Reprinted by permission of the author.*

Robertson Davies, "Keeping Faith," Saturday Night *102, 1 (January 1987), 187–92. Reprinted by permission of the author.*

George Grant, "A Platitude," from Technology and Empire: Perspectives on North America *(Toronto: House of Anansi Press, 1969). Reprinted with the permission of Stoddart Publishing, Don Mills, Ontario.*

George Grant, "The Morals of Modern Technology," abridged version which first appeared in The Canadian Forum *(Oct. 1986) of "Thinking about Technology," from* Technology and Justice *(Toronto: House of Anansi Press, 1986). Reprinted with the permission of Stoddart Publishing, Don Mills, Ontario.*

Al Purdy, "Streetlights on the St. Lawrence." From No Other Country *by Al Purdy. Used by permission of the Canadian Publishers, McClelland and Stewart, Toronto.*

Al Purdy, "Aklavik on the Mackenzie River." From No Other Country *by Al Purdy. Used by permission of the Canadian Publishers, McClelland and Stewart, Toronto.*

Mavis Gallant, "An Introduction," in Home Truths: Selected Canadian Stories *(Toronto: Macmillan of Canada, 1981), xi–xxii. From* HOME TRUTHS *by Mavis Gallant ©1981. Reprinted by permission of Macmillan of Canada, A Division of Canada Publishing Corporation.*

Margaret Laurence, "Where the World Began." From Heart of a Stranger *by Margaret Laurence. Used by permission of the Canadian Publishers, McClelland and Stewart, Toronto.*

Margaret Laurence, "My Final Hour," an address first delivered to the Trent University Philosophy Society, 29 March 1983 and published in Canadian Literature *100 (Spring 1984): 187–97. Reprinted by permission of the estate of Margaret Laurence.*

Robert Kroetsch, "No Name Is My Name." Excerpted from The Lovely Treachery of Words *©1989 by Robert Kroetsch. Reprinted with the permission of the author.*

Mordecai Richler, "My Father's Life." From Home Sweet Home: My Canadian Album *by Mordecai Richler. Used by permission of the Canadian Publishers, McClelland and Stewart, Toronto.*

Mordecai Richler, "Why I Write." From The Great Comic Book Heroes and Other Essays *by Mordecai Richler. Used by permission of the Canadian Publishers, McClelland and Stewart, Toronto.*

Robert Fulford, "How the West Was Lost," Saturday Night *100, 7 (July 1985), 5–8. Reprinted by permission of the author.*

Robert Fulford, "Foreword," in Canada: A Landscape Portrait, *by Janis Kraulis (Edmonton: Hurtig, 1982), 5–11. Reprinted by permission of Hurtig Publishers Ltd. and Robert Fulford.*

Margaret Atwood, "Writing the Male Character." From Second Words: Selected Critical Prose, *copyright ©1982, O.W. Toad Limited (Toronto: House of Anansi Press). Reprinted with the permission of Stoddart Publishing, Don Mills, Ontario.*

Margaret Atwood, "True North," Saturday Night *102, 1 (January, 1987), 141–48. Reprinted by permission of Margaret Atwood, ©1987.*

D.M.R. Bentley, "Forgetful of Former Care: Notes on the Past and Present State of Canadian Memory," Western Today *1 (March 1988): 18–25. Reprinted with the permission of the author.*

Linda Hutcheon, "As Canadian as . . . Possible . . . under the Circumstances!" An abridged version of the Robarts Lecture, John P. Robarts Centre for Canadian Studies, published under the same title in booklet form (ECW Press in association with York University). Reprinted with the permission of the author.

ILLUSTRATORS

Renée Cuthbertson: 69, 148; Kyle Gel: 172, 190, 207; Christopher Griffin: 93, 161, 268; Steve MacEachern: 113, 121, 235; Ambreen Mahmud: 11, 43, 314, 330; Allan Moon: 22, 217, 247; Liz Nyman: 59, 289.